CREATING
ANNA KARENINA

CREATING ANNA KARENINA

TOLSTOY AND THE BIRTH OF
LITERATURE'S MOST ENIGMATIC HEROINE

BOB BLAISDELL

FOREWORD BY BORIS DRALYUK

PEGASUS BOOKS
NEW YORK LONDON

CREATING ANNA KARENINA

Pegasus Books Ltd.
148 W. 37th Street, 13th Floor
New York, NY 10018

First Pegasus Books edition August 2020

Interior design by Maria Fernandez

Library of Congress Cataloging-in-Publication Data is available.

ISBN: 978-1-64313-462-8

10 9 8 7 6 5 4 3 2 1

Printed in the United States of America
Distributed by Simon & Schuster
www.pegasusbooks.us

To Kia Penso and Max Schott

CONTENTS

Foreword

by Boris Dralyuk

✳

It may at first seem somewhat paradoxical that Viktor Shklovsky, who as a youthful firebrand of formalist criticism in the 1910s and '20s railed against the naively biographical approach to the study of literature, went on to write a substantial, perceptive biography of Leo Tolstoy in 1963.[*] In truth it is no paradox: it's a concession to reality, which Shklovsky never really denied. Once they are written, literary works may enjoy a high degree of autonomy—standing outside of and, ideally, outlasting their creators—but they are, nevertheless, the works of human beings, produced in a given place at a given time and pervaded by an infinite number of outside influences. It may be useful, when analyzing literary devices or structures, to declare the author dead and buried, but a fuller understanding of any work—and especially of its creation—requires the resurrection of its creator and his milieu.

In *Creating Anna Karenina*, Bob Blaisdell manages to do precisely that, painstakingly reconstructing the artistic laboratory in which this great novel was conceived, and, more impressively still, bringing to life Tolstoy himself. Drawing on letters and memoirs, on

---

[*] For a clear rejection of the purely biographical approach, see, for instance, Shklovsky's "Letter to Tynyanov" in *Third Factory*, introduced and translated by Richard Sheldon (Champaign, IL: Dalkey Archive Press, 2002), p. 61: "One must write not about Tolstoy, but about *War and Peace*." The 1963 biography was translated into English by Olga Shartse and published by Progress Publishers in Moscow in 1978.

drafts and proofs, Blaisdell doesn't merely piece together a history, he places us inside the author's process, with its fits and starts, its bursts of inspiration and stretches of frustration. The result an intimate portrait and a journey of discovery. This sense of intimacy, this thrill of discovery set Blaisdell's surprisingly gripping book apart from the ever-growing pack of monographs on Tolstoy's masterpiece.

For readers of *Anna Karenina* who have never read a scholarly work about it, Blaisdell offers plenty of critical insight. Refreshingly, the insight is all his own. He has clearly read and absorbed tomes upon tomes of scholarship, but even when he might agree with one thinker or another, his judgment is rendered directly, without appeals to authority, in lively sentences that drive the point home—for example:

> One trouble with Tolstoy's essays and discourses is that in the midst of them *Tolstoy* seems to think they're more important, more true than his art. They're consistent but rigged, as they argue but they don't discover. Expository prose brought out Tolstoy's tendency of emphatically agreeing with himself. In his artistic productions, on the other hand, his sympathy and engagement with the imagined people and situations couldn't be settled as an argument could; writing fiction induced his deepest attention and feeling.

The opinion isn't new, but it is has seldom been expressed more engagingly, with such a winning combination of discernment and sympathy. This, too, is expository prose, but as in the best examples of the genre (certainly not Tolstoy's), the reader feels the author's mind move across the page, making discoveries as it goes.

From the very beginning, Blaisdell makes no bones about his devotion to *Anna Karenina*—his "book of books"—or about his deep admiration for its author, which borders on awe. But he is not in the least deluded about the messy, drawn-out act of composition, which doubles and redoubles on itself, or about the imperfect humanity of Tolstoy. Indeed, he is aware that the flaws are what fire the work. Had Tolstoy's argument with himself been settled before he started, had his opinions been fixed, the fiction would have lain flat—if it ever emerged at all. As Tolstoy himself knew, creation requires "the energy of delusion."* By this he meant the false belief in one's own power, in the importance of one's work, but borrowing the phrase for the title of a book of his own in 1981, Shklovsky extends the meaning: "The energy of delusion—the energy of searching freely—never left Tolstoy. [. . .] He comes up with a flawed sketch of [a historical character

---

*   Letter to N. N. Strakhov, April 8, 1878, *PSS* 62: 410-412.

for *War and Peace*], even though it contains the real facts and the real traits. [. . . T]he energy of trials, experiments, the energy of investigation compels him to describe again—a different person. This takes him years."*

Readers less learned than Shklovsky may have intuited this much, but, until now, no one had undertaken to trace the years-long trials, experiments, and investigations that brought a "different person," an Anna Karenina unlike the one Tolstoy had first envisioned, into existence. The central mystery of *Creating Anna Karenina* is indeed the emergence of that person, and its central revelation is the complex relationship between her and her "adoptive" father. As Blaisdell puts it, with customary vigor: "Anna was the character Tolstoy kept discovering, the one whose fate made him anxious and unhappy, the one whose momentum toward suicide gave her author terrifying visions of his own impulses."

Over the last half decade, I have had the pleasure of editing Bob's work for the *Los Angeles Review of Books*. He has become one of our go-to contributors, weighing in on everything from Ulysses S. Grant to Karl Ove Knausgaard, but we have particularly come to value his takes on the Russian masters—and especially on Tolstoy. In 2018, praising Viv Groskop's *The Anna Karenina Fix: Life Lessons from Russian Literature*, Blaisdell limned the traits of that volume's ideal reader: "you would have to have the confidence to know what you like, and to believe that books are like life, meant to be talked about, and that the lives of authors who have written world classics are inherently fascinating."† The same holds, of course, for the ideal reader of this book. And it is unquestionably true of the creator of *Creating Anna Karenina*, to whom all such readers owe a debt.

---

* Viktor Shklovsky, *The Energy of Delusion: A Book on Plot*, intro. and trans. by Shushan Avagyan (Champaign, IL: Dalkey Archive Press, 2007), p. 37.

† Bob Blaisdell, "Tolstoy Untangled: On Donna Tussing Orwin's 'Simply Tolstoy'," *Los Angeles Review of Books*, December 25, 2018, https://lareviewofbooks.org/article /tolstoy-untangled-on-donna-orwins-simply-tolstoy/.

A Note on the Spellings
of Russian Names

✳

Let me offer a word about the various spellings from the English-language sources I have quoted. Transliterating Russian into English has evolved in the 134 years since *Anna Karenina* was first translated into English. The name Tolstoy sometimes used to appear as Tolstoi. The Cyrillic *x* is now customarily rendered as *kh*. Constance Garnett, whose translation (titled *Anna Karenin*, not *Karenina*) from 1901 is the one I have quoted throughout, renders the painter Mi*kh*ailov as Mi*h*ailov, which to my ear is closer to the Russian pronunciation than the potentially confusing and overemphasized *k* in *kh*. Rather than regularize my sources, I use the spellings each author or translator uses. In my own translations from Tolstoy's letters and Russian sources, I try to conform to the conventions of the ALA-LC transliteration system, unless, for instance, the name through popular usage has more or less settled itself (e.g., Vronsky rather than Vronskiy; in the "Scientific Transliteration" system, sensible but odd-looking to most native English speakers, the spelling of Yasnaya Polyana becomes Jasnaja Poljana).

Introduction

✳

When reading a work, especially a purely literary one, the chief interest lies in the character of the author as expressed in the work.

—Leo Tolstoy, diary[*]

"I have nothing to hide from anyone in the world: all may know what I do."

—Leo Tolstoy to his brother-in-law Stepan Bers[†]

When Tolstoy started writing *Anna Karenina*, he was forty-four. He guessed that he would finish the novel, conceived as only a novella, in two weeks. *Anna Karenina* took him more than four years. Even after sketching out the plot, it took him several months to reconceive Anna's character. The driving motivation for him to commit to it as a serialized novel was that he was keen to buy horses; once the serialization started, however, nothing and no

---

[*]   R. F. Christian, ed. and trans., *Tolstoy's Diaries, Volume 1: 1847–1894* (New York: Charles Scribner's Sons, 1985), 73–74, October 24, 1853.

[†]   C. A. Behrs [Stepan Bers], *Recollections of Count Leo Tolstoy*, trans. Charles Edward Turner (London: William Heinemann, 1896), 2.

one, not even wild horses, could keep him on deadline. Several times he gave up or threatened to give up on the project. In about thirty of those fifty-three months he doesn't seem to have done a lick of work on it. He agonized over the procrastination, but his artistic engagement with Anna's character and her inevitable suicide probably tormented him even more.

When Tolstoy was in his seventies and was asked to reduce literature to one book, he chose *David Copperfield*. Ever since I read *Anna Karenina* for the first time when I was eighteen, my choice has been *Anna Karenina*. I read it at least twenty times in various translations before I decided to cut to the chase and learn Russian. After ten years I was able to read it in the original. Now, after repeated readings in Russian, it remains my book of books. This biographical study is the result of my quest to find out everything possible to know about what Tolstoy was doing during that period spanning the composition of this unprecedented novel. What sort of life was he living while writing—and while avoiding—the novel? During those four years, the challenges of the novel nagged at him through thick and thin, illness and health, death and birth, heaps of despair and moments of satisfaction. His biography is important because that novel is important.

In all the Russian and English biographies of him, the narrative of his *Anna Karenina* years has been recounted far too fast and loose. Even though many of his day-to-day movements and activities have been accounted for, I wanted to know them with the immediacy and depth that he continually gives us of his fictional people and places. But except in letters now and then, Tolstoy rarely described his own everyday life. It turns out that if we want to know what he, the artist, was thinking and feeling when he created *Anna Karenina*, the best source is that work itself.

Writing fiction was continually unsettling for him; the novel made him conscious of depths and fields of his thoughts and feelings. As he wrote, reread, and revised, to his surprise, despite that Anna was of a type he expressly despised, an adulterer living in high society St. Petersburg, he suddenly found her a new, real, sympathetic woman. From the point of view of the character Konstantin Levin meeting Anna for the first time, Tolstoy revealed his own personal artistic revelation:

> While he followed this interesting conversation, Levin was all the time admiring her—her beauty, her intelligence, her culture, and at the same time her directness and genuine depth of feeling. He listened and talked, and all the while he was thinking of her inner life, trying to divine her feelings. And though he had judged her so severely hitherto, now by some strange chain

of reasoning he was justifying her and was also sorry for her, and afraid that Vronsky did not fully understand her.*

And then, now that this extraordinary character had his sympathy and understanding, Tolstoy was faced with his own existential crisis. If she had everything—social standing, intelligence, beauty, love of her child, a steady marriage, vitality—how could she kill herself? Why did he, who also had everything (except beauty), find himself suicidal? It was as if he had walked into her bad dream and was sharing her fate. In his identification with her, her suicide became ominous.

The first chapter of this book shows Tolstoy trying to induce a state in which he could launch himself into a historical epic about the era of Peter the Great. The momentum he hoped would occur, as it had in the years of writing *War and Peace* (1863–1869), did not happen. He couldn't give it legs. He had recently satisfied himself with a work of great effort and the finest of touches, his children's primer known as the *Azbuka*. He had probably taken that project as far as it could go, though in the next two years, even after having started *Anna Karenina*, he would have to do a reconfiguring of it to make it popular. He was proud of the *New Azbuka*, but writing for the literacy instruction of children did not bring him to a critical realization of his own life, as *Anna Karenina* would.

Of the surviving manuscripts of drafts of *Anna Karenina*, some can be roughly dated, others can't. In the transcribed manuscripts of redacted drafts, the editors show us that we have to settle for only the date after or before Tolstoy could have written a chapter or scene, and other times we can't even know that. Despite those mysteries, we are always the lucky recipients of what he did publish, the glorious evidence that he left us on the hundreds of pages of what some of us think of as the world's greatest novel. Sofia Tolstaya recopied some of the drafts as her husband wrote them, and she witnessed startling (and occasionally disappointing) transformations in his revisions. We can see that he made corrections on one set of galleys after another. He was fiercely meticulous about and protective of the writing when he was in its midst, but once the galleys were good to go, he was notoriously sloppy about the proofreading and often asked for help in completing that task.

A few years ago, as I proceeded through the letters from and memoirs about the mid-1870s, I often felt as if I were watching him the way his wife and friends watched him,

---

* Leo Tolstoy, *Anna Karenina,* trans. Constance Garnett (New York: McClure, Phillips and Co., 1901), Part 7, Chapter 11, http://www.literatureproject.com/anna-karenina/anna_200.htm. The electronic edition from which I am cutting and pasting quotations is the 1901 two-volume edition, published as *Anna Karenin* (no concluding *a*) in New York by McClure, Phillips and Co. This is my main resource for passages from *Anna Karenina* throughout this book.

wondering why he wasn't writing. There he was, instead, going off to the Samara steppe to drink mare's milk and buy horses or into the local woods to hunt. It continues to be surprising and pleasing to read of his interactions with his many children; but it's also hard to see him and Sofia grieve over the deaths of close family members. At times he was short-tempered about the novel and while writing or trying to write it, he denounced it. We can sometimes imagine, in the face of contradictory evidence, that the novel might not survive his disgust with it. His friend Nikolai Strakhov and Sofia regularly worried that he really was going to abandon it.

✳

There are various origin stories of *Anna Karenina*, but the only one that pans out is the grisly real-life incident that occurred at the Tolstoys' local train station a year before he started the novel: "The fourth of this January [1872] at 7 in the evening an unknown young woman, well dressed, arriving at the Yasenki Moscow-Kursk railway in Krapivensky county, walked up to the rails at the time of the passing of the freight train number 77, crossed herself and threw herself on the rails under the train, and was cut in half. An enquiry has been made about the incident."[*]

Tolstoy and Sofia knew the "unknown young woman" of the news article: Anna Stepanovna Pirogova was the thirty-five-year-old mistress and housekeeper of one of the Tolstoys' closest neighbors, Aleksandr Nikolaevich Bibikov, a forty-nine-year-old landowner and widower.

Sofia soon wrote her sister Tatyana Kuzminskiy about it. Tatyana had spent many months at the Tolstoys' Yasnaya Polyana estate: "You remember, at Bibikov's, Anna Stepanovna? Well, that Anna Stepanovna was jealous of Bibikov for all the governesses. Finally, of the latest, she got so jealous that Aleksandr Nikolaevich got angry and quarreled with her, and the consequence of which was that Anna Stepanovna left him altogether and went to Tula. For three days she was lost to sight; finally in Yasenki, on the third day at 5:00 o'clock in the evening, she appeared at the station with a bag. There she gave her driver a letter to Bibikov; she asked him to get and bring her tea and gave him one ruble. Bibikov didn't accept the letter and when the driver returned again to the station he found out that

---

[*] Nikolai Gusev quotes this news story from the *Tula Provincial Gazette*, January 8, 1872. The Russian calendar was twelve days behind in the 19th century. For the rest of the Western world, the date of the suicide was January 16. See N. N. Gusev, *Lev Nikolaevich Tolstoi: Materialy k Biografii s 1870 po 1881 god* (Moscow: Izdatel'stvo Akademii Nauk SSSR, 1963), 134. (Hereafter, this reference will be listed as Gusev, *Materials*.)

Anna Stepanovna had rushed under a car and the train crushed her to death. Of course she did this on purpose. The investigators came . . . and they read this letter. In the letter it was written: 'You are my killer; you will be happy with her if murderers can be happy. If you want to see me, you can view my body on the rails at Yasenki.' What a story! For a few days we've been going around like crazies, getting together and explaining it. Bibikov is quite calm, says Levochka [Sofia's pet name for her husband], and that his nerves are strong, he'll get by. Levochka and Uncle Kostya went to look when they did the autopsy."[*]

Sofia's tone suggests that she didn't see this event as a tragedy, and apparently neither did her husband. Tolstoy never wrote about or was quoted speaking about Pirogova's suicide, but he certainly told Sofia about it. In addition to letters Sofia wrote to her sister, she noted in her diary: "Lev Nikolayevich saw her, with her head crushed, her body naked and mutilated, in the Yasenki barracks." Tolstoy was sensitive and impressionable, but if a war, a guillotining, an autopsy, or a famine was happening nearby, he wanted to see it for himself. Sofia continues: "He was terribly shaken. He had known Anna Stepanovna as a tall, stout woman, Russian in face and character, a brunette with grey eyes, not beautiful but attractive."[†]

When Anna Karenina makes her first appearance in the novel, in a scene Tolstoy wrote two years later, she dazzles us and Vronsky as she exits her train from St. Petersburg in Moscow:

> Vronsky followed the guard to the carriage, and at the door of the compartment he stopped short to make room for a lady who was getting out.
>
> With the insight of a man of the world, from one glance at this lady's appearance Vronsky classified her as belonging to the best society. He begged pardon, and was getting into the carriage, but felt he must glance at her once more; not that she was very beautiful, not on account of the elegance and modest grace which were apparent in her whole figure, but because in the expression of her charming face, as she passed close by him, there was

---

[*]   Andrew Donskov, Л. Н. Толстой—Н. Н. Страхов. Полное собрание переписки [L. N. Tolstoy – N. N. Strakhov, Complete Correspondence Vol. 1] (Ottawa: University of Ottawa, 2003), http://tolstoy-lit.ru/tolstoy/pisma-tolstomu/pisma-strahova/letter-16.htm. (Hereafter, this reference will be listed as Donskov, *L. N. Tolstoy – N. N. Strakhov.*)

[†]   Why this description does not appear in *The Diaries of Sophia Tolstoy*, I don't know. It appears in Лев Толстой в воспоминаниях современенников. [Reminiscence of Lev Tolstoi by His Contemporaries], trans. Margaret Wettlin (Moscow: Foreign Languages Publishing House), 93. No date, but this edition was published after 1960.

something peculiarly caressing and soft. As he looked round, she too turned her head. Her shining grey eyes, that looked dark from the thick lashes, rested with friendly attention on his face, as though she were recognizing him, and then promptly turned away to the passing crowd, as though seeking someone. In that brief look Vronsky had time to notice the suppressed eagerness which played over her face, and flitted between the brilliant eyes and the faint smile that curved her red lips. It was as though her nature were so brimming over with something that against her will it showed itself now in the flash of her eyes, and now in her smile. Deliberately she shrouded the light in her eyes, but it shone against her will in the faintly perceptible smile. *

Before we even know that she is, in fact, Anna Karenina, the novel's namesake, but appearing only now in the eighteenth chapter, Tolstoy has completely attracted our attention to her.† We know, but Vronsky doesn't, that she has come to try to salvage her brother Stiva Oblonsky's marriage.

The first of two inquests in the novel occurs minutes after her and Vronsky's fateful introduction to each other:

A guard, either drunk or too much muffled up in the bitter frost, had not heard the train moving back, and had been crushed.

Before Vronsky and Oblonsky came back the ladies heard the facts from the butler.

Oblonsky and Vronsky had both seen the mutilated corpse. Oblonsky was evidently upset. He frowned and seemed ready to cry.

"Ah, how awful! Ah, Anna, if you had seen it! Ah, how awful!" he said.

---

* *Anna Karenina*, Part 1, Chapter 18, http://literatureproject.com/anna-karenina/anna_18.htm.

† One advantage of being a non-native reader of Russian is that my recognition of her smile bending her lips occurs at the speed of life, rather than of frictionless instantaneousness. The first time I read the novel in Russian I was as bedazzled and transfixed as Vronsky is. "В этом коротком взгляде Вронский успел заметить сдержанную оживленность, которая играла в ее лице и порхала между блестящими глазами и чуть заметной улыбкой, изгибавшею ее румяные губы." I read that sentence something like this: "In this short glance Vronsky succeeded in noticing the held-back liveliness that played on her face and fluttered between the shining eyes and the barely noticeable smile, bending her red lips." Yes, Garnett's is better. But my herky-jerky understanding gave me something like the appreciation of a basketball player's move replayed in super slow-motion.

Vronsky did not speak; his handsome face was serious, but perfectly composed.

"Oh, if you had seen it, countess [that is, Vronsky's mother]," said Stepan Arkadyevitch. "And his wife was there. . . . It was awful to see her! . . . She flung herself on the body. They say he was the only support of an immense family. How awful!"*

Stepan ("Stiva") Arkadevich Oblonsky is as sensitive here as his author; Tolstoy often responded with tears when overwhelmed by emotions. Stiva's sensitivities, however, don't last, as Tolstoy's evidently did. By the end of the chapter, Stiva has shaken off the horror as easily as water off a duck's back; he's got his own problems, after all, for which Anna has come to his rescue. But Anna, the elegant, composed, ever-conscious, strikingly beautiful heroine, is unnerved. Though she didn't witness the guard's death, she can imagine it:

Madame Karenina seated herself in the carriage, and Stepan Arkadyevitch saw with surprise that her lips were quivering, and she was with difficulty restraining her tears.

"What is it, Anna?" he asked, when they had driven a few hundred yards.

"It's an omen of evil," she said.

"What nonsense!" said Stepan Arkadyevitch. "You've come, that's the chief thing. You can't conceive how I'm resting my hopes on you."

Anna's brother has the tact to change the subject. But she feels (and those of us who have read the novel know) that it is indeed an evil omen. Even if the incident recedes from Anna's consciousness, Tolstoy has wound up a clock whose ticking we can almost always sense.†

The other inquest is accounted for in the epilogue, Part 8, when Vronsky and Stiva, united again at a train station, recall the aftermath of *her* death:

---

* *Anna Karenina*, Part 1, Chapter 18, http://literatureproject.com/anna-karenina/anna_18.htm.

† In the ballet of the novel, conceived in 1967 in Moscow by Maya Plisetskaya and her colleagues at the Bolshoi Theater, "That scream of the brakes resonates throughout the score such that Karenina dies continually in her imagination before the train actually arrives." Simon Morrison, *Bolshoi Confidential: Secrets of the Russian Ballet from the Rule of the Tsars to Today* (New York: Liveright, 2016), 381.

For an instant Stepan Arkadyevitch's face looked sad, but a minute later, when, stroking his mustaches and swinging as he walked [. . .] he had completely forgotten his own despairing sobs over his sister's corpse [. . .]*

Stiva has his faults. But at worst, he resembles Aleksandr Bibikov, the Tolstoys' light-hearted neighbor. "There's nothing new with us," Sofia wrote her sister Tatyana, less than four months after Anna Stepanovna Pirogova's suicide, "besides that Bibikov married that same German over whom Anna Stepanovna killed herself."†

Vronsky, for his part, experiences a double dose of suffering. Vronsky has a bad toothache (as had Tolstoy at various times during the writing of the novel). Tolstoy delivers us into Vronsky's two contrasting overwhelming pains:

He could hardly speak for the throbbing ache in his strong teeth, that were like rows of ivory in his mouth. He was silent, and his eyes rested on the wheels of the tender, slowly and smoothly rolling along the rails.

And all at once a different pain, not an ache, but an inner trouble, that set his whole being in anguish, made him for an instant forget his toothache. As he glanced at the tender and the rails, under the influence of the conversation with a friend he had not met since his misfortune‡, he suddenly recalled *her*—that is, what was left of her when he had run like one distraught into the cloak room of the railway station—on the table, shamelessly sprawling out among strangers, the bloodstained body so lately full of life; the head unhurt dropping back with its weight of hair, and the curling tresses about the temples, and the exquisite face, with red, half-opened mouth, the strange, fixed expression, piteous on the lips and awful in the still open eyes, that seemed to utter that fearful phrase—that he would be sorry for it—that she had said when they were quarreling.

And he tried to think of her as she was when he met her the first time, at a railway station too, mysterious, exquisite, loving, seeking and giving happiness, and not cruelly revengeful as he remembered her on that last moment. He

---

*   *Anna Karenina*, Part 8, Chapter 2, http://literatureproject.com/anna-karenina/anna_222.htm.

†   Donskov, *L. N. Tolstoy – N. N. Strakhov*, July 23, 1874, footnote 3, http://tolstoy-lit.ru /tolstoy/pisma-tolstomu/pisma-strahova/letter-16.htm.

‡   A "*friend*"? Tolstoy somehow disassociates in Vronsky's mind the fact that Stiva, who has physical resemblances to his sister, is Anna's brother.

tried to recall his best moments with her, but those moments were poisoned forever. He could only think of her as triumphant, successful in her menace of a wholly useless remorse never to be effaced. He lost all consciousness of toothache, and his face worked with sobs.[*]

As soon as Tolstoy began the first draft in March of 1873, a draft radically different in scope, focus, and tone from what the novel became, he knew the protagonist was going to kill herself. Tolstoy may have never mentioned Anna Pirogova's suicide to anyone besides Sofia in its immediate aftermath, but writing *Anna Karenina* uncovered to him and to us its resonances. To his own continual irritation and frustration, harried by his own impulses to kill himself, he was going to spend four years describing the circumstances that led to her suicide. Anna's death in Part 7 (followed by the epilogue known as Part 8), though rewritten many times by Tolstoy, right up to the galleys of the book edition, is not the climax but the origin of the book.

---

[*] *Anna Karenina*, Part 8, Chapter 5, http://literatureproject.com/anna-karenina/anna _225.htm.

I

Readying for "a new big labor": September 1872–March 1873

✳

It always seemed to me . . . that Leo Nikolaevich was not very fond of talking about literature, but was vitally interested in the personality of the author. The questions: "Do you know him? What is he like? Where was he born?" I often heard in his mouth. And nearly all his opinions would throw some curious light upon a man.

—Maxim Gorky[*]

W hat was *Tolstoy* like? Where was *he* born? He was born at the family estate 120 miles south of Moscow in 1828, the fourth of four brothers, the lone sister being two years younger than he. He was a "count" by inheritance of his father's title. His mother, whose estate, Yasnaya Polyana, he, as the youngest boy, inherited, died before he was two. A series of aunts helped raise him and his siblings, as their father died when Tolstoy was eight. Tolstoy spent many of his teenage years with an aunt in Kazan, a thousand miles east, and became a student at the university there,

---

[*]   Maxim Gorky, *Reminiscences of Leo Nikolaevich Tolstoy*, trans. S. S. Koteliansky and Leonard Woolf (New York: B.W. Huebsch, 1920), 75.

but the brilliant boy didn't like being taught, and after switching fields of study, during which time he read voraciously on his own, he left the university at age eighteen and moved back to Yasnaya Polyana, where he indulged in gambling, women, and music. He also set up and ran a school for the peasant children but quickly abandoned it. His letters as a young man usually brim with resolution and confidence, but sometimes they're full of regret over his moral failures. He longed for military action and joined his brother Nikolai, an officer in the Russian army in the Caucasus, as a volunteer. He became an officer and a writer. At twenty-four, he published *Childhood*, the first of three semiautobiographical novels (*Boyhood* and *Youth* followed), which woke up the Russian literary community, including the most famous of them, Ivan Turgenev. Who was this new dynamo?

Meanwhile he served in the army for the next few years and saw action and wrote detailed accounts of the war in Sebastopol, which accounts were also justly admired. He left the Caucasus in 1855, and tried to make a go of literary life while still in the service in St. Petersburg but came to despise the atmosphere of the Russian capital. He returned to Yasnaya Polyana in 1856 and resigned from the army. He dreamed of marrying, but wavered. His novella *Family Happiness* (1859) looked at courtship and marriage from the point of view of a young woman. Russia's serfs were freed in 1861, and Tolstoy saw that a primary need for them was literacy. One of the most satisfying projects of his life was the school for peasant children that he set up and ran on his estate from 1859 to 1862. He publicized his and his co-teachers' work in the school in a periodical, but he seems to have grown distracted by both his longing for marriage and for writing a new fictional work. A Moscow family he and his family had known for years, the head of which was a doctor in the Kremlin, kept attracting his attention, particularly the youngest daughter, eighteen-year-old Sofia Andreevna Bers. Within months, they were engaged and married. Tolstoy gave up the running of the schools that he had set up on the estate and in the region, and in 1863 began work on what became *War and Peace*. The "family happiness" he had desired became his and Sofia's. Between 1863 and 1873 they had six children; rarely for the time, the children all survived infancy. *War and Peace* appeared in installments starting in 1865 and was published as a whole in 1869. Though his work had not yet appeared in translation in Europe, he was now the most famous and most well-regarded author in Russia.

But what was he like? He was good-humored and moody, kind and understanding, bullheaded, humble, and contrary. He had terrific energy and long periods of aimlessness. He regularly started projects that he could not sustain or finish. He continually looked for a key that would simplify the complications and confusions of everyday life. He had strong impulses for answers that his studies of science, philosophy, and religion inspired him with. He could never settle for good his own ever-critical analyses of his own and others' ideas.

For much of 1872 Tolstoy was more literarily active and productive than he would ever be again. He turned forty-four in September. Now he was bustling about with his *Azbuka*, the "ABC" book (or primer) for teaching Russia's children to read. He would eventually denigrate almost every work he ever wrote, but not the *Azbuka*, which he saw as a life raft for the uneducated. In 1870, about 85 percent of the Russian population was illiterate.[*] In 1872 he started a school again in order to try out the methods he was advocating. His eldest daughter, Tanya, remembered:

> Seryozha [that is, Sergei, the eldest sibling, born in 1863; she, Tanya, was a year younger] and I could already read and write quite passably. Ilya, then about six, could only just read and was very bad at writing; nevertheless he announced that he was going to teach the youngest class. Papa agreed, and the lessons began.
>
> They lasted for slightly over two hours every day, beginning after our dinner, which was served between five and six, and continuing till it was time for us to go to bed. Papa took the boys' class in his study. The girls were mamma's responsibility, and she taught them in another room. We three children taught the absolute beginners their alphabet. Our classroom was the hall, and fat Ilya, a big pointer clutched in one hand, would try to teach the alphabet to rows of stolid little children much the same size as himself.[†]

Ten years before, when Tolstoy had been teaching the peasant children, he realized to his dismay that there were no good primers: "To print good books for the masses! How simple and easy it looks, just like all great ideas. There is just one difficulty: there are no good books for the people, not only in our country, but even not in Europe. In order to print such books they must be written first, but not one of the benefactors will think of undertaking this task."[‡]

[*]   Max Roser and Esteban Ortiz-Ospina, "Literacy," Our World in Data, accessed July 8, 2016, https://ourworldindata.org/literacy/.

[†]   Tatyana Tolstoy, *Tolstoy Remembered*, trans. Derek Coltman (New York: McGraw-Hill, 1977), 108–109.

[‡]   Leo Tolstoy, "On Methods of Teaching the Rudiments" from *On Education*, trans. Leo Wiener (Chicago: University of Chicago Press, 1967 [originally 1904]), 33.

And so, several years later, having married and having completed *War and Peace*, he saw his own children begin to come of age as readers. He decided not to wait for some benefactor to undertake that Herculean task of writing "good books for the masses" and set about planning and composing his own primer; he adapted stories from world literature, folk literature, the Bible, local legends, science and nature studies, jokes, and, of special interest, he told or retold his own and friends' "true stories" (a genre called *byli* in Russian). These stories are just what I would advise anyone wanting to learn Russian to read. The *byli* are full of voice and wit.* They are the essence of simplicity and drama, told in the first and third person in the most conversational, plain, and direct style. "They present," writes a Russian scholar, "perfect models of the language as actually spoken."† For example, Tolstoy composed this story as told by a peasant boy:

How the Boy Told about How He Stopped Being Scared of Blind Beggarmen

When I was a boy, blind beggarmen frightened me, and I was scared of them. One time I was walking home, and sitting on some porch-steps were two blind beggars. I didn't know what they would do to me. I was scared to run away and I was scared to pass them. I thought they might grab me. Suddenly one of them (he had white eyes, like milk) got up, grabbed me by the hand, and said, "Little fellow! Are you kindly?" I tore loose from him and ran to my mother.

She sent me out with some half-kopecks and bread. The beggars rejoiced over the bread and crossed themselves and ate. Then the beggar with the white eyes said, "Your bread is good! God thanks you." And he again took my hand, and he patted it. I felt sorry for him, and after that I stopped being afraid of blind beggarmen.‡

---

* Being an amateur, I may well know Tolstoy's stories for children as well as any native English speaker could; I have crawled over them ever since I began learning Russian. I have read them on my own and with tutors; I compiled and syncretized the available English translations for a selected edition of them (*Tolstoy's Classic Tales and Fables for Children*, Prometheus, 2002) and have since published translations of several more (in the magazines *Chtenia*, *Russian Life*, and *Fungi*).

† Samuel Northrup Harper, *Russian Reader*, sixth edition (Chicago: University of Chicago Press, 1932), x.

‡ V. G. Chertkov, ed., *Polnoe sobranie sochinenii*, 90 volumes (Moscow: 1928–1958), 21: 18. Hereafter, this reference will be abbreviated as *PSS*; the numbers listed here refer to volume 21, page 18. "Kak mal'chik rasskazyval o tom, kak on perestal boyat'sya slepykh nishchikh."

The lack of initial success of the *Azbuka* when it was published in the late fall of 1872 would come to annoy Tolstoy; the criticism it would receive would also distract him from completing *Anna Karenina* in its early conception, which as it turns out, for the sake of literary history, was probably a good thing, as he recast *Anna Karenina* while he was vastly recasting the *Azbuka* into its second form, the *New Azbuka*.* He often grew disgusted with his work on *Anna Karenina*, but he never tired of trying to get the *Azbuka* right. (He was so consumed with it that in the second to last part of *Anna Karenina*, completely out of the blue but not unbelievably, he realizes that Anna herself, living with Vronsky and lonely and ostracized in Moscow, has written a children's novel.†)

In October of 1872, the *Azbuka* was at the printer's, his research into the era of Peter the Great seemed to be complete, and Tolstoy was in good spirits, raring to write a new historical epic.

One of his longtime correspondents was his distant relative Aleksandra (Alexandrine) Andreevna Tolstaya, with whom he was confessional and deferential (she was eleven years older).‡ In the early spring of 1872 Tolstoy expressed to her his amazement at his good fortune:

> My life is just the same, i.e., I couldn't wish for anything better. There are
> a few great and intellectual joys—just as many as I have the strength to

---

* This new primer would be a best seller for the rest of his life and long into the Soviet era. There were hundreds of Russian picture books of individual or thematically connected *Azbuka* stories.

† To my dismayed curiosity, Tolstoy never told us what he imagined Anna has written about. This dismay resulted, twenty years ago, in my having written one for her. Everyone who has tried to read my creation has agreed that it's terrible, which means that it's not the "remarkable" work that Anna would have written.

‡ His "двоюродная тетка" (literally "cousin aunt") Alexandrine is variously identified in biographies and notes as his "great-aunt," "second aunt," "cousin," or "second-cousin." Tolstoy sometimes took an odd tone in his letters to her; it is not the tone he took with anyone else; it doesn't seem to me especially candid; he was flirty, as if with a long-ago ex-girlfriend. Back in 1857, he had considered her as a possible wife: "In the poetical setting of a spring in Switzerland [. . .] their friendship continued to grow, and it seemed as though real feeling would develop. But the countess was eleven years Tolstoy's senior; he noticed the first lines on her sweet, animated face, and often in his diary he sadly exclaimed, 'If she were only ten years younger! . . .' They never became more than friends." Tikhon Polner, *Tolstoy and His Wife*, trans. Nicholas Wreden (New York: W. W. Norton and Co., 1945), 34.

experience—and a solid background of *foolish joys*, as for instance: teaching the peasant children to read and write, breaking in a young horse, admiring a large room newly built on to the house, calculating the future income from a newly purchased estate, a well done version of a fable by Aesop, rattling off a symphony for 4 hands with my niece, fine calves—all heifers—and so on. The great joys are a family which is *terribly* fortunate, children who are all fit and well, and, I'm almost certain, intelligent and unspoiled, and work. Last year it was the Greek language, this year it's been the Primer so far, and now I'm beginning a big, new work [that is, about Peter the Great], in which there will be something of what I told you, although the whole thing is quite different, which is something I never expected. I feel altogether rested now from my previous work and entirely freed from the influence my writing had on me, and, most important, free of pride and praise. I'm starting work joyfully, timidly, and apprehensively, as I did the first time.*

That fall of 1872, in another happy mood (evidence of such moods in the coming years is rare), Tolstoy wrote Alexandrine one of his most winning letters:

> [. . .] having finished my Primer I recently began to write the big story—I don't like to call it a novel—which I've been dreaming about for so long.†

He didn't want to jinx the Peter project by calling it a novel and he didn't want to raise his own or anybody else's expectations. He was excited, but he strove to cultivate a state of equilibrium:

> And when this folly, as Pushkin so well called it, begins to take hold of you, you become particularly sensitive to the coarse things of life. Imagine a man in perfect stillness and darkness trying to hear the sounds of whispering and trying to see rays of light in the gloom, suddenly having stinking Bengal lights let off under his nose and having to listen to a march played on instruments that are out of tune. Very painful. Now once again I'm listening and watching in the stillness and darkness, and I only wish I could describe the

---

*   Christian, *Tolstoy's Letters*, 245–246, March 31, 1872.

†   Christian, *Tolstoy's Letters*, 251–254, October 26?, 1872.

hundredth part of what I see and hear. It gives me great pleasure. So much for my confession.

Despite there being, in the fall of 1872, six children between the ages of four months and nine years old at the Yasnaya Polyana house, the noise in the morning while Tolstoy was working at his writing was supposed to be at a minimum. Aylmer Maude describes Tolstoy's morning routine at this time:

> Before breakfast he would go for a walk with his brother in-law [one of Sofia's brothers], or they would ride down to bathe in the river that flows by one side of the estate. At morning coffee the whole family assembled, and it was generally a very merry meal, Tolstoy being up to all sorts of jokes, till he rose with the words, "One must get to work," and went off to his study, taking with him a tumbler full of tea. While at work in his room not even his wife was allowed to disturb him; though at one time his second child and eldest daughter, Tatyana, while still quite a little girl, was privileged to break this rule.[*]

The Tolstoy family's room arrangements varied, and Tolstoy didn't always have the now more famous vaulted downstairs room for his writing. His private study in other periods was upstairs.

There are several drawings, paintings, and photos of Tolstoy, when he was older, composing at his desk. In a sketch by Ilya Repin from 1891, for example, Tolstoy leans closely over paper, not especially hunched but like someone who has just finished swimming laps and has raised one elbow on the edge of the pool. The bearded, balding man wears a peasant blouse. His right leg is bent under his left, his shoed right foot comfortably poking out behind him. He is sitting not on a sawn off chair, as in some images, but on a stool or crate with a plank across it, and not at his perimeter-fenced rectangular desktop, but at a circular table that has attractive bends and twists in the central post. His pen is upright. Repin shows us the author's big hands; his right gripping the pen, his left holding down the top page and the papers below it. Tolstoy's hair is uncombed. His beard hangs down his chest. He is not smiling. Though nearsighted, he is not squinting; his handwriting is probably as messy as usual, most easily decipherable by patient Sofia.

---

[*]   Aylmer Maude, *The Life of Tolstoy: First Fifty Years* (London: Archibald Constable and Co., 1908), 320.

Leo Tolstoy working at the round table, 1891, by Ilya Repin.*

"*Patient?!*" exclaims the ghost of exasperated Sofia. Her exhausting labor of recopying night after night his handwritten drafts was an act of faith and love by a devoted admirer. This man, her husband, was writing for the ages, and she was his helpmate. In the mid- and late 1860s, when the *War and Peace* galleys would be set in type by printers in Moscow from Sofia's recopied manuscripts, they would be sent back to Tolstoy, and "the work would begin all over again."

> At first only corrections, omitted letters, and stops would be marked in the margins, then occasional words would be changed, then entire sentences, and then entire paragraphs would be taken out and others substituted. When he had finished with them, the proofs looked fairly clean in places and black with corrections in others. They could not be returned because no one but the Countess was able to disentangle the maze of corrections, lines, and words. She would spend another night copying. In the morning a neat stack of pages in her small, precise handwriting would be on her desk, ready to be mailed. Tolstoy would pick them up to look them over "for the last time," and in the evening they would be back again with everything changed and covered with corrections.

---

* WikiArt.org, https://www.wikiart.org/en/ilya-repin/leo-tolstoy-working-at-the-round
-table-1891, accessed June 13, 2016.

"Sonya [Tolstoy's pet name for Sofia], darling, excuse me; again I have spoiled your work; I will never do it again," he once said with an apologetic air, showing her the pages. "We will send them off tomorrow."

Often "tomorrow" dragged on for weeks and months.*

The biographer Tikhon Polner goes on to describe Tolstoy's summer routines in times of contentedness, which means almost certainly before 1875:

Tolstoy rose quite late, came out of the bedroom in a bathrobe and, with his beard tangled and uncombed, went to dress downstairs in his study. He emerged, dressed in a gray shirt and feeling energetic and refreshed, and went into the dining room to drink tea. The children were already eating their lunch. When no guests were present, he never lingered in the dining room. Carrying a glass of tea, he went back to his study. [. . .] The Countess settled in the drawing room to sew clothes for one of the children or to finish copying a manuscript that she had not had time to get through the night before. Peasant men and women, with their children, frequently came to her with their ills; she talked to them, tried to help them, and distributed, free of charge, standard medicines, which she kept in the house [Sofia was a doctor's daughter]. Until three or four in the afternoon complete quiet reigned in the house. "Lev is at work!" Then he came out of his study, went for a walk or a swim. Sometimes he went with a gun and a dog, sometimes on horseback, sometimes on foot. At five the bell in front of the house was rung. The children ran to wash their hands. Everybody gathered for dinner. Very often Tolstoy was late. He came in much embarrassed, apologized to his wife, and poured himself a silver whiskey glass full of homemade brandy. Usually he was hungry and ate anything that was already on the table. The Countess tried to restrain him, and asked him not to eat so much cereal because the meat and vegetables were still to come.

"Your liver will bother you again!"

He never listened and kept asking for more until he had his fill.

With great animation he recounted his impressions of the afternoon. Everyone enjoyed them. He joked with the children and with anyone at the table, and no one could resist his gay mood. After dinner he worked in his

---

*   Polner, *Tolstoy and His Wife*, 92–93.

study again, and at eight the entire family gathered around the samovar. They talked, read aloud, played, sang, and very often the children who were in the same room were included. For the children the day ended at ten o'clock, but voices could be heard in the drawing room until much later. Cards and chess were always popular, and so were endless arguments. Tolstoy sat at the piano and the Countess played four-hands with him, trying desperately to keep time. Occasionally her sister Tatyana sang for them. [. . .] Summer in Yasnaya Polyana was a continuous round of festivities. Their relatives were irresistibly attracted by the charming family. [. . .]*

When he had married at age thirty-four in September 1862, Tolstoy's idea of happiness was just this: two parents, a gang of kids, activity and fruitfulness.

His friends and family associated Levin, the costar of *Anna Karenina*, with Lev Tolstoy, and, at first impression, so should we. At the beginning of the novel, Levin, thirty-four, lives on an estate that even today resembles Yasnaya Polyana. At the same age as Tolstoy was in 1862, Levin undergoes the same agonies of disappointment and hope in regard to his beloved eighteen-year-old Kitty, who resembles in many ways Sofia Tolstaya in 1862, when Sofia was eighteen. On the other hand, notes Polner, "Levin lacks Tolstoy's genius, and is therefore at times quite boring."† To remind ourselves: by the age of thirty-four, the ever-fascinating, occasionally exasperating genius Tolstoy had written the superb trilogy of novellas, *Childhood, Boyhood*, and *Youth*, as well as other world-class novellas, stories, and pedagogical essays. Levin isn't an artist; the book he is writing about Russian farming will be of no interest to anyone but three or four people besides himself.

Knowing *Anna Karenina* as it is, with the two primary storylines devoted to Anna and Levin, it can seem surprising that Tolstoy didn't invent the Tolstoy-like Levin for *Anna Karenina* until after several drafts of early chapters. It seems that he started to feel the need for a predictable character to lean on and steady himself; as the novel took hold of him, Anna was the character Tolstoy kept discovering, the one whose fate made him anxious and unhappy, the one whose momentum toward suicide gave her author terrifying visions of his own impulses; by contrast, everything that Levin does and feels was familiar to Tolstoy. Episodes about Levin allowed Tolstoy to narrate through calm seas. Even if the novel becomes *about* Levin's development, he doesn't change so much as fulfill his role.

---

* Polner, *Tolstoy and His Wife,* 100–102.

† Polner, *Tolstoy and His Wife,* 58.

In the mid-1860s, a few years into marriage, Tolstoy proudly announced to his confidante Alexandrine that he had found *happiness*:

> You remember I wrote you once saying that people are wrong when they search for a happiness that means no work, no falsehoods, no bitterness, and only serenity and bliss. I was wrong! Such happiness exists; I have known it for the last three years, and each day it becomes deeper and more serene. The material that creates this happiness is not particularly attractive: children who—excuse me—wet themselves and cry; a wife who is nursing one, leading the other by the hand, and constantly accusing me of not being aware that they are on the verge of death; and paper and ink, which are my tools for describing events that have never taken place, and emotions of people who have never existed.[*]

I like to keep these images of Tolstoy in mind; one is of him in the chaos and joy of young family life; the other is of him as the artist amazed and satisfied that he is making something real from his imagination. In the midst of his early domestic life, he was composing *War and Peace*. This is the life Sofia would remember and long for; this was the sweet privileged family life that Tolstoy would later, from guilt, try to renounce.

Even in 1872, the Tolstoy family was the happy family supposedly like all other happy families. Sofia, twenty-eight, married ten years, had been pregnant six times and had delivered safely six times. All the children were alive and well. Tolstoy was the proud papa of a huge crew that he was expecting to get even bigger.

His October 1872 letter to Alexandrine, interrupted a few pages ago, goes on. Most of Tolstoy's letters are not newsy or conversationally relaxed, but this one is. In St. Petersburg, the capital, Alexandrine at this time was the governess of Tsar Alexander II's daughter Maria, who later married the second son of Queen Victoria of England. Alexandrine never had children, but she was apparently, lately, curious about Tolstoy's. Though a relative, Alexandrine had never been a visitor to Yasnaya Polyana and Sofia only met her husband's longtime correspondent for the first time in 1877.

Tolstoy reminded Alexandrine that she had given him "a subject for my letter which I would like to write on—namely my children."

Here they are:

---

[*]   Polner, *Tolstoy and His Wife*, 75.

The eldest [nine] is fair-haired—and not bad-looking. There is something weak and forbearing in his expression, and very gentle. When he laughs, it's not contagious, but when he cries I can hardly refrain from crying, too. Everyone says he is like my elder brother. I'm afraid to believe it. It would be too good. My brother's chief characteristic was not egoism and not unselfishness, but a strict middle course. He didn't sacrifice himself for anybody, but he didn't get in anybody's way, far less do anybody any harm. He kept his joys and sorrows to himself. Seryozha is clever—he has a mathematical mind and a feeling for art, he's an excellent pupil, good at jumping and gymnastics; but he's gauche and absent-minded. There's little originality in him. He's dependent on the physical. When he's well he's a very different boy from when he's ill.

Tolstoy's favorite elder brother was Nikolai (1823–1860); for Tolstoy, Nikolai's death resounded for many years. What may seem most surprising to us in this letter is how modern and involved a father Tolstoy was. At least through the 1870s, he knew his children as deeply as his wife did. He was the one they clowned and played around with; for all her attention to and worry about them, Sofia was more reserved with them. "She rarely laughed or enjoyed jokes, and as a deeply religious woman she tended to see the business of loving and caring for her husband and children as bound up with inevitable suffering, sorrow, and sacrifice. Perhaps," speculates R. F. Christian, "this explains why the children always addressed her in the formal 'you,' even though she was always there to scold or reassure them, while their father, who was much more distant and inaccessible, was always 'thou.'"*

Tolstoy then described for Alexandrine his second son:

Ilya is the 3rd child [six years old]. He's never been ill. He's big-boned, fair-skinned, ruddy-complexioned and glowing. A bad pupil. Always thinking about what he's told not to. Thinks up games himself. Neat and tidy; possessive; "mine" very important to him. Hot-tempered, *violent*, pugnacious; but also tender and very sensitive. Sensual—fond of eating and having a quiet lie down. When he eats blackcurrant jelly and buckwheat porridge his lips smack.

Perhaps that very morning those childish lips had smacked!

---

* Sophia Tolstoy, *The Diaries of Sophia Tolstoy*, trans. Cathy Porter (New York: Random House, 1985), xxvi. From the abundance of evidence the Tolstoy children have provided us, Papa Tolstoy was demonstrably not "distant and inaccessible." *Thou* is an informal archaic English form of the second-person singular "you." The translator means to suggest that children addressed their father informally with *ty* (ты) and their mother more formally with *vy* (вы).

Original in everything. When he cries, he's angry at the same time, and unpleasant, but when he laughs everyone laughs, too.

The character in *Anna Karenina* who takes a similarly quick bead on children's personality traits is Aunt Anna, who knows and gauges her brother Stiva's gang of five:

"Merciful heavens, Tanya! You're the same age as my Seryozha," she added, addressing the little girl as she ran in. She took her in her arms and kissed her. "Delightful child, delightful! Show me them all."

She mentioned them, not only remembering the names, but the years, months, characters, and illnesses of all the children, and Dolly could not but appreciate that.

Knowing the details of the children's lives meant so much to Tolstoy, and in the beginning of the novel it means so much to Anna and to Dolly, the mother of those five children. Dolly, not her husband Stiva, however, is the parent who keenly distinguishes the characters of the children. A sign of Anna's future disengagement and loss of footing will occur with the birth of her second child, a girl. She will know less about her toddler than does Vronsky, the father, or even than her husband Karenin, who acts as a foster father.

In the letter to Alexandrine, Tolstoy was fascinated and amused by his son Ilya:

Everything forbidden has its attractions for him, and he gets to know about it at once. When still a little fellow he overheard my pregnant wife saying she could feel the movement of her child. For a long time his favourite game was to stuff something round underneath his jacket, stroke it with a tense hand and whisper with a smile: "It's baby." He would also stroke all the bumps where the furniture springs had broken and say "baby." Recently, when I was writing stories for my *Primer* he invented one of his own: "A boy asked: 'Does God go to the lavatory?' God punished him and the boy had to spend all his life going to the lavatory.'"

Tolstoy never wrote such a letter again; he never again surveyed his family in such a pleased, proud, and detailed way. At this time he expressed no regrets about their way of life, even if he betrayed the anxiety of any parent who foresees future calamities:

If I die, the elder boy will turn out a splendid fellow, wherever he gets to, and will almost certainly be top at school, but Ilya will come to grief unless he has a strict supervisor and one he loves.

Tolstoy illustrated his point about his boys in his usual brilliant, apparently simple, narrative mode:

> In summer we used to go bathing*; Seryozha would ride himself, and I would put Ilya in the saddle behind me. I came out one morning and they were both waiting. Ilya was wearing a hat and carrying a towel, all neat and tidy and beaming, but Seryozha had come running up from somewhere, hatless and out of breath. "Find your hat," I said, "or I won't take you." Seryozha ran hither and thither—but no hat. "It's no good, I won't take you without a hat. It will be a lesson for you, you're always losing everything." He was on the verge of tears. I set off with Ilya and waited to see if he showed any sympathy. None at all. He just beamed, and talked about the horse. My wife found Seryozha in tears. He'd looked for his hat and couldn't find it. She guessed that her brother, who had gone off early in the morning to fish, had put on Seryozha's hat. She wrote me a note to say that Seryozha was probably not to blame for losing his hat, and she was sending him on to me in a cap. (She had guessed rightly.) I heard rapid footsteps on the bridge leading to the bathing-place and Seryozha came running up (he'd lost the note on the way) and began to sob. Then Ilya did too, and so did I a little.

Tolstoy loved his sons but may not have been as charmed by them as he was by his daughters. And in *Anna Karenina*, Stiva Oblonsky may have shared Tolstoy's own affinity for daughters over sons:

> Two childish voices (Stepan Arkadyevitch recognized the voices of Grisha, his youngest boy, and Tanya, his eldest girl) were heard outside the door. They were carrying something, and dropped it.
>
> "I told you not to sit passengers on the roof," said the little girl in English; "there, pick them up!"

---

* I would prefer to translate the phrase Летом мы ездили купаться as: "In the summer we went swimming." We can assume, then, it happened the *recent* summer of 1872, spent at home in Yasnaya Polyana. The ambiguous "used to go" could suggest *a long time ago*, which I doubt Tolstoy would mean when he was illustrating points about the budding personalities of his boys.

"Everything's in confusion," thought Stepan Arkadyevitch; "there are the children running about by themselves." And going to the door, he called them. They threw down the box, that represented a train, and came in to their father.

The little girl, her father's favorite, ran up boldly, embraced him, and hung laughingly on his neck, enjoying as she always did the smell of scent that came from his whiskers. At last the little girl kissed his face, which was flushed from his stooping posture and beaming with tenderness, loosed her hands, and was about to run away again; but her father held her back.

"How is mamma?" he asked, passing his hand over his daughter's smooth, soft little neck. "Good morning," he said, smiling to the boy, who had come up to greet him. He was conscious that he loved the boy less, and always tried to be fair; but the boy felt it, and did not respond with a smile to his father's chilly smile.*

Tolstoy's magic with the character of Stiva is that the ever charming, ever conscious socializer, not to mention the ever calculating philanderer, never seems to be a stand-in for the author. And yet in Stiva's loving behavior as a father we do see something of his author. Tolstoy continued to Alexandrine:

Tanya is 8. Everyone says she is like Sonya [again, Tolstoy's usual affectionate name for Sofia], and I believe it, even though it's a good thing to believe, but I also believe it because it's obvious. If she had been Adam's eldest daughter and there had been no children younger than her, she would have been an unhappy girl. Her greatest pleasure is to play with little children. She obviously finds physical enjoyment in holding and touching a child's body. Her avowed dream now is to have children. The other day we went to Tula to have her portrait done. She began to ask me to buy a penknife for Seryozha, then something else for another child and something else for a third. She knows exactly what will give most pleasure to each one. I didn't buy anything for her, and she never for a moment thought about herself. On our way home I said "Tanya, are you asleep?" "No." "What are you thinking about?" "I'm thinking when we get home how I'll ask mama whether little Lev has been good, and how I'll give him a present, and somebody else a present, and how Seryozha will pretend he doesn't like it, but will really like it very much."

---

* *Anna Karenina*, Part 1, Chapter 3, http://literatureproject.com/anna-karenina/anna_3.htm.

It seems, especially in this narrative mode, that Tolstoy understands his children the way he understands his characters. He appreciates what they do and what they say, their physical manifestations, their movements and inclinations. The proud father's frank evaluations, on the other hand, might take us aback:

> She's not very clever. She doesn't like to put her mind to work, but the mechanism in her head is sound.

His next remark, about her probable conventionality, actually more reveals his own conventionality at the time:

> She'll be a splendid wife if God should give her a husband. And I'm prepared to give a huge prize to anyone who could make a *new woman* out of her.

Tolstoy had to be imagining that he would continue being the generous-hearted father he was now. He turned out, instead, in his fifties and beyond, to be rather possessive of his grown-up daughters, and, as it happened, Tanya wasn't conventional and made herself something of "a new woman" on her own: she married late, to a widower, and only had one child.*

> The 4th—Lev [three years old]. Good-looking, clever, a good memory, graceful. Any clothes fit him as though made for him. Anything other people do he can do too, and very cleverly and well. *I don't understand him* properly yet.
>
> The 5th—Masha. Two years old [actually only 20 months], the one who nearly cost Sonya her life. A weak, sickly child; milk-white body, curly fair hair, large, strange blue eyes—strange because of their deep, serious expression. Very clever, and unattractive to look at. She's going to be an enigma. She'll suffer, and search and find nothing; but she'll go on searching for ever for what is most attainable.

Masha's birth and Sofia's consequent nearly fatal puerperal fever would become part of Anna Karenina's story. (I'll discuss this unhappy connection in a later chapter.)

---

* See insert for this photograph: Tanya (Tat'yana Lvovna Sukhotina-Tolstaya) and her daughter, Tatyana Mikhailovna Sukhotina, c. 1907. Source: http://www.zapas-slov.com.ua /kiev-metro-i-lev-tolstoj-izrail-obedinyaet/.

Tolstoy has described his children's characters, but they don't seem limited or fixed. He squares them up in his vision and predicts something of their fates, and their fates are nearly their characters:

> The 6th—Pyotr [four months old]. A giant. An enormous, fascinating baby in a bonnet. He puts his elbows out and tries to crawl somewhere, and my wife gets agitated and excited and het up when she takes him in her arms, but I don't understand it at all. I know he has great physical reserves, but I don't know whether there is also anything for which they are needed. For this reason I don't like children less than 2 or 3 years old—I don't understand them. [. . .]*

By this point we should wonder about Sofia's point of view. Pyotr was the last, of course, for now. Tolstoy wanted lots and lots of children, didn't want to stop having them, while Sofia was tired and wanted a pause. Contraception was available (Sofia knew more about it than—we discover late in the novel—Stiva's wife, Dolly, knows), but Tolstoy scorned contraception, believing sex for sex's sake (as a married man) was immoral. He needed to temper his shame about his lustfulness by believing that the act could result in procreation.

After the birth of their second baby in 1864, Sofia was suffering from cracked nipples, and when she begged Tolstoy to hire a wet nurse, he threw fits. He was impatient about maintaining his complete dream of family life, and he felt nursing shouldn't include anybody but the mother and baby. Readers may remember Levin's disappointment in himself when Kitty has their baby and how its helplessness bothers him, but by 1872, Tolstoy was accustomed to his deficient understanding of infants.

However we judge Tolstoy as a father or husband, *Anna Karenina* shows us that the dynamics of family life fascinated him. Through Tolstoy we, family-focused or not, are captivated by the Oblonskys. We become thoughtful about family dynamics; we recognize the unfairness and simultaneously accept that Stiva maintains the sympathy of friends and family despite his cheating heart.

Sofia Tolstaya's husband was more dependable than Dolly Oblonskaya's, but Sofia's happiness was more obviously tied to Tolstoy's than Dolly's to Stiva's. Though Sofia had grown weary of copying out portions of Tolstoy's *Azbuka*, as it wasn't fiction for adults and didn't engage her, in the fall of 1872 she was looking forward to helping him with his grand new historical novel about Peter the Great's era.

---

* Christian, *Tolstoy's Letters*, 252–254, October 26?, 1872.

That fall, just a couple of days after Tolstoy's proud letter to Alexandrine, Sofia wrote to her sister Tatyana: "Levochka has just begun a novel and is very happy and enjoying his labor to come."*

If he was "very happy," she was very happy.

✳

In early November 1872, Tolstoy wrote to a close friend, the poet Afanasy Fet, with whom he often shared domestic news: "We've just now all gone skating as a family." (The winter freeze had already occurred in Yasnaya Polyana, 120 miles south of Moscow.) Afanasy Fet (1820–1892), one of Tolstoy's best friends in this period, was a famous poet whose work Tolstoy usually greatly admired. Fet and Tolstoy were at the time as if on the same Russian Olympic literature team. Fet was someone to whom Tolstoy never condescended. Fet never documented his friendship with Tolstoy, and neither did Tolstoy with him. They shared an interest in literature but probably an even larger one in horses. Fet was a family man, so they also regularly exchanged news about their children and wives. He mentioned to Fet, seemingly with high hopes, the impending publication of the *Azbuka*. But as for the Peter the Great novel, there was a stall: "I'm readying everything to write, but I can't say that I have begun."†

Tolstoy devoured books and kept notebooks for his research on Peter. He found that one little detail could give him the essence of a moment or of a character.

In Sofia's "Various Notes for Future Reference," which had a separate place in her diaries, she observed:

> He jots down in various little notebooks anything that might come in useful for an accurate description of the manners, customs, clothes, houses, and the general way of life in this period—particularly that of the peasants and those far from court and the Tsar. Elsewhere he jots down any ideas he may have about the characters, plot, poetic passages, and so on. It's like a mosaic. He is so immersed in the details that he came back especially early from hunting yesterday, as he wanted to go through various documents to find out whether one writer was correct in saying that they wore high collars with the short kaftan in the days of

---

* Gusev, *Materials*, 115, letter of October 28, 1872.

† *PSS* 61: 340, letter of early November 1872.

Peter the Great. L. thinks these were worn only with the long coats, particularly amongst the lower orders. [. . .]*

Amid everything that he had collected and digested about Peter the Great, he was nevertheless stymied.

Sofia had been watching him like a hawk for any sign of movement with his writing. On November 19, she wrote her younger brother, Stepan:

> Levochka sits, surrounded by a heap of books, portraits, pictures, and frowning, reads, makes marks, makes notes. At night, when the children have lain down to sleep, he tells me his plans and what he wants to write; sometimes he's disenchanted, goes into a terrible despair and thinks that nothing's going to come out, and sometimes he's so close to getting to work with great excitement; but one still can't say that he wrote, only that he prepared himself [to do so].†

Her progress report to her sister Tatyana at the end of November was more hopeful: "Now Levochka is especially heartily working on the story of Peter the Great. He gathers material, reads, writes, labors terribly, and wants to write a novel from that epoch. We're leading more than ever a solitary and laborious life."‡ Sofia, having grown up in Moscow, on the Kremlin grounds, often rued their "solitary" life. Despite that the Tolstoy family's letters and diaries make it seem as if they had a constant stream of visitors, Yasnaya Polyana was plain and simple country living; visitors necessarily came a long way; traveling there was a slow adventure until the mid-1860s, when a railroad station connected Moscow with Tula, the small city a dozen miles from Tolstoy's estate.

At the beginning of December 1872, Tolstoy took a train to Moscow for the baptism of his grandniece.§ He often declared he didn't like trains. However, to catch Tolstoy out in contradictions or seeming contradictions is easy; he was usually the first to point them out. Despite Tolstoy's dislike of trains, he continually used them and would eventually,

---

*   *The Diaries of Sophia Tolstoy*, January 16, 1873.

†   Gusev, *Materials*, 190, letter of November 19, 1872.

‡   Gusev, *Materials*, 190, letter of November 30, 1872.

§   N. N. Gusev, *Letopis' zhizni i tvorchestva L'va Nikolaevicha Tolstogo*, (Moscow: Gosudarstvennoe Izdatel'stvo Khudozhestvennoi Literatury, 1958), 397, letter of December 3, 1872. (Hereafter, this reference will be listed as Gusev, *Letopis'*.)

at the age of eighty-two, run away from home by train and finally die beside the tracks in a stationmaster's house. Trains are the locomotion that bring Anna into and out of the novel; they could bring Tolstoy up to or back from Moscow in a couple of hours. On this quick little trip, Tolstoy went to a Moscow bookstore and bought seven more books on Peter; he met with a literary friend, Pavel Golokhvastov, who gave him a list of his own Peter-related books; Tolstoy later picked thirteen of them he wanted to borrow.

Back home from Moscow a few days later, he wrote Alexandrine a newsy, cheerful note, concluding with the mention that "in the winter [we're] at work from morning to night."*

That parting line suggests he was not blocked about the writing, but he was in fact stuck.

In mid-December Tolstoy wrote to his most important friend of this decade, the critic Nikolai Strakhov, and admitted, "I have not been working. I have surrounded myself with books on Peter I and his time; I read, take notes, endeavor to write, and I *can not*. But what an age for an artist. Wherever one looks, everything is a problem, a riddle whose solution is possible only through poetry. The entire knot of Russian life rests here. It even seems to me that nothing will come of my preparations. I have already been taking aim too long, and I am too excited. I will not be distressed if nothing comes of this."† He seems to have begun preparing himself to abandon the project.

The holidays, a festive time at Yasnaya Polyana ever since Lev and Sofia's marriage, were shared with Tolstoy's old friend Dmitrii Alekseevich D'yakov (a widower) D'yakov's daughter, and a few relatives.

Tolstoy had begged his lone surviving brother Sergei to come and bring his daughter and also wondered if Sergei could lend him fifteen hundred rubles. For the next few years, it would not be unusual for Tolstoy to rummage for money to buy land or horses. This is one area where Levin seems more responsible than Tolstoy; Levin is careful about money. Tolstoy, like Stiva Oblonsky, sometimes began trying to buy before he had the money; he had more wants than means. Tolstoy explained to Sergei that the *Azbuka* had been "a fiasco" and "won't make money," and it would be best if he could pay him back in a year, with interest.‡

In the new year 1873's first letter, Tolstoy wrote to thank Golokhvastov for the books about Peter, but complained that he hadn't been able to shake off a gloomy feeling: "I'm

---

*   *PSS* 61: 344, letter of December 7–8, 1872.

†   Boris Eikhenbaum, *Tolstoi in the Seventies*, trans. Albert Kaspin (Ann Arbor: Ardis, 1982), 86, letter of December 17, 1872.

‡   *PSS* 61: 350, letter of December 17–20?, 1872.

this whole winter in so heavy, abnormal a state. I'm tormented, I'm agitated, I'm horrified by this submission, I despair, and I'm sure leaning toward that conviction that nothing besides torment is coming out of this."*

The biographer Nikolai Gusev highlights Tolstoy's attempt to light the fire of imagination, pointing out that "on this very day" of his frustrated letter to Golokhvastov, "he writes a letter to his acquaintance V. K. Istomin, working in Novocherkassk, with the request to paint 'a picture of that place' above the Azov, where the military action under Peter had taken place. He wanted to know: 'which bank of the Don [. . .] is there—where was it high, where was it narrow? Were there hills, mounds? Were there bushes [. . .] what kind of grass? Was there feather grass? Were there reeds? What kind of wildlife? And in the main currents of the Don [. . .] what was the main character it had, what kind of bank?' He asks [Istomin] to name for him the books that his questions were interested in and to indicate 'whether there was anything . . . of Peter's Azovian campaign?'"†

He wanted those eyewitness descriptions of Peter's campaign. He wanted to reengage himself the way he almost effortlessly became engaged by the people and customs in *War and Peace*. But where his imagination excitedly made connections in the mid-1860s to the first two decades of the 19th century, he was now lost and waiting. He had researched and researched, so why couldn't he transport himself in his imagination to 1700?

Gusev counts thirty-three starts of the Peter novel and divides them into six categories of focus.‡ As summarized, they seem like trial balloons that couldn't quite carry Tolstoy away. Peter was just too awful—his cruelty, his participation in torture, his killing of his own son. The whole epoch, remembered Stepan Bers, made Tolstoy feel "unsympathetic." Peter's life and character, which had been fascinating to Tolstoy, ended up disgusting him.

Meanwhile, he was also aggravated by the *Azbuka*'s poor sales and reviews, and so sure was he (he would be proved right) that the *Azbuka* deserved success, it would divide his attention and he would spend a good portion of the next year and a half revising it and recasting it.

Near the end of January, "Tolstoy journeyed to his brother's at Pirogovo for the burial of his child."§ From that bare note in the first volume of Gusev's *Letopis'* (a chronicle of almost eight hundred pages accounting for Tolstoy's day-to-day or week-to-week

---

* PSS 62: 8, letter of January 12, 1873.

† Gusev, *Materials*, 116–117.

‡ Gusev, *Materials*, 124.

§ Gusev, *Letopis'*, 399.

movements and activities from childhood to 1890), my imagination began asking for details. For starters, how did the bad news arrive? Did a servant of Sergei's carry a letter and make his way those thirty miles to Yasnaya Polyana on horseback or in a sleigh? What was Tolstoy thinking as he took the long cold midwinter journey to Sergei's? Did he become agitated about his own children's vulnerability?

As has often happened in the course of researching Tolstoy's years writing *Anna Karenina*, I wanted the details about his life presented as vividly and significantly as only he himself could present them. I wonder if Tolstoy set off similarly to how Nikita and Vasili would one day set out in his novella *Master and Man*:

> [. . .] the day was windy, dull, and cold, with more than twenty degrees Fahrenheit of frost. Half the sky was hidden by a lowering dark cloud. In the yard it was quiet, but in the street the wind was felt more keenly. The snow swept down from a neighbouring shed and whirled about in the corner near the bath-house.
>
> Hardly had Nikita ["Man"] driven out of the yard and turned the horse's head to the house, before Vasili Andreevich ["Master"] emerged from the high porch in front of the house with a cigarette in his mouth [Tolstoy smoked cigarettes even into his sixties], and wearing a cloth-covered sheep-skin coat tightly girdled low at his waist, and stepped onto the hard-trodden snow which squeaked under the leather soles of his felt boots, and stopped. Taking a last whiff of his cigarette he threw it down, stepped on it, and letting the smoke escape through his moustache and looking askance at the horse that was coming up, began to tuck in his sheepskin collar on both sides of his ruddy face, clean-shaven except for the moustache, so that his breath should not moisten the collar.[*]

While Master Vasili is venturing out into that wintry day on business, Tolstoy's purpose in 1873 was to console his brother and his brother's family.

Tolstoy wrote a letter to Fet shortly after the funeral of Sergei's child. In it he reflected on the importance of religion in dealing with death and discussed details he could not have written to his childless bachelor friend Strakhov or mentioned to his own reasonably

---

[*] Tolstoy wrote *Master and Man* in the 1890s but set it "in the seventies." Leo Tolstoy, *Master and Man*, trans. Aylmer and Louise Maude (New York: Charles Scribner's Sons, 1913; Project Gutenberg 2009), http://www.gutenberg.org/files/986/986-h/986-h.htm.

anxious wife. That is, amid the awkwardness of the ceremony of death, *what do you say, what do you do*? There's something practical to do and there's the absurdity of religious ceremony, but the ceremony somehow helps:

> [. . .] I recently visited my brother; a child of his had died and was being buried. There were priests, and a pink coffin, and everything there ought to be. My brother and I took the same view about religious rites as you do, and when we were together we couldn't help expressing to one another a feeling almost of revulsion at this ritualism. But then I began to think: well, what could my brother have done to carry the decomposing body of his child out of the house in the end? How should it have been carried out? By a coachman in a sack? And where should it be put, how should it be buried? What, generally speaking, is a fitting way to end things? Is there anything better than a requiem incense, etc.? (I, at least, can't think of anything.) And what about growing weak and dying? Should one wet oneself, s . . . *, and nothing more? That's no good.†

Tolstoy was edging toward a conviction that he would describe later in *Confession*: those human social activities that make everyday life possible for the majority of people in the world have "something" to them and shouldn't be held in contempt by nonbelievers. For now, he concluded:

> [. . .] The remarkable thing about religion is that for so many centuries and for so many millions of people it has rendered a service, the very greatest service that any human thing can render on this occasion. With such a task, how can it be logical? It is an absurdity, but the one out of many millions of absurdities which is suitable for this occasion. There is something in it.
>
> It's only to you that I allow myself to write such letters. [. . .]‡

With Fet, he sometimes extended himself and wrote his feelings directly onto the page. The postscript to this letter has been left out in R. F. Christian's English translation:

---

*   Censored as "п . . .тъ" in the Jubilee edition, *PSS* 62: 7.

†   Christian, *Tolstoy's Letters*, 256, January 30, 1873.

‡   Ibid.

My letter is wild because I'm terribly out of spirits. My work is underway—terribly difficult. Preparations of studying are not finished, the plan is completely building up, but the strength, feeling, all that is less and less. A day of health and three not.[*]

Peter's world was not where Tolstoy wanted to go. He could feel his wife and friends looking expectantly at him. It's as if his well-wishers wanted to travel with him to the launch of his new project, but instead all they were seeing was his continual repacking for it.

Meanwhile, he was so testy that he responded to Alexandrine's letter of praise of *War and Peace* by scoffing that *to him* that novel was "completely disgusting," and while trying to decide how to prepare it for inclusion in an eight-volume edition of his collected works (the last four volumes contained that novel), he had experienced "the feeling of despair, shame."[†] Tolstoy became even more irritable every time he thought about the *Azbuka* and its unhappy reception, and he warned Alexandrine off his pride and joy:

Please don't look at my *Primer*. You haven't taught little children, you're far removed from the people, and you will see nothing in it. I've put more work and love into it than into anything else I've done, and I know that this is the one important work of my life. It will be appreciated in years' time or so by those children who study from it.[‡]

He had a remedy for the chronic problem of education in Russia, and he resented the authorities for not letting him apply it.

In early February Tolstoy "read aloud with his wife the novel of Gustave Droz, *Babolain*, which T.," Sofia told her sister, "'very much likes.'"[§]

Whenever Sofia took her turn reading (assuming they took turns), did Tolstoy sit, eyes closed, nodding, murmuring approval or interest or surprise? Was it something

---

[*]   *PSS* 62: 8.

[†]   *PSS* 62: 8–9.

[‡]   Christian, *Tolstoy's Letters*, 257.

[§]   Gusev, *Letopis'*, 400. Droz's novel is readable online in an 1873 English translation from the 1872 French original that Tolstoy read. *Babolain* is narrated as a memoir; Babolain is the narrator's uncle.

like a couple watching TV together? When he read was Sofia sewing, mending, daydreaming? Was Tolstoy smoking? We can assume they were reading it in French. Their French had to be very good. From recordings made near the end of his life, we can hear Tolstoy's reedy actual voice in Russian as well as a couple of short messages that he delivered in French, German, and English.* But what about Sofia's voice? Tolstoy would soon describe Anna Karenina's "chesty laugh," but I am unaware of anything mentioned by him about Sofia's or Kitty's voices or laughs. His own laughter, recalled Aylmer Maude, "which began on a high note, had something wonderfully infectious about it. His head would hang over on one side, and his whole body would shake."†

In February, Tolstoy's brother Sergei, perhaps still grieving, visited Yasnaya Polyana. Strakhov, passing through on his way south from St. Petersburg, came to visit the Tolstoys at Yasnaya Polyana on February 18–19.

Even for some of us who love Russian literature, Nikolai Nikolaevich Strakhov might seem just a name (his name in fact means *fears*); he pops up in biographies of Dostoevsky and Tolstoy. He didn't write fiction or plays or poetry; he was not a giant or some wildman whose life would inspire his colossal friends' stories or inspire them to reconstruct him into a character. Unmarried, unreligious (though the son of a priest), he had a background in science and philosophy and wrote learned articles about them; he had argued and would continue arguing for recognizing the importance of Darwin's theories, but he was, primarily, "*a critic.*" Who needed him?

The more I learned of Tolstoy's life during his *Anna Karenina* years, the more necessary Strakhov became; obviously Tolstoy needed him! Strakhov had written long, smart, appreciative essays about *War and Peace* as it was being published. Later, in 1871, working for a journal, he wrote to Tolstoy to solicit an article, and Tolstoy straight off invited Strakhov to visit Yasnaya Polyana and become acquainted. From 1871 to the end of Strakhov's life in 1896, he was liked and valued by the entire family. Sofia appreciated his influence on Tolstoy. Strakhov was modest. He was Tolstoy's admirer without being a flatterer. Though they were the same age, Strakhov knew his literary place was far below Tolstoy's, so there was no rivalry or assumption of equality between them.

---

* "Rare! Tolstoy Reads in 4 Languages,": YouTube video, accessed June 23, 2017, https://www.youtube.com/watch?v=TXQ-KrXCAIQ. Audio available at Nekommercheskaya Elekronnaya Biblioteka "ImWerden": https://imwerden.de/publ-132.html.

† Maude, *The Life of Tolstoy: First Fifty Years*, 368.

*Nikolay Nikolayevich Strakhov (1828–1896), Tolstoy's literary conscience
and closest friend during the writing of* Anna Karenina.[*]

It's not likely that Tolstoy confessed to Strakhov this February that he had jumped ship from the Peter the Great project, because a couple of weeks later he complained to him that the writing still wasn't moving. When in mid-March Tolstoy did abandon Peter the Great for Anna the Greatest, he delayed telling Strakhov.

Two editors, having seen a news item that winter that Tolstoy was working on a novel, contacted him about their interest in publishing it. He ignored their queries.

After a letter-writing dry spell, Tolstoy, as was his habit, wrote several on one day, March 1. He was newsiest and liveliest with his sister-in-law Tatyana; he told her that they had a new English governess, Emily Tabor (Tatyana's family, living in Russian Georgia, was employing the Tolstoys' previous English governess, Hannah, whose health needed a warmer climate); he asked if Tatyana had read Alexandre Dumas *fils*'s essay about marriage, *The Man-Woman* (*L'homme-femme*). He didn't mention to her that it's a series of cynical reflections in which Dumas famously suggests that if husbands would only beat their wives at the first sign of wandering interest in another man, the wives would stay in line forever.[†] (There are a couple of references to Dumas's essay in *Anna Karenina*.)

---

[*]   Wikipedia: Die freie Enzyklopadie. https://de.wikipedia.org/wiki/Nikolai_Nikolajewitsch_
      Strachow#/media/File:Nikolay_Strakhov.jpg. Accessed June 17, 2017.

[†]   Alexandre Dumas fils, *Man-Woman; or The Temple, the Hearth, the Street,* trans. George
      Vandenhoff (Philadelphia: J. B. Lippencott & Co, 1873), see particularly pp. 59–64, https://
      archive.org/details/manwomanortempl00dumagoog.

In two of the new month's letters, Tolstoy complained about the stagnation of the Peter novel. He wrote Strakhov: "My work's not moving, and again doubt has been found."[*] He told Alexandrine he was looking forward to the family summer in Samara at his small simple farm there. Meanwhile, "My work goes poorly. Life is so good, light and short, but the presentation of it comes out so ugly, heavy and long."[†]

Strakhov, having meditated on Tolstoy's various hesitations, wrote, on March 15, all the right things: that is, his esteemed friend did not have to top himself:

> With all my soul I desire that the work that so deeply and seriously occupies you gets going finally (as I love these excitements of yours, as they excite me too!). But remember, Lev Nikolaevich, that if you don't write anything, you all the same remain the creator of the most original and substantial production in Russian literature. When there's no longer a Russian kingdom, the new people will study *War and Peace* to find out what the Russian people were.[‡]

On March 17, 1873, the day before he forsook Peter the Great for the character who became Anna Karenina, Tolstoy wrote to Fet and remarked again that "My work is not moving."[§]

---

[*]   *PSS* 62: 12, letter of March 1?, 1873.

[†]   *PSS* 62: 13.

[‡]   Donskov, *L. N. Tolstoy – N. N. Strakhov*; http://feb-web.ru/feb/tolstoy/texts/selectpe/ts6/ts62097-.htm.

[§]   *PSS* 62: 15, letter of March 17, 1873.

2

A Very Very Rough Rough Draft: March 18, 1873–June 2, 1873

❋

We know that Tolstoy's reading of a collection of Alexander Pushkin's fiction on March 18, 1873, brought on an urge to write; sometime later that day, his right hand picked up his pen and, instead of trying again to inspire himself about the court of Peter the Great in 1700, he began describing a modern high-society party where a floozy of a wife was carrying on an affair under the nose of her good, honest husband. The thought of that cuckolded husband mocked by a depraved society evoked more pity and alarm in Tolstoy than the thought that that same wife would kill herself. Her husband, who had been humiliated while she lived and cheated, would soldier on. *Or would he kill himself too?* Tolstoy wondered. How *her* suicide would happen, Tolstoy didn't know or care. *The poor husband!*

Sofia wrote, in her "Various Notes for Future Reference":

> Last night L. suddenly said to me: "I have written a page and a half, and it seems good." I assumed this was yet another attempt to write about the Peter the Great period, and didn't pay much attention.

She must have heard something like this often enough from her husband that his vague mention of that night's accomplishment did not impress her:

> But then I realised that he had in fact embarked on a novel about the private lives of present-day people.

How exactly did she realize that? Had Tolstoy stood up and walked over to her and shyly handed over the page and a half? Did she start to read it and become confused? *But, Levochka, what does this have to do with Peter's time?* That's *not true of Peter's time!*

She only remarked in the notes to herself: "So strange, the way he just pitched straight into it."

> . . . this evening he read various other excerpts from the [Pushkin] book, and under Pushkin's influence he sat down to write. He went on with his writing today, and said he was well pleased with it.[*]

In the next four years of working on *Anna Karenina*, Tolstoy would communicate having had one, maybe two more experiences of being "well pleased" with what he had written that given day. Some of the pleasure of these first two days of work may have had to do with his relief of escaping the complications of the Peter project.

Sofia added a detail concerning the second day of his work that helps dissolve the image we might conjure up of artists as relentless slaves to their work. Tolstoy was *not* working all day; sometimes he was out playing: "At the moment he is out looking at the fox with his two sons, their tutor Fyodor Fyodorovich and Uncle Kostya. This fox runs past the bridge near our house every day."[†]

That fox might be seen running through Tolstoy's procrastinating mind for the next several years; mostly in periods of feeling unable to write, he would, grumbling about his frustration, get up from his desk and go hunting.

Sofia was now excited for him, for *them*, and on March 19 wrote her sister Tatyana: "Last night Levochka suddenly unexpectedly began writing a novel of contemporary life. The subject of the novel—an unfaithful wife and all the drama proceeding from this."[‡]

After Tolstoy had been working happily on *Anna Karenina* for a week, he wrote to Strakhov. After commiserating with his friend's health problems, he shyly opened up: "Now I'll tell you about myself, but please, keep it a great secret, because nothing may come of what I have to say."

> Nearly all my working time this winter I have spent studying Peter, i.e., summoning up spirits from that time, and suddenly a week ago Seryozha, my

---

[*]   *The Diaries of Sophia Tolstoy,* 848, letter of March 19, 1873.

[†]   Ibid.

[‡]   Gusev, *Materials,* 133, letter of March 19, 1873.

eldest son, began to read *Yury Miloslavsky* with enthusiasm. I thought he was too young, and read it with him, then my wife brought up *The Tales of Belkin*, thinking she would find something suitable for Seryozha, but of course found he was too young. After work I happened to pick up this volume of Pushkin, and as is always the case, read it all through (for the 7th time, I think), unable to tear myself away and seemingly reading it for the first time. But more than that, it seemed to resolve all my doubts.*

The resolution of his doubts had to be about quitting the Peter project. The light from Pushkin's brilliance exposed Tolstoy's efforts' seeming lifelessness.

It's as if Tolstoy woke up in Pushkin-world and put on his own seven-league boots and started striding over the heads of all the other writers:†

Not only Pushkin, but nothing else at all, it seemed, had ever aroused my admiration so much before. *The Shot, Egyptian Nights, The Captain's Daughter*!!!‡ And then there is the fragment *The guests were arriving at the country house*. Involuntarily, unwittingly, not knowing why and what would come of it, I thought up characters and events, began to go on with it, then of course changed it, and suddenly all the threads became so well and truly tied up that the result was a novel which I finished in draft form today, a very lively, impassioned and well-finished novel which I'm very pleased with and which will be ready in 2 weeks' time if God gives me strength, and which has nothing in common with all that I've been wrestling with for a whole year.§

Let's consider this prediction of *Anna Karenina* being "ready in 2 weeks' time" as one of the biggest miscalculations in literary history. And what could Tolstoy have meant by "a novel which I finished in draft form"? Some of us think of *drafts* as compositions that run all the way from the beginning to end. All the material is on the page; it just needs to be rewritten, reordered, revised. But Tolstoy didn't mean that. His "draft" of the novel consisted of a few scenes and a list of notes.

---

* Christian, *Tolstoy's Letters*, 258, March 25, 1873.

† A thank-you to Kia Penso for this image.

‡ Only the first title is from *The Tales of Belkin*; the volume Tolstoy read seems to have included *all* of Pushkin's fiction, which even in collections today includes the "fragments."

§ Christian, *Tolstoy's Letters*, 258, March 25, 1873.

His first plan, a story in four parts plus an epilogue, looks like this:

> Prologue. She leaves her husband under happy "auspices." She goes <to meet>
> to console the bride and meets Gagin [the name of the future Vronsky].
> Part 1.
> Chapter 1. The guests gathered at the end of winter, and were awaiting
> the Karenins and talking about them. She arrived and conducted herself
> indecently with Gagin.
> Chapter 2. She has it out with her husband. She reproaches him for previous
> indifference. "It's too late."
> Chapter 3. <In the artels> Gagin from the riding-ring gathers himself to
> go to the meeting. His mother and brother advise him to go to her. <Party at
> her place. The husband.>
> 4th Chapter. Dinner at the Karenins' with Gagin. The husband, conversa-
> tion with the brother. St[epan] Ark[ad'ich] calms things down on the account
> of the German party and on account of his wife.
> 5th Chapter. The races—he falls.
> Chapter 6. She runs to him, reveals her pregnancy, revelation to her husband.[*]

The basic story had come to him in a few scenes. He would not hereafter be inventing
all the plot points. Those of us who have read the novel can recognize these notes' connections to it. But Tolstoy has not created the Anna we know yet. The most cinematic
pre-cinema scene in literature, the horserace, is in place—with the consequent fall. Tolstoy
never imagined Vronsky winning that race. No matter what, Vronsky will fall off his
horse, and his fall will precipitate Anna's announcement of her pregnancy to her husband.

> Part 2.
> Chapter 1. The lovers sit, and he begs her to separate from her husband.
> She separates and says that "I'm dying."
> Chapter 2. The husband is in Moscow, S[tepan] A[rkad'ich], wearing
> himself out, goes off to the club, the conversation with his wife. The family

---

[*]   *PSS* 20: 3–4. Note: The guesswork indicia < > are those of the editors of the 90-volume Soviet
     edition. They examined and attempted to decipher Tolstoy's multiple cross-outs and insertions.
     Some of the indicia open and do not close. As I have not examined the manuscripts myself,
     I have chosen to represent those incomplete marks as they left them.

of S A. The unhappiness of A[leksei] A[leksandrovich], he says that there is no way out, it is necessary to bear the cross.

<Chapter 3. He reads all the novels, studies the question. Everything is impossible. He goes to Troitsa, the meeting with the nihilists, his consolation. He fasts. The telegram. {She writes:}* "I'm dying, I ask your forgiveness. Come."

Chapter 3. Her dream again. Her terror <—the devil>. Leaving him and the son.

Chapter 4. Birth, both sob.—Safe.

5th Chapter. She steadies herself on Christian feeling, she lowers the blinds, and remembers everything and suffers. They whisper to themselves that this is impossible.

6th Chapter: St[epan] Ark proposes the divorce. The last futile [?], he agrees and leaves.

<3rd Part.>

Chapter 6: St[epan] Ark engineers the request of G[agin] and N[ana], and A[leksei] A[leksandrovich] agrees to turn the oth[er] cheek.†

Of Part 2, drifting into Part 3, we see the primary characteristic of Karenin: he will bear the suffering.

Part 3.

Chapter 1. Guffawing in society. They want sympathy. He comes; but at home he sobs.

Chapter 2. [She is] <Outcast> in society; nobody comes <except for rubbish, she shines. His scene to her.

Chapter 3. He pulls away, the son to the mother‡, and he writhes like a butterfly.

4th Chapter. Nihilists at her place. He leaves> he scolds them. <She becomes jealous. So it's necessary to leave for the country.

5th Chapter. He plays at the club. They are in the country, nothing besides animal relations; they built a life for what? He leaves. {"}So I leave, too.{"}

6th Chapter. It is established: he is in society, she is at home, her despair. §

---

*   The fancy brackets {} indicate my editorial insertion.

†   *PSS* 20: 3–4.

‡   Is this Tolstoy's creation of Anna and Karenin's son Seryozha?

§   *PSS* 20: 3–4.

Things are bad for Anna. Even if we cannot detect much sympathy from Tolstoy in these little details, we see at least her isolation.

4th Part.

Chapter 1. A[leksei] A[leksandrovich] hangs about like an unhappy person and is destroyed. His brothers. St[epan] Ark sees her and feels she is unhappy and wants to help her. The only thing—Christian love. She pushes away. The dispersal of finances. The ice melts. She complains and despairs.

2nd Chapter. He is happy, he comes. A babbler excites her jealousy. But the home is unhappy. It's impossible to go to war.

3rd Chapter. An affront from Prince M. on children. Babbler, jealousy, "debacle" feeling. Holiday [?] [indecipherable], another dream.

4th Chapter. A[leksei] A[leksandrovich] comes.> With Gag[in] a terrible scene. I'm not guilty.

5th Chapter. She leaves the house and casts herself away.

6th Chapter. Both the husband, the brother.

Finally:

Epilogue. A[leksei] A[leksandrovich] raises <the children> the son>. Gagin in Tashkent.*

These couple of pages, containing some seeds that will grow and some that won't, sprout into several hundred pages.

Later this spring, Tolstoy imagines what will become Part I of the novel. He sketchily invents Stiva's tumultuous life and in "Variant No. 4" creates Levin:

Part 1

Ch. 1 Stepan Arkad'ich wakes up and explains himself to his wife.

Ch. 2 Stepan Arkad'ich sees Ordyntsev [Levin]. Ordyntsev is full of life. A bunch of business.

Ch. 3 At the zoological garden, Ordyntsev with the bull and skates with Kitty.

Ch. 4 Dinner <and explanation about marriage> of three. Stepan Arkad'ich rides <home> to mother-in-law's, reconciliation. I'm guilty, what do you want?

---

*   PSS 20: 3–4.

Ch. 5 <Party at the Shcherbatskis'. Ordyntsev told a lie, confused.>

Ch. 6 <He goes to the country.>

Ch. 7 <Reconciliation with Dolly.>

Ch. 8 The arrival of Anna Karenina. At the railroad.

Ch. 9 She captivates everyone.

Ch. 10 The ball at the governor's and departure for Petersburg with Uda-shev [Vronsky].*

✳

Even though by 1873 Tolstoy had been a professional writer for twenty years and had had enough experience to estimate the time that a piece would require, he was never professional in the sense that he held himself to deadlines or page counts. When he was guessing that he could write *Anna Karenina* in two weeks, he must have been foreseeing a novel the size of *Childhood* or *Family Happiness* (about ninety pages). Even given two weeks, Tolstoy never composed at the terrific speed Dostoevsky could occasionally desperately summon. God or luck gave Tolstoy strength, but not the kind of strength that flows like a river. Tolstoy's power for composition was more like a thunderstorm. Here today, maybe tomorrow, but then gone for weeks or months at a time.

Professionalism is nothing to despise in an artist; Anton Chekhov and Anthony Trollope, two of Tolstoy's greatest literary contemporaries, both of whose work he admired, took pride in their ability to meet publishers' and editors' deadlines and specifications. Those two wrote so fast that the deadlines even helped them stay paced and focused. Professionalism did not make them lesser artists.

Tolstoy, on the other hand, only rushed when readying a truly finished book or a new collected edition, when he didn't have the patience or interest to proofread. But in the midst of creating a work, he never rushed, never completed something just because a deadline was looming and an editor was pleading for the promised manuscript.

What Tolstoy saw "in draft form" on March 25 and what he would finish four years later are different in focus, size, and dimension. He did not suspect in which of many possible directions the creative fires of *Anna Karenina* would burn. If he could have known the effort the novel was going to take, he probably would have stopped in his tracks and extinguished what he had started.

---

*   *PSS* 20: 8–9. *Plany i zametki k "Anne Kareninoy"* ["Plans and Notes for 'Anna Karenina'"].

Or, to try another analogy, he was like an architect designing what he thought was a summer cottage and it became, instead, a cathedral. Because it was being built on his own land, on his own dime, the transformation of its size did not inhibit him.

It's hard to think of Tolstoy as naïve, but there was something naïve about his time estimates in regard to creative works. He wrote Strakhov:

> If I finish it, I'll publish it as a separate book, but I very much want you to read it. Will you undertake to read the proofs, with a view to its being published in Petersburg?[*]

More than four years later, in January of 1878, the book edition of *Anna Karenina*, its proofreading shepherded and completed by Strakhov, would hit the bookshops.

But Tolstoy was not someone who sent hasty letters. He was self-conscious enough, self-aware enough, that he did not send this March 25 letter to Strakhov until a couple of months later.

At the end of March, twelve days after he had begun *Anna Karenina*, he took another try at outing himself about the new novel. Having exclaimed his praise of Pushkin's fiction, Tolstoy told his friend Pavel Golokhvastov: "My new study of it made a powerful impression on me. I'm working, but not at all on what I intended."[†]

But he didn't send this letter right away, either. For the first eight weeks that spring, the only people who knew what he was now working on were Sofia and her sister Tatyana. Perhaps he didn't want to set up expectations again, to be asked about the new project's progress. But it was going well, and good news can wait.

✳

There is a rival "origin" story of the novel, invented by Sofia[‡]:

> Yesterday afternoon he told me he had had the idea of writing about a married woman of noble birth who ruined herself. He said his purpose was to make this woman pitiful, not guilty, and he told me that no sooner had he imagined this character clearly than the men and other characters he had

---

*   Christian, *Tolstoy's Letters*, 258, March 25, 1873.

†   Christian, *Tolstoy's Letters*, 259, March 30, 1873.

‡   This is a follow-up to the actual originating event described in the Introduction, pages 4–8.

thought up all found their places in the story. "It's suddenly become clear to me," he said. He decided yesterday that the educated peasant he had thought up would be a bailiff.*

Sofia will prove a valuable but fitful diary-keeper and memoirist. Recounting her life in her diaries and a memoir, however, she was often content to approximate. She obliviously paraphrased or misquoted even herself; she more than occasionally related inconsistent or contradictory details; she also had bouts of willful or accidental forgetfulness.

She wrote that note above, she claimed, on February 24, 1870, but this entry was not on the pages of her usual diary. Her husband's idea does sound uncannily like *Anna Karenina*, notwithstanding the bailiff. But we know from Tolstoy's drafts over the first year of actual composition that there was *no such realization of the characters orbiting around the star Anna*.

He saw his original "Anna" as guilty as sin. He did not come to the story with sympathy or even pity for her, a cheating wife. Tolstoy would never have thought for a moment about how "pitiful" and "not guilty" Sofia would have been if she had run off with another man. As it was, Tolstoy could lose his wits if Sofia just smilingly poured tea for a male guest or sat at the piano next to an attentive male and ran her hands over the keys. Tolstoy, whose hair-trigger jealousy was well matched by Sofia's, is unlikely to have told her that he wanted to make the Anna character "pitiful, not guilty."[†] In conversation Tolstoy never expressed enlightened views about women. His art, the revelation of his deepest, best self, showed his enlightenment, and has made us realize the keenest feelings and thoughts of a brilliant, sympathetic woman, Anna; otherwise, his everyday remarks about women were those of a conventional aristocratic Russian male of the 19th century.

Tolstoy's first impulse in telling the story to a pregnant Sofia in 1870 would most probably have been to remind her what happened to women who ran off from their husbands. The real Anna Karenina was going to develop from his artistic and morally greater response. When he began the plans and drafts he condemned the Anna character and then, many pages into the drafts, began to comprehend her and, with misgivings, *love* her.

---

*   *The Diaries of Sophia Tolstoy*, 845.

†   C.J.G. Turner, author of *A Karenina Companion*, a book that has been *my* companion off and on for several years, says of the Anna character in the earliest draft: "She is here condemned, which makes it difficult to make a connection between Tolstoi's initial conception for *Anna Karenina* and the idea that he had mentioned to his wife in early 1870 of an unfaithful wife from the highest society who was to be 'only pitiful and not guilty.'" C.J.G. Turner, *A Karenina Companion* (Waterloo, Ontario: Wilfrid Laurier University Press, 1993), 15.

Tolstoy believed art happened only when the artist saw the humanity of the people about whom he was telling a story. As he wrote his fiction, Tolstoy tried to demand of himself that he deal with what he had actually created rather than with the confinements of his own initial judgments and conceptions. His art challenged his own and everyone else's conventionality.

✳

Before we meet Anna in Part 1, before Tolstoy invented that impressive introduction to the novel's protagonist, he had written hundreds of pages of drafts.

We owe to Sofia our being able to read those scattered plans, drafts, and false starts of the novel. She saved everything she could of what he wrote. However frustrating or defensive her commentary could be, she was also the greatest of Tolstoy's assistants and always expressed more sense than he about the current and future value of his work.

While most of the drafts of *Anna Karenina* are not dated, one that is is from March 27, 1873, nine days after he began. Nikolai Gusev, Tolstoy's biographer and latter-day secretary, questions the authenticity of that precise date, as it is based on an unknown hand's notation.[*] But let's look at this "Variant No. 6" anyway, which at about 1,800 words could have been composed in one day or even one sitting. It has an epigraph, "Vengeance is Mine" (the capitalization of "Mine" indicates that it is God's vengeance); the same epigraph would expand by a few words in the final version.

By this date, Tolstoy had already invented Anna's brother Stepan Arkad'ich Alabin (not yet dubbed Oblonsky or nicknamed Stiva), and had already conceived of Stepan's morning wake-up as the opening of the novel.

The tone, amused and amusing about Stepan's distress over his wife's threatening to leave him because of his affair with their children's governess, would remain through the final draft of the first chapters; the events in this March 27 draft would later span four chapters. (The *originally* conceived opening, true to Tolstoy's first plan [see above] begins with the Anna and Vronsky characters, already an item, openly flirting at a high-society party.)

Stepan, though forty-one here, is nearly the thirty-four-year-old Stiva we know in the novel.

How old should the characters be? Tolstoy took a stab; at forty-one, however, Stepan would be of almost another generation from his sister Anna, who eventually begins the novel at the age of twenty-eight but was perhaps twenty-three in the first drafts. With

---

*   Gusev, *Letopis'*, 405.

that difference of age, Stepan would not have been a child orphan, as Anna is.* We will never find out even through a draft's stray detail how their parents died. We learn in the real novel that Anna was raised as an adolescent by her aunts, just as Tolstoy was raised by his aunts from the time he was eight.

One dilemma that Stepan faces in the draft and the novel is that he needs money, but while he is in danger of being separated from his wife, Dolly, he cannot put up for sale a wood that belongs to her.

Unlike the Stiva of the novel, this early-draft Stepan is not "honest with himself." We need not feel attracted to him, nor trust his judgment. In the novel, we know he has cheated on his wife, and Tolstoy shows us that Stiva feels bad for having done so. We and all the household servants are more sympathetic to him than to Dolly; we also know that that's not fair, but Tolstoy has already got us noticing the differences between what we are supposed to feel and what we actually feel.

Here, in the draft, we don't have to believe Stepan when he reflects, upon receiving a letter from Anna that morning, "This is a woman . . . A faithful wife, a society woman and always merry and broadminded. None of this Moscow purism."† Anna, at this point in the first drafts, is still childless and wants to visit her brother and Moscow because her husband will be off on an inspection somewhere in Russia and she worries she'll be bored. Bored!

The novel's Anna, who worships her son, is never bored until after she has left her son for her lover. In the real novel, Tolstoy wants us to like and to feel the likability of Stiva Oblonsky. Here in this draft we are meant to see right through his thoughtlessness. He receives a letter from his lover, who expects him to see her that afternoon for lunch. Tolstoy would delete from the novel any new communication from Stiva's lover; she would not be a current but an ex-governess. In this draft, a touching dialogue between Stepan and his eight-year-old daughter Tanya is started but not yet perfected. As Tolstoy wrote this draft, his own daughter Tanya was eight years old. In the draft Tolstoy got locked in on "*eight* years," as Stepan, encountering his wife, recalls her "eight years ago at Moscow balls, with her strong figure and wide high chest, thin waist and small charming head on a delicate neck."‡ So the "eight years" couldn't be right, with their

---

*   In an early draft, however, they do have different patronymics, which means, if Tolstoy had thought it through and wasn't confusing the names (which he sometimes did), that at this moment he thought of them as half-siblings.

†   *PSS* 20: 81.

‡   *PSS* 20: 83.

daughter being eight (he and Dolly would not have had sex before marriage), but Stepan continues with that number when he puts his foot in his mouth, as he will similarly put his foot in his mouth in the novel: "Really, can't eight years of life atone for minutes of passion?"[*]

In the draft Dolly is too much of a pushover. We don't believe that she'll resist Stiva for long; there's no doubt she'll cave in and forgive him. In the novel, we feel her quandary and Stiva tries to have faith but doesn't really believe she will "come round."[†] "Variant No. 6" ends with Stiva leaving the chaos of the house, jumping into a carriage and cheerily calling out the directions to the driver.[‡]

The novel we all know is so seemingly perfected that its earlier drafts can seem wrong just for being different. And yet, of course, the drafts are exciting and full of life. But Tolstoy was dissatisfied with them.

He held onto the drafts and used a few early scenes more or less complete and more or less unchanged. Some of his plans (as we are seeing) bore fruit while others intriguingly or necessarily withered away. Many of the greatest scenes, however, seem to have to come to him on the spot, out of the blue.

We are indebted to the Soviet scholars V. A. Zhdanov and Z. E. Zaidenshnur for quilting together a "fifth draft" from Sofia's rescues of the drafts. Zhdanov and Zaiden-shnur call it "The First Completed Redaction of *Anna Karenina*."[§] The base of it is a draft that Tolstoy submitted to a printer in early 1874. Zhdanov and Zaidenshnur apply a lot of guesswork; they quote patches that don't transition well or can't be sewn together; they include doublings of scenes and other scenes that simply peter out. The most important of discoveries that we can make in "The First Completed Redaction of *Anna Karenina*" is that the novel is more about Karenin than Anna. Tolstoy's early Anna (her name is Tatyana or Nana in some drafts) is unpleasant and vapid, coarse and unfeeling. She is much more like Anna's high-society friends in the novel than like the real Anna.

Meanwhile, Tolstoy warmly imagines Karenin; he will cut out all the warmth and sympathy in the real novel, but the character remains mostly the same.

---

[*]   *PSS* 20: 83. See also *Anna Karenina*, Part 1, Chapter 4.

[†]   Образуется: "Come round," a coinage by the Oblonsky household servants, is translated many ways: "shape up" (Bartlett, also Pevear and Volokhonsky), "turn out all right" (Carmichael), "shape themselves" (Maude and Maude), and "shapify" (Schwartz).

[‡]   *PSS* 20: 86.

[§]   And I owe it to Professor Turner's *A Karenina Companion* for clarifying the details of this bewildering compilation.

In the "Redaction" (we'll now call it by this name), Tolstoy did not warmly imagine Anna; he did not create for her a spectacular entrance. In fact, Stiva asks the character-to-be-named Vronsky: "But you know Anna?"

"I know her; a long time ago at a ball at the minister's I was introduced to her, but it was as if, you know, I didn't say two words, and now I wouldn't even dare to bow. Then I saw her, she was acting in a French play at the Belozerskis'. She acts excellently."[*]

When in the drafts Vronsky meets her, they already know each other; this means that after Anna developed in Tolstoy's head into her glorious self, he figured out that his readers and Vronsky needed to meet her at the same moment.

In the "Redaction" she still arrives by rail. Anna, along with the reader, hears that a man has had an "immediate death" by suicide at the train station. "Immediate?" immediately asks Anna, which response Tolstoy understood was too loaded.[†] This Anna-in-the-rough is simple-minded, but, interestingly, something of a comedian:

> Every joke that Aunt Anna told had success, and the children nearly died with laughter.[‡]

Tolstoy gives no examples of her jokes. The real Anna is marvelous, but she's no Lady Glencora Palliser, Trollope's witty heroine, and a character Tolstoy was, and would continue to be, familiar with in Trollope's ongoing six-volume Palliser series (1864–1879), which Tolstoy read in English.

When Anna confesses to her sister-in-law Dolly that she "coquetted" with Gagin (the Vronsky character) and that she feels ashamed before Kitty, Dolly forgives her because she doesn't like Gagin for Kitty.[§] This is similar to the real novel, but there is no seriousness or ominousness in it. Tolstoy doesn't yet see or feel the novel's seriousness, at least in regard to Anna. This early Anna is not capable or worthy of such consideration. Tolstoy had to find in the writing the real Anna, the attractive and irreducible Anna. He had to make her life valuable enough that it was terrible she lost it.

---

[*] "Pervaya zakonchennaya redaktsiya 'Anny Kareninoi,'" in L. N. Tolstoy, *Anna Karenina: Roman v Bos'mi Chastyakh*. ["The First Completed Draft of *Anna Karenina*," in *Anna Karenina: A Novel in Eight Parts*, ed. V. A. Zhdanov and E. E. Zaidenshnur (Moscow: Nauka, 1970)], 701. Hereafter, this reference will be listed as Zhdanov and Zaidenshnur.

[†] Zhdanov and Zaidenshnur, 704.

[‡] Zhdanov and Zaidenshnur, 708.

[§] Zhdanov and Zaidenshnur, 714.

"The guests after the opera gathered at the young princess Vrassky's."* Tolstoy started his very first day's draft here, apparently, before he began recasting and searching for other starts. Although inspired by Pushkin, it's not inspiring work, as Tolstoy illustrates for the most part high-society nastiness.

Unlike Trollope or Gogol, unlike Jane Austen or his most admired Charles Dickens, Tolstoy's sarcastic or mocking presentation of aggressively nasty people is never *funny*. Anna's high-society hypocritical friends are contemptible; we don't identify with them and we don't laugh with them, or even *at* them. In the novel they're the only characters Tolstoy doesn't have us sympathize with or understand. Comic foils have no life on Tolstoy's stage.

The primary difficulty Anna's character confronts us with in the "Redaction" is that she is just another high-society hypocrite.

Does it matter that the original Anna is *not* beautiful?

> [. . .] she was unbeautiful† with a narrow forehead, short, an almost turned-up nose and a bit fat. So fat that just a little more and she would have been ugly. If not for the great black eyelashes decorating her gray eyes, black huge[?‡] hair, beautiful brow, and a not-straight stance—she had a graceful movement like her brother and short arms and legs—she would have been bad. But despite the unbeautiful face, there was something in her kind smile that made her likable.
>
> [. . .] No one could argue with a young person who called her unbeautiful when she walked into the room with her much too much squinting of her not-big narrow eyes (so that only her thick black eyelashes were visible). Narrow, very narrow forehead, small eyes, big lips and nose of an unbeautiful form.§

It seems to me that in this unflattering description, Tolstoy was imagining or remembering the neighbor woman Anna Pirogova. She had had a disturbing sexual allure, but Tolstoy didn't see the pathos of her life, just as he didn't see it of the original fictional Anna.

---

*   Zhdanov and Zaidenshnur, 717.

†   "Unbeautiful" (некрасивая) is the *literal* word; dictionaries and translators prefer to straighten out the negation into "ugly" or "plain"; I would rather stick with the language's denial of beauty than the assertion of ugly.

‡   This is the manuscript transcriber's question mark.

§   Zhdanov and Zaidenshnur, 721.

He remembered Anna Pirogova as the unattractive neighbor and in the novel pushed a character similar to hers into society.

No one could argue that a tragic novel focused on this character would be worthwhile:

> It was apparent that this course of conversation, which for most of the society people was the goal and the not-without-difficulty business, was for her a joke, not costing her the smallest effort, so little that she apparently never even thought about what to say, but spoke about whatever came into her head, and it always came out intelligently and sweetly, in all situations, lightly and seriously.[*]

The final Anna will be actually intelligent and sweet, and she will inherit the dark eyelashes and her laugh.[†] This one is thoughtless and superficial. She childishly chews on her pearl necklace. Tolstoy doesn't care about her, and we wouldn't have, either.

In one of the earliest drafts Tolstoy has Karenin confront Anna right away about her affair; in the earliest drafts they do not usually have a child (he pops up once or twice, not as a character but as a fact). Eventually Tolstoy gives them an actual child, but instead of motherhood humanizing and complicating Anna, as it does in the real novel, it makes her more contemptible; Karenin is clearly the primary and more important parent. He is the one with the sympathy and interest in their son, not she.

So what happened? How did the real Anna emerge from Tolstoy's unsympathetic conception?

We know from his earliest plans, which he conceived and described with the sparest of details, that her suicide will cause her brother, in the last chapter (before the epilogue) to sob! It's the brother's grief, not the lover's, that Tolstoy means to depict (in a draft: "Stepan Arkad'ich sobs"[‡]). It's the sobbing Tolstoy himself was doing at Anna Pirogova's inquest.

Her suicide, however, as first described in a draft by Tolstoy (and summarized by Gusev) is remarkably flippant. It comes right after her husband and lover run into each other at the house; she tells the shaken-up Karenin: "Well, you won't be suffering for long."

She goes to her room, writes a note: "Be happy. I'm crazy," and flees home. "In a day they find under the rails [in the beginning it was: 'in the Neva'] her body."

---

[*]   Zhdanov and Zaidenshnur, 722.

[†]   Zhdanov and Zaidenshnur, 741. "She laughed that sweet chesty laugh that was one of her primary charms."

[‡]   *PSS* 20: 9. This is from Variant No. 6.

Balashov [Vronsky] goes off to Tashként, that is, joins the troops in the campaign on the Khiva. This shows the real-time of the novel—the Khivan campaign came about in 1873.*

Her suicide is so little, so unrealized, so unfelt . . . but once Tolstoy finds the real Anna, her fate will become real. When her death became too terrible for him to understand, the novel sprang to life.

One unknown day in late 1873 or early 1874, Tolstoy began writing, and Anna was suddenly beautiful, elegant, intelligent, and superconscious. Her transformation immediately complicated the novel for him. She, with her fateful descent to suicide, is the character through whom Tolstoy dramatized and experienced his deepest terrors.

✳

Tolstoy continued on the novel into April of 1873 but had to apologize to both Strakhov and Golokhvastov for his long-overdue letters. "I did answer you right away," he wrote Strakhov, "but I didn't send the letter, and since then two weeks have passed."

> I didn't send it because I wrote about something that was premature [. . .]. Sometime I'll send you this letter or show you. [. . .]
>
> As for myself, that is, about myself right now, I won't write, or again I wouldn't send the letter: I'm taking on myself the highest commanded duty—I'm tormented and finding in this torment everything—not joy but the purpose of life.†

He wrote Golokhvastov as well that he had decided against telling him something that was "premature."‡

And though his dear sister-in-law Tatyana knew that he was working on a new novel, he didn't mention it in his postscript to Sofia's April letter to her except to say, "I'm very busy with work, which in no way resembles Berlin wool [a kind of embroidery]."§

---

*   Gusev, *Materials,* 264.

†   *PSS* 62: 20, letter of April 6–7, 1873.

‡   *PSS* 62: 21, letter of April 9–10, 1873.

§   *PSS* 62: 22.

Sofia noted in her diary that "Lyovochka is writing his novel, which is going well." She preceded it with two sentences that evoke the remoteness of Yasnaya Polyana and the long hold of winter: "It snowed all morning, 5 degrees above zero, no grass, no warmth, no sun, none of the bright aching joy of spring, for which we have been waiting so long. My heart is as cold, gloomy, and sad as the countryside."*

There's no indication in Tolstoy's letters of this time, however, that he felt low or that the weather was cold. His head was in the story he had begun writing, through which he was discovering "the purpose of life." Sofia was as usual watching him closely, and in her memoir she assessed his mood and health as poor.

She recalled him as having "frequent coughing spells," and that he "sometimes ran a fever at night. He became gloomy and couldn't work. And so I took the firm decision to go with him and the whole family [that summer] to Samara Gubernia to the plot of land we had recently purchased so Lev Nikolaevich could drink koumiss there, which had cured him once already. I couldn't let him go without us, remembering how hard our {earlier} separation was on me."†

Again, he himself didn't mention gloominess or coughing fits, but, as Sofia recalled, "preparations [for the trip] got underway." They invited friends and relatives to join them, and "Everybody had fun looking at these summer plans." According to Alexandra Popoff, Sofia's most recent biographer, "Tolstoy went to Moscow to buy forty-three items on Sophia's shopping list. Despite his simple tastes, he patronized the most reputable stores, making quality purchases and overspending, habits he ascribes to Pierre in *War and Peace* [and to Stiva in *Anna Karenina*]. Meanwhile, to save on expenses, Sophia was sewing clothes for the children."‡

In her memoir Sofia explained why, that spring of 1873, Tolstoy had to take over the shopping duties:

> Since I was nursing Petja at the time, I couldn't go anywhere, and Lev Nikolaevich took it upon himself to purchase in Moscow everything needed for the trip. He went there on the 20th of April and brought home things that were splendid, solid, and expensive. Marvellous trunks from Tsimmerman's, bags and belts. He bought hats for the children and a beautiful grey

* *The Diaries of Sophia Tolstoy*, 50, April 17, 1873.

† Sofia Andreevna Tolstaya, *My Life,* trans. John Woodsworth and Arkadi Klioutchanski, ed. Andrew Donskov (Ottawa: University of Ottawa Press, 2010), 188.

‡ Alexandra Popoff, *Sophia Tolstoy: A Biography* (New York: Free Press, 2010), 72.

felt *Mousquetaire* hat for me, replete with grey feathers. In a fine store he ordered for me an expensive grey alpaca coat with a cape, and shoes to go with it.

He showed my outfits to Mme Sushkova and Mlle Tjutcheva, asking their opinion. They approved. At the time I paid little attention to my appearance and realised that Lev Nikolaevich wanted me to be fashionably dressed (*comme il faut*), and this meant a lot to him. I, however, was tormented by a single thought: to get everything done in time. [. . .]*

Sofia was pleased and flattered (she mentions "expensive" twice). She wrote that she didn't concern herself with her appearance "at the time," but it's impossible to find a photo or painting of her where she doesn't seem conscious of and comfortable with her fashionable self.†

In *Anna Karenina*, Stiva Oblonsky seems to know and appreciate shops; he knows the best ones. Though we never see Stiva shop, we know that he has many decided opinions about where to get what is needed for his dinner party. We know Anna has a dressmaker, and perhaps we could imagine her shopping in Petersburg or Moscow or Italy, but Tolstoy never describes her doing so. In one draft he seems to have been about to write a description of Karenin in a toy shop (more on this later), and we know in the novel that Anna has shopped for and bought toys for Seryozha's ninth birthday. In the 1880s and for the rest of his life Tolstoy would become so committed to simplicity and feel so much guilt about his wealth that it's hard to imagine him in 1873 enjoying himself in a shop. We'll see, however, that for the next several years he would be an impulsive buyer of horses and property.

The most poignant detail of Sofia's recollection of this April, though, is about her baby at the breast, Petja. For Sofia, her husband's shopping expedition brought to mind the little son who would die that fall.

Having returned home with the goods, Tolstoy went back to Moscow at the beginning of May, "finishing his arrangements with the printing of the new edition of his works in eight volumes," writes Gusev. "Tolstoy decided to publish himself, without the use of a publisher. In this edition there had to be everything that was in the edition of 1864, plus *War and Peace*, some material from the *Azbuka* and some pedagogical articles from *Yasnaya Polyana*, not included in the 1864 edition."‡

---

* Tolstaya, *My Life,* 188.

† For example, see photo insert, Sofia Tolstaya with her toddlers Seryozha and Tanya in 1866, http://tolstoy.ru/media/photos/index.php?topic[]=301.

‡ Gusev, *Materials*, 138.

At the printer's to discuss those eight volumes, Tolstoy seemed to feel that he shouldn't have to look at or touch the material again. He was petulant about proofreading this edition and groaned in anticipation of the job.

He was glad the family would be going away for the summer; he planned for them to depart on May 15.

Though he had had a breakthrough with *Anna Karenina*, he doesn't seem to have thought of it as a major or consuming project, as the Peter the Great novel was to have been, or as revising and repackaging the *Azbuka* would be. He liked the thought of this novella-sized *Anna Karenina*, perhaps because he figured that it would not consume his time or energy. He believed that he could put it aside for the summer and resume it without a hitch.

In early May, Tolstoy took his three oldest children with him to bid farewell to his sister, Maria, and his brother Sergei at their estates while Sofia stayed home with the youngest three.

After Tolstoy and the children had returned home, Tolstoy received a woeful letter from his sister-in-law Tatyana about her four-year-old daughter, Dasha. He later recounted to Tatyana herself and her husband, Sasha Kuzminskiy, how he broke the news to Sofia:

> I'm coming from Tula with the letters. Sonya happily meets me. And I say: "Big sorrow, big, big sorrow!" She says: "Hannah died [their former governess now working for Tatyana's family]." I say: "From Kutais, but not Hannah." Not thinking for a moment, she said, as if she had read the letter, namely these two words: "*Dasha died.*"
>
> How is this? How was she able to know this?
>
> She was terribly upset, so much so she isn't able to talk about it.
>
> [Our son] Seryozha is sorry for you. And [our daughter] Tanya lay down for a long time on the bed and cried.
>
> Goodbye, dear friends, let God help you pass well through this heavy stage in life.

Any set of parents would reflect on this event and grieve, fearing for their own; Lev and Sofia had to look at each other and at their lively brood and count their lucky stars. Tolstoy's condolences were full of grief and perhaps also of foreboding:

> Beloved friend Tanya! I can't describe to you the impression that the news produced on me about the death of my charming cutie (as it pleases me to

think now), my favorite Dasha! I never would have thought this death would so strike me. I felt it, as you and your children are close to me. The whole day I could not think about her and about you without tears. I'm experiencing the feeling that, probably, now torments you: to forget or remember and with horror to ask yourself, Is it really true?*

He described reading her, Tatyana's, letter and crying. Having expressed all his sympathy, he began recommending religion. He said that he knew how she felt by remembering his brother Nikolai's death but that of course the death of a child was more "majestic and mysterious."

※

A week before that letter to his sister-in-law, Tolstoy finally confessed to Strakhov that he was writing something new; he withheld, however, even a vague description of its subject: "I'm writing a novel which has no connection at all with Peter the First. I've been writing for more than a month now [eight weeks, in fact], and have finished it in draft form [or "*roughly*," he should have said, as in *I have dozens of pages and a rough idea of how it goes*]. This novel—I mean a novel, the first in my life [for his own reasons, Tolstoy didn't categorize *War and Peace* as a *novel*]—is very dear to my heart and I'm quite absorbed by it, but in spite of that, philosophical problems have been occupying me very much this spring. In the letter which I didn't send to you, I wrote about this novel and about how it came to me unwittingly, thanks to the divine Pushkin, whom I happened to pick up and reread with new enthusiasm."†

In a postscript, he requested: "Please don't tell anyone that I'm writing." Strakhov answered that he of course wouldn't and was enthusiastic in any case about whatever this novel was.

Tolstoy was pleased by the thought of a long, work-free summer on the Samaran steppe, but he was distracted by Sofia's ill health; and she was distracted, she recalled, by her husband's and Petya's poor health and Tatyana's terrible news. The trip was postponed to early June.

---

* This sincere, difficult letter is unfortunately not included in R. F. Christian's *Tolstoy's Letters*, the only collection in English of Tolstoy's personal correspondence to various recipients. See *PSS* 62: 27.

† Christian, *Tolstoy's Letters*, 261, May 11, 1873.

In the meantime, Tolstoy tried to make hay with his collected edition's version of *War and Peace*. Back in late March, when he was too shy to send the letter to Strakhov about the birth of *Anna Karenina*, he explained: "I've started to prepare a second edition of *War and Peace* and to strike out what is superfluous—some things need to be struck out altogether, others to be removed and printed separately. Give me your advice if you have time to look through the last 3 volumes. And if you can remember, remind me of what is bad. I'm afraid to touch it, because there is so much that is bad in my eyes that I should want to write it again after refurbishing it. If you could recall what needs changing and if you could look through the arguments in the last 3 volumes and tell me that this and that needs to be changed, and that the arguments from page so and so to page so and so need to be cut out, you would oblige me very much indeed."[*]

Tolstoy considered Strakhov the most astute critic of *War and Peace* and knew that his own proofreading and revising of *War and Peace* was going too far. He needed to restrain himself and felt that with Strakhov's help he might do so. But it was not as if he could ever put himself in a good or contented frame of mind by rereading his published work. By habit, by character, he was a renouncer. Tikhon Polner, one of his biographers, remarks:

> Other people's thoughts and opinions on any subject served only as a starting point for the independent workings of his mind. In almost every instance the material was discarded. He was never satisfied to say, "No"; he always had to add, "No, it's impossible." He had a habit of saying, "Not only has it never been that way, it never could have been." He settled in every one of his thoughts as if it were a fortress, and no efforts of adversaries could dislodge him from the position he occupied. As time went on, new ideas appeared. Ideas just as arrogant, just as self-confident, just as final—and then, without a struggle, the old ideas gave up the stronghold to the newcomers and disappeared without leaving a trace.[†]

Tolstoy almost always eventually renounced not only others' ideas but the best ideas he himself ever had, from writing fiction to raising a family to advocating for education and social change.

While he composed a work, his judgments were ruthless, but his published work almost always became immediately stale, "bad in my eyes." He would become so agitated by it

---

[*]   Christian, *Tolstoy's Letters*, 258, March 25, 1873.

[†]   Polner, *Tolstoy and His Wife*, 24.

that he could not read it the way he would have read anybody else's book. He couldn't keep his nose to the page and plow ahead; he couldn't stop second-guessing his earlier self's artistic decisions and personal opinions. He never reread for pleasure the final versions he had made of *War and Peace* or *Anna Karenina.*[*]

He knew, somewhere in his real pride, that *War and Peace* was an astounding feat. But he could never not feel smarter *now* than he had been when he wrote the narrative. The deep and comprehensive way he appreciated other authors, he never managed with his own work. He wept and laughed over others' creative works; and as he composed his own, he felt them deeply: "I often feel more strongly not what I have actually felt, but what I have written and felt in describing my characters. They too have become my memories, as if they had been actual experiences,"[†] he told a late-in-life friend, the composer Alexander Goldenweiser. But he didn't or couldn't reread his books. He worked on his fiction until it was "ready," and then he published the book and his sense of it got tangled up with, it seems, unpleasant memories. In 1873 Tolstoy didn't admire the energy and vitality of *War and Peace*. He saw its errors and waywardness.

As we encounter Tolstoy's peeved denunciations of *Anna Karenina* and its heroine, we will realize that his expressing dissatisfaction with his work was habitual, and that his criticisms are only contrary or bewildering rather than illuminating.

On May 4, he made it clear how much he counted on Strakhov's help: "I'm still busy correcting *War and Peace*. I'm cutting out all the arguments [that is, the long discourses on history] and the French [about 12 percent of the text, which he was hastily translating into Russian, *not* cutting]; and I would dearly like your advice. May I send it to you to look through when I've finished?"[‡] Strakhov agreed to do so; he never seems to have turned down any of Tolstoy's many requests for help.

At the very end of May, when the family was practically ready to set out on the 900-mile journey to the farm in Samara, Tolstoy wrote Strakhov: "I'm very, very grateful for your offer to look through *War and Peace*. You wouldn't believe how valuable it is to me.[. . .] I haven't finished volumes 4, 5, and 6 yet, and I've been cutting out bad things here and there. I would have sent you my corrected copy of those parts which are finished straightaway, but the books have gone to Samara with half our possessions.

---

* He absentmindedly or irritatedly proofread them, but I have yet to come across a description or account of him happily reading his published novels.

† A. B. Goldenweizer, *Talks with Tolstoy*, trans. S. S. Koteliansky and Virginia Woolf (New York: Horizon Press, 1969), 161.

‡ Christian, *Tolstoy's Letters*, 261, May 11, 1873.

I'll very soon correct the rest in Samara and send it to you, taking advantage of your invaluable offer."

He admitted to Strakhov that he was in a rush, unable to maintain creative focus, and for the first time acknowledged, in writing, the likelihood of *Anna Karenina*'s delay: "My novel is also at a standstill, and I'm losing hope of finishing it by autumn."[*]

He then groused about the *Azbuka* (called "Primer" below), which Strakhov, a former schoolteacher, had already helped him proofread:

> The *Primer* is an inscrutable mystery to me: if I meet anyone, especially anyone with children, I hear genuine praise, and complaints that there's nothing of mine to read, but nobody buys the *Primer*, therefore nobody needs it. I've now thought of sending it to the zemstvos and having it sewn up in 12 small booklets. As you can see from my letter, I'm in a very cold, practical frame of mind, which is always the case with me in summer; I'm worried about the sale of books, printing, the harvest etc.

He asked Strakhov to tell him which parts of the *Azbuka* he should include in the collected edition.

His routine of getting into a "very cold, practical frame of mind" seems to mean that he didn't mix the creation part of writing with the business side. He customarily took the summers off. He would read, ride, welcome guests, but he wouldn't "work" on the writing. We should be awed by how much Tolstoy wrote; yet we will keep noticing how unsteadily he worked at *Anna Karenina*, how often he took time off from it. Writing was one of Hercules' labors for him. He did it, as did Hercules, because, being the greatest in the world, he *had* to.

On June 2, 1873, writes the biographer Rosamund Bartlett, "sixteen members of the Tolstoy household gathered in the drawing room, shut the doors and sat in silence for a few moments to prepare for the journey ahead, then completed the ritual by getting up and crossing themselves."[†]

Before Tolstoy hustled out of the door of his study, what had he done with the *Anna Karenina* manuscript? Had he set it on his desk under a paperweight or perhaps tucked it into an envelope or folder in a drawer or tossed it on a shelf? Had it been sent ahead in a trunk with the *War and Peace* galleys? The exact situation of it was unremarked on

[*]   Christian, *Tolstoy's Letters*, 262, May 11, 1873.

[†]   Rosamund Bartlett, *Tolstoy: A Russian Life* (London: Profile Books, 2010), 210.

by Tolstoy or, in their memoirs, by Sofia or the children. Wherever that *Anna Karenina* manuscript was, he did not work on it all summer. Bartlett resumes: "A caravan of carriages and carts then transported them to Tula to catch a train, and in Nizhny Novgorod they boarded the steamer for Samara."

Before he hopped aboard, Tolstoy wrote to the *Moscow News* about his "sound" method of teaching literacy and asked the editors to publish the letter, which they did on June 7 while the Tolstoy family was riding on the steamer on the Volga. He declared in this public letter that he had figured out what the best method was twelve years ago, had written about it in his *Yasnaya Polyana* magazine, and that he could demonstrate it to the Moscow literacy committee (and he would in the early winter of 1874). Even though he had got that grievance off his chest, the lack of public understanding of his pedagogical theories and experiences would continue to stick in his craw.

3

Summering in Samara

❋

I had come to believe that the serious biographer must physically pursue his subject through the past. Mere archives were not enough. He must go to all the places where the subject had ever lived or worked, or traveled or dreamed. Not just the birthplace, or the blue-plaque place, but the temporary places, the dream places.

—Richard Holmes[*]

T he steppes of the Samara region in summer!

From Yasnaya Polyana it took about a week in June of 1873 for the sixteen members of the household to arrive at the farm Tolstoy had bought in the Samara countryside.[†]

Those treeless arid steppes!

---

[*] Richard Holmes, "A Quest for the Real Coleridge," *New York Review of Books*, December 18, 2014, 61.

[†] By Sofia's account in *My Life* (page 192), those sixteen included "the nanny, the cook, the valet, the chambermaid and the tutors" and her brother and "the Englishwoman," by whom Sofia must mean Hannah Tarsey, the Tolstoys' former governess and now the governess for her sister Tatyana's children; she wished to try the koumiss cure.

"Were I to begin describing, I should fill a hundred pages with this country and my own occupations," Tolstoy had told Fet two summers before.* And if he had ever done so, we would all of us imagine them as vividly as everything else he described.

Tolstoy had journeyed to Samara for the first time in 1862 for a fermented-milk health cure—koumiss therapy. Koumiss, variously spelled by its translators, is a slightly alcoholic potion of mare's milk, made by the formerly nomadic native people of the region, the Bashkirs. For all of Tolstoy's physical energy, for all of his loudly and consistently expressed mistrust of medicine, he seems to have had a streak of hypochondria. He hated listening to doctors but followed their advice in the end. In 1862 he had felt worn out from his efforts running the school for peasant children and advocating for pedagogical reform in his magazine, *Yasnaya Polyana*. He understandably worried he could have tuberculosis, which two of his brothers had recently died of. His late father also had gone to the steppes for the koumiss cure.† After a month in that summer of 1862, Tolstoy felt himself coughing less and regaining weight. Although he had hired a clerk, he told Alexandrine Tolstaya in a letter back then, "I do not dictate or write much. Laziness quite overpowers one when taking koumiss."‡

The biographer Aylmer Maude says that in 1862, during the thirty-three-year-old Tolstoy's health-restoration visit, the envious landowner "noticed how extremely cheap and how fertile was the land in those parts. He therefore wished to purchase an estate there, and visited the district in the autumn of 1864, probably with that end in view."§

Tolstoy returned to Samara in 1871. He had had such a nightmarish experience traveling on his own in 1869 (this came to be referred to as the "Arzamas Horror," during which Tolstoy hallucinated a voice telling him to kill himself—more on this

---

* Maude, *The Life of Tolstoy: First Fifty Years*, 337, letter of July 16–17, 1871. See *PSS* 61: 256.

† Behrs, *Recollections of Count Leo Tolstoy*, 89.

‡ Paul Biryukoff [Pavel Ivanovich Biriukov], *Leo Tolstoy, His Life and Work: Autobiographical Memoirs, Letters and Biographical Material* (New York: Charles Scribner's Sons, 1911), 354, letter of June 28, 1862.

§ Maude, *The Life of Tolstoy: First Fifty Years*, 300. Neither does Gusev, in the *Letopis'*, seem to know how long Tolstoy was there in 1864, and Tolstoy's correspondence (see *PSS* 61) does not mention this trip.

later) that Stepan, Sofia's fourteen-year-old brother, was enlisted as his traveling companion.*

There is much to like in Stepan Bers's memoir of his brother-in-law, from whom he only grew disaffected when Tolstoy renounced the family's privileged life in the early 1880s. Bers was generous about and fond of Tolstoy. The biographer Maude writes: "Tolstoy furnishes an example of the well-known fact that men of artistic temperament are often untidy. Though he acknowledges the advantages of neatness in general, he often remarked that it is a quality most frequently found in shallow natures. He himself simply could not, and therefore did not try to, keep his things in order. When he undressed he let his clothes or boots drop where he stood; and if he happened to be moving from place to place, his garments remained strewn about the room, and sometimes on the floor." Maude quotes Stepan:

> I noticed that to pack his things for a journey cost him great effort, and when I accompanied him I used very willingly to do it for him, and thereby pleased him very much. I remember that once, for some reason, I did not at all wish to pack for him. He noticed this, and with characteristic delicacy did not ask me to, but put his things into his portmanteau himself; and I can assert positively that no one else, were they to try, could have got them into such fearful disorder as they were in, in that portmanteau.†

Tolstoy's trip in the summer of 1871 took him away from Sofia, the children, and Yasnaya Polyana for eight weeks. From Samara he, his "man-servant" Alexei, and Stepan (often referred to by his nickname Styopa) rode horses along the Karalyk River to the village of Karalyk, where he had stayed in 1862.

---

* Sofia Tolstaya noted in her diary on December 9, 1870: "All this time of inaction, of what I should have called intellectual repose, he has been much tormented. He has kept repeating that his conscience bothered him because of his idleness, before me, others, and people in general. Occasionally he seems to think that he is being inspired again and then he is happy. At other times it seems to him—but this always occurs when he is out of the house and away from the family—that he will go mad, and his fear of insanity becomes so intense that afterward, when he has told me about it, I too am terrified." Quoted by Alexandra Tolstoy in *Tolstoy: A Life of My Father*, tran. Elizabeth Reynolds Hapgood (New York: Harper and Brothers, 1953), 191–192.

† Maude, *The Life of Tolstoy: First Fifty Years*, 324.

At first Tolstoy was blue and could not shake his mood. He wrote Sofia: "I would say that I'm completely healthy if not for the sleeplessness and the very depressed state of my soul. Really, Styopa is of use to me and I feel that with him the Arzamas horror won't happen."*

A few days later, he wrote to tell her: "I can't give you any pleasant news. My health is still not good. Since I came here, I've begun to get a feeling of depression like a fever at 6:00 o'clock every evening, a physical depression, the sensation of which I can't convey better than by saying that soul and body part company. [. . .] I don't understand my condition: either I've caught a cold in the tent during the first cold night or else the koumiss is bad for me, but I've been worse in the three days I've been here. The main thing is weakness, depression, and wanting to play the woman and weep, and it's embarrassing, whether with the Bashkirs or with Styopa." Tolstoy went on, however, to describe the satisfactions of lacking comforts:

> We're living in a tent and drinking koumiss, Styopa as well, everybody treats him; the discomforts of life would strike terror in your Kremlin heart: no beds, no crockery, no white bread, no spoons. As for you, you would find it easier to endure the misfortune of underdone turkey or undersalted Easter cake. But these discomforts aren't at all unpleasant, and it would be good fun if only I were well. As it is, I make Styopa depressed, and I can see that he's bored. The hunting is quite decent. I went out once and killed two ducks. [. . .]
>
> The most painful thing for me is that because of my poor health, I only feel 1/10 of what exists. There are no intellectual pleasures, especially poetic ones. I look at everything as though I were dead—the very thing for which I used to dislike many people. And now I myself can only see what exists; I understand and grasp it; but I can't see through it, as I used to, with love. And if I'm sometimes in a poetic mood, it's only a very sour and tearful one—I just want to cry.†

But to everyone's relief, he came around. Embarrassedly, he wrote Sofia:

> I'm glad to write to you, my dear, with good news about myself, i.e., that two days after my last letter to you where I complained about depression and ill

---

*   *PSS* 83: 176, letter of June 14, 1871.

†   Christian, *Tolstoy's Letters*, 234–235, June 18, 1871.

health, I began to feel fine, and ashamed that I had alarmed you. I can't, from habit, either write or say to you what I don't think. [. . .]*

That last admission is quite a boast. He described for her his and Stepan's routines:

There is much that is new and interesting; the Bashkirs who reek of Herodotus, and Russian peasants, and villages which are especially charming for the simplicity and kindness of the people. I bought a horse for 60 rubles and Styopa and I go riding. Styopa is fine. Sometimes he's in high spirits and keeps abusing Petersburg with an important air, sometimes he hangs around me and I'm sorry for him because he's bored, and sorry he's not at Yasnaya. [. . .] I shoot ducks and we have them to eat. We've just been riding after bustards and only scared them away as usual, then we came on a wolf's litter and a Bashkir caught a cub there. I'm reading Greek, but very little. I don't feel like it. Nobody has ever described koumiss better than the peasant who said to me the other day that *we are out at grass*—like horses. I don't feel like anything which might harm me: vigorous exercise or smoking (Styopa is trying to cure me of the habit of smoking, and now gives me 12 cigarettes a day, reducing the number all the time)—or tea or sitting up late.

I get up at 6, drink koumiss at 7, go to the village where the koumiss drinkers live, have a talk to them, walk back, drink tea with Styopa, then read a bit, walk about the steppe in my shirtsleeves, go on drinking koumiss, eat a piece of roast mutton, and either go hunting or riding, and in the evening go to bed almost as soon as it's dark.†

Aylmer Maude notes that "Tolstoy was extremely fond of the Bashkirs, associated much with them, and strictly followed their diet: avoiding all vegetable foods and restricting himself to meat and animal products. Dinner every day consisted chiefly of mutton eaten with the fingers out of wooden bowls."‡

Tolstoy occasionally recounted his dreams to Sofia:

Sleep here, more than anything, brings me closer to you. The first night I dreamed of you, then of Seryozha. I showed the portrait of the children to the

---

*   Christian, *Tolstoy's Letters*, 235–236, June 23, 1871.

†   Christian, *Tolstoy's Letters*, 236, June 23, 1871.

‡   Maude, *The Life of Tolstoy: First Fifty Years*, 335.

Bashkir men and women [. . .] In the dream I saw that Seryozha was being naughty and I got mad at him; in reality it was probably the opposite.[*]

Awake, he continually looked out for Stepan's comfort in a comfort-limited place, doling out to him candies and marmalade that Tolstoy had bought in the town of Samara.[†]

He and the boy camped all summer; they slept in a sweltering tent and Tolstoy took doses of koumiss. In the village, Tolstoy had found a priest with whom he could study ancient Greek, which pursuit Sofia was sure had been and would continue damaging his health. (She said she persuaded his friends to write him and tell him to desist.) Though I'm skeptical about Greek study–induced illness, she had come to the conclusion that his intellectual exertions tended to weaken his physical health.

In late June of 1871, Tolstoy, about to ride eastward with Stepan across the steppes to Buzuluk for a seasonal fair, refined for Sofia his description of the daily routine: "I wake very early, often 5:30 (Stepa sleeps until 10:00). I drink tea with milk, 3 cups, I walk around the little kibitka, I look at the herds returning from the mountain, which is very beautiful, about a thousand horses."[‡]

The Buzuluk fair became a summer highlight for the Tolstoy family. In 1871, however, Tolstoy was so tired from *not* sleeping well in the tent that on the road at an inn, he wrote Sofia, "I slept so that I didn't sense the bedbugs which (when I woke up and saw them) had fallen all over me."[§]

Stepan remembered this adventure and reminds us that Tolstoy, for all his sociability, had a reserve of dignity[¶]:

> The fair attracted a strange motley of different nationalities and races, Russian moujiks [peasants], Ural Cossacks, Bashkirs, and Khirgese. As usual, and thanks to his natural affability, Leo Nicholaevitch was soon on the best

---

[*] PSS 83: 183, letter of June 23, 1871. In *Tolstoy's Letters* R. F. Christian did not translate the last forty lines of the letter.

[†] PSS 83: 190.

[‡] PSS 83: 189, letter of June 27, 1871.

[§] PSS 83: 192–193, letter of June 29, 1871.

[¶] "Contrary though he may have been, ornery and overly dogmatic at times, I cannot think of a single instance in his life when Tolstoy consciously schemed on his own behalf or kowtowed to others. His aristocratic integrity was phenomenal, and a main source of his appeal down to this day," writes Donna Tussing Orwin, *Simply Tolstoy* (New York: Simply Charly, 2017), 99.

terms with them all. Some of the frequenters of the fair were generally drunk, but, for all that, the Count would chat and laugh with them. Once a drunken moujik, inspired by a superfluous excess of affection, wished to embrace him, but a stern look from the Count was sufficient to make him draw back, as he muttered a kind of apology, "No, pardon me, I pray you."[*]

When Tolstoy wrote to Sofia that summer of 1871 to ask her permission to invest in land near Patrovka, "he went ahead anyway, even before he had received her reply," writes the biographer Rosamund Bartlett. "As it happened, she was not at all enthusiastic: 'If it's profitable, that's your business, and I don't have an opinion on the matter. But it would have to be extreme necessity that would want to force a person to live in the steppe without a single tree for hundreds of miles [Sofia exaggerated the treelessness], as one would never go there willingly, particularly with five children.'"[†] Bartlett reminds us: "A primitive Bashkir village in the middle of nowhere was not every Russian's idea of the ideal health resort."[‡]

Confusingly to Sofia (she may have wondered, *If you love me so much, why did you choose to leave?*), Tolstoy wrote her during the 1871 trip more than a dozen tender letters, with notes to the children as well. To Ilya, who was only five, he wrote:

> Ask Seryozha, he'll read to you what I'm writing. Today a Bashkir was riding and saw three wolves. He wasn't at all scared and jumped right down from the horse at the wolves. They began biting him. He shot two but caught one and brought him to us. And tonight, maybe the mother of this wolf will come. And then we'll shoot her. I kiss you.[§]

Sweet dreams, Ilya! (By the way, Tolstoy gave up hunting about a dozen years later.)

Once the Tolstoys had worked out a correspondence system, which involved his sending a hired man to Samara, letters took about eight or nine days to arrive. When Tolstoy requested Sofia's approval of his scheme to buy thousands of acres of farmland, he excitedly pitched to her all of its advantages ("Ten times more income than ours, ten times less bustle and

---

[*]   Behrs, *Recollections of Count Leo Tolstoy,* 93–94.

[†]   Bartlett, *Tolstoy,* 209.

[‡]   Bartlett, *Tolstoy,* 208.

[§]   *PSS* 83: 183, letter of June 23, 1871.

work"*), with Sofia shaking her head and resigning herself to her husband doing what he wanted to do, no matter her doubts about the farm's profitability. "Don't be mad, sweetie," she wrote him, "if I oppose you in something, but do in any case what you want."†

Having already done what he wanted, he tried to reassure her in his response: "Living without trees for 100 versts would be terrible in Tula; but here it's another thing: the air and grass and dryness and heat makes it so you grow to love the steppe."‡

His daughter Alexandra Tolstaya remarks in her biography: "Whether it was because Tolstoy loved the steppes, the Bashkirs and the koumiss, or because he had a passion for acquiring new property, or a desire to build up some capital for the benefit of his growing family, his trip to the province ended with his making a most advantageous purchase of 2,500 desyatins [6,750 acres] of land [. . .] for 20,000 rubles."§

Tolstoy and Stepan returned to Yasnaya Polyana in early August 1871. Tolstoy made a short trip to the steppe the following summer to make arrangements about building and plowing.¶

✳

Until July of 2018, I had to take Tolstoy's descriptions of the Samara region in pieces, from different years of Tolstoy's life, as well as make use of descriptions by other travelers and family members, because how else does a writer describe a place where he has never been?

Feeling abashed before the dogged biographer Richard Holmes, who desired to leave no stone unturned in his pursuit of the poet and critic Samuel Taylor Coleridge, I finally traveled to the easternmost bend of the Volga and made it to the city of Samara. Then Aleksandr, a driver-photographer, drove me the final ninety miles from that city to the "treeless" countryside on the steppe, where Tolstoy bought thousands of acres of farmland. Thanks to a local historian, Valentina Petrovna Salazkina, who met me at the Patrovka village library, which was originally established in 1893 from a gift of books and money from Tolstoy himself, I was shown the brand-new, in-the-making monument to Tolstoy and his son Ilya (who was instrumental in relieving the region during the famine of 1891). Salazkina then guided me and the driver to the site where Tolstoy and his family spent

---

*   *PSS* 83: 191, letter of June 27, 1871.

†   *PSS* 83: 191, Letter of July 10, 1871.

‡   *PSS* 83: 203, letter of July 20, 1871.

§   Tolstoy, *Tolstoy: A Life of My Father*, 197.

¶   Maude, *The Life of Tolstoy*, 337.

the summer of 1873 (a marker is laid at the spot), and then on foot, across the dry lively steppe, to the marker at the site of the second house.

I understand now why Tolstoy so adored the region. The sky, the air, the dots of yellows and purples amid the dry grasses, the rugged pockets of scrappy brush and low trees immediately caught my fancy. I could imagine Tolstoy sighing with delight at the rolling vistas and seemingly endless space.

So to continue back to June of 1873, when the whole Tolstoy family set out for Samara to their farm and its ramshackle farmhouse: They left Yasnaya Polyana on June 2 and seem to have stayed one night in Moscow. The boys' tutor, Fedor Fedorovich, went ahead of the rest to Samara with a carriage "and most of our things." Sofia wrote: "As I recall, the rail trip from Moscow to Nizhnij Novgorod was most unpleasant." They were all in one "compartment," and they couldn't leave that compartment either: "[I was stuck with] little children and filth." They took a steamer down the Volga eastward to Kazan, which journey she liked, "in spite of my fussing over the children."

Sergei, the eldest child, remembered: "The great spaces of water, the dark forest slopes, the yellow sand beaches, the spray that splashed up from the ship's wheels, the fish and the smell of fish, the trading at the ports, the different types of vessels, barges, cargo boats, and rafts—all these were new and vivid impressions."*

On board Sofia made the acquaintance of Princess Elizaveta Aleksandrovna Golitsyn (the princess title in Russia was not on a par with that title in England), whom she liked very much. The princess was accompanying her sick lover and their two children.

Anna Karenina might accustom us to taking for granted the shunning of high society women in out-of-wedlock relationships, yet the Tolstoys were quite used to and accepting of them—Sofia's maternal grandmother had been the product of a second family; Tolstoy's brother Sergei had several children with his common-law wife before he married her (and during which time was even briefly engaged to Sofia's sister Tatyana!), and Tolstoy's sister, Maria, had a longtime partnership with her illegitimate daughter's father. The Tolstoys, like most aristocrats, were familiar with unsanctioned relationships. (Why then, Tolstoy may have begun to wonder, was Anna Karenina going to have to suffer so much for hers?)

Sofia relates that Princess Elizaveta married young, and her husband left her after two weeks. All he had wanted was to sleep with her and he had been willing to marry her to do so. Elizaveta, abandoned by him, eventually got her own lover, became pregnant, and

---

*   Sergei Tolstoy, *Tolstoy Remembered by His Son Sergei Tolstoy*, trans. Moura Budberg (New York: Atheneum, New York, 1962), 17.

left home. She was now forty. As a plot, it's more intriguing than what Tolstoy had come up with for Anna and Vronsky.

Sofia surprisingly doesn't connect the next scene that she narrates to the death scene of Levin's brother Nikolai in *Anna Karenina*:

> [Elizaveta] later told me, when I visited her in Moscow, just *how* Kiselev [her lover] died. He had already grown completely cold and motionless, the priest had recited the prayer for the dying, and Princess Elizaveta Aleksandrovna covered his eyes with her hands. The priest approached, took one look at him and said, "It's over!" Suddenly from somewhere out of the depths, as though from the grave itself, came a voice: "Not quite!"
>
> Both gave a shudder and, as the princess said, the effect was terrifying.*

In *Anna Karenina*, "the effect" of Levin's brother Nikolai's last peep is not "terrifying" but grimly comic:

> Towards night the sick man was not able to lift his hands, and could only gaze before him with the same intensely concentrated expression in his eyes. Even when his brother or Kitty bent over him, so that he could see them, he looked just the same. Kitty sent for the priest to read the prayer for the dying.
>
> While the priest was reading it, the dying man did not show any sign of life; his eyes were closed. Levin, Kitty, and Marya Nikolaevna [Nikolai's companion] stood at the bedside. The priest had not quite finished reading the prayer when the dying man stretched, sighed, and opened his eyes. The priest, on finishing the prayer, put the cross to the cold forehead, then slowly returned it to the stand, and after standing for two minutes more in silence, he touched the huge, bloodless hand that was turning cold.
>
> "He is gone," said the priest, and would have moved away; but suddenly there was a faint stir in the mustaches of the dead man that seemed glued together, and quite distinctly in the hush they heard from the bottom of the chest the sharply defined sounds:
>
> "Not quite . . . soon."

---

* Tolstaya, *My Life*, 190–191. (Note: the brackets in *My Life* are supplied by its 21st-century editor, Andrew Donskov.)

And a minute later the face brightened, a smile came out under the mustaches, and the women who had gathered round began carefully laying out the corpse.[*]

Was Sofia remembering the scene from *Anna Karenina* and mixing it up with her own memories?

At first I imagined she must have told the princess's story to Tolstoy and he had said, "Wonderful! I'll use that."

But maybe, just as Sofia misremembered the first words of his first draft of *Anna Karenina* (which she only could have remembered from the final version[†]), she mixed this up, and drew the *Anna Karenina* scene into her recollection of Princess Elizaveta's story.

I wish I could find a polite way to challenge some of Sofia's memories. After all, it's only because of her account of this summer vacation that it has become real in my imagination. For example, when the Volga steamer docked at Kazan, still a couple of hundred miles north of Samara, Tolstoy went out in the morning with his two older sons, Sergei and Ilya, to show them where he had lived as an adolescent. We can imagine that the boys must have been so pleased to be out with their vigorous dad in this historic, exotic city. The steamship embarked again. Sofia, preoccupied with the baby, her daughters, and the servants, says she only later noticed that her husband and two older sons were not on board. And now how confused the boys must have been when they saw their father confronting the empty space at the pier. Did Tolstoy know the English expression "missing the boat"? Did he laugh? Did he groan? I expect that he did both. Meanwhile Sofia offered the captain money to go back, which he did (though he didn't accept the money):

As we made our approach, there was Lev Nikolaevich standing on the dock with his arms upraised, in a guilty pose. Serezha was standing on one side of him while Iljusha stood on the other, sobbing for all to hear.[‡]

Just now typing up those two sentences by Sofia, it occurred to me that this misadventure had probably become a family story repeated many times by everyone concerned.

When they got off the steamer for good at the town of Samara they stayed "at a splendid hotel,"[§] and Sofia was pleased to encounter Princess Elizaveta again.

---

[*]   *Anna Karenina*, Part 5, Chapter 20, http://literatureproject.com/anna-karenina/anna_144.htm.

[†]   Tolstaya, *My Life*, 188.

[‡]   Tolstaya, *My Life*, 191–192.

[§]   Tolstaya, *My Life*, 192.

Sergei, almost ten years old, remembered the horse-drawn vehicles in which they drove ninety miles southeast from Samara to the farm:

> Shortly before our journey an old friend of my father, Sergei Urussov, in order to make the journey easier for my mother, presented her with his large dormouse that seated six people. It was the classical vehicle of these times, in which our ancestors travelled before the railroad existed. It was pulled by six horses—two in front and four in a row behind; a boy, the so-called Vorreiter, rode on one of the front horses. A kind of trunk was fixed on the roof of the carriage; behind was a two-seated bench, and the coachman's seat was large enough to hold three people. In the carriage sat all our women with the youngest children, the others drove in wicket carts with straw carriage-bodies. Halfway we stopped for the night in a large hut where we suffered greatly from bedbugs. . . .

Sofia also remembered this portion of the trip and that it was a native Mordovian family's hut. The woman whose hut it was didn't speak Russian. There were bedbugs, Sofia confirms, and some members of the Tolstoy contingent slept elsewhere on the grounds. "I went out of the hut into the spacious farm-yard," she recalled, "looking for Lev Nikolaevich. He had prepared some accommodation for the two of us in a small out-barn. But somehow it didn't turn out all that well: it was stuffy, and there were mice running around. I went over to the hut to visit the children and feed Petja, and when I came out, I saw Lev Nikolaevich dragging a large bale of hay out of the out-barn and preparing to spend the night in the open air. So the two of us went to sleep in the hay in the middle of the farm-yard. But there was no freshening of the air during the night. A tepid stillness hung over everything, and the wind kicked up the dust."*

Sofia's descriptions here are vivid, though she had not noted them in a diary, which she rarely opened during these years of *Anna Karenina*. In the memoir she evoked herself and Lev and the way they were:

> I remember our mood at the time being happy, even amorous. Nothing could disturb our sense of quiet joy. All the children I had borne were alive, healthy,

---

* Tolstaya, *My Life*, 192. As for the Mordovians, the editor of *My Life* explains in a footnote (192), they belong "to the Volga-Finnic branch of the Finno-Ugric people, approximately one-third of whom live today [2010?] in the Mordovian Republic of the Russian Federation."

and right here with us. Our love had in no way been affected by anything. We were young, strong, and energetic, and, most importantly, friends and kindred spirits in every respect.[*]

When she wrote her memoir, she was contrasting these memories with the heartaches and grief that she didn't know in 1873 were on the horizon, and probably she also had in mind the disaffection and out-of-sync relations that she and Lev had had for much of the last thirty years of his life.

She remembers that night—the place, the air, being surrounded by family and feeling happy. She remembers "at the time" they were "even amorous." How much would Tolstoy have blushed had he read this passage? Everything Tolstoy ever wrote about sex disintegrated him into a heap of shame. Sofia was more candid. Can we hope for them that on this long journey to the farm on the steppes that they had an "amorous" night for themselves "in the hay in the middle of the farm-yard"?

Let's remind ourselves that she was the one fondly remembering this night. *Everything was good!* The family was whole, complete. None of her children had died yet—but in the next three years one and then another and another were going to. For now she and Lev were on an adventure. Where the family was, there life was, buggy and mousy though it was.

Gusev thinks that the Tolstoys arrived at the farm on June 8,[†] while Sofia's biographer Alexandra Popoff calculates that the trip took eight days, which would make it June 10 at the earliest.

Son Sergei later described the farm's layout:

> Our property was divided into twelve fields of which only two were sown; the first, on hard soil, with Turkish wheat, the second with Russian wheat. Sometimes corn would be sown in the third year. The other nine or ten fields were left for pastures and meadows. The first two years after ploughing, the fields were overgrown with coarse, wild grass, but the next years they gave very good hay. The hay was gathered into stacks spread all over the steppe. There was no wood in that neighborhood, and bricks of dried manure were used for fuel. Pyramids of these bricks were stacked around the villages and huts.[‡]

---

[*]   Tolstaya, *My Life*, 192.

[†]   Gusev, *Letopis'*, 409.

[‡]   Tolstoy, *Tolstoy Remembered by His Son*, 18.

In the chapter "Homestead on the Tuchkov Land" from her memoir, Sofia remembers, "our little house there turned out better than I had anticipated." Even so, according to their impressionable first child, Sergei, "There was not enough room in it for all of us; so Fedor Fedorovich [the tutor], my two brothers and I spent the summer in an empty shed, and my father and Stepan Bers in a Bashkir caravan, a sort of felt tent, which my father had bought."[*]

Their big barn, Sofia noted, would remain empty of crops because of the drought. She described how the Bashkirs made koumiss. Koumiss did everyone who drank it some good, but she herself wouldn't drink it. The children sometimes had lessons with her, but mostly they romped. A piano had been brought from Yasnaya Polyana. No one mentions whether they hauled it back home in August or not, and no one that summer describes any music flowing from it. Sergei remembered Sofia having a harder time than the others: "My mother was at that time nursing Peter [Petja] and she bore with difficulty the discomforts of life on the farm. The house was drafty, the roof leaked, the bricks stank and burnt badly, the incredible number of flies made eating and sleeping a misery, the post came rarely, and had to be fetched by messenger from Samara. There were no neighbors, except Bashkirs and peasants, and the doctor lived far away."[†]

Sofia remembered: "Behind the homestead rose a sharp-peaked mountain known as the Shishka."[‡] She collected "marine fossils"[§] and studied English on her own with a big volume of Shakespeare; apropos of no particularly recalled incident, she wrote that she identified with Desdemona. She recalled realizing (she was not quoting a diary): "*How many* there are of us—young wives with jealous husbands, just as innocent as Desdemona, who spend years trying to figure out what our men are angry at us for!"[¶]

If there was a jealous scene that summer, it was not noted by anyone. She writes that she remembered "even though Lev Nikolaevich left this work [*Anna Karenina*] alone for a time, he never ceased thinking about it and being fascinated by it."[**] She provides no details of nor evidence for his continuous mental activity about the novel. Could she really know that he "never ceased thinking about it"? Of course what he had already written was knocking around or hibernating somewhere within him; but it was not on his mind.

---

[*]   Tolstoy, *Tolstoy Remembered by His Son*, 17.

[†]   Tolstoy, *Tolstoy Remembered by His Son*, 18.

[‡]   It's still there: See photo insert for an image of the Shishka from Tolstoy's time on the steppe and a contemporary view from the site-marker of Tolstoy's farmhouse.

[§]   Tolstaya, *My Life*, 192–193.

[¶]   Tolstaya, *My Life*, 194.

[**] Tolstaya, *My Life*, 188.

He *definitely* didn't mention *Anna Karenina* in his letters that summer while he was in Samara. Sofia was, I'm guessing, just theorizing from the distance of decades, and I think most of us would have made such a guess ourselves. After all, how could he *not* have been thinking of *Anna Karenina*? (Two years later, again in Samara, he would brag to his friends that he hadn't let himself think about writing all summer long.)

Two weeks after their arrival on the farm they sent a messenger to Samara with letters. Sofia wrote her sister Tatyana. Meanwhile, in Tolstoy's first letter of the summer, he asked Strakhov about helping him with "correcting" *War and Peace*, the galleys of which were tormenting his thoughts like a rash: "We are enjoying life in the Samara steppes, thank goodness, despite the heat, the drought and the children's illnesses, which are not serious, but are a worry to us. The primitive state of nature here and of the people with whom we are in close contact have a good effect on my wife and children."*

Tolstoy had been scrawling over the galleys of *War and Peace* that he was sending to Strakhov:

> I'm afraid that the calligraphic side of things is bad and will be impossible for the printers—I couldn't do any better, what with the Samara flies and the heat.†

His editorial work on *War and Peace* aggravated him: "I very rarely like it when I reread it, and for the most part it excites disgust and shame."‡ We learn that it was in this state of mind that he translated the novel's French conversations into Russian "drily and sometimes even incorrectly," says Gusev.§ Tolstoy also extracted information from the text and placed it into footnotes; he gathered some of the essay-like passages into a section of their own and reduced some material. "All these changes were made in a great hurry so as not to hold up the volumes for the printer," writes Gusev, "and, besides which, were done with him not fully convinced and sometimes even reluctantly."¶

It is characteristic of him that his disconnection from *War and Peace* led him to make hasty editorial changes; he was willing to give up solid ground that he had fought for at the time of writing and revising and first publishing the complete novel.

---

* Christian, *Tolstoy's Letters*, 263, June 22, 1873.

† Ibid.

‡ *PSS* 62: 34, letter of June 22, 1873.

§ Gusev, *Materials*, 139.

¶ Gusev, *Materials*, 140.

He wrote to Strakhov: "The obliteration of the French sometimes seems a pity, but on the whole, it seems to me better without the French. The judgments of war, history, and philosophy seem to me, removed from the novel, to improve it and don't deprive it of interest on their own."[*]

Gusev writes: "Tolstoy asked Strakhov to look through his corrections and delete those of them that Strakhov judged as 'bad,' and, besides this, to fix what Strakhov found 'conspicuously and noticeably bad.'"[†]

Strakhov answered Tolstoy exactly correctly: "It seems to me that you poorly value *War and Peace*."[‡] Tolstoy probably should have paid Strakhov to edit it, and then, with due deliberation, accepted or declined each particular change.

Tolstoy's next bit of surviving correspondence from that summer of 1873 is a postscript to Sofia's July 8 letter to her sister Tatyana. He noted: "Sonya has gone off to feed [the baby], I am finishing off the writing."[§] He was glad to know that Tatyana would be coming to Yasnaya Polyana. He told her that the life there in Samara was better for everyone, that they relied on themselves. The "facilities" weren't like the ones Tatyana had in the Caucasus, but they were better than he had expected.

As of July 8, there had been no mention of Lev's or Sofia's distress about the drought-provoked "famine." In long retrospect, Sergei, their son, though sympathetic to the native Bashkirs for the loss of their nomadic way of life, pointed out the drawbacks of the Bashkirs' farming practices, which worsened the effects of the drought:

> All their efforts were concentrated on sowing as much wheat as possible. They sowed little corn, and no oats or hemp, no vegetables or potatoes. Therefore if there was a bad crop of wheat, which depended on whether it rained in May, they not only suffered great losses but even hunger. It was an irregular form of agriculture.[¶]

This was the third straight poor harvest. The local governor hadn't done anything to help (so Tolstoy would tell Strakhov on September 4) but instead had demanded all the back taxes from the impoverished farmers.

---

[*]   *PSS* 62: 34.

[†]   Gusev, *Materials,* 140.

[‡]   Donskov, *L. N. Tolstoy – N. N. Strakhov,* 127, after September 3–4, 1873, http://feb-web.ru /feb/tolstoy/texts/selectpe/ts6/ts62097-.htm.

[§]   *PSS* 62: 35.

[¶]   Tolstoy, *Tolstoy Remembered by His Son,* 19.

I keep having to remind myself that Tolstoy was on vacation, unwinding, and yet, just as he would do whenever new disasters struck the people, he threw himself into relieving their suffering:

> When A. S. Prugavin eight years later, in 1881, was in the Buzuluskiy region, in which was Tolstoy's estate, he heard from those peasants there many stories about the "hearty care" that Tolstoy showed, living among them at the time of the famine in 1873, how he "personally went around to the most needy peasant-yards, with care in their interests and needs, how he helped the poor, supplied them with bread and money, and gave them means for buying horses and so on."
>
> But of course this wasn't enough for Tolstoy.*

That is, Tolstoy exerted his energy and surveyed farm families to determine what they actually had on hand. Then he wrote to a Moscow newspaper about the regional disaster and explained to the readers that it wasn't, as they were told, that the peasants were drunk, but that there had been these terrible harvests. He contributed his own money and solicited readers' and governmental contributions. Tolstoy was so regularly giving and generous that I had forgotten this instance. He would again and again do such fund-raising and rallying for people whose lives had been devastated.

And while he was doing this, what was he thinking? Could he have been thinking of *Anna Karenina*, as Sofia believed? I don't think so.

Did he dramatize in his fiction such philanthropy as he himself provided?

No.

Levin doesn't ever rescue any famine-stricken peasants; if Levin had gone on vacation and encountered people in need, we can guess he tenderheartedly would have helped them, but Levin doesn't go to the steppes. Tolstoy did help the poor but wrote about other things for his characters. How great and good was Tolstoy? He saw suffering and did his utmost to relieve it. But if we want to feel superior to him we can remind ourselves, for example, that Tolstoy wasn't always a super husband or father, that he was born into wealth, which he squandered, that he wanted to live right and often failed . . .

And all of these failings are ones that he pointed out to us about himself!

There are no letters or notes by the Tolstoys between July 8 and the completion of his famine-relief article on July 28. This may be understandable, as they were busy:

---

* Gusev, *Materials,* 142.

Crops at the Tolstoys' farm were meager, but elsewhere, around distant villages, fields were bare and there was not enough water for the cattle. [. . .] Their farmstead became a center for the locals [. . .]. The Tolstoys refused no one: several hundred laborers "set up their tents in the field, grazed the oxen, and harvested wheat." Some families camped in the yard, sleeping near the barns, in or underneath their carts.[*]

In his article datelined "farm on the river Tananyka,"[†] Tolstoy explained in his usual clear way the situation year by year from 1871, and how the poorer peasants began to go into debt after having a bad harvest. The next summer things got worse, and the poor peasants had to sell their cows and horses, and then the next rung of peasants went into debt. Now in 1873 even the "rich" peasants didn't have any crops and ninety percent of the population was hungry. The people depended on the crops and farm work. There was nothing growing; there was almost no bread. He had gone out into the countryside seventy versts (about forty-five miles) in three directions, and all the fields were bare:

> In the villages, in the farmyards where I went, everywhere it's one and the same: not absolute famine but a situation close to it, all signs of a coming famine. There are no peasants anywhere, they're all leaving to look for work, homes of skinny women with skinny and sick children and old people. There's still bread, but just barely; dogs, cats, calves, chickens are hungry, and beggars, nonstop, come up to the windows and they're given crusts or are refused.[‡]

Then he described a prosperous peasant family, by whose example he refuted those who said the dire situation was the shiftless peasants' fault. He detailed his surveys of one of every ten families (not one village in three, as Stepan remembered): how many inhabitants, children, workers, cows, chickens, how much land, what was growing.

Reading to the end of Tolstoy's article, I began to understand for the first time why novel-writing could have seemed to him a kind of self-indulgence. As he went out among poor people in a devastated place, his doubts could naturally creep in that a long story about a married woman who runs off with an army captain could only be an entertainment

---

[*]   Popoff, *Sophia Tolstoy: A Biography*, 75.

[†]   Translated from Хутор на Тананыке.

[‡]   *PSS* 62: 37.

for the upper classes, and that such a novel does nothing for relieving the suffering that the majority of the world experiences.

Does consciousness of the world's suffering mean that we ought, from humility, from decency, to give up deriving pleasure from the arts? Tolstoy would wonder about this question for the rest of his life. Twenty years later he wrote a fellow novelist: "I was about to begin further work on a certain piece of fiction, but believe me, it hurts my conscience to write about people who never existed and who never did anything of the kind. Something is wrong. Is it that the form of fiction has outlived itself, or that stories are outworn or that I am outworn? Do you experience anything like this?"[*]

We all wrestle with that thorny problem of enjoying ourselves while the world seems to be collapsing, but in the meantime we go on reading *Anna Karenina* with excitement and tears. And, after all, Tolstoy, with his heavy conscience, went on writing it.

Witnessing and imagining the peasants' suffering, Tolstoy felt guilty for his pleasures and advantages. He wrote in the article:

> The situation of the people is terrible when looking at and considering the coming winter; but it's as if the people don't feel or understand this.
>
> As soon as one talks with a peasant and asks that he consider himself and consider the future, he says: "We don't know how our headmen think," but he seems absolutely calm, as usual; so for a person who condescendingly looks now at the people, distributed across the steppes, picking the stubble barely seen from the ground, elsewhere sprouted wheat, one might see a healthy, always merry working people, and one might hear songs and laughter here and there, to whom it would even seem strange that in the midst of this people is one of the worst poverties. But this poverty exists and its signs are far too clear.
>
> The peasants, despite that they sow and reap more than other Christians, live by the Testament's words: "The birds of the heavens don't sow or reap, and the heavenly father feeds them"; the peasant firmly believes that by his eternal heavy labor and the smallest requirements his heavenly father feeds him, and so he does not value himself and when such a terrible impoverished year comes, he only humbly bows his head and says, "We've angered God, apparently for our sins!"

* Hugh McLean, *Nikolai Leskov: The Man and His Art* (Cambridge, MA: Harvard University Press, 1977), 452, letter to Nikolai Leskov, July 10, 1893.

From this count, it's clear that ninety percent of the families don't have enough bread. "What are the peasants to do?" First, they will mix in the bread in cheap and non-nutritious bad-stuff: chaff, quinoa (as they told me, in some places they're already doing that); in the second, the strong members of the peasant family are leaving this fall or winter for work, and from hunger the old and the women and exhausted and feeding mothers and children will suffer. They will die not straightaway from hunger but from disease, by reason of the food will be bad and not enough, and especially because the Samaran population of various generations is accustomed to good wheat bread.

Last year even, in some places mothers had to nurse the wheat bread for the young children; this year there is already none and the children are getting sick and dying. What is there to do when it is already beginning, there is not enough pure black bread?

It's terrible to think about the poverty that awaits the biggest part of the population in Samara Gubernia if it's not given help by the government or community. A subscription might be opened, in my opinion, for two things: 1) a subscription for contributions and 2) a subscription for grant money for provisions on credit, without interest for two years. The subscription of the second kind, that is, grant money without interest, I propose, in order to more quickly reach that sum that will provide for the suffering population of Samara Gubernia, and probably the zemstvo of Samara Gubernia could take on itself the labor of distributing bread bought with this money and debt collection in the first harvest year.*

✳

Tolstoy wrote movingly to Alexandrine Tolstaya in St. Petersburg on July 30. The situation—now that he knew firsthand the peasants' condition—was indeed dire. First he apologized for bothering her and then, in the excerpt below, he explained why he felt he had to:

With all my characteristic inability to write articles, I've written a very cold, clumsy letter to the papers, and for fear of a polemic, I've presented the matter as less terrible than it really is, and I've written to some of my friends to get things

---

*   *PSS* 62: 42.

moving, but I'm afraid that no headway will be made or that it will be slow, and I'm turning to you. If you wish to, and are able to interest the good and the mighty of this world, who are, fortunately, the same people, then headway will be made, and yours and my joy will be such insignificant grains of sand in that enormous good that will be done for thousands of people, that we won't even give it a thought. I don't like writing in a plaintive tone, but I've lived for 45 years in the world and I've never seen anything like it, and never thought it possible. When one pictures vividly to oneself what it will be like in winter, one's hair stands on end. [. . .] It's particularly shocking and pathetic to someone who is able to understand the Russian's forbearance and humility in suffering—his calmness, and submissiveness. There's no good food—well, there's no point in complaining. If he dies—it's God's will. They aren't sheep, but good, strong oxen ploughing their furrow. If they fall—they'll be dragged away, and others will pull the plough.* [. . .]

He notes Alexandrine's own charity work with "Your Magdalens," that is, prostitutes, but he argued, "pity for them, as for all spiritual suffering, is more of the mind, of the heart, if you like; but one's whole being feels pity for simple, good people, who are physically and morally healthy, when they suffer from deprivation; when one looks on their suffering, one is ashamed and grieved to be a human being. So there, I put this important matter, dear to our hearts, into your hands."†

Tolstoy's article was published on August 17, prefaced by an editorial note about Tolstoy and the situation in Samara. It had "many number of responses," says Gusev. "Tolstoy's letter appeared as if not the first then in any case one of the first instances of statistical description of Russian village reform; it spoke in terms of numbers and so it produced such a strong effect."‡ Gusev believes that Tolstoy was right in making the article a "cold, clumsy" argument: "Tolstoy's call for help provided by contributors saved Samara's peasants from destruction."

> The letter about the Samara famine was Tolstoy's first public display [in which he was] revealing a disastrous situation of the Russian peasantry in the post-reform period. It set the beginning of many others of Tolstoy, of even worse effects on the given question in the '80s and '90s.§

---

* Christian, *Tolstoy's Letters,* 264, July 30, 1873.

† Ibid.

‡ Gusev, *Materials,* 144.

§ Gusev, *Materials,* 146–147.

Sofia's memoir's story of the famine-relief is so very different from her husband's that I need to account for it. She was anxious that they had no doctor nearby and that bread was scarce. She says that as a result of her observing the impending famine and worrying about the winter for the region's poor that she "decided to write an article for the papers with an appeal for help."[*]

> I showed the article to Lev Nikolaevich.
> "Who'll believe you without all sorts of statistics?" was his reaction.
> Whereupon he decided right off to go around the nearest villages, along with my brother Stepa and taking a survey of the families and mouths to feed hut by hut.[†]

She has claimed that the article was her idea. Tolstoy never suggested this, and their surveying, as she understood it, is different from what Stepan and Tolstoy actually did.

She didn't in her memoir seem to take pride that she had prompted *his* effective work. She has left it to us to believe that her husband took over her idea.

Her own brother Stepan did not mention her input or article and credited only Tolstoy. "It is impossible to give an adequate idea of the misery and sufferings the poorer peasants had to endure," Stepan recalled. "With his wonted kindliness and energy, Leo Nicholaevitch came to their aid, and was the first to open a subscription fund for the starving population. I accompanied him to two of the neighboring villages, and helped him to make an inventory of all the grain and property actually in their possession."[‡]

I will ungenerously doubt that Sofia wrote any article. She may have said, "I will write an article," and explained to her husband what she might say in it. And then he would have said (as she said he said), "Who'll believe you without all sorts of statistics?" And then he and Stepan went and did the legwork (not, as she said, "hut by hut"), and then Tolstoy made the right decision about how to present it, "coldly."

Because he wrote the article, Russia learned about the famine, news that the governor himself didn't want known, and a heap of money was donated, some of it actually directed to the particular families that Tolstoy had mentioned.

Tolstoy did much good for the sake of the hungry in rural Samara, but what else did he do that summer? What were his routines? The contrasting presentations of the famine

---

[*]   Tolstaya, *My Life*, 196.

[†]   Ibid.

[‡]   Behrs, *Recollections of Count Leo Tolstoy*, 98–99.

from Sofia and Lev remind us that in the meantime family life was going on. Even if we're responding to emergencies and donating food and money, we all still have our home life. Sergei and the other children remembered nothing unpleasant.

Sofia recalled that despite having the book of Shakespeare for her English improvement, she didn't read much; the children demanded a lot from her, she recalled, and they were often sick from the heat:

> I would send to Samara 130 versts distant and they would bring stale white bread loaves, which I would slice. I would dry rusks and store them away (preferably in a drawer) so they wouldn't get mouldy. This is what we lived on, and sometimes we also ate Albert biscuits.[*]

Sofia's editors provide a note about the biscuits, which were British and "very popular in Russia at the time."[†] Were they a gift sent from governess Hannah's family back in England? Just what sorts of products could upper-class Russians like the Tolstoys buy? I'm guessing they had more "Western" products available to them than would be available to Soviet citizens.

But they were caught by the drought, too. They had no water in their wells. They "drank either boiled water or dirty water . . . Only those who drank koumiss didn't get sick," recalled non-drinking Sofia.[‡]

She fondly, heartbrokenly remembered her baby son Petja as he was then, "big, chubby, and thirsty. I even wrote my sister about him: 'My little bull keeps tugging at me. I'm growing thin, but I shan't wean him until we return home from Samara.'"[§]

Meanwhile . . .

> Lev Nikolaevich would drink quantities of koumiss and then walk or ride far into the steppes, walking completely naked, as he said, in the sun. He didn't write anything, he read practically nothing, and lived a purely animal life, building up his strength and health.[¶]

---

[*]   Tolstaya, *My Life*, 194.

[†]   Ibid.

[‡]   Ibid.

[§]   Tolstaya, *My Life*, 196.

[¶]   Tolstaya, *My Life*, 195.

We have to travel now in our imaginations to the steppe, a hundred and forty-seven years ago. We venture outside in the woozy early afternoon and we notice off in the grassy distance, perhaps with the pinecone-shaped Shishka hill behind him, a figure, a burly fellow striding along. Is he wearing an animal skin? . . . That *naked* man there is the author of *War and Peace*!

As far as I have found, Tolstoy did not express horror or shame at male nakedness. (But *female* nakedness? Kitty in *Anna Karenina* is humiliated by having to undress for medical examinations, and Tolstoy almost stutters with astonishment at the unashamed society women whose dresses reveal something of their bosoms.) Still, this naked detail surprised me. Sofia's "as he said" is important. She was emphasizing, *I didn't see this. He told me so. If Lev wants to stride about the steppe like Adam, let him!*

She did not begrudge him the recovery of his vitality. Her statement that he didn't write and hardly read is untrue, though. He conducted the survey of the peasants and he wrote the article, and at least for the first week or two he had read or tried to read and correct the *War and Peace* volumes.

Tolstoy wanted the family to stay through the harvest, but that year "the harvest was absolutely pitiful." There was a big gathering with people they had hired "in the large village of Zemlijanka," "hundreds of people with their children, cows, dogs and even chickens."[*] Sergei remembered that his father set up recreational races and events in early August, though not as he more grandly and famously did in 1875.[†]

There are no more surviving letters by Tolstoy after the one on July 22 to Alexandrine until he got back to Yasnaya Polyana. They left the farm in Samara on August 14. "The steamer voyage wasn't as much fun as before," Sofia remembered, "since we spent a long time on the river, there was fog, and Tanja and I felt very much under the weather." They arrived home on August 22, her birthday.[‡] We don't know anything more from the family about the excitement or resignation of returning or about the return journey. On August 23, Sofia weaned baby Petja. A month later she was pregnant again.

---

[*]   Tolstaya, *My Life*, 195.

[†]   "In the summer [1873] my father organized races on the farm, like ancient Bashkir races. I
       won't write about these because the races which my father organized in 1875 were much more
       spectacular . . ." Tolstoy, *Tolstoy Remembered by His Son*, 20.

[‡]   Tolstaya, *My Life*, 196.

4

Distractions and Family Woes: August 22–December 31, 1873

※

The return to Yasnaya Polyana brought Tolstoy back to attempting to resume *Anna Karenina*. There is no evidence that as he took walks or rode around the estate he tried to conjure up situations for the novel. He seems to have worked and created with his right hand dipping the pen into the inkwell and skritching it across the paper. So we can imagine him now, in late August of 1873, thinking or hoping that being at his desk would get the novel rolling again. He felt physically restored.

From his personal correspondence, we see that he wanted to want to write. He wrote two letters on August 24—one to Strakhov and one to Fet. He told Strakhov he didn't know how to thank him for the summer's "boring work on *War and Peace*."

> You write that you're awaiting from me something in a more severe style—like my attempts in the *Azbuka*; but I, to my shame, ought to confess that recorrecting and finishing off now that novel, about which I wrote you, is in the lightest least severe style.[*]

He still had not described the plot of *Anna Karenina* to Strakhov and had no suspicions that his novel's "lightest least severe style" was going to darken and concentrate itself into a most severe style.

---

[*]   *PSS* 62: 45.

I want to play around with this novel and now I can't finish it and I'm afraid that it's coming out poorly, that is, you won't like it. I will await your judg-ment when I finish; but unless you or I are going to be in Petersburg, I won't be able to read it to you. Our whole big happy family has come back, returned from Samara, having acquired physical and spiritual health. I say nothing of myself: I'm healthy as a bull, and, like a dammed mill, I've built up water. If only God gives enough strength to use in this business. Where are you preparing your trip for? Over to our side? That would be so joyful for me. I don't dare daydream about it.*

He was ready to burst with this novel. His summertime had indeed been his restoration.

And there was that "big happy family" of his.

To Fet, Tolstoy wrote a note apologizing that it was *not* a letter. His third sentence (of four) reads:

Despite the drought, losses, discomfort, we're all, even the wife, happy with the trip and even more happy with the old frame of life and accepting the respective labors.†

The perfect summer vacation.

He had family happiness there and back home, and *Anna Karenina* was, as far as he knew, simply a lark that wouldn't cost him or his readers much involvement.

But, even into September, he still had to think about the revised *War and Peace* for the collected works. Back in June, we might remember, he had asked for Strakhov's help with it. Strakhov's letter in response to that one has not survived, but "pointed out some judgments (probably in the epilogue), which he thought excessive." Though Tolstoy had given his friend full power to eliminate what seemed "excessive, contradic-tory, unclear," Tolstoy backpedaled in early September with, as Gusev says, "a char-acteristic qualification": "I give you this full-power and I thank you for the taken-up labor, but, I confess, I'm sorry. It seems to me (I'm probably wrong) that there's not anything excessive there."‡

---

*   *PSS* 62: 45.

†   *PSS* 62: 46.

‡   Gusev, *Materials,* 140–141.

I imagine Strakhov receiving this letter and twisting his mouth at the thought of the earnest work he had put in at Tolstoy's request. I imagine Tolstoy, professing his regret but deciding on second thought that, after all, *War and Peace* is a pretty good book, and that he shouldn't monkey with it—*even if Strakhov is right.*

Strakhov wrote him back that there was in any case an error in an astronomy reference. He justifiably scolded Tolstoy again for not valuing *War and Peace* highly enough. Tolstoy told him he remembered that passage and Strakhov should have taken it out, but that he would write the printer that very day to get it removed. Dutiful Gusev, following up on this point, writes: "However, either the letter wasn't written or it didn't reach the printer, and the 1873 edition's paragraph 12 remained in its place and was reprinted in all the further editions."*

Tolstoy finally realized, or maybe Sofia told him, or maybe Strakhov's critical admiration convinced him, that he himself was not the best option for the *War and Peace* editing job. This early September letter from Tolstoy to Strakhov is full of personal feeling and gratitude. When I had read only Gusev's quotations from this letter they didn't give me a sense of the friendship. Reading the whole letter, there is more loving-friendship feeling in it than in any friendship Tolstoy describes in *Anna Karenina*. After thanking Strakhov again for all his work on *War and Peace*, Tolstoy declared: "I fully believe in you."

> Right now I told my wife that one of the happinesses for which I thank fate is this, that N. N. Strakhov exists. And it's not because you help me, but for making it pleasant to think and write, knowing that there is a person who wants to understand not what he wants to but everything that wants to be expressed by him who expresses it. You are so good to me to have written about your place in the library that I see you there and dream about it [. . .]†

Strakhov, having made his living as a schoolteacher and then as a freelance writer, now had an adequately salaried job at a library in St. Petersburg. Tolstoy had a thing against journalists:

> I am very glad for you that you sit on that chair and are not needing to write in the newspapers. Today is a superb fall day, I went out the whole day alone

---

*   Gusev, *Materials,* 141.

†   *PSS* 62: 46, letter of September 3–4, 1873.

on the hunt and several times remembered you [. . .] and the whole time it's been annoying to me to think that you're a journalist.[*]

Tolstoy then confessed that he was embarrassed to say he himself had taken to the newspapers, but because of the famine he had just had to! He explained that the Samara governor only found the news and publicity inconvenient for the government's sake: "The letter achieved its goal if it caused a bit of noise."[†]

※

On September 5 the painter Ivan Kramskoy, who had never met Tolstoy, arrived at Yasnaya Polyana to try to persuade the famous novelist to sit for a portrait for the collector Pavel Tretyakov's gallery in Moscow. Previous attempts by others to persuade Tolstoy to sit for a painting had failed.

Gusev narrates Kramskoy's point of view:

> Finding out from a servant that the count was absent, off somewhere, Kramskoy walked along looking for him. Seeing in a barn a worker sawing wood, Kramskoy turned to him with a question:
>
> "Would you know, my dear fellow, where Lev Nikolaevich is?"
>
> "Why do you need him? I'm he."
>
> "I'm the artist Kramskoy; I came to ask permission to do your portrait for the Tretyakov Gallery."
>
> "No need for that, but I'm glad to see you. I know you. Come along with me."[‡]

Good story! Probably too good.

Tolstoy seems to have enjoyed being taken for just another workman, and maybe Kramskoy sensed that and indulged the great man. Everyone noticed how earnestly

---

[*] *PSS* 62: 46–47.

[†] Writing irrepressibly to his pal, Tolstoy also complained about the *Azbuka*'s reception: "I truly know that this is the best book by which it's ten times easier and better to learn than by the others, and all Russian children will continue to learn by the bad ones, which makes me angry every time when I am on an empty stomach and not in good spirits." *PSS* 62: 47.

[‡] Gusev, *Materials*, 148. Gusev's reference for this: И. Гинцбург. Художники в гостях у Л. Н. Толстого. I. Gintsburg. [*L. N. Tolstoy's Artist-Guests*], volume 11 (1916), page 192.

Tolstoy worked, and Tolstoy's brother Sergei teased him that he was constantly picking up the idiosyncratic mannerisms of his peasant farmhands. Tolstoy wanted to seem like an honest working man, to be approachable. Like Levin, Tolstoy ecstatically mowed with the workers. We know that he could enjoy labor for labor's sake, for its physical exercise, for bringing him to a state of unselfconsciousness. Kramskoy right away was attracted and amused. That same day, Kramskoy reported to Tretyakov:

> We talked for more than two hours. I returned to the question of the portrait four times, and all to no avail. None of my pleas or arguments had any effect on him. Finally I began to make all kinds of concessions, and went to the utmost extremes. One of my last arguments was: "My respect for the reasons which keep your grace from sitting to me prevents me from insisting any longer; I shall, of course, have to relinquish all hope of ever doing your portrait, and yet—your portrait should and will hang in the gallery." "How so?" "Why, very simply. To be sure, I shall not be the one to do it, and none of my contemporaries either, but in thirty, forty, or fifty years it will be painted, and then it will be a cause for regret that it was not done by a contemporary." He thought it over, but still refused, though with hesitation. To clinch our talk, I again began to make concessions and presented the following terms, to which he agreed: first, the portrait was to be painted, but if for any reason it did not please him, it was to be destroyed; then, the time when it was to be sent to your gallery would depend on him, although the portrait was to be your property. This last condition was so generous that he was even taken aback and had to accept it. Then it appeared from our subsequent conversation that he would like to have a portrait for his children, but did not know how to arrange it; he asked about making a copy and whose consent was required if it was to be made later, that is—the copy, which he felt should also be sent to you. To forestall the possibility of his beating a retreat, I made haste to explain that an exact copy was out of the question and could not be executed even by the same artist, and that the only solution was to do two portraits from life; it would depend on him which he would keep for himself and which would be sent to you. At that we parted, having decided to begin sittings tomorrow, that is, Thursday. *

---

* I've typed the complete contents of the September 5, 1873, letter. Ivan Nikolayevich Kramskoi, "Letters to P. M. Tretyakov," in *Reminiscences of Lev Tolstoi by His Contemporaries*, 275–276.

Kramskoy must have been clever and patient; he was for certain a good salesperson. In Sofia's memoir's account of the portraits, she recalled there was just something about Kramskoy or because he came in person that made it so he "quite endeared himself to Lev Nikolaevich."[*]

Ten days later, Kramskoy reported to Tretyakov:

> Now that I have started work on the portrait and have come to know the count better, I see that he feels obliged not to impose his choice upon me. That is clear from everything that has passed between us. For instance, after his third sitting, he and his wife expressed satisfaction with the portrait; the next time I came with another canvas and started another, larger portrait,[†] allowing the first to dry. When that portrait was underway, the countess said to me, "It could not be better!" The count agreed and added that his conscience would not permit him to keep the better one for himself. I said nothing and bade my time, confining myself to the remark that both portraits should be so good as to make preference difficult. Then I resumed my work on the first. The count doubted that it would come up to the second. But I went on working, and yesterday the results were so satisfactory that it was adjudged by all to be better than the second.[‡]

How about this account from Sofia's memoir?

> I recall going into the small drawing room and watching these two "artists" at work—one of them on a portrait of Tolstoy, the other on his novel *Anna Karenina*. Their faces were serious and concentrated on their respective tasks. Both artists were genuine, larger than life, and I felt such respect for them in my heart.

This would be a good scene for a movie. Tolstoy is sitting for a portrait *and* writing the novel. We can see the speed (the pace anyway) of his writing, the movements of his

---

[*]   Tolstaya, *My Life*, 197.

[†]   The portrait at the Tretyakov Gallery is 98 x 79.5 cm (https://www.wikiart.org/en/ivan-kramskoy/portrait-of-leo-tolstoy-1873). I haven't found the dimensions of the portrait at Yasnaya Polyana.

[‡]   Ivan Nikolayevich Kramskoi, "Letters to P. M. Tretyakov," in *Reminscences of Lev Tolstoi by His Contemporaries*, September 15, 1873.

pen, his eyes, his shifting in his chair, his feet. (Does he have one leg tucked under him?) And how fine it is to also catch the famous painter at work!

However, it's Sofia's imagination that created this scene.* Tolstoy, by every other account, including evidence from Sofia's own letters of the time and from her own memoir a page later, was not working on the novel. He wanted to but just couldn't. She remembered: "It happened that same autumn [. . .] I do recall being upset that Lev Nikolaevich was not continuing work on his novel *Anna Karenina*, which I liked so much and got more and more interested in as I continued my transcribing of it."†

Sofia's next memory about her husband and Kramskoy might have a basis in reality:

> One time I happened to find them engaged in a conversation about art. They were in a heated argument but, unfortunately, I do not recollect what they said.‡

It's the absence of re-created dialogue and particular details that persuades me of its plausibility.

Sofia remembered the portraits taking two or three weeks, but as of September 23–24, when Tolstoy wrote to Strakhov, the sittings were still going on. Are we to assume the sittings were every day from September 6 (the day after Kramskoy's visit that secured Tolstoy's cooperation) through the 23rd or 24th? Kramskoy says that he went back and forth, letting one painting dry while he worked on the other.

Sofia, who would be under the gaze of one of Kramskoy's portraits hanging on a wall at Yasnaya Polyana for the next forty-five years, was not, after all, enamored with the results:

> He partially spoilt them because, after painting the head and hands from life, the whole torso was done in absentia. That was because Lev Nikolaevich was off hunting with [Dmitrij Dmitrievich] Obolenskij and refused to sit for the artist. As if hunting were somehow more important than a portrait which would last hundreds of years.

---

* Gusev states: "Sometimes during the sittings Tolstoy instead of conversations wrote *Anna Karenina*." [Иногда во время сеансов Толстой вместо беседы писал "Анну Каренину."] He doesn't give a source for this, which is unusual for him; so it seems to me he must have been summarizing Sofia's account. Gusev, *Materials*, 150.

† Tolstaya, *My Life*, 198.

‡ Tolstaya, *My Life*, 197.

Even now I can see Kramskoj stuffing Lev Nikolaevich's grey shirt with some kind of white cotton rags and sitting this headless scarecrow on a chair, girded with a belt. If you examine the portrait carefully, it is quite apparent how unnatural the bulging chest appears, along with the gatherings in the shirt, and how small the head is in comparison to the body.[*]

Offering us uninhibited reflections, Sofia has managed to get in digs at both her husband and Kramskoy: *Tolstoy wouldn't sit still and Kramskoy couldn't paint straight!*[†]

Some of us (I, for example) have stood before both portraits, which hang on walls one hundred miles apart, and not for a moment realized that they were different. Sofia claimed if we could "examine the portrait carefully," we would notice what she noticed. Let's look again then at the Yasnaya Polyana portrait: the chair back appears behind his right shoulder and his right elbow could be leaning on the chair's arm. Yes, he seems more reluctant to be sitting; he's thinking about . . . if his actions speak louder than Sofia's recollections, not *Anna Karenina* but *hunting*. In the favored image for reproduction, the one hanging in Moscow, Tolstoy seems to be engaging with the viewer. He is

[*] Tolstaya, *My Life*, 197. The portrait on the left, better known and displayed at the Tretyakov Gallery in Moscow, is the one she did not select.

[†] Gusev discusses Kramskoy and future remarks about these portraits and the sessions in *Materials*, 149–152.

not speaking but is surely ruminating about something. I cannot decide which of the two is the one Sofia believed was done from a stuffed scarecrow body.

Even though Tolstoy had not yet conceived of Anna Karenina's portrait-painter Mikhailov, this episode of sitting for Kramskoy can put us in mind of Mikhailov's sessions and his portrait of Anna. Everyone who sees Mikhailov's portrait of Anna is struck by it, by how revealed she is, by how they know her now better than they knew her before. The artist has revealed what they all could see but hadn't really noticed. What is art? One example is Mikhailov's portrait of Anna, a revelation of what we didn't know but could have known.

In the novel, Tolstoy likes to show us the limitations of Vronsky's self-awareness; though he is not stupid, he is dense:

> From the fifth sitting the portrait impressed everyone, especially Vronsky, not only by its resemblance, but by its characteristic beauty. It was strange how Mihailov could have discovered just her characteristic beauty. "One needs to know and love her as I have loved her to discover the very sweetest expression of her soul," Vronsky thought, though it was only from this portrait that he had himself learned this sweetest expression of her soul. But the expression was so true that he, and others too, fancied they had long known it. *

In that letter of September 23–24 to Strakhov, Tolstoy implied that he had resumed *Anna Karenina*:

> I've made good progress in my work, but I'll hardly finish it before winter—December or thereabouts. As a painter needs light for the finishing touches, so I need inner light, of which I always feel the lack in autumn.

But how much "progress" had Tolstoy made by now? He accepted that his "inner light" had insufficient wattage "for the finishing touches," but he was far far far away from finishing. He said absolutely nothing about his actually sitting down and writing—and he protested that it wasn't his fault that he hadn't finished. He knew that Strakhov (who had asked in his last letter, "Please, as soon as possible, your novel! And

---

*   *Anna Karenina,* Part 5, Chapter 13, http://literatureproject.com/anna-karenina/anna _137.htm.

if still not soon, say at what stage it is"*) would be disappointed if the novel-writing hadn't begun again:

> Besides, everything has been arranged so as to distract me: acquaintances, hunting, a court session in October with me as a juryman and then the painter Kramskoy who is painting my portrait for Tretyakov. Tretyakov tried to send him to me a long time ago, but I didn't want him, but now this Kramskoy has come himself and talked me round, particularly by saying "your portrait will be painted anyway, but it will be a bad one." Even this wouldn't have persuaded me, but my wife persuaded him to do another portrait for her, instead of a copy. And now he's painting it, and very well according to my wife and friends. [. . .]

And then, changing the subject again, Tolstoy related a topic from his sittings with Kramskoy that truly excited his interest:

> He was telling me today about the murder of Suvorina. [R. F. Christian's note on this: "Suvorina, the first wife of the publisher and journalist A. S. Suvorin, was shot in a hotel by a certain Komarov, a friend of the family, who then committed suicide."] What a significant event!
>
> Werther shot himself and so did Komarov and the schoolboy who found his Latin lesson difficult. The one is important and noble, the other sordid and pathetic. Write and tell me if you find out any details of the murder.[†]

Tolstoy was explicit that he considered that a suicide could be "important and noble," notably Werther's romantic suicide. He was fascinated by the idea of such a suicide. He wanted to know more.[‡]

---

[*] Donskov, *L. N. Tolstoy – N. N. Strakhov*, 127, September 3–4, 1873, http://feb-web.ru/feb/tolstoy/texts/selectpe/ts6/ts62169-.htm.

[†] Christian, *Tolstoy's Letters*, 265, footnote 5.

[‡] Whether Strakhov sent him news stories or if Tolstoy learned the gory details elsewhere is not apparent. See Donskov, *L. N. Tolstoy – N. N. Strakhov*, 131, footnote 6. Donskov quotes from the September 22, 1873, issue of the newspaper *Golos* (*The Voice*) on the September 19 murder-suicide.

His correspondence of September 23 to Fet is a "What's wrong? Why haven't you written?" letter, friendly and intimate. "Obviously we, truly, I and the wife, are not only your friends but we love you. If everything's well and good, write how're your chicks, things, plans. [. . .] We're as of old; strongly planted another eleven years (it's eleven years now that we're married)." He was writing this letter on the anniversary of his marriage. He said that he was resuming the novel, "that is, I'm soon finishing the novel I started."* He mentioned Kramskoy's two portraits, and added: "If you don't come to me on the road to Moscow, I'll be angry and come to you."†

As of this date the happy family that was like all other happy ones was still Tolstoy's own.

※

On October 3, he went hunting at Obolenskii's again. On October 4, Sofia noted in her diary that Kramskoy "is doing two portraits of L., and this tends to prevent him working. But to make up for it there are long discussions and arguments about art every day."‡ Was Kramskoy possibly still around, four weeks after starting? She used the present tense in her entry. She also noted on this date that "Throughout the summer, which we spent in the province of Samara, L. did no writing, but he is now polishing, revising and continuing with the novel." She didn't say that she had seen his hand moving over the manuscript; and if she were now recopying his manuscript she would proudly have mentioned it.

Sofia briefly accounts for October 1873 in *My Life*. She didn't like Lev's return to hunting or that, as she *remembers* recording§ in her diary of October 11, "he had caught three hares. The children, upon seeing their father's serious attitude toward hunting and not realising that for him it represented a vital respite after his intellectual labours, were all infected with the hunting bug, which I was terribly sad to see. One time on a walk in October they ferreted out a hare and became wildly ecstatic."¶

So she accepted his hunting as something that he needed, but she didn't like that her children had a new excited interest in it. She did not explain whether it was because she

---

* *PSS* 62: 48.

† Ibid.

‡ "Various Notes for Future Reference," *The Diaries of Sophia Tolstoy*, 848.

§ It is *not* noted, however, at least on that date, in *The Diaries of Sophia Tolstoy*.

¶ Tolstaya, *My Life*, 198.

felt pity for the animals, or that she considered hunting a pastime whose indulgence had to be earned.

Tolstoy, in any case, was crazy for it.

I started reading one of Tolstoy's letters from this period (a letter over which Gusev spends a while arguing why he thinks it was written in October) and, when I was thinking it was written to Strakhov, I was surprised by how gleeful and playful it was. *What's gotten into Tolstoy?*

What had gotten into him was that he was writing not to Strakhov but to his brother Sergei, that's what. How different we are around our siblings compared to how we are with the rest of humanity. In the novel Tolstoy will show us Levin's particular anxiety when he is around his brother and half-brother. Tolstoy's tone when writing to his brother Sergei is different from the tones he used to Fet or Strakhov; it's intimate and looser:

> How's everything with you, lively, healthy, well? Mashenka [their sister] not long ago sent a telegram! [. . .] Hunting you, I think, I'm not kidding. There's such a drought there's not been a hunting day. I caught three hares at the same time. Don't you need some money? Generally the thought torments me that we're not agreeing in when to pay you interest.
>
> If you could think it over and write, that would be good. I would have come to you if it weren't such a valuable time. But maybe you're coming over and then we'll talk.[*]

The next time they talked, Tolstoy was in no ways cheerful.

When Tolstoy was actually writing *Anna Karenina*, he did not at the same time conduct other business or do other projects. So if Sofia was accurate about his having started revising in early October, this distracted letter about his distractions shows that he must have almost immediately stopped revising. On October 16, Gusev, citing Sofia's letter to Tatyana, says that at Yasnaya Polyana "for a week," there were "teachers from the people's schools (about twenty people) for discussion of the topic on applying with the peasant children the method of teaching grammar, laid out by Tolstoy."[†] In *My Life* Sofia remembered that Tolstoy "summoned twelve rural teachers" to Yasnaya

---

[*] *PSS* 62: 51–52.

[†] Gusev, *Letopis'*, 413.

Polyana: "He brought kids from neighbouring villages to the annexe—kids who had never gone to school—and conducted some experiments on them."[*]

Much more significant in Sofia's October 16 letter to Tatyana was the news that Tolstoy had "completely abandoned" the novel.[†]

Did Sofia make herself patiently listen to him whenever he announced, "That's it! I'm done! I quit!"? Sofia was so much a part of Tolstoy's life and has provided us with so much information that I wonder about her reactions when she doesn't tell us what she was feeling. How many days or weeks did it have to be before she nudged him, "Lev, please get back to the novel!"

This was the first of Tolstoy's declared abandonments of *Anna Karenina*.

✳

On October 23, the president of the Moscow Literacy Committee, answering Tolstoy's bold early June public letter about pedagogy, invited Tolstoy to present to the committee members an account of teaching reading by his method. This polite invitation led to work that would distract him from resuming the novel. To make a case for himself in public after having made the case in writing was going to take up a lot of Tolstoy's time. Kramskoy's coming to paint him had made him feel awkward and distracted, but at least at times it was interesting to him and even flattering, and he could have kept himself writing had he been in the mood. This beckoning to him to defend his pedagogy, however, would relieve him from attempting to fix his attention on the novel.

The pedagogue D. I. Tikhomirov thought that "the committee should not take up Tolstoy's proposal, because 'a 10-day experiment won't convince anybody of the validity of its use, because if everyone is convinced that the theoretical basis of the usefulness of [Tolstoy's] teaching is incorrect, the most brilliant results that come from the proposed experiment, by the method's inventor, will show only that in his hands it can be very good.'"[‡]

Tikhomirov was giving Tolstoy credit for what Tolstoy didn't want factored into a pedagogical judgment—that is, his big personal presence. Was it Tolstoy's fault that he hadn't been able to explain himself in a way that convinced the committee members? Or maybe the committee understood better than he that he simply loved the work and was

---

[*] Cathy Porter's wording of the last phrase would alarm most 21st-century parents. Tolstaya, *My Life*, 198.

[†] Gusev, *Letopis'*, 413.

[‡] Gusev, *Materials*, 160.

brilliant doing it, and that a brilliant teacher is not actually tied down to any method, that she or he sensibly uses any method to help a student learn? While Tolstoy believed his method rather than his personal charisma and tact should have been enough to win the argument, we'll see that he would encourage his protégé to use *any* effective methods. Tolstoy's real method (I would argue) was to be smart, sensitive, and excited about the immediate discoveries he made in his classroom. Preparing for and overseeing the pedagogical experiment would take up the bulk of Tolstoy's attention in January and February of 1874.

✳

The Tolstoy children were home-schooled for the most part, at least until early adolescence. What Sofia and Tolstoy didn't have time or ability to teach them, tutors and governesses did. Sofia explained in *My Life* that their nice old French governess at this time was a bit of a thief; they caught her stealing and had to fire her.* Sometime that fall Tolstoy wrote to N. M. Nagornov, his niece's husband, asking if he could go to a particular office in Moscow (near where the State L. N. Tolstoy Museum is now) and ask for a French or Swiss governess or governesses, "not so old as Mademoiselle Raoux," he said. She needed "to look after Tanya and give lessons to the little ones."†

The Tolstoys' seemingly perpetual search for governesses lets us see, when the novel opens, something of the Tolstoy family situation in the Oblonsky family.‡ "All was confusion in the *Tolstoy* household" would still fit, if just for the number of children and for the household problems. A few problems obviously not in *Anna Karenina* are Tolstoy's involvement with the *Azbuka*, the teaching-methods dispute, his trying to write *Anna Karenina*, and, in a few weeks, the death of baby Petya.

For *My Life*, Sofia probably had to steel herself to relate the chapter "The Puppy and the Death of Petja":

At the end of October 1873, or possibly the beginning of November, someone brought to Lev Nikolaevich a tiny but well-bred borzoi puppy as

---

* Tolstaya, *My Life*, 198–199.

† *PSS* 62: 51.

‡ In the novel, Tolstoy does not explain how, why, or when the governess with whom Stiva has been carrying on the affair stopped working for the Oblonsky family. In an early draft she seems *not* to have left her job.

a gift [perhaps Sofia knew but couldn't bring herself to name and blame the "someone"?]. [. . .] The children had great fun with this little doggie, and my chubby little Petja was especially fond of it. [. . .] One time this dog began to wheeze and cough, almost like a bark, and little Petja, after visiting him, came and declared that "amka bobo" [Cathy Porter's footnote says this is baby talk for "the doggie's sick"]. I told the nanny to stay away from the dog, and after a two-days' illness, the puppy passed on.*

Three days later Petya was sick; they gave him medicine for croup; he died two days after that, on November 9.

Though I was in the same room [writes Sofia], I could not bear to see my boy's passing. It was Lev Nikolaevich who was sitting at Petja's bedside at the moment of his death. We had sent for the doctor during the night, and by the time he arrived in the morning, the boy was already dead. The doctor said Petja had caught the croup from the puppy, and that infections from animals, chickens and such like, were a common occurrence. I was completely overwhelmed by an unanticipated feeling of loss over my child for the first time in my whole life. I could feel a very painful rupture, practically a physical experience of suffering. [. . .]

Sofia quoted from Tolstoy's letter to Tatyana's husband:

"Even Petja, just a noisy kid and still devoid of any kind of charm from a father's point of view . . . yet, apart from the sorrow associated particularly with his passing, he has left a feeling of great emptiness in our home which I had not anticipated."†

That sounds not very feeling. We know that Tolstoy said he didn't care much about the children until they could talk, and late in *Anna Karenina* we see Levin's confused disgust with his and Kitty's baby. Children had to be able to talk to have "any kind of charm" for Tolstoy.

---

*   Tolstaya, *My Life*, 199.

†   Ibid.

And yet, let's look at his *entire* letter to Sasha Kuzminskiy, which the editors of the Jubilee edition guess as having been written between November 18 and 25:

> We rarely exchange letters with you, dear friend, and every time only about misery. Your letter came without me [being here], and Sonya read it through. I was in Moscow. And in your little note, which Sonya wrote to me with the horses that met me, she wrote me about your misery [the Jubilee edition note explains Tatyana had suffered a miscarriage or "unsuccessful delivery"]. I can't tell you how that hurts me. However many times I've noticed this strange law of luck: good and bad, not in a single game, but in the most important matters of life. It seems we with you—and we're so close by wives and friendship—are stuck in this vein of bad luck. We'll be strong. Again we're awaiting the happy vein, which for me stands only in nothing changing. *Even Petja, just a noisy kid* not yet having *any kind of charm from a father's point of view . . .* yet, *apart from the sorrow associated particularly with his passing, he has left a feeling of great emptiness in our home which I had not anticipated.*[†]

Tolstoy went on and poured out *more* feelings:

> How many times have we remembered how he was! I hope that now your letter will come with other news, if not good then not bad about Tanya. Please write if you haven't already. As far as we are from each other, I feel that you are truly also on the same roads, in family joys and miseries, nobody takes such part as we with each other.[‡]

Reading the whole letter makes quite a different impression. His remembrance of Petya is moving. Tolstoy does not seem cold as much as like someone trying to moderate the presentation of his feelings. He was a father, he was reminding himself and Sasha; it's *different*. It's not as bad as what a mother feels. He was not cold in feeling but tempered about his grief when he compared his feelings to Sofia's.

---

[*]   The translator Cathy Porter's ellipsis may reflect Sofia's text, but there does not seem to be anything missing from Tolstoy's actual letter.

[†]   *PSS* 62: 56. The italics represent Porter's translation.

[‡]   Ibid.

At this moment in *My Life*, much of which was composed decades after the fact, Sofia mounts her own defense of this period of the mid-1870s, when their relationship became unhappy. She had plenty to complain about and a lot of their mutual agony was his fault. But she took revenge here—the way people do at divorce hearings—by denying him feelings that he actually had.

But back to Sofia's heartsick recounting. She had "a vivid memory of the funeral: there was a heavy frost. Lev Nikolaevich and I placed the coffin on our sleigh and took it to the church ourselves. During the service I looked at that little face, which had been quite untouched by the brief illness, and I tried my best to keep my spirits up. [. . .]"

> But the most terrible moment was when we placed the little coffin on the
> snow beside the freshly dug grave, and in this heavy frost I saw his little body
> clothed in a light white shroud—that same little body that I had fed with my
> breasts and just recently weaned, which I protected from the slightest draft
> of air, coddled and kept warm, and now grown stiff partly from death and
> partly from the frost.*

On the day of the funeral, Tolstoy wrote his brother: "[. . .] after your departure, that is, last night, Petya died, and today he's been buried. His throat suffocated him, what's called croup."†

According to the Mayo Clinic: "Croup refers to an infection of the upper airway, generally in children, which obstructs breathing and causes a characteristic barking cough. The cough and other symptoms of croup are the result of inflammation around the vocal cords (larynx), windpipe (trachea), and bronchial tubes (bronchi). When a cough forces air through this narrowed passage, the swollen vocal cords produce a noise similar to a seal barking. Likewise, taking a breath often produces a high-pitched whistling sound (stridor). Croup usually isn't serious and most cases can be treated at home."‡

Tolstoy knew what he was talking about to Sergei in calling it croup:

> This (comes) to us again very heavily, especially Sonya.—Yesterday I received a
> letter from the printer that the twelfth edition is coming out. And the D'yakovs

---

*   Tolstaya, *My Life*, 199–200.

†   *PSS* 62: 52, letter of November 10, 1873.

‡   Mayo Clinic, "Croup," http://www.mayoclinic.org/diseases-conditions/croup/basics/definition /con-20014673, accessed March 17, 2015.

came today. He has gone now to Moscow and leaves Masha and Sofie with us. I'd be much better if I went to Moscow now. Sonya will stay alone. If you can, come now, that is the day after tomorrow, the 12th. You'll eat with us or we'll eat on the train? Answer, how and what?[*]

At first I misread and thus mistranslated "Sonya will stay alone" as *"Sonya can't be left alone,"* because that's what I thought he should and would say. But the note by Gusev is unmistakable ("Tolstoy left YP November 12 and returned on the 16th," which Gusev learned from a letter from Sofia to Tatyana[†]). Tolstoy left!

Maybe Tolstoy did know Oblonsky rather deeply within himself? Stiva would or could leave Dolly alone shortly after a child's death, and so also, apparently, could Tolstoy leave Sofia.[‡]

In *My Life*, however, Sofia didn't blame him: "Lev Nikolaevich went to Moscow to sell an edition of his complete works." (She was mistaken in that he wasn't "selling" it, it was being released.)

> It was very hard for me to live without Lev Nikolaevich, but there was so much to do, especially teaching the children, that willy-nilly I was obliged to plunge once more into my family duties. Once again the lessons proceeded according to an established timetable. Once again every evening I would transcribe Lev Nikolaevich's work.[§]

Her baby was dead; she was pregnant; the other children needed her. Her husband went back to his routine—earning money, resuming *Anna Karenina*—and she went back to hers, work for which we readers owe her thanks.

This next passage from Sofia's memoir humbles me (and anybody who thinks they really know Tolstoy and his work), just as I believe Sofia meant for it to do:

> The transcribing of *War and Peace*—and, indeed, all Lev Nikolaevich's works—was a source of great aesthetic pleasure for me. I fearlessly looked

---

[*]   *PSS* 62: 52, letter of November 10, 1873.

[†]   Gusev, *Letopis'*, 414.

[‡]   See Tolstoy's November 18, 1873, letter to Fet [*PSS* 62: 55], which confirms that Tolstoy left the D'yakovs there with Sofia, to stay with her and console her, while he went off on business.

[§]   Tolstaya, *My Life*, 200.

forward to my evening labours, and joyfully anticipated just *what* I would derive from the delight of becoming further acquainted with his work as it unfolded. I was enthralled by this life of thought, these twists and turns, surprises and all the various unfathomable aspects of his creative genius.

I would ask myself: why did Lev Nikolaevich substitute a new word or phrase for one which appeared to be perfectly suitable already? It often happened that the galley proofs finally sent to Moscow for printing would be returned and corrected yet again. Sometimes he would telegraph an instruction to change some word or other—even just *a single word*.

Why were whole beautiful scenes or episodes deleted? Sometimes, in transcribing, I felt so terribly sad at deleting splendid passages he had crossed out. Sometimes he restored what he had crossed out, and that made me happy. It happens that you get so involved with all your heart and soul in what you're transcribing and you become so familiar with all the characters that you yourself begin to feel you can improve it: shorten an overly long passage, for example, or rearrange punctuation marks for better clarity. And then you come to Lev Nikolaevich with the work you've copied all ready, and you show him the question marks you've made in the margin, and ask him whether it might not be better to substitute this word for that, or delete frequent repetitions of the same word, or something else besides.

Lev Nikolaevich would explain to me why it had to be a certain way, or sometimes he would listen to me as though he were actually glad of my observation. But when he wasn't in a good mood, he could get angry and say *that's just a trifle,* or *that's not important, it's the overall thought that's important,* etc.[*]

She was almost always on the job, right there, the sympathetic, forbearing midwife to artistic creation.

※

*   Tolstaya, *My Life,* 83–84. Touchingly, after devoting a couple of thousand words on her decades of work as his copyist and transcriber, Sofia shakes herself and announces: "While describing my participation in Lev Nikolaevich's works, I got distracted from the description of our lives, and so I shall now return to the first year of our marriage, 1862–63" (Tolstaya, *My Life,* 85).

The day after his return home from Moscow, Tolstoy wrote to Strakhov. His first paragraph was loving and grateful, which would make it obvious again if we didn't already believe it that he adored Strakhov. Tolstoy then told Strakhov about Petya's death . . . and the progress that he was making with *Anna Karenina*:

> I didn't answer you for a while, at first because of negligence, and then for some time our whole life was destroyed. Our little child died—Petya. This was the first death after 11 years. The meaning of this death is impossible for a childless person to understand.[*]

(True, how impossible it is to comprehend a child's death! And yet it seems tactless to tell a dear friend, "You, having different circumstances, couldn't possibly understand mine.")

> My work up to this was going well, even very well. I can say that seven sheets are ready for printing, and the rest are all kneaded in dough, so that the finish is only a question of time. I've already begun thinking about the process of printing, and all my hope is on you. And if you agree to take on the corrections I will publish it in Petersburg and will publish the first volume, not waiting for the second.[†]

So what had he been coming up with for *Anna Karenina*? That "ready for printing" should be taken with a grain of salt, considering Tolstoy's track record with "finishing" writing, and as for "the rest are all kneaded in dough," he might have meant only that he had dozens of pages in the dough-bucket of his mind, the yeast of the dough being some of those notes we read in Chapter 2 (e.g., "She has it out with her husband. She reproaches him for previous indifference. 'It's too late.'"). We know the "light" novel he planned has no chance of coming to light because his life, becoming more and more unhappy, was going to flow, transmuted, into the novel, including, for a sentence or two, his recent heartache over the baby.

It seems hard to comprehend now, with our sense of the final *Anna Karenina*, how he could still be so mistaken about its length and estimated time of completion:

---

[*]   *PSS* 62: 53, letter of November 17, 1873.

[†]   Ibid.

It could be ready in December, and maybe not ready. Please, answer, as always, simply and straight, would you take on this work and on what terms.[*]

He was impatient: the baker wanted to bake the dough. He did not mind now the thought of committing to publication before the novel's completion. (Most of the rest of the letter is about physics, specifically gravity, about which he was puzzled. He asked Strakhov, his go-to person for science, if he understood him and agreed with him.)

Tolstoy's manner of mentioning Petya's death to Strakhov was dramatically different from how he discussed it with Fet, who had his own children:

> We have a misery: Little Petya got sick with the croup and in two days died, on the 9th. This is the first death after 11 years in our family, and for my wife it's very heavy. It's possible to console oneself that if one of us eight had to be chosen, this death is the lightest of all and for all; but the heart, especially a mother's—this is the most amazing revelation of God on earth—doesn't judge, and my wife is very miserable.
>
> For some days I was in Moscow on business, making use of the presence of the D'yakovs with us in order not to leave Sonya alone, and now we're in a little way becoming used to the emptiness that Petya left behind.
>
> [. . .] I have one of the best, joyful occupations—these math and Greek lessons with the children that we've begun.
>
> Pass on our sincere greetings and hello to Marya Petrovna.[†]

In another letter to Strakhov, on December 12–13, he discussed science and philosophized until the last few lines. He knew Strakhov wanted to hear news of his creative work, so at the end he condescended to address that: "My work with the novel a few days ago was going well in progress. But then I was all unhealthy and out of sorts."[‡]

A few days later, he wrote Strakhov again:

> I waited the whole year, sufferingly awaited the arrangement of the soul for writing—it came—I am using it in order to finish my favorite thing. Now what can I do to satisfy the pleasure of Prince Meshcherskiy, and to bring

---

*   *PSS* 62: 54.

†   *PSS* 62: 61.

‡   *PSS* 62: 61, letter of December 12–13, 1873.

about a good cause? 1) Either to cut off work in order to write *une bluette* [a trifle], I even for a minute thought of doing this. But this would be a crime concerning my present duty.—2) To publish a chapter from this novel; but I constantly redo them and even so am unhappy with them, and again this passage. 3) *From this portfolio* give *something*—I cannot let go muck with my name. For such a purpose to do such a thing would be disgusting. [. . .]*

He would like to be distracted, it seems, by working on that "bluette," a piece Gusev calls the "beginning of a tale." It opens with the phrase (". . . and I lost consciousness"). Wouldn't it make sense that this fragment would have something to do with *Anna Karenina*?

It would, but it doesn't. It's the opening of a dreamlike science-fiction tale of about five hundred words, perhaps a Swiftian satire intended for children.[†]

Sofia wrote her sister Tatyana on December 19 and mentioned that Tolstoy was "writing a lot" on *Anna Karenina*.[‡] On December 28, Gusev notes that Tolstoy recorded his last diary entry until April 17, 1878. It seems that Tolstoy didn't really need a diary once his thoughts and feelings were permeating *Anna Karenina*.

---

*   *PSS* 62: 61–62, letter of December 16–17, 1873.

†   *PSS* 17: 135–136.

‡   Gusev, *Letopis'*, 416.

5

Anna Karenina's False Start: January 1–August 14, 1874

❋

The figure from a lifeless imagined thing had become living, and such that it could never be changed. That figure lived, and was clearly and unmistakably defined.

—*Anna Karenina*[*]

A t the beginning of January, writes Gusev, "T. tells his children in French the contents of a Jules Verne novel."[†] Sofia's memoir explains: "Lev Nikolaevich would tell stories in the evenings from the illustrated editions. Later on these stories served for our reading after evening tea, and we eagerly awaited this time. One time Lev Nikolaevich went to Moscow and tried to buy something else by Jules Verne, but couldn't find any illustrated edition, so he bought *Le Tour du monde* without illustrations. Then he began doing very primitive ink drawings to go with this work, which, I would say, delighted the children even more. I kept these drawings, and they are preserved in the Historical Museum in Moscow along with his manuscripts."[‡]

---

[*] *Anna Karenina*, Part 5, Chapter 10, http://www.literatureproject.com/anna-karenina/anna _134.htm.

[†] Gusev, *Letopis'*, 416. Gusev cites Sofia's January 9, 1874, letter to her sister Tatyana.

[‡] Tolstaya, *My Life*, 202.

Here was Tolstoy as a dad and entertainer. Here was Sofia understanding that these drawings were *important,* that is, more important to her (and to me) than what he was gleaning at the time from his readings of Schopenhauer and Henry George. Tolstoy had to read ahead in *Around the World in Eighty Days* and choose the scenes he anticipated the children would respond to and he could render best.

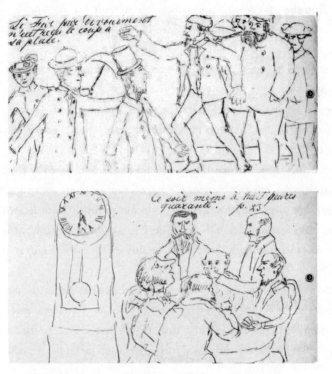

Two of Tolstoy's several illustrations for his children from
Jules Verne's *La Tour du Monde* (Around the World in Eighty Days)*

---

*   Top illustration from http://cultureru.com/category/visual-arts/pictorial-souvenirs-of-russian
    -writers/l-tolstoy-1828-1910/. Accessed July 7, 2017. The text from Chapter 25 reads: "Si Fix,
    par devouement, n'eut recu le coup a sa place." [As translated by Charles F. Horne: "If Fix,
    throwing himself in the way, had not received the blow in his place."] Bottom illustration from
    Josh Jones, "The Art of Leo Tolstoy: See His Drawings in the *War & Peace* Manuscript & Other
    Literary Texts," Open Culture, November 14, 2014, http://www.openculture.com/2014/11
    /the-art-of-leo-tolstoy.html. Accessed July 7, 2017. The text reads "Ce soir meme a huit heures
    quarante. p. 23" [This very night at eight-forty.] Stuart and Fogg are discussing the train from
    Douvres that leaves at 8:45, which Fogg says he's going to take.

❊

Sofia, in her otherwise undated entry from her memories of 1874, noted:

> I wrote my sister [. . .] "[. . .] My evenings are spent in a lot of transcribing.
> Levochka's novel keeps progressing. Occasionally we play four-handed piano
> pieces, and have supper at one {in the morning}* (I sometimes heat up supper
> myself on the gas cooker), after which I'm exhausted to the limit and go to
> bed and read English novels until three {a.m.}. . . ."†

Sofia was proud of herself and pleased with their intimacy; she was helping him with
his writing again.

On January 9, Sofia wrote her sister that she was recopying the novel "a lot," and it
was "completely changing."‡ Unfortunately for family happiness, Tolstoy left for Moscow
on January 15.§

That day, before the public meeting to which he had been invited by the literacy committee, Tolstoy had a "conversation with Katkov's typographer concerning the printing
of *Anna Karenina* in a separate edition."¶ He meant to finish his little novel and put it
behind him. Having taken care of that printing business, he made his way to the meeting.

Tolstoy was famous enough that the session was standing-room only:

> It differed in an unusual way for a meeting of the committee by the crowd: 31
> members of the committee and 65 outsider attenders (usually at meetings of
> the committee there were no more than 15–20); in the space of the hall there
> was not enough space—they stood in doorways and sat on the window-sills.**

Tolstoy was asked to demonstrate his method, and he answered that it was all laid out
in the *Azbuka*, and he could explain to the committee anything that was still unclear. He

---

* The fancy brackets { } indicate words or phrases supplied by the editor of *My Life*, Andrew
  Donskov.
† Tolstaya, *My Life*, 201.
‡ Gusev, *Materials*, 159.
§ Gusev, *Materials*, 160.
¶ Gusev, *Letopis'*, 416.
** Gusev, *Materials*, 160–161.

answered a questioner who pointed out that one of the best features of his method was that the children quickly learned to read, while the "advocate of the sound method, D. I. Tikhomirov, explained that the speed of learning was a secondary matter. Much more important was the development of the children, achieved by the conscious work of the sound method."

> To this Tolstoy said that the teacher's obligation was to satisfy the wishes of the people, and the people wished for their children to be taught reading and writing as quickly as possible. "But as for development," said Tolstoy, "the parents are not asking [for that], for this they won't pay a salary, consequently, the teacher does not have any right to develop the pupils . . . I don't consider I have the right to produce development, because all development suggests its own known direction."*

Based on Tolstoy's experience with actual students, this was a weak argument. As a teacher, Tolstoy was so deeply involved that he *did* "develop" the students. He *did* change them. "Education is violent; because it is creative," wrote ever-practical G. K. Chesterton.† "It is creative because it is human. It is as reckless as playing on the fiddle; as dogmatic as drawing a picture; as brutal as building a house. In short, it is what all human action is; it is an interference with life and growth."‡

Tolstoy didn't believe teachers had the right to inculcate students, but he knew very well that any involved charismatic teacher is shaking up souls—Tolstoy did this himself and had described it in his *Yasnaya Polyana* articles of 1861–62. And of course speedy learning *is* better, all other things being equal. But Tolstoy couldn't have taught a fast, catchy system if he weren't so dynamic—so Tikhomirov's criticism of his method was fair. From a distance, we can regret his wasting his time and energy on an academic shoe-tying dispute. Both Tolstoy's and Tikhomirov's methods worked, but Tolstoy's pride was wounded and he got caught up in the arguments for one side.

His method worked best if he was the one carrying it out, and we also know, from his own mouth (and pen), that in the moment of teaching he used *anything* that worked:

---

*   Gusev, *Materials,* 161.

†   Chesterton (1874–1936) was one of the few literary Englishmen of the early 20th century who was not besmitten by Tolstoy.

‡   G. K. Chesterton, "Authority the Unavoidable," in *What's Wrong with the World* (New York: Dodd, Mead and Co., 1910).

To the question of how he conducts the teaching of reading, Tolstoy answered, "I first of all mark on the wall with charcoal or chalk giant letters, and with a stick point at the letter and name it, and the children repeat it. In such a way, I in one lesson get through the whole alphabet, and already by the next day all the children know it without an error."*

The biographer Ernest Simmons points out that these "assembled pedagogues were naturally confused, for in part Tolstoy obviously employed the very oral method that he professed to scorn."† All of us teachers have been at meetings where a colleague asserts the effectiveness of a particular teaching method, while neglecting to mention the primary difficulty that had to be overcome: exciting interest in actual students. The professional teachers at this meeting would have understood that it was not Tolstoy's method as much as that Tolstoy had a knack with the students and that they raptly attended to him. Even a great teacher, however, doesn't want *that* to be true—that her method might matter less than the medium.

The questions went on, and Tolstoy was rambling. He was trying to prove something that he could only truly prove in his own classroom and that he could really only describe through narrative:

Tolstoy in detail answered his opponents on why he counted the sound method unacceptable in a Russian school. "When eight- to twelve-year-old students come to school," he said, "you begin the lessons with turning their attention on what's contained in the room that surrounds them. You ask them about such subjects that they have long known, so in such a way even the most unintelligent student answers you. So you say you begin your lessons with conversations, but I count those absolutely harmful, as in order for the conversations not to be boring demands genius from the teacher; then you give the children the word 'au,' demand they name it and ask what is heard in the beginning of the word and what at the end. But this very word they do not understand . . . Then you go over a whole bunch of exercises and conversations, but all these conversations only confuse the child, push him off and create a disbelief in the parents toward teaching, because they see that the child studied but all the same doesn't know anything. So here, finally, in

* Gusev, *Materials,* 161.

† Ernest Simmons, *Leo Tolstoy,* Volume 1 (New York: Vintage, 1960), 348.

three weeks the child comes home and to the parents' question, What did you learn, what do you know?, the child answers, 'The sound 'oo.'"*

Tolstoy showed in his education articles of 1862 that he was never restrained by a method; he always trusted the moment. He registered what was working and what wasn't. He couldn't persist with a lesson if it wasn't feeling successful. Here, on the other hand, he was imagining *what would happen* if he persisted in stupidity, in futility; in a real classroom he would have rerouted the lesson plan.

> Speaking out publicly, Tolstoy, as always, was shy and felt uncomfortable; in the words of the *Russian Herald* reporter, he spoke "awkwardly, passionlessly, and with frequent hesitations." [. . .]†

He was awkward, in part, because, like his character Levin, he was trying to concentrate while being watched and feeling self-conscious. He would not have spoken by rote.

> At the conclusion of the debate the president said a final conclusion might be taken only "after experience of the advantages of the one or the other method."‡

That is, it was a tie, and thus required a contest.§

Tolstoy went ahead (he liked contests) even though he knew this dispute couldn't be decided the way a horse race is; the reading method depended on the particular student and the particular teacher.

He wrote Sofia that evening:

---

*   Gusev, *Materials,* 161–162.

†   Gusev, *Materials,* 159–194.

‡   Gusev, *Materials,* 162.

§   "The entire stenographic record of the meeting was published" in No. 10 of the Moscow Dioscean Statements of 1874 (Gusev, *Materials,* 163). This meeting was recorded and Gusev seems to have had his hands on it. As much as I poke through the library's Internet holdings, I can't find the article. The Russian Government Public History Library [Государственная публичная историческая библиотека] has 1869 and 1877 but not 1874's Полная стенограмма заседания напечатана в № 10 "Московских епархиальных ведомостей" за 1874 г. См. также т. 17 настоящего издания, стр. 594 и сл.

I'm keeping my promise. I arrived well. All the important business about the printing [. . .] and the meeting in the committee, all this finished favorably. Only one thing was not good: this is that I promised tomorrow and the day after to give model lessons, and this will take up all my evening, which I would have spent pleasantly. And, I'm afraid, there will not be benefits, that is no one will be convinced, there is too much stupidity and stubbornness. I didn't get angry, and D'yakov and others said that I spoke well. And tomorrow I hope to escape so that on Thursday I don't go to the meeting. My health is well. The D'yakovs are very sweet.—I kiss you, darling, and the children.

I ask the three older ones to behave so you don't complain about but praise them.[*]

The next day, the first day of the contest, he was sick. On the 17th he did a demonstration of the method at a factory. Gusev writes: "The gathering was a group of illiterate workers. Tolstoy started teaching them literacy by his method. He wrote with chalk on the board the letters of the Russian alphabet, named them and had the students repeat them in order to explain to the students the turning of the sounds into syllables." Gusev quotes Tolstoy's opponent Tikhomirov's memoir:

"Besides the difficulty and novelty, the whole atmosphere of the lesson was not favorable: the presence of strangers, the stuffiness in the confined room distracted and wearied the students. And sweat rolled from the students and the teacher. Tolstoy could not further continue the lesson. The first lesson remained unconvincing."[†]

The president of the committee decided that the question of which method was better was still open.

Although Tolstoy's lesson had been a bust, the committee wanted the contest to proceed anyway. On the 17th (or perhaps, Gusev says, the 18th) Tolstoy returned home to Yasnaya Polyana.

---

*   *PSS* 83: 214, letter of January 15, 1874.

†   I couldn't track down on the web Tikhomirov's article, either. Gusev, *Materials*, 162–163. [Ref: Д. И. Тихомиров. Из воспоминаний о Л. Н. Толстом. "Педагогический листок", 1910, 8, стр. 557.]

I was expecting Tolstoy to begin to feel guilty about having wasted not only his own but everybody else's time, but apparently not. He had Pyotr Morozov, one of the teachers at his school in the early 1860s, complete his method's lessons over the next several weeks.

This is an unpleasant episode, as unpleasant as any academic dispute, because finally it settled nothing and Tolstoy, a great principled pedagogical theorist and teacher, comes off poorly. Almost the only thing at stake was that he wanted to win the contest, and he allowed himself to badger his stand-in Morozov to stick to the declared methods ("firmly maintain my instructions"*), when to send the pupils to the board, when to dictate, and what to do when things weren't working . . . "and write me how it's going."† The letters are undated, but according to the Jubilee editors they fall between February and March 15. Morozov's letters in reply no longer exist. "First off, write me as often as possible," commanded Tolstoy. "I write every day . . . and receive one a week."‡

Tolstoy was uncomfortable appearing in public, and this was one of those tasks wherein his conscience was sending him plenty of messages to desist. A bad conscience is something he would depict in Oblonsky:

> Stepan Arkadyevitch, with the same somewhat solemn expression with which he used to take his presidential chair at his board, walked into Alexey Alexandrovitch's room. Alexey Alexandrovitch was walking about his room with his hands behind his back, thinking of just what Stepan Arkadyevitch had been discussing with his wife.
>
> "I'm not interrupting you?" said Stepan Arkadyevitch, on the sight of his brother-in-law becoming suddenly aware of a sense of embarrassment unusual with him. To conceal this embarrassment he took out a cigarette case he had just bought that opened in a new way, and sniffing the leather, took a cigarette out of it.
>
> "No. Do you want anything?" Alexey Alexandrovitch asked without eagerness.
>
> "Yes, I wished . . . I wanted . . . yes, I wanted to talk to you," said Stepan Arkadyevitch, with surprise aware of an unaccustomed timidity.
>
> This feeling was so unexpected and so strange that he did not believe it was the voice of conscience telling him that what he was meaning to do was wrong.

---

*   *PSS* 90: 232–233.

†   *PSS* 90: 233.

‡   *PSS* 62: 76.

Stepan Arkadyevitch made an effort and struggled with the timidity that had come over him.

"I hope you believe in my love for my sister and my sincere affection and respect for you," he said, reddening.

Alexey Alexandrovitch stood still and said nothing, but his face struck Stepan Arkadyevitch by its expression of an unresisting sacrifice.[*]

Just so Tolstoy, his conscience being shrugged aside, kept pushing poor Morozov: "All this is possible, Petr Vasil'evich, and you'll be quite a fellow if you do it all."[†] The misgivings and anxiety were the signals Tolstoy either should have given up the whole thing or done the work himself.

The Jubilee editors say that Morozov, in the course of these two months, paid several visits to Tolstoy at Yasnaya Polyana,[‡] where Tolstoy had resumed writing *Anna Karenina*.

In a late January letter, this one to Fet, we learn about a letter-reading habit Tolstoy had:

I was overjoyed at your letter and began, as usual, to read it from the end: it seems to me you're promising to come.[§]

We don't know if it's also Anna's habit, but she does this too when she receives her husband's icy letter and starts reading at the end:

A footman brought in a thick packet directed in Alexey Alexandrovitch's hand.

"The courier had orders to wait for an answer," he said.

"Very well," she said, and as soon as he had left the room she tore open the letter with trembling fingers. A roll of unfolded notes done up in a wrapper fell out of it. She disengaged the letter and began reading it at the end. "Preparations shall be made for your arrival here . . . I attach particular significance to compliance . . ." she read. She ran on, then back, read it all through, and

---

[*] *Anna Karenina*, trans. Garnett, Part 4, Chapter 22, http://www.literatureproject.com /anna-karenina/anna_123.htm.

[†] *PSS* 62: 77.

[‡] Ibid.

[§] *PSS* 62: 66.

once more read the letter all through again from the beginning. When she had finished, she felt that she was cold all over, and that a fearful calamity, such as she had not expected, had burst upon her.[*]

Tolstoy and Anna were reading letters from the end because they were looking for an answer, a decision, the final word.

In early February, Sofia wrote and told her sister, "Apart from the children's lessons, I hardly let my pen out of my hand, spending the whole time transcribing Levochka's novel (*Anna Karenina*), which he keeps endlessly revising, as always . . ."[†] As for those lessons, recalled Sofia, her children "were also making good progress in French, but they didn't like being compelled to speak foreign languages. English was closer to them than any other, since all the nannies they had were English, and little Masha didn't even know any other language and could barely understand Russian." In the area of foreign-language learning, we can see the Tolstoy family as the Oblonsky family, at whose pretentiousness or wrongheadedness Levin looks askance:

> ". . . What have you come for, Tanya?" she [Darya Alexandrovna, "Dolly"] said in French to the little girl who had come in.
>
> "Where's my spade, mamma?"
>
> "I speak French, and you must, too."
>
> The little girl tried to say it in French, but could not remember the French for spade; the mother prompted her, and then told her in French where to look for the spade. And this made a disagreeable impression on Levin.
>
> Everything in Darya Alexandrovna's house and children struck him now as by no means so charming as a little while before. "And what does she talk French with the children for?" he thought; "how unnatural and false it is! And the children feel it so: Learning French and unlearning sincerity," he thought to himself, unaware that Darya Alexandrovna had thought all that over twenty times already, and yet, even at the cost of some loss of sincerity, believed it necessary to teach her children French in that way.[‡]

---

[*]   *Anna Karenina,* Part 3, Chapter 16, http://literatureproject.com/anna-karenina/anna_85.htm.

[†]   Tolstaya, *My Life,* 201, February 6, 1874.

[‡]   *Anna Karenina,* Part 3, Chapter 10, http://literatureproject.com/anna-karenina/anna _79.htm.

I wonder if Sofia, on first recopying this passage, looked askance at Tolstoy and reminded him that they had both *agreed* on the matter of the benefits of English language acquisition for their children.

In either January or February, Tolstoy turned down Nikolai Nekrasov's offer to publish *Anna Karenina* in *Notes from the Fatherland*: "I don't think I can start publishing in journals, and so I'm very sorry that I cannot fulfill your wish."* Why, by March 1, would he change his mind? He would agree then, if he was going to publish it in a periodical, to publish it in Katkov's *Russian Herald*.

In mid-February, in the midst of writing the novel and directing the literacy contest from afar, Tolstoy wrote Strakhov. He was annoyed by Strakhov's less critical, more accepting attitude of, among other things, the genre of criticism:

> [. . .] criticism which you are so fond of is a terrible thing. Its only importance
> and justification is to guide public opinion, but this is the joke—when criti-
> cism talks rubbish it guides public opinion, but if it is the result of genuine
> and serious (ernst) thought it has no effect, and may just as well have never
> been written.†

Despite his renunciation of criticism, Tolstoy would go on to write criticism that was "the result of genuine and serious thought." For example, in the 1880s he would write introductions of writers' selected works for a publishing company that he and Vladimir Chertkov started in order to print inexpensive editions of classics and wholesome works for the newly literate populations in Russia. When Tolstoy spoke or wrote about literature, his listeners and readers learned not just his lightning-strike opinions but how sharply and engagedly he read. Reading Tolstoy's critical essays on Chekhov, Ruskin, the Bible, Shakespeare, and Maupassant, it can seem as if he as a reader has a bigger and better lens than ours: it's got panorama-vision with heat sensors and radar. We can aspire to reading with his power and perception (just as we can hopelessly aspire to write with his power and perception), but probably the most important benefit of such criticism as Tolstoy's is that we are provoked to go read the work that he discusses.

When the characters in *Anna Karenina* read, on the other hand, they are almost always distracted; they don't take in more than they want to; they're reading to pass the time or in order *not* to think. This shows that Tolstoy doesn't take fully engaged or perceptive

---

*   *PSS* 62: 69.

†   Christian, *Tolstoy's Letters,* 266, February 13, 1874.

reading for granted. Tolstoy's most admiring depiction of reading would occur in 1885 in a moral tale that he adapted from the French, "Where Love Is, There God Is Also":

> When Avdyeich read these words, there was joy in his heart. He took off his glasses, put them on the book, leaned his arms on the table, and fell to musing.*

Shoemaker Avdyeich's reading experience of the Gospels is not the result of criticism and could not have been inspired by criticism. So in that sense, Tolstoy might ask, what is the use of writing or reading criticism? Avdyeich's thoughts and actions *are* the "criticism."

In any case, to Strakhov, Tolstoy went on and changed the subject, unusually to his own writing habits:

> You guessed that I'm very busy and am working hard. I'm very glad that I didn't start publishing a long time ago when I wrote to you. I can't draw a circle except by joining it up and then straightening out the initial irregularities. And now I'm joining up the circle and straightening it out, and straightening it out . . . It's never happened before that I've written so much without reading anything to anybody and not even talking about it, and I terribly want to read it out. What I would give to have you here!†

Tolstoy creates the marvelous image of an artist drawing a circle by hand. By repeated applications, he tries to smooth out the rough curves through handwork. The second revelation is that Tolstoy needed to read aloud his own writing and hear it himself. Maybe he couldn't imagine a reader unless there was a reader in the room with him. With somebody listening, he himself could listen to it and appraise it:

> But I know that that's mean and I'm only deluding myself. I'm tired of working—revising, putting on the finishing touches—and I'd like someone to praise it and I don't want to work on it any more if possible.

We can believe he was "tired of working"; Tolstoy was not a literary workman. He was not Anthony Trollope knocking out one novel after another. Though we know that Tolstoy read many of Trollope's forty-seven novels, one of which, *The Way We*

---

*   Translation by Leo Wiener.

†   Christian, *Tolstoy's Letters*, 266, February 13, 1874.

Live Now, would be appearing in translation in some of the same issues of the *Russian Herald* as *Anna Karenina*, we don't know if he ever read Trollope's posthumously published *An Autobiography* (1883) or what he made of workman-like artists. Trollope writes:

> I always had a pen in my hand. Whether crossing the seas, or fighting with American officials, or tramping about the streets of Beverley, I could do a little, and generally more than a little. I had long since convinced myself that in such work as mine the great secret consisted in acknowledging myself to be bound to rules of labour similar to those which an artisan or a mechanic is forced to obey. A shoemaker when he has finished one pair of shoes does not sit down and contemplate his work in idle satisfaction. "There is my pair of shoes finished at last! What a pair of shoes it is!" The shoemaker who so indulged himself would be without wages half his time. It is the same with a professional writer of books. An author may of course want time to study a new subject. He will at any rate assure himself that there is some such good reason why he should pause. He does pause, and will be idle for a month or two while he tells himself how beautiful is that last pair of shoes which he has finished! Having thought much of all this, and having made up my mind that I could be really happy only when I was at work, I had now quite accustomed myself to begin a second pair as soon as the first was out of my hands.[*]

Tolstoy, in contrast, can make us feel that his god's gift of talent was a burden. It's amusing that he wanted "someone to praise" this draft; later, he regularly told Strakhov that he did not want any praise of the work from him. Strakhov, he sometimes suggested, was too predictably encouraging:

> I don't know if it will be all right. I rarely see things in such a light that I like everything about them. But so much has already been written and polished up and the circle has been almost joined, and I'm so tired of revising, that I want to go to Moscow after the 20th and deliver it to Katkov's printing press. [Christian's note: "Tolstoy went to Moscow on 2 March to deliver the first part of *Anna*

---

[*]   Anthony Trollope, *An Autobiography* (New York: Dodd, Mead and Company, 1916), Chapter 17.

Karenina to the printer's."] I've changed my mind about troubling you. I'm very grateful to you but I must correct the proofs myself.*

Tolstoy had rushed along with the novel, but then he suddenly became uncertain about its value and decided that he wanted to publish it in parts. Strakhov immediately and enthusiastically answered Tolstoy's letter: "What wonderful news, inestimable Lev Nikolaevich! The event that is occurring in Yasnaya Polyana is so important and so precious for me that I am afraid of something all the time, as used to happen, when you are afraid and do not believe that a woman loves you. But you write that everything is ready: for God's sake, do protect the mss and pass it on to the press."†

Again and again Strakhov shows us the proper or sensible response to Tolstoy's composition of this novel: "protect the mss" *with your life*. Tolstoy was giving birth to something "so important and so precious"! (An artist who speaks of his own work as precious is probably contemptible; but if we're artists' friends, anxious for the appearance of their work, we can be fully justified in our assessment of its preciousness.)

As a change of pace, on February 27, Tolstoy wrote in a notebook at Yasnaya Polyana what Gusev calls "the opening of a religious-philosophical work."‡ I would call it, instead, the beginning of his multiyear revision and development of *Confession*, the philosophical rumination about his suicidal impulses in the mid-1870s:

> There is a language of philosophy and I will not speak it. I will speak a simple language. The interest of philosophy common to all society and the judgment of all.
>
> Philosophical language is invented for counter-objections. I'm not afraid of objections. I'm looking for them. I don't belong to any camp. And I ask the readers not to belong to one.—This is the first condition of philosophy. I need to object to materialism in the preface. It's said that besides earthly life there is nothing. I need to object because if that's so, there's nothing for me to write about. Having lived nearly 50 years, I'm convinced that earthly life gives nothing, and the smart person who looks at earthly life seriously, the difficulties, fears, reproaches, fights—for what?—out of craziness, right away will

---

* R. F. Christian's note: "Tolstoy corrected the proofs with the help of Yury Samarin [. . .]" *Tolstoy's Letters*, 266.

† Eikhenbaum, *Tolstoi in the Seventies*, 112, letter of February 22, 1874.

‡ Gusev, *Letopis'*, 418.

shoot himself, and Hartmann and Schopenhauer are right. But Schopenhauer gave the feeling that there is something, as he did not shoot himself. So this something is the task of my book. Why do we live?—Religion.—*

Was this the real book that Tolstoy first imagined Levin working on, instead of the one that Levin eventually got stuck on about the economics of contemporary Russian farming?
No.
Why?
Because Levin is ten to twelve years younger than Tolstoy in 1874, not a writer, and not yet a father.

On the other hand, Levin, by the end of *Anna Karenina*, is tempted to shoot himself; he doesn't figure out the answer of *why* he shouldn't, but by managing to avoid it, he gets past the "feeling" that he ought to. As did Tolstoy. Perhaps the value of *Anna Karenina* was that it was the "something" task that kept Tolstoy from shooting himself. It was not, to his thinking, the reason to stay alive, but his dramatization of Anna's despair may have prevented his own self-destruction.

The day before going to Moscow to submit the first part of *Anna Karenina* to the printer for publication as a separate edition, he wrote to the editor of the *Russian Herald*, Mikhail Katkov:

> As for the proposition for publishing in the *Russian Herald*, if I decide to publish in a magazine, generally speaking, the desire will always be to give it to the *Russian Herald*. My conditions are 500 rubles a sheet.†

He was wavering about the novel even as he was submitting it. Should he publish it as a book, part by part, as he had *War and Peace*, or serialize it in a journal instead? Was he anxious as he rode on the train that something would happen to the manuscript? Was he satisfied? Did he look it over some more? I imagine him confident and proud, knowing he had indeed worked hard at it and that the material itself was about as good as anyone could produce. The first part of the manuscript that wasn't yet but would be

---

*   *PSS* 48: 347. R. F. Christian includes a snip of this work as a *diary* entry for this date: "Schopenhauer gave people to feel that there is something, which stopped him from shooting himself. What that something is is the purpose of my book. What do we live by? *Religion*." Christian, *Tolstoy's Diaries*, 191.

†   A "sheet," printed and cut, became sixteen pages. *PSS* 62: 70, letter of March 1, 1874.

his great work was in his hands or tucked into his bag. Was he thinking of the story and of how he would be reading it aloud to those specially selected listeners, or was he contemplating the literacy-teaching contest?

It was that first night in Moscow, on March 2, when, according to Gusev he read "aloud some chapters of the novel."[*] He wrote about this experience a few days later, back in Yasnaya Polyana, in a letter to Strakhov:

> [. . .] I read a few chapters out for the first time to Tyutchev's daughter and Samarin. I chose them both as being very cold, intelligent, and shrewd people, and it seemed to me that it made little impression on them . . .[†]

Tolstoy sometimes brought his art out into the air in order to get a new sense of it, to assess it, to be surprised by it, to replan it. But how keenly did he read those friends' responses? *"I chose them both as being very cold, intelligent and shrewd people"*!

Imagine that you, you cold, intelligent, shrewd person, have been chosen by the author to listen to the beginning of *Anna Karenina*. You don't know that it's going to be *Anna Karenina*. You are distracted perhaps by Tolstoy's excitement or manner. He's even told you, perhaps, that he has chosen you because you're "very cold, intelligent, and shrewd," which seems simultaneously complimentary and insulting. You are a test audience. He is not an actor. He is not, likely, reading it with obvious self-admiration. You have to guess what it is he wants to hear from you; you are not his equal. You cannot be totally frank. But if you are completely bowled over, gasping with awe, will he think you're a sycophant?

This is in contrast to Strakhov, who could react as enthusiastically as he felt; he could fall off his chair in amazement and insist that the great chapters he had just heard read to him were sublime—and he would have been right. Strakhov had enough confidence in his literary opinions to be able to state that Tolstoy's writing was extraordinary. But here the poet Tyutchev's daughter and Samarin[‡] were a special panel, whose "coldness"

---

[*]   Gusev, *Materials*, 159.

[†]   Christian, *Tolstoy's Letters*, 267, March 6, 1874.

[‡]   Tolstoy was once "attracted to" Tyutchev's daughter in 1857–1858, writes Andrew Donskov, and "there was talk of their marriage." (Donskov, *L. N. Tolstoy – N. N. Strakhov*, 157.) As for Yury Fyodorovich Samarin, R. F. Christian says: "Tolstoy first met Samarin in Moscow in 1856, and was struck by his 'cold, supple and educated mind.' He is reported to have referred to Samarin as '. . . one of the pleasantest people I've known'" (Christian, *Tolstoy's Letters*, 210). Samarin was nine years older than Tolstoy and died in 1876. Samarin never knew *Anna Karenina* in its final form or that he had been let in on a singular literary experience.

would perhaps keep Tolstoy from getting distracted. He could read to them and feel as if he had exposed the novel without having to care deeply about their responses. Tolstoy's account of the evening continues:

> . . . but so far from being disenchanted, I set about revising and touching it up with even greater enthusiasm. I think it will be good, but it won't be liked and it won't be successful because it's very simple. Samarin has agreed to correct the proofs. I'm very glad about this, but I'll do some correcting myself as well.*

But what could Tolstoy have meant by its being "very simple"? It means that he still hadn't discovered the real novel yet. For the moment, he thought that he was going to finish and ditch it before it could consume him.

While in Moscow, he visited the school where the children were learning reading by his method, but he did not remark in writing about that experience.

On March 5, as Tolstoy returned to Yasnaya Polyana by train, did the motion of the train remind him of Anna and her fate? Did he try to read, as he would depict Anna trying to? Did he drift off into a nap and wake up two or three hours later in Tula or at the Kozlova Zaseka station, the train stop nearest Yasnaya Polyana?

Besides the letter to Strakhov on March 6 about his business in Moscow and the reading aloud of those *Anna Karenina* chapters, he wrote, in a different vein, to his relative Alexandrine:

> [. . .] This year sorrow has afflicted us. We lost our youngest son, the 6th child. Now we have 5 and are expecting another around Easter. Of all the intimate losses we could have suffered, this was the easiest to bear—a little finger, but painful just the same, especially for my wife. Death never has a very painful effect on me (I felt this at the loss of a dearly loved brother). If you yourself don't approach nearer to your own death with the loss of a being you love, if you don't become disillusioned with life and don't cease to love it and expect good of it, then these losses must be unbearable; but if you submit to this approach to your own end, then it's not painful, but important, significant, and beautiful. That is the effect death has on me, yes, and on everyone, I think.†

---

* Christian, *Tolstoy's Letters*, 267.

† Christian, *Tolstoy's Letters*, 268.

This is what Tolstoy in a philosophical frame of mind said about death. Such philosophy was an aspirational pursuit for him. How should it feel? Like *this*. But this had not been how he acted or would act when the thought or reality of death hovered near. His fear of annihilation was soon going to disable him. His imagination would in fact "become disillusioned" and anticipating death would definitely not seem "beautiful" to him. Tolstoy was of two minds about death: (1) wise and philosophical and (2) petrified.

> A small example. When burying Petya, I was concerned for the first time about where I am to be laid. And, apart from a mother's special, almost physical pain, it had the same effect on Sonya, despite her youth.
>
> We're living in the same old way, so busy that there's never enough time. The children and their upbringing take up more and more of our time, and it's going well. I try not to, but I can't help being proud of my children. Besides that, I'm writing and have started publishing a novel which I like, but which is unlikely to be liked by anyone else, because it's too simple. [. . .]

Again with the "simple" and unlikable *Anna Karenina*! And how about his "Besides that" ("*krome togo*"*)! *Anna Karenina* as a "besides that"! Besides that, writes Albert Einstein, I have come up with a theory of relativity . . . Besides that, writes Mozart, I have jotted down an opera, *The Marriage of Figaro* . . . etc.

For his relative, he was bringing together death and the novel. He even mentioned the happy state of his happy family. All happy families are . . . on the verge of unhappiness. Does being conscious of family happiness break the spell? It's not clear that he ever again expressed his interest, happiness, and pride in the family.

Throughout March, Tolstoy continued his backseat driving of his substitute Morozov's teaching. It could not have been easy to work as Tolstoy's stand-in: "I just received your letter, and I still know little and it's short. How did the little ones read? Were they able to recite? [. . .] Write me in more detail about everything that I wrote you. Were you able to use everything that I advised you in the last letter and how did it work?"†

The nagging persisted: "You ask me whether I accept that the exams were intense? I can't answer that at all because I don't know anything about the success of the pupils from the time of my leaving Moscow. You don't write me anything or you write me what I don't need to know; the smallest details are what interest me in the school's progress. You

---

*   *PSS* 62: 73.

†   *PSS* 90: 233, letter of March 18–19, 1874.

don't even answer the questions in my letters. How does the dictation go with the young ones? How are they reading?"* He told Morozov to test the comparison group's students.

It could have been this contest that prompted Tolstoy's bitter regrets in *Confession* about imposing his pedagogy on the world: "I naively imagined that I was a poet and artist and could teach everybody without myself knowing what I was teaching, and I acted accordingly."

> [. . .] I acquired a new vice: abnormally developed pride and an insane assur-
> ance that it was my vocation to teach men, without knowing what.
>
> To remember that time, and my own state of mind and that of those men
> (though there are thousands like them today), is sad and terrible and ludicrous,
> and arouses exactly the feeling one experiences in a lunatic asylum.
>
> We were all then convinced that it was necessary for us to speak, write,
> and print as quickly as possible and as much as possible, and that it was all
> wanted for the good of humanity. And thousands of us, contradicting and
> abusing one another, all printed and wrote—teaching others. And without
> noticing that we knew nothing, and that to the simplest of life's questions:
> What is good and what is evil? we did not know how to reply, we all talked at
> the same time, not listening to one another, sometimes seconding and praising
> one another in order to be seconded and praised in turn, sometimes getting
> angry with one another—just as in a lunatic asylum.†

In the first week of April, Tolstoy was still caught up in the teaching contest and traveled back and forth between Yasnaya Polyana and Moscow despite the fact that Sofia was due at any time and despite the anxiety-causing news that his brother Sergei's wife had just miscarried.

In a chapter about 1874 titled "Disease and Death," Sofia remembered: "I always feared a premature birth, and was constantly thinking that I would certainly die therefrom. I became so nervous that I wrote my sister: 'I've become so nervous, fearful and timid that the slightest thing can set me off and even drive me to despair.' [. . .] I was especially afraid for my eldest son, Serezha. I loved him very much and wrote about him: 'As the eldest,

---

* *PSS* 90: 235, letter of March 20–21, 1874.

† Leo Tolstoy, *Confession*, trans. Aylmer Maude (London: Oxford University Press, 1971),
   10–11.

and smartest, and kindest, he is dearer to me and gives me greater cause for concern than any of the others . . .'"*

This might remind us about *Anna Karenina*, and the premonition Anna has when pregnant with Vronsky's baby. Anna, after all, has some connections to Sofia. Anna's hysterical fears about her second pregnancy are Sofia's actually much more reasonable fears about her seventh. Sofia's devotion to Seryozha is Anna's to her own Seryozha.

While Kitty shares conspicuous traits and characteristics with the Sofia of ages eighteen and nineteen, there are also measures of Sofia in Anna, who is the same age as Sofia as the novel proceeds. And once the vital "real" Anna existed, maybe Sofia began to take after *her*. Life imitates art, as Oscar Wilde enjoyed pointing out. In the next three decades Sofia would threaten to kill herself a half-dozen times. Experiencing the death of several of her children perhaps made her feel less frightened of dying herself.

By April 11 Tolstoy was home for Sofia and quite anxious. He wrote his friend Golokhvastov that "Up to now all is well, but I'm awaiting my wife's childbirth, and for some reason I'm afraid this time."[†] Perhaps he was afraid because his sister-in-law had just had a miscarriage or because Sofia had told him that she was afraid. He also wrote a short note, sometime pre-delivery in April, to Fet: "We every day wait and worry ever more and more."[‡]

Even so, he once more rushed off to Moscow and made his final appearance on April 13 before the literacy committee, where he learned the committee would not offer an official decision.[§]

On that date, there was no stenographic record taken of the meeting, and the president of the committee asked Tolstoy to write an article about what had been said there. Tolstoy didn't write it, but he did query Nikolai Nekrasov about providing *Notes of the Fatherland* with an article about his argument with "the Moscow pedagogues."[¶] This argument became instead his important essay "On Popular Education" that he published in September.

He complained to Strakhov:

---

* Tolstaya, *My Life*, 202.

† *PSS* 62: 79, letter of April 11, 1874.

‡ *PSS* 62: 84, letter of April 1–21, 1874.

§ Gusev, *Letopis'*, 419.

¶ Gusev says this was the content of Tolstoy's letter, but the letter has not survived. *Letopis'*, 420.

> I've been recently occupied with something quite different—schools of literacy. The Moscow Literacy Committee got me involved in the cause, and made the old pedagogical ferment rise in me again.[*]

Strakhov tried to remind him of the folly of fighting this pedagogical battle, but Tolstoy wouldn't listen. It's hard not to feel, with Strakhov and Sofia, how fruitless this pursuit was. Tolstoy was wanting to be distracted. His friend and his wife were right, all of it came to nothing, and he eventually renounced it himself.

On the other hand, I believe it would have been sensible for the committee to have listened to Tolstoy on these matters, despite his losing his temper. He fussed about being called names ("a reactionary and a Slavophile"), and delivered a couple of shots about school systems that I believe must have been true then because they're true today:

> [. . .] People who know nothing and have no talents—who don't even know the people they have undertaken to *educate*—have got their hands on the whole business of public education, and what they are doing makes your hair stand on end.[†]

He had just written and redone his *Azbuka*, the most influential book there would ever be for Russian literacy. He was hands down an expert, and he couldn't resist the bait of an argument. It's true that this particular educational dispute came to nothing and that *Anna Karenina* came to something. We know what he should have devoted himself to, but it turns out he was able to do it all.[‡]

He concluded his touchy letter to Strakhov:

> But don't forget your promise—come and see us in summer. There is something ironical about the tone of your last letter. Please don't allow this with me, because I love you very much.[§]

---

[*]   *PSS* 62: 83, letter of April 18–19, 1874.

[†]   Ibid.

[‡]   And yet I realize that if there had been a "Tolstoyan" movement in education, if it had been taken up by disciples and channeled into a system, he would soon have been excluded from it, because he would have continually criticized it and would have wanted to modify it. He could never have been an obedient soldier even in his own army.

[§]   *PSS* 62: 83, letter of April 18–19, 1874.

Tolstoy responded with annoyance here to Strakhov's tone and once in a while elsewhere. Their friendship was imbalanced, affectionate but a bit condescending on Tolstoy's part; on Strakhov's, affectionate but awed and earnest. In any case, we don't know what Strakhov said, because the letter that spurred Tolstoy's reproach hasn't survived, but Strakhov's immediate reply to Tolstoy's letter was: "It means I wrote you very poorly if you find something ironical in me. Maybe I jokingly spoke of the Academy, but not about *you*. [Tolstoy was recently made a member.] . . . You're mistaken." Strakhov promised to come to Yasnaya Polyana on July 1. "Then finally I'll become acquainted with your new novel. How I await this!" How surprising that Strakhov, who would regularly be rolling up his sleeves to proofread the galleys of the novel, still didn't know its contents. Strakhov directly and forcefully addressed Tolstoy's pedagogical ideas, rightly complimented the old *Yasnaya Polyana* articles, and then got some of his dignity back by chiding Tolstoy about the literacy contest: "And now you undertake to wrestle with this filth. I will say straight off that this is unpleasant for me in regard to you. [. . .] It'll be sad for me if your strength and time is wasted on an argument and repelling all the mud. [. . .]"*

Anna Karenina seemed nowhere in Tolstoy's mind when Sofia gave birth to their fifth son, Nikolay, on April 22, and Tolstoy wrote his brother to beg him to come for Nikolay's christening.† The week after Nikolay's birth, Tolstoy drafted "A Grammar for Village Schools."‡ "The attraction of pedagogy corresponded with the cooling to the begun novel," writes Gusev.§ He had also gotten himself involved in governance of the Krapivensky County school board.¶

In May, Tolstoy wrote Strakhov about what would become the long essay "On Popular Education":

> Now I'm even writing an article, that is my pedagogical profession de foi. [. . .]
> Whether I'm mistaken or not, I'm firmly convinced that I can put the business
> of the people's education on such footing that it isn't now and hasn't stood
> anywhere in Europe, and that for this nothing is needed besides [not having]
> someone who doesn't love or know this business undertake it. [. . .]
> My novel lies there. [. . .]**

---

* Donskov, *L. N. Tolstoy – N. N. Strakhov*, 160–161, May 10, 1874.

† *PSS* 62: 85.

‡ Gusev, *Letopis'*, 420–421. (Also, *PSS* 21: 412–424.)

§ Gusev, *Materials*, 159–194. (The letter to Strakhov is here: *PSS* 62: 88–89.)

¶ *PSS* 62: 89.

** *PSS* 62: 88–89, letter of May 10, 1874.

Educational issues had detached Tolstoy from the novel and now he seemed to want to kill the story in his imagination. By May 20, he was asking Strakhov, who was champing at the bit to read *Anna Karenina*, to read the education article. He concluded: "Tell me, please, and advise."*

Strakhov's answer is unknown, but we can guess what it was. *Sure*, Strakhov must have said, *why not?*

At the end of May, the Kuzminsky family arrived; sister-in-law Tatyana and her children would stay until the end of August. The obvious and neat parallel, as Sofia would point out in *My Life*, is Levin's hosting of his sister-in-law Dolly's family, the Oblonskys. Sasha Kuzminskiy and Stiva Oblonsky were otherwise engaged, Stiva in Moscow, Kuzminskiy in the Caucasus. Sofia made no pretense that situations in *Anna Karenina* had nothing to do with their lives. She was proud of how their family life made its appearances in the novel. Of "The Summer of 1874," for example:

> We were all terribly delighted by the arrival of the Kuzminskijs, and our customary happy summer life started up with all the bathing, wagon rides, jam-making, children, and everything Lev Nikolaevich describes in his novel *Anna Karenina*, with certain variations. For example, the thunderstorm that caught Kitty and her child in the forest was the same kind of storm that caught Serezha and me in the forest closest to our house, i.e., Chepyzh, while Levin's fright was Lev Nikolaevich's.
>
> Again, when I took two of our children to communion, it wasn't Tanja, but Lelja, who said to the priest in English: "Please, some more for Lelja." And there were many variations like that.†

For Sofia, a happy summer took place at home, not in Samara.

Tolstoy wrote Strakhov, "I have now finished my article and it seems to me it successfully speaks clearly and truly."‡ More importantly, he told Strakhov he was writing to the printer to suspend publication of *Anna Karenina*: "I can't think about that writing now."§

Tolstoy had pressed the pause button in the hope that his responsibility for the novel would disappear—a miscarriage. What would continue for three more years was his

---

*   *PSS* 62: 91.

†   Tolstaya, *My Life*, 204.

‡   *PSS* 62: 92, letter of end of May, early June, 1874.

§   Ibid.

feeling of the novel being not only a burden on him but less important than other activities in his life.

Perhaps as he moved toward his realization of the Anna we know in the novel, he saw a portend of his own depression. His *Confession* will describe suicide's pull on him during this coming period. His "light," "simple" novel became heavy when he seriously contemplated suicidal Anna.

Sometime between June 10 and 15, Tolstoy wrote a consoling letter to his sister Maria about an injury he heard she had suffered. He said that he and his family were fine, not counting the death of Petya and the now imminently expected death of Auntie Tatyana Alexandrovna, which came on June 20.*

On the day of Auntie's death he apologized in a letter to Strakhov for asking him for favors when Strakhov was busy. Please, he wanted to know, was the public education article okay? "The request is that you read it through with a pencil in hand and making use of cross-outs tell me whether it's worth publishing somewhere? [. . .] As for myself, of course, everything you do I will be happy with. Even if you burn the article or do nothing.—The closer comes the time of meeting with you [which is two weeks], the more I'm joyful and expectant, how very important (you are) for me and for my writing that is and will be."†

That very day, writing from St. Petersburg, Strakhov determinedly leaned on Tolstoy to return to *Anna Karenina*, which Strakhov still hadn't lain eyes on. And it was not because Tolstoy's educational work wasn't important. Strakhov wrote:

> I'll be in Moscow on July 3, estimable Lev Nikolaevich. Decidedly, it's impossible to wander about more than a month and I need to be in Petersburg again by July 29. I propose now to be at your service; couldn't I help you with the editing of the novel?
>
> I read with terror that you were stopping publication—you're torturing us with expectation. That which you write about the importance of your pedagogical work, it shows how ardently you're attracted by it. Sometime in 1862 I first read your *Yasnaya Polyana* with excited praise (this was in *Time*); consequently you cannot doubt my sincere sympathy with your pedagogy; but you exaggerate it, leaving behind your higher art.

---

* Born in 1792, Tat'yana Aleksandrovna Ergol'skaya was Tolstoy's father's second cousin.

† *PSS* 62: 93–94, letter of June 20, 1874.

About both I terribly want to speak with you, and I don't even want to write because it feels like everything can't be written.[*]

Strakhov knew that as much as he loved the man and appreciated the education articles, the best thing he could do was help Tolstoy do what Tolstoy could do better than anyone. Tolstoy wrote Sergei about their aunt's death and asked him to come to the burial on June 22.[†] After the funeral, he wrote a confession to Alexandrine:

[. . .] Yesterday I buried Auntie Tatyana Alexandrovna. [. . .] she faded away little by little, and had already ceased to exist for us 3 years ago, so much so that (I don't know whether this was a good or a bad feeling), I avoided her and couldn't see her without a feeling of agony; but now that she's dead (she died slowly, and painfully—like a childbirth), all my feeling for her has returned with still greater force. [. . .] All's well with my family. You predicted a girl for me, but a boy was born, just like the one we lost, and although he's called Nikolay, we involuntarily call him Petya, like the other. I'm in my summer mood—i.e., I'm not occupied with poetry and have stopped publishing my novel and want to give it up, I dislike it so much. [. . .][‡]

His haunting image of Auntie had become, it seems, a waking nightmare. Dread seems to have descended on him; he made an effort to regain the philosophical attitude about death that he had had on March 6.

To his brother Sergei, he wrote again: "I didn't think I'd be so sad about Auntie. It's impossible to learn about dying from her. She lived like a child and so she died—at least for us. What she thought in her last moments, no one knows. She only said when she was asked how she wanted to be shifted, 'Just a moment, just a moment, and soon you can shift me as you like and all will be well.'"[§]

Tolstoy wanted *something* to be revealed about death, not simply calm resignation after the slow, painful descent that preceded it. (Her quiet acceptance would become in the next decade exactly what he would celebrate in his fictional characters.) In one of his

---

[*]   Donskov, *L. N. Tolstoy – N. N. Strakhov,* 169, June 20, 1874; http://feb-web.ru/feb/tolstoy /texts/selectpe/ts6/ts62169-.htm.

[†]   *PSS* 62: 94, letter of June 20, 1874.

[‡]   Christian, *Tolstoy's Letters,* 270, June 23, 1874.

[§]   *PSS* 62: 97, letter of end of June 1874.

summer letters to Sergei, he told him that the house was full, and it was "boring." He mentioned their sister, who was back in Europe and in need of money.* Maria, with her out-of-wedlock daughter, was dependent on them for financial support, and they both worried about her. She would soon closely identify herself, installment by installment, with the heroine of her brother Lev's novel.

In early July, Strakhov made his visit to Yasnaya Polyana. Strakhov read the novel for the first time and was crazy about it, and in consequence Tolstoy became momentarily reinspired and began reviewing the typeset chapters.

Then he again threw them down.†

Tolstoy worked instead on the education essay, but, as we see in his letter to Golokhvastov, all was confusion in the Tolstoy house: "We now have no one besides an English nanny and we need a master for the boys and a governess for the girls."‡ As if of no importance, or perhaps to parry Golokhvastov's asking again about *Anna Karenina*, he mentioned at the end: "I'm stopping my publication, and I cannot force myself to deal with it in the summer."§

Usually the summer travels and the suspension of routine freed him; this summer so far, though, he was home conducting business, and the novel promised only more obligation.

In a fretful mood, he wrote Fet: "I'm amazed that you didn't receive my letter, dear Afanasy Afanasich. [. . .] It's terribly sad when you arrive at this present age, as you and I have, to feel oneself more and more alone [. . .]. This is not a depression. [. . .]"¶ That is, he knew Fet would presume it was a depression, but he needed to tell Fet to resist saying so. "Strakhov spent five days with me, and despite his awkwardness speaking, I was pleased with him, but constantly, I think, annoyed him by remembering you."**

In the letters to Fet and Golokhvastov, it seems that Tolstoy was having his revenge on the snake who had tempted him to go back to the novel.

Strakhov, his ears probably burning from Tolstoy's peeved mentions of him, undauntedly wrote to Tolstoy on July 23 with full accurate critical praise of *Anna Karenina*. Tolstoy wanted to condemn the novel to the trash; in good conscience Strakhov wouldn't let him do so. He told Tolstoy that he had another meeting to attend and so wouldn't be back to

---

*   *PSS* 62: 103–104, letter of June–July 1874.

†   *PSS* 62: 100.

‡   *PSS* 62: 98, letter of mid-July 1874.

§   Ibid.

¶   *PSS* 62: 99, letter of July 12–18, 1874.

**   *PSS* 62: 99.

Yasnaya Polyana until the 6th or at the latest the 8th of August. (It's not clear that Tolstoy's trip to Samara with his son Seryozha had been planned for that time yet.) Ever since reading *Anna Karenina* two weeks before, wrote Strakhov, "Your novel hasn't left my head. Every time you write I'm struck by the amazing freshness, the absolute originality, as if I've suddenly leapt over from one period of literature into another. You correctly noticed that in some places your novel recalls *War and Peace*; but this is only where there are similar subjects. As soon as there's another subject, it appears in a new light, even never seen, never having happened before in literature. The development of Karenina's passion is a miracle of miracles. It's not complete, I think, what you have shown of (many parts are not written) the relations of the world to this event. The world enjoys (what an amazing feature!) the temptation tempting him; but the reaction presents itself partly false, hypocritical, partly sincere and deep. I don't know very well what you will have there, I don't dare or think to—to develop your theme; but it has to be something very interesting, very deep; on this point, everything turns its attention and will demand from you a decision, judgment."

In the manuscript that Strakhov had in hand, it was *complete*, more or less: Anna has *died*:

> As for me, the inner story of passion is the main thing and explains it all. Anna kills herself from the egotism of the idea, serving completely that very passion; this is an inescapable outcome, a logical deduction from that direction which drew her from the very beginning. Oh, how strong, how irresistibly clear!
>
> All this is taken by you with the very highest point of view—this is felt in every word in every detail, and you probably don't value this as you ought, and maybe you don't notice it. [. . .]

Strakhov appealed to Tolstoy's competitiveness:

> You are obliged, in the full thought of the word, to publish your novel in order to kill off this [i.e., Turgenev's "falseness" in *Smoke*] and similar falseness. How aggravated Turgenev has to be! He is a kind of specialist in love and women! Your Karenina at once kills off all of his Irinas and similar heroines (as they're called in *Torrents of Spring*). And for Boborykin, Krestovskiy, and other such novelists this will be a useful and fruitful lesson. But reading you will be endlessly insatiable—really, such a topic!
>
> With all my soul I wish you resolve and strength. For me now it's very clear the story of your novel. You got heated up writing it, got distracted, and it became boring to you. [. . .]

By some of your words I see that you are thinking through various things, in comparison with which the subject of your novel sometimes seems to you insignificant (as for me it has essential, first-level importance!). Here there's one way—get down to business and don't leave off until you finish. If you don't finish your novel, I will blame you simply for laziness, an unwillingness to force yourself a little bit. [. . .]*

"Strakhov's praises did not have much effect on Tolstoi," says the biographer Boris Eikhenbaum.† But I think Strakhov's praises did indeed have quite a bit of an effect. Strakhov made Tolstoy confront what was really and truly there—the miraculous creation of Anna and how her depression leads to her suicide.

Tolstoy answered the novel's champion:

Even before I received your letter, I took your advice, that is, I took up the work on the novel; but what was printed and typeset, I so much didn't like, that I finally decided to destroy the printed sheets and redo everything from the start concerning Levin and Vronsky. And they will be as they are but better.‡ I hope as of the fall to take up this work and finish it.§

Ambitious. Hopeful. That's the spirit!

Except that he still didn't feel like actually working on it.

While putting it off, was it tumbling around in his head? For Tolstoy, composition was not divine or beautiful. He didn't think of his fiction as a gift to the world, though Strakhov correctly thought of it that way. The novel *troubled* Tolstoy. And if, as he said, he was seeing new possibilities for Vronsky and Levin, that meant a lot was going to have to change.

He wrote to Alexandrine on that same semi-hopeful day, but not about the novel: it was about his despairing hunt for tutors and governesses: "I have a German-uncle and

---

* Donskov, *L. N. Tolstoy – N. N. Strakhov*, 171–172.

† Eikhenbaum, *Tolstoi in the Seventies*, 116.

‡ One detail about Levin that did not survive the revision in the real *Anna Karenina* but that could have, without disturbing the plot while also filling in a time of Levin's life, is that Levin at the end of his coursework at the university started working at a ministry; he was displeased with what he encountered there and after a half-year returned to his estate. We get this summation of the contents at http://feb-web.ru/feb/tolstoy/texts/selectpe/ts6/ts62174-.htm.

§ *PSS* 62: 100, letter of July 27, 1874.

English-nanny, but the older children have outgrown them and we are looking for a master and governess." He apologized repeatedly for annoying her with his requests for help, but he knew that she, the governess of a Romanov princess, had connections to others in her field in Switzerland and England. He was pulling out all the stops.

"My desires here," he wrote Alexandrine, "are that the person have good morals, as much as possible a high soulful mood, without being pedantic or a Pharisee. And best of all a husband and wife, childless or with a child from six to eleven years old. There are no other requirements. Nationality is of no matter: German, French, English, Russian—as long as it's European and Christian. Salary—everything I can give, that is, from one to two thousand rubles for two. Education—all the same—the more the better—especially language, but if they don't know any, besides proper language, I'm fine. I can—as I've done all along—teach them myself the mathematics and the classical languages. Age? It's all the same, from 20 to 70."

He added: "If necessary, I would go to Switzerland or wherever necessary in order to see those who might come under my requirements. The needs for the children had suddenly changed—as if onto a new stage. This especially seems so for the girl [Tanya was nine]. They develop earlier." In the 1870s Tolstoy continued to seem like a 21st century father, involved in all aspects of the children's lives: "How much I think over and feel about them, with so much effort—for what? So that in the best case, they're not very bad or stupid people."*

Those are the sentiments of an involved but realistic parent.

And at the same time he was vacillating over whether or not to write his novel.

How a two-week getaway to Samara with his son Seryozha got planned, I don't know. Perhaps it was a spur-of-the-moment idea. Muttering to Sofia about his yearning for Samara, did she suggest that he take a short trip there? Her brother could stay to help with the kids, but maybe he could take their oldest boy this time? Seryozha had just turned eleven. The first written mention of the trip is in Tolstoy's letter of July 29, on the eve of his and Seryozha's departure for Moscow and from there to Samara, when he wrote Golokhvastov just as humbly and desperately as he had written to Alexandrine about help finding a tutor and governess. Concluding his letter, he complained: "The other day Strakhov was at my place; he almost got me interested in my novel again, but I just dropped it. It is terribly disgusting and nasty."†

This was *two* days after his hopeful remarks to Strakhov!

---

*   *PSS* 62: 101, letter of July 27, 1874.

†   Eikhenbaum, *Tolstoi in the Seventies*, 116, letter of July 29, 1874.

What does Tolstoy's repulsion from the novel that he himself had created mean?

Tolstoy has taught me almost everything I think I know about psychology, and I wonder at this moment, in his repeated mentions of his disgust with the novel, how much of this reluctance had its roots in depression? He didn't know or couldn't imagine where his vitality for writing was going to come from.

Sofia remembered this journey in her memoir as "Lev Nikolaevich's Trip with Serezha to Samara—The Children at Home": "It was frightening for me to let [Serezha] go off so far away, but I also considered it harmful to keep the boy his whole life just with me and his nannies."[*]

The Tolstoys' Seryozha and *Anna*'s Seryozha are growing up over the time of the novel; and while Karenin and his Seryozha have a poor relationship (in the *final* draft, but not in the early drafts, when Karenin is a good dad and has a magic touch with children), Tolstoy saw this as a chance to develop a better relationship with his boy. Sofia remembered:

> At that time Lev Nikolaevich, too, had begun taking an interest in his children, and I even detected a degree of concern in him that he was missing out on opportunities, that he must hasten to hire a good teacher and begin getting the older boys studying ancient languages. [. . .][†]

On July 30, Tolstoy and Seryozha stayed with the Perfil'evs in Moscow. Tolstoy was finishing up accounts with the printer of that abandoned separate edition of *Anna Karenina*, for which thirty chapters of Part 1 had been set in type.[‡] As a reassuring husband and father, Tolstoy wrote Sofia right away: "We arrived fine. [. . .] Polin'ka [Praskov'ya Fedorovna Perfil'eva] suggested Arkady [a servant] taking Sergei to the zoo garden, and I called and went myself with them."[§] (That zoological garden is an important place for Levin in Part 1, Chapter 9; he goes there, in winter, to see Kitty, and he displays his skating prowess; however, when he gets to skate with her he communicates too much about his feelings and she freezes him out, preparing us, if not him, for her impending rejection of his proposal.)

On with the parental report: "Seryozha slept little and was limp, but I lay him down to sleep, and he's sleeping now. Very soon I'll wake him to eat and to leave. [. . .] Seryozha

---

*   Tolstaya, *My Life*, 205.

†   Ibid.

‡   Gusev, *Letopis'*, 423.

§   *PSS* 83: 216, letter of July 30, 1874.

has woken. He's sleepy, but hasn't much of an appetite."* Seryozha's own note to his mother was written on Tolstoy's letter. They traveled by train to Nizhni-Novgorod on July 31 and got on the Volga steamer August 1, when Seryozha added: "Dear Mama, we're now on the steamer, and my handwriting is bad from that, because the steamer rolls so much. We went straight onto the Nizhni Gorod train; it was a very comfortable space for us, because in our compartment sat a German and a Jew. I slept on the floor, but I slept better than on a sofa. In the morning we went to Nizhni. There it was terribly crowded, because there was a fair. We went on the *Alexander II* steamer, which is very big and is two stories. We're now between Nizhni and Kazan and we ought to be in Samara after tomorrow morning. In this steamer is a very big wheelhouse and cabins, not below but on the same level with the wheelhouse. [. . .]"†

Tolstoy followed Seryozha's informative note: "Well, here, he's written everything. Traveling for us is going well and the company is simple and not unpleasant. The main thing is that the steamer runs all night and on Saturday morning we'll be in Samara. This saves us time, but don't expect us before the 15th. Maybe we'll stay longer on the farm.—I had been very tired, but on the steamer I have already succeeded in resting. Seryozha's very sweet, and this trip has brought us together. I'm always looking at him with affection. I said that it's boring on a steamer, but now I take that back; I'm sitting on a balcony, I look around and am joyful and think about how next year we'll all go together. Only if for you it would be beneficial. [. . .] I won't have any melancholy with Seryozha. The whole time it's as if I'm with the family."‡ Apparently, Sofia had been remembering his low mood when he went for a koumiss cure in 1871 with her little brother Stepan.

Even if depressed, he was careful to reassure her.

He wrote her again from the farm: "I slept poorly in the night and so slept through into Samara, and the steamer was late, so that in Samara I was very rushed and didn't manage to send you this letter."§ He had heard from the housekeeper that the bread was especially bad at their place.¶

---

* *PSS* 83: 216, letter of July 30, 1874.

† *PSS* 83: 218, letter of August 1?, 1874.

‡ Ibid.

§ Seryozha's note about the last leg of the steamer-trip was more detailed and must have upset poor Sofia: "Our steamer tonight collided with another steamer and broke our wheel, and now we sit atop a sand bank. I and Papa didn't see or hear anything because we were sleeping . . . Our steamer was late because the wheel needed fixing and because in some places it was very small." *PSS* 83: 219, letter of August 3, 1874.

¶ Ibid.

At the Samara farm, Tolstoy's goal was "to look at what was growing and to settle accounts." While there he finished preparing "On Public Education"* for publication.

How about that? He wouldn't work in the summer . . . except on public service writing. Evangelizing knows no rest. Art, on the other hand, demanded something else from him, namely creation, not the sharp explication of what he already thought, and it required a cool mind.

But when and how did he work on the essay? Did he share any of his thoughts about education with Seryozha? After all, he had assigned the boy teaching duties in 1872 when he was using the *Azbuka* to teach the peasant children.

In any case, Seryozha was "delighted" to be on the steppe with his father, but he remembered decades later being chagrinned there when Tolstoy lost his temper:

> I was surprised to hear my father reprimand a local peasant very angrily for appropriating about 13 dessiatines to his plot. Altogether the affairs on the farm were not too prosperous. My father had appointed an ignorant peasant, Timofei, as bailiff and he proved totally inadequate. My Uncle Sergei used to say about it: "Leo can allow himself the luxury of taking on bad bailiffs; for instance, Timofei will cause him one thousand rubles damage; Leo will describe him in a book and receive two thousand rubles for the description—so he'll be one thousand to the good."[†]

Father and son returned to Yasnaya Polyana by August 14, the date on which Tolstoy wrote his brother: "I especially want to see you and find out that everything is fine, because five days ago I saw [something] so terrible and lifelike in a dream that I can't forget it. When we see each other, I'll tell it to you."[‡] This reminds me of the scene when Anna tells Vronsky *her* frightening dream, and she manages to terrify him more than she ever did by any other action:

> "[. . .] I have had a dream."
>
> "A dream?" repeated Vronsky, and instantly he recalled the peasant of his dream.
>
> "Yes, a dream," she said. "It's a long while since I dreamed it. I dreamed that I ran into my bedroom, that I had to get something there, to find out

---

*   Gusev, *Materials*, 169.

†   Tolstoy, *Tolstoy Remembered by His Son*, 22.

‡   *PSS* 62: 104.

something; you know how it is in dreams," she said, her eyes wide with horror; "and in the bedroom, in the corner, stood something."

"Oh, what nonsense! How can you believe . . . "

But she would not let him interrupt her. What she was saying was too important to her.

"And the something turned round, and I saw it was a peasant with a disheveled beard, little, and dreadful looking. I wanted to run away, but he bent down over a sack, and was fumbling there with his hands . . ."

She showed how he had moved his hands. There was terror in her face. And Vronsky, remembering his dream, felt the same terror filling his soul.

"He was fumbling and kept talking quickly, quickly in French, you know: *Il faut le battre, le fer, le brayer, le petrir.* . . . And in my horror I tried to wake up, and woke up . . . but woke up in the dream. And I began asking myself what it meant. And Korney said to me: 'In childbirth you'll die, ma'am, you'll die. . . .' And I woke up."

"What nonsense, what nonsense!" said Vronsky; but he felt himself that there was no conviction in his voice. [*]

Dreams resonate throughout *Anna Karenina*, but we will never know what terrible dream it was that Tolstoy intended to tell his brother.

---

[*] *Anna Karenina*, Part 4, Chapter 3, http://literatureproject.com/anna-karenina/anna_104.htm.

6

For Love or Money?: August 15–December 31, 1874

✳

By August 15 Tolstoy was conducting business and catching up with friends, but for the next two weeks there was no mention of trying to resume *Anna Karenina*.

He told Sofia his "On Popular Education" article was ready for publication; he would be paid 150 rubles a "sheet" in the September or October issue.* "Tolstoy also thanked the editor of *Notes of the Fatherland* for his readiness to help him in his fight with the pedagogues," writes Gusev, "and concluded his letter with the words: 'I firmly believe that if the editorial office turns its serious attention on this question, that it will become absolutely aligned with my point of view.' Nekrasov without delay answered his agreement to all of the conditions."†

As for Tolstoy's statement that "the editorial office" would certainly agree with him, this was not his rhetorical trick for confirming solidarity with his views but his customary attitude. He always believed what he said and always agreed, if just for the moment, with his own arguments. It was typical for Tolstoy to argue like so: "If you really think about it, you'll finally draw the very same conclusions that I have drawn."

---

* Each *sheet* was cut into 16 pages. In 1904, for an English complete works edition of Tolstoy, the Harvard professor Leo Wiener translated almost the entire article (seventy-two pages). Wiener skipped only the four-page *Notes of the Fatherland* introduction, which contains Tolstoy's contemporary justification for the article. If we round up the pages to *eighty*, Nekrasov would have paid Tolstoy 750 rubles.

† Gusev, *Letopis'*, 169.

Even if he should have been working on *Anna Karenina* instead, Tolstoy's essay is one of the most stirring works on education ever published. He brings us to think about the fundamentals of education; he shows us why we ought to question any system or trend or fad.

In the introduction, he explains that the transcription of his remarks as provided him by the committee was mistaken; he also makes excuses for why his method did not prove its superiority, among them that his method required ten- and eleven-year-olds, not younger or older students, as well as that the school was "stuffy," and that, furthermore, Popotov, his opponent and the proponent of the sound-method, in fact used Tolstoy's methods and Tolstoy's *Azbuka*!

Strakhov and Sofia were still disappointed that he was not writing the more important *Anna Karenina*, but all his many writing gears were meshing. His nonfictional exposition was at its usual height of brilliance. As a critic, Tolstoy's vision showed him huge holes and fault lines in his opponents' arguments, and he almost always had the confidence in himself to offer remedies:

> Should I teach according to the sound alphabet, translated from the German, or from the prayer book? In the solution of this question I was aided by a certain pedagogical tact, with which I am gifted, and especially by that close and impassioned relation in which I stood to the matter.
>
> . . . because compulsion in education, both by my conviction and by my character, are repulsive to me, I did not exercise any pressure, and, the moment I noticed that something was not readily received, I did not compel them, and looked for something else. . . .
>
> . . . Consequently, the question of what the criterion was as to what to teach and how to teach received an even greater meaning for me; only by solving it could I be convinced that what I taught was neither injurious nor useless. This question both then and now has appeared to me as a cornerstone of the whole pedagogy, and to the solution of this question I devoted the publication of the pedagogical periodical *Yasnaya Polyana*. In several articles (I do not renounce anything I then said) I tried to put the question in all its significance and to solve it as much as I could. At that time I found no sympathy in all the pedagogical literature, not even any contradiction, but the most complete indifference to the question which I put. There were some attacks on certain details and trifles, but the question itself evidently did not interest anyone. I was young then, and that indifference grieved me. I did not understand that

with my question, "How do you know what to teach and how to teach?" I was like a man who, let us say, in a gathering of Turkish pashas discussing the question in what manner they may collect the greatest revenue from the people, should propose to them the following: "Gentlemen, in order to know how much revenue to collect from each, we must first analyze the question on what your right to exact that revenue is based." Obviously all the pashas would continue their discussion of the measures of extortion, and would reply only with silence to his irrelevant question.

This example, so effortless and vivid, reminds us that Tolstoy may be the greatest master of metaphor since Homer. The images are natural, immediate, none too worked over, the genius mind revealed at its moment of making connections. And it's *funny*! The point is so serious, however, that Tolstoy doesn't let up:

> But the question cannot be circumvented. Fifteen years ago no attention was paid to it, and the pedagogues of every school, convinced that everybody else was talking to the wind and that they were right, most calmly prescribed their laws, basing their principles on philosophies of a very doubtful character, which they used as a substratum for their wee little theories.
>
> And yet, this question is not quite so difficult if we only renounce completely all preconceived notions. I have tried to elucidate and solve this question, and, without repeating those proofs, which he who wishes may read in the article, I will enunciate the results to which I was led. "The only criterion of pedagogy is freedom, the only method—experience." After fifteen years I have not changed my opinion one hair's breadth . . .*

As a student under the direction of tutors and professors, Tolstoy was a Samson who burst whatever bonds anyone put on him. In Kazan in the early 1840s, the brilliant adolescent Tolstoy could not be compelled to read what he was told to read, but he read passionately anything that attracted him. He would not follow the mandated course of studies. Having switched fields of study a few times, he dropped out of the university.

By the time he began writing *Anna Karenina*, Tolstoy had been teaching his own children for several years. Despite having hired tutors for them, he kept teaching. For the

---

*   "On Popular Education," in *Tolstoy on Education*, trans. Leo Wiener (Chicago: University of Chicago Press, 1972), 286–289.

most part, his children fondly remembered those lessons, but his eldest daughter, Tatyana, described one of his failures:

> The hardest lessons of all were the arithmetic ones with papa. Outside the schoolroom I was never particularly in awe of him and even played with him sometimes in a way my brothers would never have dared. But during our arithmetic lessons he was a stern, impatient master. I knew that the slightest hesitation on my part would make him start to get angry, raise his voice, and reduce me to a state of total idiocy.[*]

Hence most of us teachers send our children to school. We need separation; we need a different relationship, a "formal" one to give us and our children space and freedom. There might have to be some abstraction to teach others, and parents and children have a built-in *lack* of abstraction; we flow into each other.

Tolstoy knew this about himself: he had to be excited and interested and curious about his subject to be able to teach it. He knew that this was true of others, including Anna, when we find her explaining to Levin, in Part 7, Chapter 11, to Levin's complete sympathy, why her venture into girls' education did not pan out:

> "I was just telling Anna Arkadyevna," said Vorkuev [a publisher], "that if she were to put a hundredth part of the energy she devotes to this English girl to the public question of the education of Russian children, she would be doing a great and useful work."
>
> "Yes, but I can't help it; I couldn't do it. Count Alexey Kirillovitch [i.e., Vronsky] urged me very much" (as she uttered the words Count Alexey Kirillovitch she glanced with appealing timidity at Levin, and he unconsciously responded with a respectful and reassuring look); "he urged me to take up the school in the village. I visited it several times. The children were very nice, but I could not feel drawn to the work. You speak of energy. Energy rests upon love; and come as it will, there's no forcing it. I took to this child [the English girl Hannah]—I could not myself say why."

---

[*]   Tolstoy, *Tolstoy Remembered*, 133. We see Tolstoy illustrate a similar scene involving Maria and her father, Prince Bolkonsky, in *War and Peace* (Part 1, Chapter 22), with not a trace of sympathy for the overbearing, short-tempered prince.

And she glanced again at Levin. And her smile and her glance—all told him that it was to him only she was addressing her words, valuing his good opinion, and at the same time sure beforehand that they understood each other.

"I quite understand that," Levin answered. "It's impossible to give one's heart to a school or such institutions in general, and I believe that's just why philanthropic institutions always give such poor results."

She was silent for a while, then she smiled.

"Yes, yes," she agreed; "I never could. *Je n'ai pas le coeur assez large* [I don't have a big enough heart] to love a whole asylum of horrid little girls. *Cela ne m'a jamais reussi* [I could never work like that]. There are so many women who have made themselves *une position sociale* in that way. And now more than ever," she said with a mournful, confiding expression, ostensibly addressing her brother, but unmistakably intending her words only for Levin, "now when I have such need of some occupation, I cannot." And suddenly frowning (Levin saw that she was frowning at herself for talking about herself) she changed the subject.[*]

By the time Tolstoy wrote that scene, sometime late in 1876, he had renounced the confident opinions he expressed in "On Popular Education."

He had been hoping for and expecting a strong response on its publication, hence his requirement that Nekrasov publish it within two months.

To continue with Tolstoy's busy August 15, he wrote Golokhvastov to ask him to thank Madame Golokhvastova for her help in trying to find the Tolstoy children a governess and, by the way, he was passing along to Golokhvastov *Anna Karenina*, "as much as isn't hateful,"[†] to read through for corrections. (Imagine Johannes Vermeer in 1658 writing a friend to come over to look at his painting of a young woman pouring water from a pitcher, or at least glance at as much of it as "isn't hateful.")

He wrote to Alexandrine to thank her for her help in having found him and Sofia a Swiss governess and also to tell her the latest about his money-draining farm in Samara:

> [. . .] This year there was a very abundant harvest throughout the whole Samara province, and, as far as I know, the only place in the whole Samara province that was missed by the rains was my estate, and I had again sowed

---

[*] *Anna Karenina*, Part 7, Chapter 10, http://www.literatureproject.com/anna-kareninaanna_199.htm.

[†] *PSS* 62: 105.

> a big area and again suffered a big loss. I went there and couldn't believe my eyes, and I felt hurt, as though I'd been put in the corner when I'd done nothing wrong. [. . .]*

We should be grateful that his financial losses in Samara may have compelled him to keep writing *Anna Karenina*. But perhaps he felt some cynicism about the novel for its being driven, in part, by financial considerations.

Finally, he wrote his sister about their financial business and asked for *her* help in finding a classically educated governess who could speak French or German.†

At the end of August he traveled with his sister-in-law Tatyana to the D'yakovs' Cheremosh estate. What a sociable man! But is it the way Tolstoy writes—from his own singular viewpoint—that makes us forget how sociable he was? In *Anna Karenina*, even as singular and isolated as Levin sometimes seems, old friends and acquaintances pop up everywhere, at every turn. Levin knows the peasants, the officials, the real estate sharks, *everybody*. Tolstoy was not a writer who sat in his den and rarely ventured forth. His writing, at times, was simply a duty, not the task that defined him. That is why there can be so many autobiographical details in common between him and Levin. Levin himself is working on a big, long complicated book on Russian farming that he too keeps finding excuses to break off from. Where Tolstoy and Levin most importantly do differ is that Tolstoy could create Levin, but Levin could not have dreamed up Tolstoy.

Tolstoy sent "On Popular Education" to *Notes of the Fatherland* on August 30, with instructions to send the corrected copy to Strakhov. He worried to Nekrasov that the censor would get at it. In fact it escaped censorship and suffered no changes.

The same day, he anxiously wrote to Strakhov to ask him if he would have time to look over the essay's galleys for corrections. He had to apologize as well for not having responded to Strakhov's last letter because, "Believe me, ever since that day I haven't had a free minute. I only just got back from Samara, where there was an amazing event: there was growth everywhere, except for mine; I had to go to Novosil'skiy District in the south, to buy more land! ["How Much Land Does a Tolstoy Need?" could have been the title of this unfateful trip], and then I returned and found a house full of guests [the Kuzminskiys and Golokhvastovs], and only yesterday I saw off the difficult guests and felt the freedom of thought. It's a terrible shame I missed

---

the chance of seeing you. I'll try to arrange this trip to Petersburg in winter, which for various circumstances I might need to do."[*]

Strakhov always accommodated Tolstoy's requests, and yet writing to Strakhov for favors also seemed to require that Tolstoy update his admiring friend with apologies and, usually, excuses about the state of *Anna Karenina*: "My novel's not moving, but thanks to you I believe that it's worth finishing, and I hope to do so this year."[†]

Somewhere near September 9, according to Gusev, Tolstoy went to Moscow on his continued hunt for a governess; he also brought a manuscript copy of *Anna Karenina* to the *Notes of the Fatherland*'s printer and asked that the typeset copy be sent to Strakhov.[‡] Had Tolstoy been sneaking in some work on *Anna Karenina*? Was it brand-new revised work that he brought to the printer or was it what was left over from his attempts to work on it during and immediately after Strakhov's July visit? I'm inclined to believe that it was old material Tolstoy wanted to see freshly in type. Neither he nor Sofia mentioned him having done any writing on it, and after all Gusev says the purpose of the trip was not the delivery of the manuscript but the hiring of a governess.

But can we imagine Tolstoy interviewing potential governesses? Wherever the meetings in Moscow took place, Tolstoy could have interviewed French, English, Swiss, or German women in their native languages, and even if they knew he was a well-known writer in Russia, they would have had no idea of the future worldwide stature of this intense gray-eyed man. Was he alarmingly serious? Awkward? Stiva Oblonsky, we know, would be eyeing them for a potential liaison. Tolstoy would not have seriously thought of philandering with his daughters' governess, would he?

He also saw P. M. Leont'ev at the *Russian Herald* about the novel and about his desire to receive the payment ahead of publication, a negotiation that, according to Gusev, was not settled, but Tolstoy needed the money.

On September 10, he wrote Strakhov to ask him if it was okay to have the corrected copy of the new *Anna Karenina* chapters sent to him. "I wait with impatience and agitation for your answer," he wrote, though he couldn't have doubted Strakhov would do it, as he had already asked the printer to send it to his friend. "I don't dare ask you to set the compensation, but if you could set it, I would count myself even more obliged to you. You encouraged me to publish and finish this novel, and you're saving it from disfigurement."

Of course Strakhov came through again, but there is no evidence in their correspondence of Strakhov actually being financially compensated by Tolstoy.

In mid-September "On Popular Education" came out. Strakhov would write from St. Petersburg: "The noise from your article is tremendous."[*]

Tolstoy was happy with the noisy article. Through "On Popular Education," he "established thinking on pedagogical questions," says Gusev, "even among people that never before thought about them."[†]

Tolstoy wrote to Fet that he had been buying mares and that he and Sofia were leaving for the D'yakovs' the next day and that he would go hunting with Obolenskii. As for *Anna Karenina*, Tolstoy announced, "That Tolstoy who writes novels has still not come, and I expect him with particular impatience. He's also a downcast person."[‡]

Even when he was gloomy, going hunting invigorated him, and he hunted wolves during the September 17–24 week at the D'yakovs'. There are, curiously, no wolves or any wolf-hunting expeditions in *Anna Karenina*.

Strakhov sent him a letter that must have been awaiting him when he returned to Yasnaya Polyana. It continued a plea that the world's readers would have joined in had they only known: "Write, write, inestimable Lev Nikolaevich! This is my primary request."[§]

Tolstoy's annual fall excuses for not working on *Anna Karenina* popped up whenever he mentioned the novel at all. Sofia didn't understand or believe his excuses; Strakhov was more sympathetic about his difficulties with resuming work but also more emphatic about his need to do so anyway.

Tolstoy didn't see it as making excuses. He needed to know what life's purpose was. He describes this philosophical dilemma in *Confession*:

> Before occupying myself with my Samara estate, the education of my son, or the writing of a book, I had to know *why* I was doing it. As long as I did not know why, I could do nothing and could not live. Amid the thoughts of estate management which greatly occupied me at that time, the question would suddenly occur: "Well, you will have 6,000 desyatinas[¶] of land in Samara Government [district] and 300 horses, and what then? . . ." And I was quite

---

[*]   Donskov, *L. N. Tolstoy – N. N. Strakhov*, 186, November 8, 1874.

[†]   Gusev, *Materials*, 174–175.

[‡]   *PSS* 62: 112, letter of September 12–16, 1874.

[§]   Donskov, *L. N. Tolstoy – N. N. Strakhov*, 180, September 22, 1874.

[¶]   Footnote by Aylmer Maude: The desyatina is about 2.75 acres.

disconcerted and did not know what to think. Or when considering plans for the education of my children, I would say to myself: "What for?" Or when considering how the peasants might become prosperous, I would suddenly say to myself: "But what does it matter to me?" Or when thinking of the fame my works would bring me, I would say to myself, "Very well; you will be more famous than Gogol or Pushkin or Shakespeare or Molière, or than all the writers in the world—and what of it?"

And I could find no reply at all.[*]

Tolstoy knew but didn't mention in *Confession* that part of the "What of it?" of writing *Anna Karenina* was because he wanted the money. When he was down in the dumps, he, like many people, bought things. (He never mentions *Anna Karenina* by name in the final draft of *Confession*. He deleted his one mention of it from a draft when he published the tract in 1882, as if it were the name of an old shameful liaison.)

His vacation at the D'yakovs' did not settle him down enough to work on the novel. On September 26, he wrote to Strakhov: "I am out of sorts with tasks and the children, for whom we still don't have teachers[†], and (my) health, and so I look at this novel as if at someone else's business."[‡]

In mid-October, he requested the Krapivensky regional school board to supply teachers for the new peasant schools. At the end of October he resumed work on a grammar book for the schools.

When Tolstoy wrote to Fet it was to apologize for not having answered Fet's last letter; he wanted to go visit him, but he had been busy with farm business, the schools, and his family. He also needed to ask his friend for a loan: "An indispensable purchase of land in Nikolskoe has come up, for which I must borrow ten thousand for a year on the security of the land. It may be, perhaps, that you have money that you have to invest."[§] As Tolstoy seemed to half-expect, Fet turned him down.

Craving sympathy, Tolstoy explained in a letter to his relative Alexandrine how overwhelmed he was:

---

[*]   *Confession,* Chapter 3, 16–17.

[†]   He also complained to Golokhvastov on the 25th or 26th that they still didn't have a governess or master. See *PSS* 62: 114.

[‡]   *PSS* 62: 115, letter of September 26, 1874.

[§]   Eikhenbaum, *Tolstoi in the Seventies,* 117–118, letter of October 22, 1874.

I have not answered you [. . .] for so long because the more I live the more I feel that I'm turning like a squirrel in a wheel, and there is less and less time. There is so much bustle, worry, business, activities, which keep me from you.

You, probably, feel the same, even without a family.

My novel, really, is starting printing. But it is surely going to take four months, and I do not have the time to continue correcting it. Besides bringing up and teaching the children, whom I occupy myself with (and with remorse, I think, when I gave them paid teachers), besides work (I am writing—you will be amazed—a grammar); besides school business, which I teach in my school and in the district, and fights with members, money business (the purchase of land, which was necessary), besides all of this, the family adversity. My wife was feverish while breastfeeding, which is her torment, and a few days ago, my oldest daughter was running to me on the parquet, and tumbled, and broke her collarbone. But we only now have begun to think about and worry about the fractures. The striking of her head was so strong that the doctor and we were frightened for her life and sanity.—It is true that the autumn is always a heavy time for me. I hope that when the snows begin falling on us, I will write again of that happy situation of peace, the hard growth of life that I so love.*

A parent's life is fraught, and Tanya's accident (dated by Sofia as October 27) would continue to cause anxiety for another two weeks.

Sofia's account of Tanya's accident is more scattered but more medically observant and detailed:

> . . . I was sitting downstairs in the children's room and breastfeeding Nikolushka when all of a sudden someone came running up, saying that Tanja had fallen on the parquet floor and severely injured herself. I ran upstairs. Tanja had just been lifted up and laid down {on a bed}. She was cross-eyed and her face looked frightening. She soon began vomiting.
>
> Tanja had been sliding over the parquet as though on ice-skates, in her silly Tula boots with copper heels (as was the cheap provincial fashion of the time), and had fallen flat on her back. These boots had been bought on impulse, as we always bought footwear for both ourselves and the children at Shumakher's in

---

* *PSS* 62: 118, letter of October 29, 1874.

Moscow. And in this case, as though on purpose, nobody had been to Moscow for a long time, and a servant had picked up these clogs in Tula.

When the vomiting started, I realised right off that there had been a concussion of the brain, and we sent for Doctor Knertser, who had always treated our family, and while waiting for him we applied ice to her head. Upon his arrival the doctor also ordered us to place leeches behind her ears. By nighttime she was running a high fever and showing signs of delirium.

I can no longer describe the horror we went through that night. I recall my hands shaking and my heart pounding as I took a leech in a towel and tried to place it in the exact spot the doctor had indicated.

Apart from the concussion of the brain, the doctor also found a fracture in the left collarbone and applied a bandage.[*]

The only good news of the time was that on October 29, the Teaching Committee of the People's Ministry approved for school use the *New Azbuka*, which was now on its way to continuous success.[†]

While still at Yasnaya Polyana Tolstoy wrote to Golokhvastov:

We're tormented with bustle, worries, but mainly illnesses in the family: now the wife, now the children. My daughter Tanya a week ago fell on the back of her head on the parquet and was near death. Now she is out of danger, but her collarbone is broken and tomorrow I'm taking her to Moscow. [. . .] As for the novel, I am not working on it.[‡]

In sum, he was busy with everything except *Anna Karenina*.

"From letters of 1874 one might think that *Anna Karenina* had been abandoned forever," calmly observes the Soviet critic Boris Eikhenbaum. "But early in November, during a sojourn in Moscow, the thought of printing the novel appears anew. From all indications the cause of this new decision was simply the need of money."[§] Though Anna's fate is unavoidable, the fate of the novel seems to have come down to fluky circumstances; if Tolstoy hadn't needed the money, he may well have given up on *Anna Karenina* as he

---

[*]   Tolstaya, *My Life*, 206.

[†]   Gusev, *Letopis'*, 428.

[‡]   *PSS* 62: 119–120, letter of November 1–2, 1874.

[§]   Eikhenbaum, *Tolstoi in the Seventies*, 117–118.

had on the Peter the Great epic. Perhaps Sofia was nudging him, reminding him: *We're strapped for cash! Levochka, write the novel!*

Catching up on correspondence, apologetic, he wrote Strakhov:

> I'm guilty only that you are doing so much for me. But this guilt you can for-
> give, because I so highly value your help. I'm also guilty that I'm not sending
> you the corrections of the novel. I cannot, and I cannot take it up. [. . .] My
> cares now are the family—all of them one after the other, children, wife, are
> sick, and financial business. I have to buy the land surrounding my estate
> and I need to borrow money, and petition the courts, and raise the children
> (for six months we haven't been able to find a governess and tutor), and the
> Krapivensky district schools [. . .]

He went on to describe his duties as a school board member and the preparations he had needed to do for the *New Azbuka*, which would come out at the end of May 1875. In Moscow, he said, where he was going with his daughter the next day, he needed to negotiate with the *Russian Herald* for *Anna Karenina* at 500 rubles a printer's sheet and a 10,000-ruble advance that he needed for his land purchase.[*]

Sofia remembered that on November 4, "Once Tanja had recovered, got up and was in fairly good spirits, Lev Nikolaevich took her along with the Englishwoman [Emily Tabor, the governess] to see a fine surgeon in Moscow, who set the bone [. . .]"[†]

Imagine them on the train: Tolstoy trying to cheer up Tanya. Perhaps he made small talk in English with Emily. With his wife ill, his daughter injured, and his mind as preoc-cupied as Stiva's in his quest for money, did he listen to Tanya and Emily's English chatter? During Tolstoy's days in Moscow he was on a quest to raise money and sell a novel that he didn't want to write, but he had to comfort Tanya and have her looked after.

When they returned from Moscow on November 7, Tolstoy resumed his correspon-dence about selling the novel.

Sofia wrote her sister that despite their tight circumstances, it had become neces-sary to pay debts; they had decided to cut down the Zakaz wood near Yasnaya Polyana and sell it. This is one more instance where it is useful to remind ourselves that there is something of Tolstoy in Stiva Oblonsky, the spendthrift who always needs more

---

[*]   *PSS* 62: 121, letter of November 3, 1874.

[†]   Tolstaya, *My Life*, 206.

money—including, to his embarrassment, needing to sell off a portion of his wife's inherited property.* Sofia also told her sister:

> Levochka is selling his novel in a magazine, is asking for 500 rubles a sheet, and they will probably give it. But he doesn't occupy himself with it; he passionately takes up the school and is busy with all the business; I almost never see him, either he's in the school, or on the hunt, or downstairs in his room with the teachers, whom he teaches how to teach.[†]

On that same day, Tolstoy, while in negotiations with Katkov at the *Russian Herald*, also offered the novel to Nekrasov's *Notes from the Fatherland*:

> A need for ten thousand has forced me to retreat from my intention to print my novel in book form. I considered myself bound by an accidentally given promise to *Russky vestnik* [the *Russian Herald*] to publish it with them, if I did decide to publish in a magazine, and therefore made them an offer to give their magazine twenty printer's sheets of my novel,[‡] at the rate of 500 rubles per sheet and payment to me of ten thousand in advance, with the commitment, in case I did not turn in the manuscript within a specified time, to repay this money, and with the right to print the novel separately after the publication of the last parts in the magazine. They began to haggle, and I was very glad that by this they freed me of my promise. I am now making the same offer to you, informing you beforehand that I will not yield from my stated terms, and at the same time, knowing that the terms offered by me are difficult for a magazine, I will not be at all surprised if you do not accept them, and your refusal will in no way, I hope, change those good relations that I have again entered into with you. The novel will probably consist of forty printer's sheets. The printing of the conclusion, whether in your magazine or separately, will depend on our future agreement.[§]

---

*   *PSS* 62: 112, letter of November 8, 1874.

†   Gusev, *Materials*, 190, letter of November 8, 1874.

‡   He had now for the first time realistically estimated (though still *short*) the size of the novel—about 640 pages.

§   Eikhenbaum, *Tolstoi in the Seventies*, 118, letter of November 8, 1874.

The Jubilee editors say that Tolstoy did not send this letter to Nekrasov, but if that's true, how did Nekrasov know the terms Tolstoy was asking for? On that same day, Nekrasov wrote to Tolstoy agreeing to Tolstoy's conditions for the novel . . . but it was too late!* The *Russian Herald* after all agreed to all of Tolstoy's terms and would pay him 20,000 rubles to publish the entire novel in the magazine and grant Tolstoy some leeway about missing deadlines.

Strakhov, concerned about Tolstoy's negotiations with the *Russian Herald*, squawked:

> Your intention to sell the novel to *Russky vestnik* disturbs me very much: I have a foreboding that you will not come to an agreement. *Russky vestnik* has too few subscribers and from their dealings with Dostoevsky I know how stingy they are. And did not Nekrasov start negotiations with you? He asked me to make you an offer and even to help him out, "since Tolstoi is a self-willed person; he very likely will be obstinate." I was in no hurry to write you about this, knowing that Nekrasov himself is in correspondence with you; as far as concerns my persuading you in his favor—I do not want to.[†]

Strakhov's foreboding was mistimed and slightly misplaced. Tolstoy's troubles with Katkov, the editor at the *Russian Herald*, would only come to a head three years later with the Epilogue (Part 8) of the novel, which Katkov would refuse to print. But Strakhov's main point in this letter was his praise of *Anna Karenina*: "I return to your novel. As usual with me, the more I read the more I begin loving and understanding it. How charming—the scene of Levin's declaration of love! The scholarly conversation of Levin's brother—also inimitable! How fresh all this is, new and endlessly true and sharp! The conversation in the restaurant seemed to me a little long. Of course, that does not matter, as it still has all your worthy skill."[‡]

When Tolstoy wrote his brother Sergei sometime shortly after his return with Tanya from Moscow, he did not seem relieved of his worries, responsibilities, or gloominess: "We could die soon and in that world God knows whether we'll see each other again."[§]

For most of November, Tolstoy, though now contractually obligated to write, remained uninspired about resuming the novel.

---

* Gusev, *Letopis'*, 430.

† Eikhenbaum, *Tolstoi in the Seventies*, 118, letter of November 8, 1874.

‡ Donskov, *L. N. Tolstoy – N. N. Strakhov*; web.ru/feb/tolstoy/texts/selectpe/ts6/ts62185-.htm.

§ *PSS* 62: 125.

Sofia wrote her brother Stepan: "Levochka has gone completely into public education, schools, teacher training, that is where he will teach the teachers for public schools, and all this occupies him from morning to night. I with confusion look at all this, I'm concerned for his strength, which he spends on these activities, and not on writing the novel. And I don't understand how far this is useful, as far as all this action is extended over a little corner of Russia—Krapivensky Uezd."*

In retrospect, Sofia's completely reasonable concern was needless. Gusev suggests that Tolstoy found her concerns easy to ignore, but without her anxious pressure, would Tolstoy have definitely returned to the novel?

In the midst of training teachers, of planning for the district schools, of going hunting, it's impossible to tell if he was also reconceptualizing *Anna Karenina*.

Besides the first dozen or so chapters that he would send the *Russian Herald* on January 4, 1875, he had hundreds of pages of very rough drafts. He was avoiding the grind of the novel—but not other hard work.

In her search for occupation, Tolstoy's heroine will eventually expend her energy writing a children's novel; perhaps in his search for occupation, Tolstoy spent his energy on *not* writing a novel.

Sofia wrote her sister Tatyana: "The novel is not being written, but letters are showering us from all the editors: ten thousand before and five hundred silver rubles per sheet. Levochka doesn't speak about this, and it's as if the business doesn't touch him."† She went on: "Never mind the money, it's his vocation, writing the novels, which I love, value, and feel so enthusiastic about, while these ABCs, arithmetics, and grammars I despise . . . What's lacking in my life now is Lyovochka's work, which I always enjoyed and admired. You see, Tanya, I am a true writer's wife, so close to my heart do I keep our creative work."‡

Tolstoy was avoiding confiding in or explaining to Sofia his difficulties with the novel.

On the 11th of December Tolstoy again went to Moscow to look for tutors for his children; he also saw Katkov about the novel.§

Ten days later he sent Katkov a piece of the manuscript via his nephew. Tolstoy told the editor that he would send more "tomorrow, or at the latest the day after tomorrow,"⁵ but

---

*   Gusev, *Materials*, 190, letter of November 20, 1874.

†   *PSS* 20: 615, letter of December 10, 1874.

‡   Popoff, *Sofia Tolstoy: A Biography*, 80.

§   Gusev, *Letopis'*, 431.

⁵   *PSS* 62: 128, letter of December 21, 1874.

he does not seem to have done so. Katkov would have to get used to Tolstoy's many missed deadlines, but the novel would indeed begin coming out at the very end of January 1875.

In his December letter to Alexandrine, we see that Tolstoy continued to avoid working on the novel:

> [. . .] You say that we are like a squirrel in a wheel. Of course. But you mustn't say it or think it. I, at least, whatever I do, am always convinced that *du haut de ces pyramides, 40 siecles me contemplent* [from the top of these pyramids, 40 centuries contemplate me], and that the whole world will perish if I come to a stop.*

What a wonderful image of energizing vanity! I *must*! I have a quest! I am important! He had used this phrase in reference to Napoleon's self-admiration in *War and Peace*, and though Tolstoy despised Napoleon, he understood his vanity. We can believe that Tolstoy, when he wasn't badmouthing himself, really did feel himself on the heights, obliged to complete his work, whether it was the novel or, as he preferred for the moment, plans for revamping education:

> True, an imp sits there winking and saying that it's all just threshing the water, but I don't let him have his way, and you mustn't, either. [. . .] I've now moved over entirely from abstract pedagogics to a matter which is on the one hand practical and on the other hand very abstract—the matter of schools in our district. And I've again taken a great liking, as I did fourteen years ago, to the thousands of children that I'm concerned with. I ask everyone why we want to educate the people; and there are five answers. Tell me your answer when you have a chance. This is mine. I don't reason about it, but when I enter a school and see this crowd of ragged, dirty, skinny children with their bright eyes and often angelic expressions, alarm and terror come over me, not unlike what I'd feel at seeing people drowning. Ah, goodness me!—how can I pull them out, and who should I pull out first and who next? And what is drowning here is what is most precious—just the very spiritual qualities that strike one so obviously in children. I want education for the people simply in order to save those drowning Pushkins, Ostrogradskys, Filarets, and Lomonsovs. Every school is teeming with them. [. . .]†

---

*   Christian, *Tolstoy's Letters*, 273, December 23?, 1874.

†   Ibid.

As touching as his image of saving the drowning children is, his letter is still only a clever excuse for not working on *Anna Karenina*. He wanted *this* reason to be the primary reason, but he himself couldn't love "thousands of children." He will soon have Anna herself say so to Levin.* There is no one that Tolstoy liked who is an abstraction.

Tolstoy concluded his letter to Alexandrine, again trying to justify his lack of movement with *Anna Karenina*:

> I've promised to publish my novel in the *Russian Herald*, but so far I've been quite unable to tear myself away from living people in order to devote myself to imaginary ones.[†]

Tolstoy was feeling as if *Anna Karenina* would be taking him away from his real work, his good work—and how could one justify making art in the presence of "drowning children"? Why shouldn't one sacrifice making art for the sake of "the people"?

But with the deadline coming and the money needed, he finally had to work on the novel. He dashed off a brief letter to Strakhov:

> [. . .] I've delivered my novel to Katkov (verbally[‡]), and your advice to do so made me decide. As it was, I was hesitating. I'm still busy with the Primer, a Grammar, and the schools in the district, and I haven't the heart to get down to the novel. However, I must do so now, since I've promised. [. . .][§]

---

* *Anna Karenina*, Part 7, Chapter 10, http://literatureproject.com/anna-karenina/anna _199.htm.

† Christian, *Tolstoy's Letters*, 273. Meanwhile, Gusev shows us that Tolstoy liked this argument about the would-be "Pushkins": "This very view about the goal of the school Tolstoy expressed in a letter to S. A. Rachinskiy on April 5, 1877: 'These children have to be taught in order to give them a plank of salvation out of that ocean of ignorance in which they're floating and no salvation—they, maybe, swim better than we—but such equipment as a means of which they reach to our shore, if they want. I could not and cannot enter a school in relation to the little ones and not experience straight away a physical disturbance, as if I had seen Lomonosov, Pushkin, Glinka, Ostrogradskiy and not recognized what they need.'" *Materials*, 192.

‡ I'm unhappy with R. F. Christian's translation of "verbally" (Christian, *Tolstoy's Letters*, 272); I would rephrase that as "I gave Katkov (on my word) the novel." Cf. *PSS* 62: 128: "Я отдал (на словах) роман Каткову."

§ Christian, *Tolstoy's Letters*, 272, December 23, 1874.

Sofia remembered: "The year ended very quietly. For the holidays we had a family Christmas tree party which included the servants' and peasants' children. [. . .] All the presents and toys Lev Nikolaevich bought in Moscow, where he went not long before Christmas."*

This means that on December 11, in the midst of negotiations about the novel and searching for teachers, Tolstoy was also toy shopping for his children. Today, visitors to Yasnaya Polyana and the Tolstoy house-museum in Moscow can't help noticing the abundance of charming children's toys on display in the bedrooms. The biographer Rosamund Bartlett says, however, that Tolstoy "was not at all keen on toys, which were banished from the nursery, forcing Sonya to produce horses and dogs out of cardboard, and sew rag-dolls herself so the children had something to play with." She adds: "Christmas in Russia was about the only time the Tolstoy children were allowed toys. Tanya in particular cherished the dolls her godfather Dmitry Alexeyevich [D'yakov] gave her . . ."† I believe that the evidence of the actual toys means the children did have plenty of toys and that Tolstoy had enjoyed shopping for them. (In December of 1872, Tolstoy told his sister-in-law Tatyana of their Christmas preparations, "toys everywhere in boxes,"‡ and of the children looking where they were *not* supposed to.)

Before New Year's Day, Tolstoy wrote to Fet, encouraging him to write and to visit. As for news, he told Fet that he and the family had had a tough winter, but, thank God, they had returned "to our normal life."§

---

*　Tolstaya, *My Life*, 207.

†　Bartlett, *Tolstoy: A Russian Life*, 203, 206.

‡　*PSS* 61: 350–351, letter of December 22, 1872.

§　*PSS* 62: 129, letter of December 28, 1874.

7

Anna Karenina: The Serial: January–June 1875

✳

"You and your novels—for already a long time are the best parts of my life."
—Nikolai Strakhov[*]

I n early January, Tolstoy opened the mail and read Strakhov's New Year's wishes: "There's nothing I so desire as that you work on your novel." Strakhov was in Petersburg having read (in galleys or manuscript, it's not clear) the first part of *Anna Karenina*, and he was marveling at it. "This image of passion in all its charm and in all its humiliation does not go out of my head. You didn't tell me or write whether it's true I understand your novel; but I understand it like so. Karenina is so sympathetic and good in her soul that the first exposure, the first signs of the fate awaiting her don't yet carry her away. She gives her whole soul to one desire—she gives herself to the devil, and there's no exit for her. You have an endless most original exhibition of passion. You don't idealize her or humiliate her, you are the *only fair* person, so that your Anna Karenina excites an endless pity for her and yet it's wholly clear that she is guilty. If I don't understand it right, please write me."

---

[*] Donskov, *L. N. Tolstoy – N. N. Strakhov*, 324, April 4–5, 1877.

Knowing his friend's tendencies to put off the artistic work for other projects, Strakhov added the nudge: "The most beneficial thing for the novel will be if it appears uninterrupted—how good that would be!"* Strakhov's advice was on the money (in the same letter he also complimented Tolstoy "on the money" that he was going to earn for the magazine publication).

On the other hand, we don't have to agree with Strakhov's judgment that Anna is "guilty." Quibbling over the English translation, if one translates his "*vinovata*" as "blameworthy" or "at fault," we could agree that she's to blame, *too*. She's partly at fault. But to blame for what? The novel, after all, is full of "I'm to blame" or "I'm guilty" statements, and yet each time it happens, we wonder and the characters wonder, "Is being to blame simply being oneself? I am I and *that's* my fault?" Tolstoy has Stiva provide us the first example of this philosophical quandary in Part 1, Chapter 1:

> "Ah, ah, ah! Oo! . . ." he muttered, recalling everything that had happened. And again every detail of his quarrel with his wife was present to his imagination, all the hopelessness of his position, and worst of all, his own fault.
>
> "Yes, she won't forgive me, and she can't forgive me. And the most awful thing about it is that it's all my fault—all my fault, though I'm not to blame. That's the point of the whole situation," he reflected.[†]

On January 4, Tolstoy wrote an excuse letter, without quite blaming himself, to editor Katkov: "I've been sick—and could only finish three sheets; I'll send the rest, I hope, in about three days."[‡] He probably did not send the rest in three days; he could have brought the rest ten days later when he took the train to Moscow and met with Katkov.[§]

Perhaps while he was in Moscow he wrote the lone letter to Sofia that survives from 1875. It was about the business he had been conducting, but he also mentioned that he was sick, hadn't eaten all day, and was suffering a migraine, the first migraine he had noted since a letter in 1867.

For the next several months, Tolstoy's attention would now and then be distracted from *Anna Karenina* by looking after the printing of the *New Azbuka*; his niece Varya's husband, Nagornov, continued serving as the business manager of that project.

---

*   Donskov, *L. N. Tolstoy – N. N. Strakhov*, 190, January 1, 1875. Or http://feb-web.ru/feb /tolstoy/texts/selectpe/ts6/ts62189-.htm.

†   *Anna Karenina*, Part 1, Chapter 1, http://literatureproject.com/anna-karenina/anna_1.htm.

‡   *PSS* 62: 132.

§   Gusev, *Letopis'*, 432.

At the end of January, simultaneously with the first installment of *Anna Karenina* appearing in the *Russian Herald*, Katkov's brother killed himself. Tolstoy wrote the editor a letter of condolence: "I only just heard, dear Mikhail Nikiforovich, about the unhappiness befallen you. Believe, from my entire soul, how I feel your woe and understand the heaviness of your loss. However rarely I met up with the deceased, I understood clearly how highly I valued him when I received this sad news. From my whole soul, I wish you the strength for moving beyond your woe and I ask you to believe in the sincerity of my feelings for you."*

He was properly sympathetic, but the timing did not seem to Tolstoy an ominous coincidence. There really had been a rash of suicides in Russia, and Katkov's brother had had a history of violence and mental illness. Soon this "trend" of suicide would only confirm for Tolstoy the presence of a universal despair.† In his own depression that would descend on him this year, the country's increasing number of suicides would make him wonder why there weren't more.

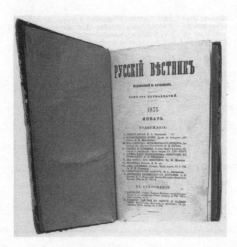

1875 cover of *Russkiy Vestnik*‡

---

* *PSS* 62: 135.

† "In his writing, Tolstoy was in some ways following a trend as it was just at this time that the incidence of suicide in Russia reached what has been described as epidemic proportions." Bartlett, *Tolstoy: A Russian Life*, 230.

‡ The caption by the State Museum of L. N. Tolstoy reads: "The journal *Russian Herald* with the first publication of Tolstoy's novel *Anna Karenina*." http://tolstoymuseum.ru/museums /funds/scarce_book.php.

The January issue of the *Russian Herald*, the first of 1875, came out on January 28. This was usual during Tolstoy's time (and common enough in ours in academic journals); that is, the publication date caught (or missed) the end rather than the beginning of the stated publishing month. The first installment of *Anna Karenina* contained Chapters 1–14 (1–23 in the book edition), which make up the first two-thirds of what we know as Part 1.

Can we imagine ourselves well-off educated Russians and that it's the middle of winter, 1875? There's a fat issue of the *Russian Herald* that has been delivered in the mail. Being bookish sorts, we're going to survey the table of contents (printed on the front). And yes, here, what we had heard rumors of, is the beginning of a novel by Lev Tolstoy!

Anna Karenina? The title indicates a heroine, not a theme like *War and Peace*.

Let's open to it!

There's an epigraph, which are usually so obscure, but this one looks plain enough: "Vengeance is Mine, and I will repay."

Vengeance? Who's going to pay back whom? Oh, right, the uppercase "Mine" means it's God Himself.

And now the first sentence: "Happy families are all alike; every unhappy family is unhappy in its own way."*

Is that true?

That is true!

Well, let's see if that's true.

It's the middle of winter. We can get away with reading these chapters before anybody else in the house gets his or her hands on the copy. And we do read them; it takes a couple of hours, but we, having just experienced one of the greatest literary pleasures of our lives, exclaim with wonder and want to start reading it all over again:

The confusion in the Oblonsky house. The kids running around like crazy. The servants looking for positions elsewhere. Stiva waking up to his sweet dream of attractive women dancing around and his hearing an operatic voice. Then he remembers why he has woken up in the wrong room. He recalls the scene of three nights ago when he came home and his wife confronted him with the love letter to him from his mistress, the children's ex-governess! He blames himself but also his, as if independent of him, *stupid smile*! How can we be so delighted by this rascal? But *everyone* in the novel who knows him is similarly charmed. He tries to restore to himself the pleasure he had in the dream, but duties call. He talks to his valet and sees his barber and reads his mail and telegrams, learning that his sister, Anna Karenina herself, has responded to his plea for help and will be arriving

---

* *Anna Karenina*, Part 1, Chapter 1, http://literatureproject.com/anna-karenina/anna_1.htm.

in Moscow from Petersburg the next day. He dresses and Tolstoy tells us something of Stiva's "liberal" political background and work habits.

Despite Stiva's waywardness as a husband, he is an effective government bureaucrat. We learn about his past; we'll eventually know more of his past probably than of any other character. As he eats breakfast he hears the clamor of his five children, and he betrays his favoritism for his eldest daughter over his eldest son; he queries his daughter Tanya about her mother's mood. He helps a woman with a bureaucratic request and, before leaving for the office, goes to see his wife, who is packing. Tolstoy, who will invariably be sympathetic to Dolly, shows us how miserable she is. She knows but Stiva doesn't that she and the children probably will *not* leave. Stiva tries to work his charm on her, but, out of guilt, he can't see his way to her forgiveness and even makes an uncharacteristic mistake of tactlessness about the affair, and Dolly becomes furious. She tells *him* to do the arranging for his sister's stay. We don't blame her at all . . . but we feel for Stiva.

At Stiva's office, a surprise visitor, Levin, arrives, all dressed up but with his nose out of joint. Levin is an old friend from university days who has come to Moscow to make a marriage proposal to Dolly's sister Kitty.

We learn of Levin's previous retreat from Moscow, when he had failed to propose to Kitty. After Levin agrees to meet Stiva later for a meal, Levin goes off to visit his academic, older half-brother, Sergei. From there Levin goes to see if he can find Kitty skating at the pond at the zoo, where Stiva will be meeting him. She is there, and he is overwhelmed with love for her; he skates with her and blurts out too clearly his hopes. She clams up. Confused, he goes off to eat with Stiva. Stiva bucks him up about Kitty, and Levin is soaring before Stiva brings him crashing to the earth with the news that Levin now has a rival: the likable, rich army captain Alexei Vronsky. When Levin goes to see Kitty that evening, her mother is leery of him, because she has hopes that Vronsky will propose to Kitty. When Levin proposes, Kitty apologetically tells him, "It can't be." Before Levin can flee in shame, Vronsky shows up. He has none of Levin's self-consciousness or modesty; he is not reflective, but he is bewildered by Kitty's father's contempt for him. The Levin-Vronsky rivalry is a sore spot between Kitty's parents. Kitty's mother is pleased, nevertheless, that Levin seems to be out of the picture now for good.

We learn of Vronsky's background. He is not a dishonest or bad man. He is confident but not quite arrogant; he has a conservative bent; he has an easy social manner. We follow Vronsky as he goes to the train station to meet his mother, about whom he doesn't allow himself to acknowledge his lack of respect for. And all of a sudden, stepping down from the train carriage in which his mother has ridden from Petersburg is a graceful, strikingly beautiful woman.

Anna Karenina strikes us and Vronsky the way a goddess would. After introductions all around (she has chatted with Madame Vronsky on the ride down), Anna starts to leave with Stiva, but there's been a terrible, ominous accident. A station worker has been crushed and killed by a train. Vronsky shows off his generosity before Anna and Stiva by leaving money for the worker's widow and family. Stiva takes Anna home, where Anna sits with Dolly and the children, winning all of them over. She then listens to Dolly's account of the situation with Stiva, and Anna sympathizes with *her*. Anna's sympathy opens up the possibility of reconciliation, and Stiva gets his chance to make up. Kitty, who is staying with Dolly, is infatuated by poised Anna's beauty and personal attention to her. Vronsky drops by the Oblonsky house one evening, but only Anna divines that it was to see her that he has happened to come over. At the ball that week, where Kitty expects Vronsky's proposal, Anna captivates him; Kitty realizes Vronsky isn't interested in her anymore and she is devastated.

※

While his readers were devouring the first issue, Tolstoy was, according to Sofia's letter to her sister, hurriedly readying the next installment for the February issue.[*] (Each installment was roughly half a "Part.")

From the beginning to the middle of February, Tolstoy wrote Katkov four undated letters about the *Anna Karenina* chapters that he would be submitting; he repeatedly apologized for their lateness and made promises about the submission of further chapters.

The last of the four letters to Katkov concerns Tolstoy's argument about the necessity of preserving the scene depicting Anna and Vronsky's postcoital anguish after their first time making love:

> I am sending you some proofs, dear Mikhail Nikiforovich. I'm very sorry that there are so few, especially as the next 5 or so printer's sheets are certainly ready, and I'll send them to you in a few days.
>
> The second part is one of 6. I need this division because of the interval of time that has passed and the internal division of the book.
>
> I can't touch anything in the latest chapter. Vivid realism, as you say, is the only tool, since I can't use either pathos or argument. And this is one

---

[*]   Gusev, *Letopis'*, 433, letter of January 30, 1875.

of the passages on which the whole novel stands. If it is false, everything is false.* I tried to do the correcting so as to avoid setting up new type; I don't know if I've succeeded, but all the corrections are necessary.†

Tolstoy argued what almost any author argues when challenged by an editor about an episode, section, or scene: *I have to have to it!* Katkov relented. We'll look at this scene in its publication time, late February.

※

In St. Petersburg, Strakhov wrote Tolstoy about the reception there of the first installment of the novel: notwithstanding a comment that Strakhov heard from one dense reader, it was being admired. Strakhov, pleased to be the bearer and predictor of all the enthusiasm, concluded: "So it is. Goodbye and I entreat you one thing—don't make a stop, let the novel appear uninterruptedly in each issue. Then my prediction will come true—an unheard of and immeasurable success!"‡

Tolstoy immediately vexed Strakhov, perhaps on purpose. Answering his friend, he thanked him for the news, and confessed that he had not expected success and had prepared himself for a fall. In addition to all his school business, the *New Azbuka*, and a grammar and a math book, "just very recently," he wrote, "I conceived the idea of a new poetic work which gives me great pleasure and excitement, and which will probably be written if God gives me life and strength and for which I need my reputation."§

He had another six hundred pages or so of *Anna Karenina* to revise and write, but he claimed that he was thinking *past* that; and he must have guessed that this announcement would not be not pleasing to Strakhov. (Gusev says we don't know what "poetic work" Tolstoy had in mind.¶) Tolstoy continued then to perversely (and characteristically)

---

*   The editors of *PSS* (see 62: 139) say in a footnote that Tolstoy is referring to Chapter 11 of Part 2, "wherein is depicted the convergence of Anna with Vronsky" ("где изображено сближение Анны с Вронским").

†   Christian, *Tolstoy's Letters*, 274, middle of February 1875.

‡   Donskov, *L. N. Tolstoy – N. N. Strakhov*, 193, February 13, 1875; http://feb-web.ru/feb/tolstoy/texts/selectpe/ts6/ts62193-.htm.

§   Christian, *Tolstoy's Letters*, 274, February 16, 1875.

¶   Gusev, *Letopis'*, 435.

critique his new novel; if we didn't know which work he was criticizing, we wouldn't guess it was *Anna Karenina*:

> I don't believe it will be a great success. I know how much you want it to be a great success and you think it is. But I completely agree with the people who don't understand what there is to say about it. It's all—I don't say *simple* (simplicity, if it is there, is a tremendous virtue which it is difficult to attain), but low-grade. The idea is such a private one. It can't be, and it oughtn't to be a great success, particularly the first chapters which are decidedly weak. Besides, it's poorly finished. I can see that, and it hurts me. [. . .]*

Tolstoy added that as far as he knew the *Russian Herald* wouldn't publish more than three issues containing the novel this year, and, despite Strakhov's hopes that Tolstoy would keep the momentum going, "there will be a break." I don't like to think of Tolstoy being disingenuous, but in regard to Katkov's journal, Tolstoy often seemed disingenuous. As would any editor, Katkov wanted the hit novel to keep rolling out on a regular schedule.

Tolstoy was conducting frantic literary and pedagogical activity while under a dark cloud of family unhappiness. He continued to Strakhov:

> I've been living in a strange and awful state of excitement this winter. In the first place I've had a cold all the time—toothache and a feverish condition—and I've been staying at home. Then there has been practical work—managing 70 schools which have been opened in our district and which are going wonderfully. Then the pedagogical work I spoke about. Then the older children whom I have to teach myself, since I haven't found a tutor yet. Then the printing of the novel, the proofs of the novel and of the *Primer*, which are urgent, and now at the same time a family sorrow and a new plan. The family sorrow is the terrible brain disease of our 9-month baby in arms. For over 3 weeks now he has been going through all the stages of this hopeless disease. My wife is feeding him herself and is in despair one minute that he will die, and the next that he will live and be an idiot. And it's strange: I feel the need and the joy of work as never before. [. . .]†

---

*　Christian, *Tolstoy's Letters*, 274, February 16, 1875.

†　Christian, *Tolstoy's Letters*, 275, February 16, 1875.

In the midst of grieving, Tolstoy sometimes found relief in writing. But depression had its heavy hands on him and would soon bring him to a standstill.

Tolstoy fondly concluded to Strakhov, "Goodbye: why do you write nothing about yourself? I remember, you were staying with us this time three years ago. How we enjoyed ourselves."*

Tolstoy had a lot on his mind and too many things to do when, in the middle of February (Tolstoy often didn't date his letters), he wrote to the Baroness Y. I. Mengden, who had written to Sofia to ask Tolstoy for his permission to publish translations of his works: "I'm answering for my wife, esteemed Lizabeta Ivanovna, because we have a very dangerously sick little baby, and she's not able to think about anything else in her condition. I'm answering two points that very much interest me: a people's journal and the translation of my works into English."† He critiqued what he had seen of "journals for the people." They needed what he himself demanded of writing: *clarity*‡:

> [. . .] Intelligibility, comprehensibility, is not only a necessary condition if people are to read willingly, but is, I am firmly convinced, a check which prevents what is foolish, inappropriate, or untalented from appearing in a journal. If I were the editor of a popular journal, I would say to my colleagues: write what you will, preach communism, the Flagellant faith, Protestantism, what you will, only in such a way that every word should be intelligible to the carter who takes the copies round from the press; and I am certain that the journal would contain nothing that is not honest, wholesome and good. I am not joking, and I don't wish to talk in paradoxes, but I know this well from experience. It is impossible to write anything bad in completely simple and intelligible language. Everything immoral will seem so ugly that it will be discarded at once: everything sectarian, whether Protestant or Flagellant, will appear so false if expressed without unintelligible phrases; everything would-be educational, popular-scientific, but not serious and for the most part false, which popular journals are always full of, also expressed without such phrases but in intelligible language, will seem so stupid and impoverished that it will also be thrown out. If a popular journal seriously wishes to be a

---

*   Christian, *Tolstoy's Letters*, 275. The Jubilee edition editors say Tolstoy was mistaken about the year of his friend's visit: it was *two* years before, not three. (*PSS* 62: 142.)

†   *PSS* 62: 143, letter of February 10–19, 1875.

‡   *PSS* 62: 143.

popular journal, it only has to try to be intelligible and it is not difficult to achieve this. On the one hand it has only got to filter all the articles through the censorship of yardmen, cabmen, and kitchen cooks. If the readers don't stop over a single word which they don't understand, the article is fine. But if after reading an article none of them can tell what they have read about, the article is useless. [. . .]*

Tolstoy wanted there to be a people's journal, he assured Mengden, but it was not an easy task to publish good writing for the people because, he believed, there was so little of it. In the 1880s he would produce, edit, and publish such material himself in inexpensive booklets.†

Tolstoy gave Mengden his formal permission, written in French, to translate his work (Mengden had told Sofia that in England translations were done only with the permission of the author): "I authorize the baroness to translate everything into English. I authorize the translation from Russian."‡ *Anna Karenina* was not published in English until 1886, a year after it first appeared in French. Countess Mengden had no hand in its English translation.

Meanwhile, Fet wrote Tolstoy about *Anna Karenina* that "The hero Levin is the person Lev Nikolaevich (not the poet) . . ."§ It's no surprise that a close friend immediately recognized the original of Levin, but how many other readers in 1875 would have recognized facets of young Tolstoy in the character of self-conscious, honest, deep-thinking, serious, intense Levin?

Some short time before February 20, Tolstoy wrote his brother: "We're very bad. Nikolin'ka, that is, the one at the breast, for three weeks already has been sick with a brain illness, and there's no hope for recovery. At the beginning there was vomiting, then began the convulsions—his eyes became fixed, and hiccoughs—and now everything continues such; he only steadily and slowly weakens. Sonya is very oppressed; she feeds and walks him and awaits his death. It's oppressive, especially for her. And besides this I've not left here for 3 or 4 weeks and I sit constantly in flannels and am tormented with pain from my remaining teeth."

---

*   Christian, *Tolstoy's Letters*, 276, February 1875.

†   But, my 21st-century reader, what of that notion of absolute *intelligibility* and *clarity*? *I* believe it. I *want* to believe it even though the exceptions I think of, advertisements, political sloganeering, flummox me.

‡   *PSS* 62: 145.

§   Gusev, *Letopis'*, 436.

Tolstoy was grieving, yet the agony of his bad teeth distracted him. Tolstoy would revive this double torment two years later when he was concluding the novel and imagining *Vronsky's* grief.[*]

"On the whole it's really sad for us," Tolstoy wrote his brother Sergei. "You've lost children from this same illness, so you know."[†]

The Tolstoys' ten-month-old baby, Nikolai, died on February 20. Sofia recalled that, "Two days later Lev Nikolaevich and I took him in a covered cart to be buried. Neither of us were completely healthy, there was a twenty-degree frost and a fearful snowstorm blowing. When we put the open coffin down on the snow, the wind tore the headband from his [the baby's] head, along with the muslin cloth covering him. Our fur coats were flapping in the howling, strange-sounding wind. We were no longer in any position to cry or even to think. We proceeded hastily with the burial, the one concern for both of us being not to catch cold. I was concerned for Lev Nikolaevich and he for me."[‡] Sofia's sheer grief is communicated here in Tolstoy's ideal "completely simple and intelligible language."

Tolstoy wrote again to his fellow family man Fet and provided his own brief, humbled account:

> We have one sorrow after another. You and Marya Petrovna will certainly pity us, especially Sonya. Our youngest son, 10 months old, fell ill about three weeks ago with the terrible disease which is called water on the brain, and after 3 weeks' terrible torture died the day before yesterday, and we buried him today. I feel it hard on account of my wife, but for her, nursing him herself, it was very difficult.[§]

The deaths of their children always affected Sofia more than Tolstoy, naturally enough, as he suggested here. His pity and helplessness about the deaths, however, brought him eventually to a belief that the initial grief had been in vain, a belief in which Sofia, and some of us who find such a philosophy cold comfort, could not share.

Tolstoy confessed to Fet:

---

[*] See Part 8, Chapter 5 of *Anna Karenina*, or Chapter 13 of this book for a discussion of this scene.

[†] *PSS* 62: 141, letter of the middle of February.

[‡] Tolstaya, *My Life*, 208.

[§] Christian, *Tolstoy's Letters*, 277, February 22, 1875.

You praise *Karenina*, which pleases me very much, and other people praise her, so I hear; but assuredly there never was a writer so indifferent to his own success, *si succes il y a* [if success it is], as I am. [. . .]

Tolstoy was not in the mood to remember his own most lofty ambitions as an author. He actually had never been "indifferent to his own success," for which "vanity" he would mock himself in *Confession*.

Tolstoy told Fet of the same vague idea for a new project that he had shared with Strakhov: "On the one side, school business, on the other—a strange business—the subject of a new writing, overwhelming me in this very heavy time of the illness of the baby."* He praised "the embryo" of a beautiful new poem by Fet, which had an "absolutely clear poetic thought, but is absolutely unclear as far as the words go."†

Meanwhile, "I have received from Turgenev a translation of Two Hussars printed in *Le Temps*, and a letter in the 3rd person asking me to let him know that I received it, and that M. Viardot and Turgenev are translating some other stories, both of which things were completely unnecessary."‡ In the next few decades, many copies of his translated works would be sent to him at Yasnaya Polyana by the translators or publishers.

Tolstoy ended the letter with an invitation to Fet and his wife to come visit them for a day, and with a word about Tolstoy's favorite of all topics with Fet, horses: "The money will be sent the 1st of April. I very much thank Petr Afanas'evich [Fet's brother] for the nice horse.—I'm afraid only that he won't be a solid and trotter enough young stallion. I would much more like the old stallion."§

By February 23–24, Tolstoy was writing Strakhov about business concerning *Anna Karenina* and the *New Azbuka*. He didn't mention the death of baby Nikolai:

I've just received the proofs for the 2nd issue, and there are many things I'm dissatisfied with. You have ruffled my author's self-esteem about the novel, dear Nikolay Nikolayevich, and so if you have the time and the inclination, please let me know anything intelligent you hear or read by way of criticism of these chapters. There are many weak passages in them. I'll mention them to

---

* Regarding the "new project," see Tolstoy's letter of March 16–20, 1875, to the Archimandrite Leonid in Christian's *Tolstoy's Letters*, 278–279; *PSS* 62: 149.

† *PSS* 62: 149.

‡ Christian, *Tolstoy's Letters*, 277.

§ *PSS* 62: 149.

you: *Anna's return home, and Anna at home* [Pt. I, Ch. 22–23]. *The conversation in the Shcherbatsky family after the doctor's visit up to where the sisters have it out. The Petersburg salon,* and others. If there are criticisms of these passages, please let me know. [. . .]*

What if Strakhov had answered a couple of weeks later like so: "Oh, yes, Lev Nikolaevich, a slew of wise critics and readers have been saying that *all* those parts are terrible"? What was Tolstoy fishing for? What does it mean when an artist or performer at the top of his game reveals his anxiety about the project he's working on? Since 1875 there has been only one reader of the novel's many million readers who ever criticized those passages as "weak": Tolstoy himself.

Meanwhile, the despondent, grieving Sofia was proud when she heard of the excited response to the appearance of the first serialized chapters of *Anna Karenina*:

> On this subject [*Anna Karenina*'s success] I wrote my sister soon after Nikolushka's death: "Levochka's novel is out, and they say it's enjoying fantastic success, but I have this strange feeling welling up inside me, here we are in the midst of such {personal} grief, yet are being celebrated everywhere."[†]

She would forever speak fondly, admiringly, and sensibly of the novel. She was more level-headed than her husband about its supreme place in the world. Her daughter Alexandra narrates:

> Tolstoy was working intensely, revising completed parts for publication and adding chapters; Sophia was copying daily. Daughter Tanya, then eleven, would recall Sophia settling down at her desk in the evenings. Although behind her was a long day, it was clear "from the expression of concentration on her face, that for her the most important time . . . was just beginning." Occasionally, Tolstoy approached her as she was copying and looked over her shoulder. "Then my mother would take his big hand and kiss it with love and veneration, while he tenderly stroked her dark, shining hair then bent to kiss the top of her head."
>
> Only a few months after Nikolai's death, Sophia was pregnant again.[‡]

---

[*] Christian, *Tolstoy's Letters,* 277, February 23–24, 1875.

[†] Tolstaya, *My Life,* 210.

[‡] Popoff, *Sophia Tolstoy: A Biography,* 82.

✷

When the second 1875 issue of the *Russian Herald* arrived shortly after its publication date of February 28, did Sofia read it, or did she tap her finger on the journal's cover and say with veneration, "I don't need to read it there. I already know it through and through"?

Here are the February 1875 chapters in summary:

Levin, comprehending Vronsky's superiority as a romantic rival, goes to see Nikolai, his tubercular, difficult, unhappy, and irritable brother. Then Levin goes home to his estate and tries to reconcile himself to this familiar place and all his responsibilities to it. He sits reading and daydreaming in his study while the family retainer, Agafya, talks about recent local events.

Then we turn to Anna, who, ashamed of having enjoyed conquering Vronsky, leaves Moscow. She thinks that she is in the clear, that the flirtation is over, but Vronsky has followed her and rides the same train back, and during a brief station stop confronts her on the platform and tells her his feelings. At the train station in St. Petersburg, Vronsky awkwardly presents himself to Karenin, Anna's husband. Anna is surprised by her disappointment in her renewed sight of Karenin and even of her new impressions of her beloved son, eight-year-old Seryozha.

Tolstoy has us follow Vronsky to the apartment that he shares with his regimental mates; Vronsky rearranges his life to be wherever Anna socializes.

Part 2 of the novel opens with Kitty seeing a doctor and *being seen* by him—an excruciating image to Tolstoy, a naked young woman (modeled on Sofia) before a man who doesn't know her. Kitty's father is embarrassed and angry because he has correctly sensed that Kitty's illness is the result of her shame at having been rejected by Vronsky. Dolly goes to her parents' house to commiserate with her little sister Kitty, which leads to Kitty expressing her disgust at Dolly for having accepted Stiva's philandering as a fact of their marriage. After Kitty's blow-up, the sisters make up.

Tolstoy jumps us to Petersburg, where we learn about the highest levels of society and that Anna and Karenin are in the second-highest level. But they can and do also interact with the next level down, which includes Anna's friend Betsy, who is Vronsky's cousin. Betsy is a frivolous, sharp-witted, cheating wife. Tolstoy shows Anna descending into Betsy's atmosphere. Betsy conspires with Vronsky and Anna to arrange opportunities for their social meetings. In Part 2, Chapter 6 (of the book publication), we see the framework and many details of Tolstoy's original draft's opening scene—a party at Betsy's with the gossips wondering when Karenin is going to notice the obvious love between Anna and

Vronsky. The deliriously smitten couple scarcely care or notice that they're being observed. Anna tries to pretend to Vronsky that she is not in love, but he repeatedly proudly declares himself to her. They ignore Karenin's entrance at the party, but he notices the attention that Vronsky and Anna attract from the other guests, and he resolves to speak to her about it. She remains at the party, and her husband goes home. Karenin is resolute about *not* being jealous. We learn Karenin's background and about his career climb through governmental ministries. His lone friend was his brother, who has died. It's clear that Anna is his only friend. He is a disconnected father. Awaiting Anna's return from the party, he paces. When she arrives home, he broaches the topic of her overly intimate conversations with Vronsky, and she dismisses his remarks and they go to bed. She almost hates him. Though partially blind in regard to social life, Karenin realizes that he seems to have lost her.

Tolstoy wraps up the second installment of the novel with Vronsky and Anna sleeping together for the first time. This event is the passage of "vivid realism" that Tolstoy so absolutely defended to his editor Katkov. It is the only passage in the novel about which we have to blush in embarrassment and admit that our favorite author has artistic and personal limitations. Confronted with sex, Tolstoy loses his wits. Tolstoy told Strakhov of a conversation that he had had with Yiury F. Samarin about the punctuation marks that precede the chapter:

> Samarin told me: "There, where you have two lines of periods, I guess that there ought to be two chapters, and it's a pity there's not." I answered: "It's a pity that all that's missed is filth. If I wrote it 100 times I wouldn't at that spot change anything." I thought that this was only my opinion, and you won't believe how pleased I was to find out that people like Danielevskiy understood purity. (Not to mention you.)[*]

I will take from this that even at the time some readers knew that Tolstoy was way off track in his attitude about sex, that "purity" was an idea that short-circuited his creative imagination. Tolstoy was convinced that everyone shared or should share his shame about sexual intercourse, so instead of allowing Vronsky and Anna their long-anticipated bliss, he imagines what he thinks he would have felt:

> That which for Vronsky had been almost a whole year the one absorbing desire of his life, replacing all his old desires; that which for Anna had been

---

[*]   *PSS* 62: 164, letter of March 30–31, 1875.

an impossible, terrible, and even for that reason more entrancing dream of bliss, that desire had been fulfilled. He stood before her, pale, his lower jaw quivering, and besought her to be calm, not knowing how or why.

"Anna! Anna!" he said with a choking voice, "Anna, for pity's sake! . . ."

But the louder he spoke, the lower she dropped her once proud and gay, now shame-stricken head, and she bowed down and sank from the sofa where she was sitting, down on the floor, at his feet; she would have fallen on the carpet if he had not held her.

"My God! Forgive me!" she said, sobbing, pressing his hands to her bosom.

She felt so sinful, so guilty, that nothing was left her but to humiliate herself and beg forgiveness; and as now there was no one in her life but him, to him she addressed her prayer for forgiveness. Looking at him, she had a physical sense of her humiliation, and she could say nothing more.

As he wrote this scene depicting the aftermath of Anna and Vronsky's first act of passionate love, Tolstoy's personal nightmare overwhelmed his imagination:

He felt what a murderer must feel, when he sees the body he has robbed of life. That body, robbed by him of life, was their love, the first stage of their love. There was something awful and revolting in the memory of what had been bought at this fearful price of shame. Shame at their spiritual nakedness crushed her and infected him. But in spite of all the murderer's horror before the body of his victim, he must hack it to pieces, hide the body, must use what he has gained by his murder.

And with fury, as it were with passion, the murderer falls on the body, and drags it and hacks at it; so he covered her face and shoulders with kisses. She held his hand, and did not stir. "Yes, these kisses—that is what has been bought by this shame. Yes, and one hand, which will always be mine—the hand of my accomplice." She lifted up that hand and kissed it. He sank on his knees and tried to see her face; but she hid it, and said nothing. At last, as though making an effort over herself, she got up and pushed him away. Her face was still as beautiful, but it was only the more pitiful for that.

"All is over," she said; "I have nothing but you. Remember that."

"I can never forget what is my whole life. For one instant of this happiness . . ."

"Happiness!" she said with horror and loathing and her horror unconsciously infected him. "For pity's sake, not a word, not a word more."

She rose quickly and moved away from him.

"Not a word more," she repeated, and with a look of chill despair, incomprehensible to him, she parted from him. She felt that at that moment she could not put into words the sense of shame, of rapture, and of horror at this stepping into a new life, and she did not want to speak of it, to vulgarize this feeling by inappropriate words. [. . .]*

A hundred years later, the American critic Marvin Mudrick observed of this scene:

Strong stuff, this moment of truth ("'What bliss?' she said with disgust and horror"†), which, coming to it in so celebrated a novel, we don't dare question because we're afraid to seem coarse and ignorant: certainly the authoritative voice wouldn't say it if it weren't true (and how do we check it, do we take a poll of murderers' row or the girls at the office?). Only it isn't God talking, it's Tolstoy, who unreasonably needs to assert that this particular married woman [. . .], voluntarily clasped for the first time in the arms of her lover, will of course find the sex act frightful and revolting (if she can't manage to close her eyes and think of England), will experience it as the "spiritual" equivalent of rape and murder, will see "her bewitching dream of happiness" crumble instantly. Tolstoy is at odds here not only with common sense but with his own creature. Anna gives evidence by everything else she thinks and says and does that she is physically and passionately in love with Vronsky; she was before and will continue to be after; she never regrets her love for him except when she suspects he doesn't return it; nothing in her nature or circumstances suggests that this time as well as innumerable times afterward she wouldn't enjoy the act; and whatever her apprehensions it isn't likely, the bewitching dream having come to pass, that she would react to Vronsky's first completed pass as old Tolstoy hopes [. . .]. Tolstoy the novelist has created a woman alive to pleasures which Tolstoy the bluenose implausibly denies her.‡

---

* *Anna Karenina*, Part 2, Chapter 11, http://literatureproject.com/anna-karenina/anna_45.htm. The remainder of the chapter contains an account of one of Anna's dreams, about which there has been much appreciative commentary.

† Mudrick quotes Louise and Aylmer Maude's translation.

‡ Marvin Mudrick, *Books Are Not Life But Then What Is?* (New York: Oxford University Press, 1979), 99–100.

Perhaps the best we can say for Tolstoy here is that, however bad the depiction, however nonsensical and out of character (for Anna) the scene, Tolstoy, in arguing for it, was simply pushing back against an editor. Who was Katkov to object to anything the greatest author of his time had written? Who are we to be disappointed by Tolstoy's compulsive prudery? (On the other hand, Katkov was arguing against a truly lousy, shameful scene. It was indeed, as Katkov said, "false.") Tolstoy, as the bridled but not broken author, was going to publish what he wanted, because it was "necessary." The novel was also behind schedule, overdue, its readers were clamoring for more . . . so perhaps Katkov felt that he had to relent.

But the shame of the sexual act that Tolstoy depicts! How to explain it?

It is, unhappily, all too explicable: Writing this baffling scene about Anna and Vronsky's terrible first sexual experience, Tolstoy was remembering his and Sofia's terrible wedding night in 1862. Sofia recalled:

> [. . .] even there at the station, the torments began which every young wife must go through. Not to mention the terrible physical pains, and just think of the shame! How torturesome it was, and unbearably shameful! All of a sudden there awakened within me a new, crazy but involuntary feeling of passion which had been dormant in the young not-yet-developed maiden.
>
> It was good that it was dark in the carriage, good that we could not see each other's faces. It was only close, very close that I could feel his breath, which was fitful, quick and passionate. His whole strong and powerful being overwhelmed my whole self, which was meek and loving, but suppressed by tormenting pains and unbearable shame.
>
> Again and again, the whole night the same trials, the same sufferings.[*]

It wasn't just the shame of the act that bothered Sofia and Tolstoy, it was that the act "awakened . . . a new, crazy but involuntary feeling of passion." The first act led to many more acts. Alexandra Popoff continues the story of the brutal wedding night in her biography of Sofia:

> Tolstoy made a crude entry in his diary: "She was in tears. In the carriage. She knows everything and it's simple. At Biryulevo. Her timidity. Something morbid." Sophia would never forgive him his impatience: three decades later,

---

she described their first night as a rape: "Violence had been committed; this girl was not ready for marriage; female passion, recently awakened, was put back to sleep."*

When Sofia eventually got around to writing her description of that night, she was detached enough to analyze her horrified experience. Tolstoy, on the other hand, could not write about it even in a *novel* about *other* people without his shame pinkening the pages. *She* could describe its wretchedness. For Tolstoy sex was too personal to describe imaginatively, sympathetically, appreciatively. His personal shame about sex and seemingly of his own wedding night overpowered his artistry and leached here into the novel.

❋

In early March, Tolstoy wrote Strakhov to thank him for his help with the *New Azbuka* money accounts, about which his brother-in-law Petya Bers was no use. Now he would like Strakhov's assistance in getting "On Popular Education" published as a "mini-book." Tolstoy followed up with Nagornov in an exasperated letter on March 8 about the corrections needed for the *New Azbuka*: typefaces of various sections and stories, including "The Three Bears," and formatting the book.

He wrote Nagornov again in mid-March and apologized for all the changes he was making in the children's reader, and meanwhile, "Every day I'm receiving telegrams from Katkov—hurrying me with Karenina, which disgusts me, and all the time I'm awaiting news from Varya. Sonya and I kiss her."† (Tolstoy's niece Varya would have a baby on March 22.)

Very late again with his *Anna Karenina* chapters, Tolstoy in March declared to Katkov: "I will never promise beforetime concerning my writing, most esteemed Mikhail Niki-forovich, which as it goes on, it seems so ready, but when I took it out to send it, it was unavoidable to correct it, and I held onto it. Now it's all ready, and I wanted to send it already by post, even though it's not recopied, but my nephew came from Moscow and tomorrow night he is taking the train back. He will bring you the manuscript at 9 in the morning on Monday, and this will give me time to recopy it and review it."‡

---

*   Popoff, *Sophia Tolstoy: A Biography*, 30–31.

†   *PSS* 62: 159, letter of March 16, 1875. Information about Sofia's note to her brother and Varya's giving birth to a daughter are in the footnotes on this page.

‡   *PSS* 62: 159–160, letter of March 1–20?, 1875.

Is there an editor or teacher who hasn't heard such an excuse?

"Now it's all ready," and yet he would still like to get the proofs back for a day! He worried there might be some geographical errors concerning St. Petersburg (if there were, Katkov should fix them), and he apologized again and signed off.

From Petersburg Strakhov responded to Tolstoy's curiosity about readers' reactions to the novel: "The excitement doesn't lessen; at first I thought that the second installment was having less success, but now I think that it's even more. [. . .] *About the weak places*, which you point out, nobody speaks. [. . .] The progressives—Stasov, Polonskiy are amazed that Anna feels dirty shame, and they suppose that it is because you are a defender of the old morality."[*] (Stasov and Polonskiy were on to something, but Tolstoy never answered them, except perhaps indirectly in *The Kreutzer Sonata,* Tolstoy's novel of the late 1880s, wherein the protagonist blames his murder of his wife on the jealousy agitated by the indulgence of marital sexual intercourse.)

After finishing off the March pages, Tolstoy had to work on the April installment; on March 29 Sofia wrote her sister Tatyana that Tolstoy "is only writing Anna Karenina."[†]

❋

The end of Part 2 (Chapters 12–29 of the book version) came out on March 31.

If it's the evening of the last day of March 1875, and we have finished poring through this installment in the *Russian Herald,* what do we know now about Anna, Vronsky, Karenin, Levin, Kitty, Stiva, and Dolly?

At the beginning of springtime, Levin, on his estate, is still smarting over Kitty's rejection. He supervises and plans the farm work and is vexed by some of his workers. Stiva visits and they go hunting. Levin asks Stiva about Kitty and learns that she is unmarried, very ill, and has gone abroad for treatment. Levin can't help thinking that she deserves her suffering. To Levin's annoyance, Stiva sells Dolly's property to a land speculator.

We turn again to Vronsky and his and his wanton mother's backgrounds. Madame Vronsky disapproves of her son refusing career opportunities because of his fidelity to Anna. Vronsky doesn't consider their relationship only an affair. There is a big horserace that he is going to compete in against other military officers. Vronsky prepares himself on that day, but wants to see Anna, and decides to do so, even though they haven't arranged a pre-race meeting. First he visits the English groom in charge of his racehorse

---

[*]   Donskov, *L. N. Tolstoy – N. N. Strakhov,* 202–203, March 21, 1875.

[†]   Gusev, *Letopis',* 440.

Frou-Frou. Vronsky takes a carriage to Anna's house in the country and sees her for a few tender minutes while her son, Seryozha, is out with a nanny. Anna tells him that she's pregnant, and Vronsky is glad—too glad from her perspective, because she thinks that he thinks that it means she will have to leave her husband. Vronsky departs for the race.

At the racetrack Vronsky's brother intercepts him in order to confront him about Anna, seconding Madame Vronsky's disapproval, and Vronsky tells him off. The thrilling race proceeds and Tolstoy puts us in the saddle with Vronsky on his adored Frou-Frou:

> [. . .] Once more he perceived in front of him the same back and short tail, and again the same swiftly moving white legs that got no further away.
>
> At the very moment when Vronsky thought that now was the time to over-take Mahotin, Frou-Frou herself, understanding his thoughts, without any incitement on his part, gained ground considerably, and began getting along-side of Mahotin on the most favorable side, close to the inner cord. Mahotin would not let her pass that side. Vronsky had hardly formed the thought that he could perhaps pass on the outer side, when Frou-Frou shifted her pace and began overtaking him on the other side. Frou-Frou's shoulder, beginning by now to be dark with sweat, was even with Gladiator's back. For a few lengths they moved evenly. But before the obstacle they were approaching, Vronsky began working at the reins, anxious to avoid having to take the outer circle, and swiftly passed Mahotin just upon the declivity. He caught a glimpse of his mud-stained face as he flashed by. He even fancied that he smiled. Vronsky passed Mahotin, but he was immediately aware of him close upon him, and he never ceased hearing the even-thudding hoofs and the rapid and still quite fresh breathing of Gladiator.
>
> The next two obstacles, the water course and the barrier, were easily crossed, but Vronsky began to hear the snorting and thud of Gladiator closer upon him. He urged on his mare, and to his delight felt that she easily quickened her pace, and the thud of Gladiator's hoofs was again heard at the same distance away.
>
> Vronsky was at the head of the race, just as he wanted to be and as Cord had advised, and now he felt sure of being the winner. His excitement, his delight, and his tenderness for Frou-Frou grew keener and keener. He longed to look round again, but he did not dare do this, and tried to be cool and not to urge on his mare so to keep the same reserve of force in her as he felt that Gladiator still kept. There remained only one obstacle, the most difficult; if he could cross it ahead of the others he would come in first. He was flying

toward the Irish barricade, Frou-Frou and he both together saw the barricade in the distance, and both the man and the mare had a moment's hesitation. He saw the uncertainty in the mare's ears and lifted the whip, but at the same time felt that his fears were groundless; the mare knew what was wanted. She quickened her pace and rose smoothly, just as he had fancied she would, and as she left the ground gave herself up to the force of her rush, which carried her far beyond the ditch; and with the same rhythm, without effort, with the same leg forward, Frou-Frou fell back into her pace again.

"Bravo, Vronsky!" he heard shouts from a knot of men—he knew they were his friends in the regiment—who were standing at the obstacle. He could not fail to recognize Yashvin's voice though he did not see him.

"O my sweet!" he said inwardly to Frou-Frou, as he listened for what was happening behind. "He's cleared it!" he thought, catching the thud of Gladiator's hoofs behind him. There remained only the last ditch, filled with water and five feet wide. Vronsky did not even look at it, but anxious to get in a long way first began sawing away at the reins, lifting the mare's head, and letting it go in time with her paces. He felt that the mare was at her very last reserve of strength; not her neck and shoulders merely were wet, but the sweat was standing in drops on her mane, her head, her sharp ears, and her breath came in short, sharp gasps. But he knew that she had strength left more than enough for the remaining five hundred yards. It was only from feeling himself nearer the ground and from the peculiar smoothness of his motion that Vronsky knew how greatly the mare had quickened her pace. She flew over the ditch as though not noticing it. She flew over it like a bird [. . .]*

The first many times I read this thrilling chapter I didn't think of sex. And then the first time I did think of it, I didn't want to. Now I've given up resisting. It *is* a horserace, but it's also like sex. And I eventually couldn't help wondering: Did Tolstoy really overlook the obvious sexuality?

And now I can't help concluding: *Yes, he was unconscious of its obvious sexuality.* Vronsky is not responsible for confusing horseracing with sex; Tolstoy is.

Let's imagine a Tolstoy who wasn't ashamed of human sexuality. That Tolstoy couldn't have written this without blushing and realizing, "Oh, yeah, that *is* like . . ." But if this

---

* *Anna Karenina*, Part 2, Chapter 25, http://www.literatureproject.com/anna-karenina/anna _59.htm.

unashamed Tolstoy had been able to write about sex as frankly as writers a hundred years later, what a marvel *that* could have been: Tolstoy describing sex would have been as gorgeous and thrilling as this race. We would all recognize something about our consciousness in the act. His *unconscious* description survives, and we do know something that he didn't know he was making us conscious of.

Vronsky's excited race ends terribly; he has to shoot the horse to put it out of its misery. Tolstoy knew just what would most pain a horse-lover, and we are upset for Vronsky.

After Vronsky falls and curses himself for his maiming of Frou-Frou (and his therefore necessary destruction of her), we switch to Anna's point of view, back at her house earlier in the day, on her husband's return. We learn of their spoken and unspoken arrangements for keeping up appearances. Karenin means to take her to the race, but Betsy calls for her and whisks her away herself. At the races, Karenin finds himself watching Anna instead of the horses. When she hears that Vronsky has fallen she becomes almost hysterical with worry, and Karenin insists that she return home with him. In the carriage, when he scolds her for her reaction, he suddenly wants her to lie and tell him that it's nothing. Instead, she tells him that she in fact loves Vronsky and is his lover.

✳

"How annoying, dear friend Tanya, that it's impossible to write without letters, without paper and ink, or you would have received every day long letters from me, especially this winter," Tolstoy wrote his sister-in-law Tatyana at the end of March. "How often I remember you and so want to see you, in both good and bad moments.—I'm terribly busy this year, and except for one woe and now another, some sort of doubtful condition of Sonya's health, I would be very happy myself this winter. I received your long letter, Tanya, at the time of the heaviest illness of Nikol'inka, but I appreciated it. As for Anna Karenina, if only I had your talent of description. I would pay someone to put in the commas. [. . .] No, no joke, you won't believe how I read, with such great joy, your so very descriptive letters. [. . .] Judging by your silence about your health, I suppose and am glad that it's fine. [. . .] So don't think you're right or think that if I don't write I don't love you. I love you very much and am not an egotist, as you, I know, swear I am."[*]

In *Confession* Tolstoy paints with a broad bold brush a picture of his mood during this time as continuously frighteningly gloomy. But there he was, in the letter above, lively and playful with his sister-in-law, and in a letter around the same time to Strakhov he

---

[*]   *PSS* 62: 162–163, letter of March 29?, 1875.

was unusually friendly and newsy. Tolstoy wished him a good trip to Rome, and believed his friend must be as excited as a boy: "I would very much like to see you. You think that I only think about myself. Not at all. I feel for people whom I love, and I feel for you [. . .]"* Then Tolstoy recounted for Strakhov the conversation he had had with Yury Samarin about the scene that he couldn't possibly modify: Anna and Vronsky having murderously miserable sex.[†]

Unusually, Tolstoy mentioned his actual effort on the book, though unfortunately he didn't pinpoint which chapters he had in mind:

> In the last installment a few chapters came to me which I put in and about which I really struggled. Tell me what you think about them.[‡]

Tolstoy was finished for now with his work on *Anna Karenina*. For the next eight months he would at first deliberately put it off and then, in the midst of composing the first draft of *Confession*, uselessly try to proceed with the novel. His attention went at first to the *New Azbuka* and educational issues.[§] Tolstoy wrote his assistant Nagornov at the beginning of April and gave him three choices for the new title of the revised *Azbuka*: "Children's Azbuka," "New or Children's Azbuka," or "New Azbuka." We have Nagornov's choice.[¶]

Tolstoy wrote the editor of the *Notes of the Fatherland*, Nekrasov, to ask about the journal's interest in another education article as well as expressing hope that Nekrasov would give the *New Azbuka* some serious notice; and though Tolstoy seemed full up with arguments about education, and assured Nekrasov that the article would be ready for the May issue, nothing would come of it, except perhaps Nekrasov's consternation and the beginning of the end of their correspondence.[**]

But horses! From late March through April Tolstoy continued an anxious correspondence with Fet about the logistics of getting a stallion that he was buying from Fet brought

---

*   *PSS* 62: 164, letter of March 30–31, 1875.

†   See above, in this chapter, p. 164.

‡   *PSS* 62: 164.

§   As impressive an accomplishment as the *New Azbuka* is, I have given it too little attention in this book.

¶   Gusev, *Letopis'*, 441.

**   *PSS* 62, 170–171, letter of April 2, 1875.

to Yasnaya Polyana in time to mate with a special mare: "Please don't be mad at me for my impatience."[*]

He was *busy*, as he kept saying. He was worried about what the censors would do with the *New Azbuka*; Tolstoy told Nagornov: "I won't be able to make all the necessary changes before the trip to Samara [in early June]."

At the end of April, Tolstoy wrote three drafts of a letter promoting the *New Azbuka*.[†] Promotion was another one of those things that Tolstoy did that does not seem characteristic of him, yet with characteristic focus and skill he did it well. He contacted a dozen journals and newspapers.

For some reason, though, he had the hardest time hiring tutors for his older children. His eagerness to do so was clear when a tutor came into range. He wrote to May Perrot, a Swiss to whom (on Alexandrine Tolstaya's recommendation) he had asked for help finding a tutor and governess: "We're awaiting an answer concerning Rey. We're leaving June 7."[‡]

❋

On May 2, the April issue of the *Russian Herald* appeared; it contained the fourth installment of *Anna Karenina*: Chapters 28–31 of Part 2 and Chapters 1–10 of Part 3 (corresponding in the book edition to Chapters 30–35 in Part 2 and Chapters 1–12 in Part 3).

Here, in summary, is what we could have devoured that early May day:

The Shcherbatskys are at a German spa, and Kitty becomes attracted to the selfless, saintly, slightly older Varenka, the foster daughter of a mean old Russian invalid, Madame Stahl, who lives in that town. Kitty's mother arranges an introduction, and the young women become friends. In Kitty's effort to be "good" by emulating Varenka, she helps a sickly Russian painter and his family. The painter, to her embarrassment and the wife's anger, falls for her, which mishap shows Kitty that she is not cut out for Varenka's saintly selflessness. In frustration and envy, she blows up at Varenka, but Varenka understands and forgives her. Kitty's spirits are restored, and the family returns to Moscow.

Part 3 opens with Levin's half-brother Sergei Ivanovich Koznishev, the academic philosopher. He goes to visit Levin to unwind, even though for Levin it's the farm's busiest time. Sergei wants to chat and argue, but Levin just feels oppressed. Levin breaks free by announcing his intention to take up a scythe and mow a meadow with the peasants.

---

[*] *PSS* 62: 177, letter of April 21–25?, 1875.

[†] *PSS* 62: 178–180, letter of April 1875.

[‡] *PSS* 62: 180.

No one can read these mowing scenes without joy. Who has communicated as potently as Tolstoy the ecstasy of rhythmical athletic movement?

> Another row, and yet another row, followed—long rows and short rows, with good grass and with poor grass. Levin lost all sense of time, and could not have told whether it was late or early now. A change began to come over his work, which gave him immense satisfaction. In the midst of his toil there were moments during which he forgot what he was doing, and it came all easy to him, and at those same moments his row was almost as smooth and well cut as Tit's. But so soon as he recollected what he was doing, and began trying to do better, he was at once conscious of all the difficulty of his task, and the row was badly mown.[*]
>
> The longer Levin mowed, the oftener he felt the moments of unconsciousness in which it seemed not his hands that swung the scythe, but the scythe mowing of itself, a body full of life and consciousness of its own, and as though by magic, without thinking of it, the work turned out regular and well-finished of itself. These were the most blissful moments.[†]

Meanwhile, Stiva has sent his wife and children to their dilapidated house in the country, not so far from Levin. Dolly, with the help of her servant woman, gets the place organized and habitable. Stiva writes from Moscow to ask Levin to go help Dolly. Levin travels there one day and does indeed help. His feelings are confused, though. He is attracted by the family life but put off by some of the upper-class pretensions. He is thrown way off by Dolly's significant hinting to him that Kitty is back, and due to visit, and available again. He becomes cranky with her and her handling of the children (why teach them French?!), and he abruptly, unhappily leaves. He meets a wealthy peasant on his way back; the peasant's son has married and Levin sees how happy the young man and his lively wife are. Levin thinks maybe he ought to marry a hardworking, unpretentious peasant woman, but by chance that very next early morning he glimpses from afar a sleepy Kitty in a carriage on her way to Dolly's and he realizes that he can't, because "I love *her*."

※

---

[*]   *Anna Karenina*, Part 3, Chapter 4, http://www.literatureproject.com/anna-karenina/anna_59.htm.

[†]   *Anna Karenina*, Part 3, Chapter 5, http://www.literatureproject.com/anna-karenina/anna_59.htm.

Readers of the April issue of the *Russian Herald* didn't know that they would have to wait until the end of January 1876 for the next installment. Tolstoy didn't know it would be quite that long, either.

He must have resolved to get off some letters on May 5 before his and Sofia's two-day trip to Moscow. He was in a tender and repentant mood. He not only wrote to Nagornov to apologize if his last, pushy letter had angered the young man, he wrote a note to Fet anticipating Fet's visit to Yasnaya Polyana. That same day he also wrote a letter to his sister-in-law Tatyana and her husband Sasha Kuzminskiy, wherein at first he sounds like the incarnation of Stiva Oblonsky: "Still I'm very glad that you're pregnant. This is divine." And then Tolstoy sank back into his weird, sex-averse self: "But to me there's something unpleasant."* He informed his sister-in-law of "Our important family business—concluding dealings with the Swiss Monsieur Rey for 5,000 francs." Rey would be "master, teaching Latin, Greek, mathematics, German and French. [. . .] His [that is, Rey's] sister will come to Tanya after August." Tolstoy thought that Rey was twenty-three, but according to the Jubilee editors, Rey, born in 1848, was twenty-seven. Rey would work for the Tolstoys from June 1875 until January 1878. As for *Anna Karenina*, Tolstoy told Tatyana and Sasha, "until fall I won't write or publish anymore."

Not working on the novel was a promise that was easy for him to keep. Meanwhile, his printing of the *New Azbuka* cost him only 2,000 rubles.† It would continue to earn him money through twenty-eight editions in his lifetime.‡

Finally, having written all of those necessary business and personal letters, he concluded with one to Strakhov that may make Tolstoy, the model usually of literary consciousness, seem unconscious:

> Don't be angry, dear Nikolay Nikolayevich, because this letter will be short. I've already written 8 letters and this—intimate—letter to you I was putting off to the end. And now there's no time. Still, better a short one than nothing at all. I know how nice it is when abroad to get letters from Russia.
>
> I particularly want to reply to what you write about yourself. The state of your soul has been partly revealed to me, but that is all the more reason for wanting to penetrate further into it. And my wish is a legitimate one; it isn't based on intellectual interest, but on heartfelt attraction toward you. There

---

*   *PSS* 62: 181, letter of May 5, 1875.

†   *PSS* 62: 181–182, letter of May 5, 1875.

‡   *PSS* 21: xxxvii.

are souls whose only doors lead straight into living rooms. There are big doors and small ones, open doors and closed ones, but some are at the end of entrance halls, back and front staircases and corridors. You have winding corridors, but your apartments are good, and the main thing is, I love them. And I always wanted to penetrate them. You always speak, think, and write about the general—you are objective. And we all do this, but really it is only deceit, legitimate deceit, the deceit of decency, but still deceit, like clothing. [So Tolstoy's naked strolling in Samara may have seemed to him a freedom from "deceit"?] [. . .] And you wear too much objectivity, and so spoil yourself, at least for me. What criticism, judgments, or classifications can compare with an ardent, passionate search for a meaning for one's life? [. . .]*

With almost everything Tolstoy wrote, the distance between our life and his seems to disappear. We know exactly what he means because he knows and conveys exactly what he means. Even if we don't like what Tolstoy is saying, we *know* what he's saying. No evasiveness, no hinting, no special obscure personal meaning.

Except there in that second paragraph.

Tolstoy was in an elated mood, as we see from the letters that he wrote earlier that day to Fet and Tatyana. He was wanting the doctor in Moscow to assure him and Sofia that her health could handle another pregnancy. The trip was unusual, if not unprecedented, in that the two of them, absent the children, went *together* to Moscow.

How can we explain, though, Tolstoy's expression of "heartfelt attraction" to Strakhov and his wish for penetrating his friend's private spaces? Why all that about the "deceit" of clothing?

It's not that we need care if Tolstoy had homosexual feelings. All power to him! But if he didn't know it, *that's* what brings us back into Tolstoy's blind spot. The letter continues:

Objectivity is decency, as necessary to the masses as clothing. Venus de Milo can go about naked, and Pushkin can talk frankly about his personal impression of her. But if Venus goes about naked and an old cook does as well, it will be disgusting. And so people decided that it would be better for Venus to be clothed, too. She doesn't lose anything, and the cook will be less ugly.

---

*   Christian, *Tolstoy's Letters*, 279, May 5, 1875.

This compromise seems to me to exist in things of the mind, too. Extremes, ugliness, *surcharge* of clothing often do harm, but we are used to them. And you wear too much objectivity, and so spoil yourself, at least for me.[*]

So, really, Tolstoy was just asking his friend to not cover up, to *reveal* himself, right?— as Tolstoy, unconsciously, was revealing himself here, and as Tolstoy consciously reveals himself in almost every other instance.

Tolstoy continues: "What criticism, judgements, or classifications can compare with an ardent, passionate search for a meaning for one's life?"

The search for the meaning of life is the purpose for Levin and for Anna.

Wouldn't Strakhov, the shy bachelor, like to join Tolstoy in that search?

Tolstoy concluded the letter with a delighted recognition of coincidental desires:

> How strange that you are seeking out the monks and want to go to the Optina Monastery. That's just what I wanted, and still do.
>
> How can we see each other? I'm going to Samara with the family at the end of May and come back in August. If you could only come to see me!
>
> In any case, please write to me.[†]

He included the general delivery address for Samara and added: "I've sent something for the 4th issue [of *Anna Karenina*] and won't touch it again till autumn."[‡]

On the same day, Tolstoy went from flirting with his sister-in-law to confessing his intellectual and emotional love to his devoted friend Strakhov. And he was about to go to Moscow with his wife for two days, without the children. And she would give birth to a premature baby in six months.

I don't know what to make of it.

Was Tolstoy simply supercharged with attraction for his loved ones that day?

Strakhov, in the meantime, had written Tolstoy a two-part letter from Italy, dated April 22 and May 5. Once Strakhov sent it, it took perhaps two weeks to reach Tolstoy. The friends were negotiating just what their relationship was or ought to be. In the April-dated letter, Strakhov made a perplexed start:

---

[*]   Christian, *Tolstoy's Letters*, 279, May 5, 1875.

[†]   Christian, *Tolstoy's Letters*, 280, May 5, 1875.

[‡]   Ibid.

You give me a few questions and even reproach me for those thoughts (as if they're mine) that you yourself think about one of them. No, Lev Nikoaevich, this is not my thought; I know how kind you are and I feel your love. But I write you only about you, just about you, because I sincerely go into your interests and thoughts. I start so with almost everything, even sometimes with simple people; with you I count myself in your debt, for joy. But what's true is true; I hide myself from you, and I haven't uncovered, speaking about myself. Why not? I say straight off—I would be ashamed to uncover to you that lowness, that fall of spirits that covers me. [. . .]

Maybe I'm living through that period and am redoing my youth, but now I don't see a way out. For two years I have been looking for it and I haven't found it. Everything interests me weakly, nothing catches fire that might light the soul. On this theme I might write without end, but this is shameful to me—and this subject is absolutely useless and would interest no one. At the end of your letter you express a very good desire: *be strong*, you write. Yes, this is just what I should desire. [. . .]

On May 5, Strakhov added:

I still need to answer your questions. I wrote you that it's necessary to com-municate something to you. You ask me—what?—I don't remember, posi-tively don't remember, about what business; so many impressions have passed through my head.[*]

They were wrestling over questions that were troubling Tolstoy more than Strakhov. Strakhov was in low spirits but wasn't exactly having a crisis, as Tolstoy was. Tolstoy's loving assurances and wishes to "penetrate" Strakhov's reserve wouldn't ever appear so plainly in his letters again.

In *Anna Karenina*, however, the minor character Sviazhskiy, a friend of Levin's, is a family man but isn't, it seems, much of an intellectual, though he reads a lot. Sviazhskiy is modest, as was Strakhov, and both were widely and deeply educated, but the real-life Strakhov was also an important literary critic and science writer. He was a shy man but not a shy critic. For all that, the editors of the Jubilee edition direct us

---

[*] Donskov, *L. N. Tolstoy – N. N. Strakhov*, 207–209, April 22 and May 5, 1875; http://feb-web.ru /feb/tolstoy/texts/selectpe/ts6/ts62207-.htm?cmd=2.

from Tolstoy's May 5 letter to Strakhov and the chapter where Levin tries to "penetrate" Sviazhskiy:

> If it had not been a characteristic of Levin's to put the most favorable interpretation on people, Sviazhsky's character would have presented no doubt or difficulty to him: he would have said to himself, "a fool or a knave," and everything would have seemed clear. But he could not say "a fool," because Sviazhsky was unmistakably clever, and moreover, a highly cultivated man, who was exceptionally modest over his culture. There was not a subject he knew nothing of. But he did not display his knowledge except when he was compelled to do so. Still less could Levin say that he was a knave, as Sviazhsky was unmistakably an honest, good-hearted, sensible man, who worked good-humoredly, keenly, and perseveringly at his work; he was held in high honor by everyone about him, and certainly he had never consciously done, and was indeed incapable of doing, anything base.
>
> Levin tried to understand him, and could not understand him, and looked at him and his life as at a living enigma.
>
> Levin and he were very friendly, and so Levin used to venture to sound Sviazhsky, to try to get at the very foundation of his view of life; but it was always in vain. Every time Levin tried to penetrate beyond the outer chambers of Sviazhsky's mind, which were hospitably open to all, he noticed that Sviazhsky was slightly disconcerted; faint signs of alarm were visible in his eyes, as though he were afraid Levin would understand him, and he would give him a kindly, good-humored repulse.[*]

Strakhov never mentioned seeing himself in Sviazhsky and no one among their acquaintances did, either. This should persuade us that Tolstoy thought better of Strakhov than he does of Sviazhsky.

For the most part, Strakhov's Italian letters describe Rome and his trips out from Rome, and as if only because he knew Tolstoy was reading between the lines, they include an occasional personal detail.

✳

---

[*] *Anna Karenina,* Part 3, Chapter 26, http://www.literatureproject.com/anna-karenina/anna_95.htm.

Tolstoy and Sofia's visit to the doctor in Moscow brought the welcome professional opinion that her pregnancy would be safe.

The other good news Tolstoy received was that the censorship committee didn't interfere after all and had let the *New Azbuka* through, and it was published May 19 or 20.[*] In his continued effort to promote interest in the children's reader, he wrote to Katkov, hoping to get a plug for it: "Such an *Azbuka* there never was, not only not in Russia but anywhere! And each little page of it cost me more work and has more meaning to me than all the writings for which I have been so undeservedly praised."[†]

The politically disreputable Katkov, a sort of 19th-century Fox News bloviator, deserves some credit here. He told Tolstoy that he would pass the *Azbuka* on to the Reading Committee member who could do it the most good. Then, favor granted, he discreetly added: "We're waiting from you a portion [of *Anna Karenina*] for the June issue. Is there the concluding part of the first half of the novel? I'm afraid I'm besieged by subscribers."[‡]

Tolstoy doesn't seem to have answered Katkov to tell him that his subscribers would have to just keep on waiting, but he did tell Nagornov to get Katkov, who was also a Reading Committee member, a copy of the *New Azbuka* as soon as possible.

Tolstoy could busily and anxiously promote the *New Azbuka* but could not engage himself in writing *Anna Karenina*. He continued with follow-up letters to the committee and an education journal editor.

We don't know what Tolstoy bought or whom he saw when he was in Moscow around May 22–24, but when he returned home he wrote his brother to ask him to send money to their sister. Answering Sergei's concern about Sofia's poor health (which Tolstoy had mentioned in his last letter), he clarified: "Sonya's health isn't as bad as I thought, but it's not good. The main thing is that she's pregnant, and so it's hard to judge."[§] He then reviewed accounts with him, and at the end of May there was one more letter, including a legal statement that Sergei had received 7,660 silver rubles from Lev. He caught up on news, and said it was good that Sergei hadn't come to visit: "We have Madame Menglen [the old acquaintance and a translator] with her daughter, and it's a terrible boredom. But how great it would be if you came to us for a visit in Samara." Sergei did not ever visit his brother there.

---

[*] *PSS* 62: 178, editorial note 3.

[†] *PSS* 62: 186, letter of May 17, 1875.

[‡] *PSS* 62: 186, footnote 4.

[§] *PSS* 62: 189, letter of May 27–28, 1875.

Eager to be free of business, of farming, of supervision over schools, Tolstoy became relentless in planning his summer getaway. He must have been convinced that the uprooting would benefit the whole family, particularly Sofia, though she remembered her personal disgruntlement with it:

> By springtime both my health and Lev Nikolaevich's had deteriorated so badly
> that we decided we must definitely go for koumiss treatments to the new plot
> of land we had bought from Baron Bistrom in the Buzuluk Uezd of Samara
> Gubernia, six versts from the village of Gavrilovka.
>
> Even though we spent some time there, I didn't have the opportunity to
> drink any koumiss, on account of a new pregnancy which had begun—the
> tenth, including the two miscarriages. I was thirty years old then, but this
> endless child-bearing had quite drained me. Everything was difficult for me,
> and I had become indifferent to it all. I did not look forward to leaving Yasnaya
> Polyana for the challenging trip to Samara for koumiss.*

Did she tell him what she tells us, her readers in *My Life*, that she didn't want to be pregnant any more or as often?

In an unhappy episode in Part 6 of *Anna Karenina* (not published until February 1877), we read how Dolly disapproves of Anna's having somehow rendered herself impregnable. Tolstoy, the author in the wings, almost audibly echoes Dolly's disapproval. Dolly, uncomfortable in Vronsky's and Anna's luxurious home, confused by her own regrets and unhappiness in marriage, tells Anna in a tête-à-tête about her tête-à-tête with Vronsky:

> "He said that he was unhappy on your account and his own. Perhaps you will
> say that it's egoism, but what a legitimate and noble egoism. He wants first of all
> to legitimize his daughter, and to be your husband, to have a legal right to you."
>
> "What wife, what slave can be so utterly a slave as I, in my position?"
> [Anna] put in gloomily.
>
> "The chief thing he desires . . . he desires that you should not suffer."
>
> "That's impossible. Well?"
>
> "Well, and the most legitimate desire—he wishes that your children should
> have a name."
>
> "What children?" Anna said, not looking at Dolly, and half closing her eyes.

---

*   Tolstaya, *My Life*, 209.

"Annie and those to come . . ."

"He need not trouble on that score; I shall have no more children."

"How can you tell that you won't?"

"I shall not, because I don't wish it." And, in spite of all her emotion, Anna smiled, as she caught the naive expression of curiosity, wonder, and horror on Dolly's face.

"The doctor told me after my illness . . ."

How mysterious that ellipsis is! What exactly did the doctor tell Anna? What do the drafts tell us? Nothing.* Tolstoy, as free as a writer in Russia could be at this time, could not or would not let us overhear Anna. But when, several years later, he did discuss contraception in *The Kreutzer Sonata*, it was in the mode of grim disgust. Dolly and Anna's conversation continues:

"Impossible!" said Dolly, opening her eyes wide.

For her this was one of those discoveries the consequences and deductions from which are so immense that all that one feels for the first instant is that it is impossible to take it all in, and that one will have to reflect a great, great deal upon it.

This discovery, suddenly throwing light on all those families of one or two children, which had hitherto been so incomprehensible to her, aroused so many ideas, reflections, and contradictory emotions, that she had nothing to say, and simply gazed with wide-open eyes of wonder at Anna. This was the very thing she had been dreaming of, but now learning that it was possible, she was horrified. She felt that it was too simple a solution of too complicated a problem.

"*N'est-ce pas immoral?*" was all she said, after a brief pause.

"Why so? Think, I have a choice between two alternatives: either to be with child, that is an invalid, or to be the friend and companion of my husband—practically my husband," Anna said in a tone intentionally superficial and frivolous.

---

* In the Zhdanov and Zaydenshnur edition of the novel, p. 535, there are 38 periods in this ellipsis. Preceding Anna and Vronsky's lovemaking-as-murder chapter, p. 129, there are 84. What the significance could be of the number of dots, I don't know. These are the only two extended ellipses in the novel. Zhdanov and Zaidenshnur, 129 and 535.

"Yes, yes," said Darya Alexandrovna, hearing the very arguments she had used to herself, and not finding the same force in them as before.

"For you, for other people," said Anna, as though divining her thoughts, "there may be reason to hesitate; but for me. . . . You must consider, I am not his wife; he loves me as long as he loves me. And how am I to keep his love? Not like this!"

She moved her white hands in a curve before her waist with extraordinary rapidity, as happens during moments of excitement; ideas and memories rushed into Darya Alexandrovna's head. "I," she thought, "did not keep my attraction for Stiva; he left me for others, and the first woman for whom he betrayed me did not keep him by being always pretty and lively. He deserted her and took another. And can Anna attract and keep Count Vronsky in that way? If that is what he looks for, he will find dresses and manners still more attractive and charming. And however white and beautiful her bare arms are, however beautiful her full figure and her eager face under her black curls, he will find something better still, just as my disgusting, pitiful, and charming husband does."

Dolly made no answer, she merely sighed. Anna noticed this sigh, indicating dissent, and she went on. In her armory she had other arguments so strong that no answer could be made to them.

"Do you say that it's not right? But you must consider," she went on; "you forget my position. How can I desire children? I'm not speaking of the suffering, I'm not afraid of that. Think only, what are my children to be? Ill-fated children, who will have to bear a stranger's name. For the very fact of their birth they will be forced to be ashamed of their mother, their father, their birth."*

I had always thought that the doctor must have sterilized Anna, but it is also possible that Anna had begun using some sort of birth control, which was uncommon but still a possibility at that time.

If that's so, how does Vronsky not notice? That very day Vronsky has told Dolly that he anticipates more children: "We have a child, we may have other children."†

Could some portion of Tolstoy's guilt about sex have come from knowing that he was disabling a woman with the pregnancy? That for all his sexual "need," the consequences of it landed on the woman? (The plot of Tolstoy's last long novel, *Resurrection,*

---

*   *Anna Karenina*, Part 6, Chapter 23, http://literatureproject.com/anna-karenina/anna_180.htm.

†   *Anna Karenina*, Part 6, Chapter 21, http://literatureproject.com/anna-karenina/anna_178.htm.

turns on this fact. The woman, not the man, is punished for the "crime" that the man instigates.) Tolstoy had to keep facing the knowledge that pregnancy and childbirth were life-threatening for Sofia.

But back to the most sympathetic mother in any of Tolstoy's novels, Dolly, as she muses to herself, muses for the first time in what seems to her like years. For a couple of days she is free of her children and has room to *think*:

> "It's very well that I'm teaching Grisha, but of course that's only because I am free myself now, I'm not with child. Stiva, of course, there's no counting on. And with the help of good-natured friends I can bring them up; but if there's another baby coming? . . ." And the thought struck her how untruly it was said that the curse laid on woman was that in sorrow she should bring forth children.
>
> "The birth itself, that's nothing; but the months of carrying the child—that's what's so intolerable," she thought, picturing to herself her last pregnancy, and the death of the last baby. And she recalled the conversation she had just had with the young woman at the inn. On being asked whether she had any chil-dren, the handsome young woman had answered cheerfully:
>
> "I had a girl baby, but God set me free; I buried her last Lent."
>
> "Well, did you grieve very much for her?" asked Darya Alexandrovna.
>
> "Why grieve? The old man has grandchildren enough as it is. It was only a trouble. No working, nor nothing. Only a tie."
>
> This answer had struck Darya Alexandrovna as revolting in spite of the good-natured and pleasing face of the young woman; but now she could not help recalling these words. In those cynical words there was indeed a grain of truth.
>
> "Yes, altogether," thought Darya Alexandrovna, looking back over her whole existence during those fifteen years of her married life [when the novel was published in book form in 1878, Sofia and Tolstoy had been married fifteen years], "pregnancy, sickness, mental incapacity, indifference to every-thing, and most of all—hideousness. Kitty, young and pretty as she is, even Kitty has lost her looks; and I when I'm with child become hideous, I know it. The birth, the agony, the hideous agonies, that last moment . . . then the nursing, the sleepless nights, the fearful pains. . . ."
>
> Darya Alexandrovna shuddered at the mere recollection of the pain from sore breasts [this had been one of Sofia's afflictions during nursing, about

which her husband had given her little sympathy] which she had suffered with almost every child. "Then the children's illnesses, that everlasting apprehension; then bringing them up; evil propensities" (she thought of little Masha's crime among the raspberries), "education, Latin—it's all so incomprehensible and difficult. And on the top of it all, the death of these children." And there rose again before her imagination the cruel memory, that always tore her mother's heart, of the death of her last little baby, who had died of croup [*croup*! I think of poor Sofia copying these words; she must have wept]; his funeral, the callous indifference of all at the little pink coffin, and her own torn heart, and her lonely anguish at the sight of the pale little brow with its projecting temples, and the open, wondering little mouth seen in the coffin at the moment when it was being covered with the little pink lid with a cross braided on it.

"And all this, what's it for? What is to come of it all? That I'm wasting my life, never having a moment's peace, either with child, or nursing a child, forever irritable, peevish, wretched myself and worrying others, repulsive to my husband, while the children are growing up unhappy, badly educated, and penniless. . . .

"Why, even if we suppose the greatest good luck, that the children don't die, and I bring them up somehow. At the very best they'll simply be decent people. That's all I can hope for. And to gain simply that—what agonies, what toil! . . . One's whole life ruined!" Again she recalled what the young peasant woman had said, and again she was revolted at the thought; but she could not help admitting that there was a grain of brutal truth in the words.[*]

It's not that the novel is autobiographical here and that details of Dolly's life fit into the Tolstoys' lives; but Tolstoy is completely sympathetic to Dolly's hard-earned thoughts. Sofia also saw the parallels between her situation and Dolly's, and she knew that even if, as she would complain, her husband didn't understand her and wasn't particularly or correctly sympathetic to her, he at least understood her plight via his fictional characters. He could sympathize, on paper, with the conflicts and miseries of motherhood.

Sofia recalled about the summer of 1875: "Life with its complications, deaths, and illnesses threw both Lev Nikolaevich and myself into a state of total apathy, and we began

---

[*] *Anna Karenina*, Part 6, Chapter 16, http://literatureproject.com/anna-karenina/anna_173.htm.

to fear that our country life was completely degrading us both morally and physically."* (This may have been true for Sofia, but Tolstoy never expressed a belief that "country life" could degrade him or others.) She continues:

> We needed to go off somewhere, either abroad or {at least} to a city. But our lives at the time were totally under the control of Lev Nikolaevich, and we continued living at Yasnaya Polyana and taking trips to an even more difficult life, on the Samara steppes. [. . .]†

She now concludes that *he wasn't listening to her concerns* about not wanting to go to Samara.

We know that he took her to the doctor in Moscow just before the trip, and that the doctor assured them that she was in good enough health to go. If he agreed with her and believed that country life was degrading, why would he have left Yasnaya Polyana for a much more rustic life in Samara? This was a family debate that Sofia lost, and then, in recollection, she confounded the story. Simply, he wanted the whole family to go to Samara; she wanted a different kind of trip. She narrates:

> On the 4th of June Lev Nikolaevich went off to Moscow, and the whole family was supposed to leave for koumiss on the 6th. Lev Nikolaevich would meet us in Moscow, from where we were to go on all together. [. . .]
>
> We hadn't planned to stop overnight in Moscow, but, upon meeting us [on June 6], Lev Nikolaevich announced that we would be spending a day there, stopping over at the Obolenskijs' flat on the Arbat, and that Professor Zakhar'in would be coming by that evening to give me advice on how to cope with my ill health over the summer.‡

Sofia was put out about Tolstoy's arrangements, but on the other hand he did listen to her complaints and arranged again for a doctor to see her. The doctor, Sofia notes, scolded Tolstoy, "But you haven't been taking care of her!" and insisted that she stop transcribing this summer, due to her nerve-damaged right shoulder. Tolstoy had to have agreed easily to that, because, as was his summer habit, he had no intention of writing:

---

*   Tolstaya, *My Life*, 209.

†   Ibid.

‡   Ibid.

Apparently, Lev Nikolaevich got a little frightened, and became very kind toward me, and took care of me as best he could. This was difficult for him—he wasn't accustomed to it.[*]

Oh, Sofia! While giving Tolstoy credit for taking care of her, she also has to mention that he didn't know very well how to do so.

In Moscow, she remembered, the children went to the zoo—some of them for the first time—and to the Kremlin "with their new tutor." This tutor, in the position Tolstoy had long been striving to fill, was Jules Rey, who had just arrived from Switzerland.

Everywhere, Sofia remembered, Tolstoy was lauded for *Anna Karenina*. On June 7, the entire Tolstoy family, joined by Sofia's little brother Stepan Bers and the tutor, departed from Moscow. Sofia recalled: "The trip to Samara was quite difficult and not a joyful venture this time. At Nizhnij Novgorod we boarded a wretched little steamer which was very cramped and rocked quite a bit, so that Tanja and I were nauseous the whole time. Seeing my poor condition, the captain took pity on me and gave me the executive cabin upstairs, where Tanja and I settled in."[†]

---

[*]   Tolstaya, *My Life*, 210.

[†]   Ibid.

8

Summer, Fall, Winter 1875

✳

I. Samara: June–August

On June 11, "The carriages were already waiting for us at Samara," recalled Sofia. "We spent the night there, and twenty-four hours later we were already at our homestead."

A week later, she wrote her sister Tatyana: "Levochka is sipping up the koumiss, he walks the precipices. He's healthy, tanned to black; of course, he writes nothing and spends days either on the steppe or in the tent of the Bashkir Mukhamed Shakh . . . Today Levochka, Monsieur Rey, and the children went to the fair in Pokrovka. Levochka bought a very frisky horse for racing. The races will be on August 6 [Lev's Saint's Day]."*

Tolstoy may have seemed half-Levin, half-Vronsky to Sofia. He was pleased to renew his friendship with Shakh and keen to buy a fancy horse. Tolstoy would continue having a fine vacation: two months of pursuing horses, games, and exotic forms of farming—and no writing. Son Sergei remembered: "The untrammeled, wild life of the semi-nomadic Mongol tribes, with their special habits and customs, the wide horizon, the expanse of the steppes carpeted with soft feather grass, the special breed of Kirghiz horses with their thick manes and tails—all this attracted Tolstoy. He liked the mettle, the strength and

---

*   *PSS* 62: 193, footnote 2, letter of June 20, 1875.

the spirit of these horses of the plains, and he even considered setting up a stud farm on his estate to crossbreed them with racehorses."*

As she was recalling that summer, Sofia may have been shaking her head. "Life on the steppes was exactly the same as during our previous stay," she wrote.† But the children were happy, apparently, and Sergei remembered this summer fondly: "On June 29 there was always a fair in Busuluk. My father went there partly to buy mares for the stud farm he intended to start, partly because he liked to see new places. My mother, [Uncle] Stepan, and we three older children went with him. My impressions of this trip were: a bad hotel with bedbugs, brown ewes with funny crinolines on their backs, herds of untrained horses . . . Behind Busuluk was a monastery where a hermit, a simple peasant, lived in a cave he had dug himself. My father was very much interested in him and talked to him at length."‡

Tolstoy had sponsored horse races in 1873, but this summer he planned a grander festival at his farm. Having already promised the contestants prizes, and not wanting to disappoint them, he wrote his niece's husband on July 4 to ask him to buy and send, as soon as possible, a rifle and a silver watch. He suggested prices that Nagornov should or could pay for them and expressed "a new debt of thanks."

> We're living well here, praise God, only my wife is still a bit sick. The harvest promises to be good, but for me it's been very little.
>
> Ever since we left Moscow, soon a month now, we haven't received a single piece of news and we know nothing of what's happening beyond the region and, mainly, with all those close to us. When you write and have Varya write, don't spare the ink and write a lot about both of you.§

After Nagornov answered him, Tolstoy wrote again on July 22 to instruct him further about promoting the *New Azbuka*, and added: "We're living just as we were

---

*   Sergei further explains: "My father had planned to have a large stud at the Samara farm. By crossing trained English and Russian trotters with wild Kirghiz, Kalmik, and Bashkir animals it was hoped to get strong, enduring horses, particularly suitable for cavalry. The conditions in the Samara steppes for such a stud were very favorable. The steppe hay, grown on almost virgin soil, was as nourishing as oats, and there were plenty of meadows. To fulfill this plan my father bought several beautiful pedigree horses and a great number of steppe mares." *Tolstoy Remembered by His Son*, 25.

†   Tolstaya, *My Life*, 210.

‡   *Tolstoy Remembered by His Son*, 23.

§   *PSS* 62: 193.

when I wrote the last letter, that is, well, except for the health of my wife, which is still threatened."*

Besides worrying about Sofia, Tolstoy was enjoying long days of not writing a word and scarcely reading.

On July 24 or 25, he wrote to Strakhov the only surviving wholly non-business letter of the summer. Tolstoy was persisting in suggesting that if Strakhov would just be more candid, more revealing, more trusting, less shy, their friendship would be greater. He himself was relaxed and content:

> I drink koumiss with the Bashkirs, buy horses, choose land to plow, I hire reapers, I sell wheat and sleep. Around August 15 we will be, God willing, at Yasnaya, and then, looking around, I'll write you and will await our seeing each other.†

This letter and other details of Tolstoy's life make me question my belief in *Confession* and Tolstoy's claims about the depths, duration, and totality of his depression in this period. How depressed could he have been if he was organizing with apparent excitement a race and festival?

Perhaps Tolstoy had more vitality while depressed than most of us do when we're fine. Sofia, on the other hand, was depressed and restless, perhaps in the way that Anna is when she, out of place in the countryside, waits for Vronsky to sow his wild oats in politics. This summer Tolstoy felt cheerful on the steppe, free of Yasnaya Polyana's demands and of his writerly responsibilities.

We know, but he didn't, that he was going to crash-land into stupefaction, if not full-on depression when they returned home.

For now, he celebrated one of the happiest public activities in which he ever participated. In her role as a biographer, his daughter Alexandra, who wasn't even born until 1884, writes: "On the appointed day people began to arrive from all quarters with their sheep, their camp equipment, kettles, tubs of koumiss: the local peasants, Kirghiz, Bashkirs in quilted coats, in clean white shirts and loose trousers, sheepskin caps, in fezzes and soft leather boots. Four distinguished Mohammedan women, who normally would have remained in seclusion, were driven to the races in the Count's carriage.

---

*   *PSS* 62: 193.

†   *PSS* 62: 194–195, letter of July 24–25, 1875.

"The crowd of several thousand persons spread out their rugs, installed themselves in picturesque, colorful groups and orderly fashion along the heights from where they could see the races. Plaintive Oriental songs were intoned, bagpipes were played and dancing alternated with wrestling."[*]

Son Sergei, who *was* there, describes a game of "fight and tug with a stick," a contest that Tolstoy won every time except when "a fat man" out-tugged him. As for the race, Sergei describes it fondly and clearly:

> On an even place in the steppe a circle of five versts was marked out with a deep furrow, which had to be raced round ten times. Thirty-two horses were in the race, among them one of ours, four or five belonging to Russian peasants, and the rest were Bashkir horses. The jockeys were young boys [Stepan Bers says they were about ten years old and rode saddleless[†]] who were distinguished by the various colored kerchiefs they wore round their heads.
>
> The organization of the race was not very efficient. When the horses had already started, my father moved the finish to a considerable distance from the start (so that the distance should be exactly fifty versts) and this upset the calculations of the participants. Then the mounted Bashkirs who were not in the races dashed about the circle, encouraging their horses and bewildering the others. Only seven horses reached the end, the others having moved out of the circle. The first prize was won by a Bashkir horse that had raced the distance in one hour thirty-nine minutes; the second winner was our horse; the other prizes were won again by Bashkir horses and only one Russian horse got a prize. The Russians were disgruntled and said that the Bashkirs had upset their horses.[‡]

Stepan Bers adds: "The festival lasted two days, and passed off very gaily, and in the most perfect order. What, probably, pleased the Count most was the complete absence of the police."[§]

We can wish Tolstoy had described the two-day party of racing and drinking with native peoples himself, but he never did, and he never again tried to put on a public festival.

---

[*]   Tolstoy, *Tolstoy: A Life of My Father*, 211.

[†]   Behrs, *Recollections of Count Leo Tolstoy*, 100–101.

[‡]   *Tolstoy Remembered by His Son*, 24–25.

[§]   Behrs, *Recollections of Count Leo Tolstoy*, 101.

What we can enjoy imagining, I think, is Tolstoy being Stiva-like: that energetic person who gets things started, who likes to create a jolly community event. (I wonder if the latter-day pacifist ever regretted the gift of the rifle?) On the other hand, Tolstoy so loved horses that he never renounced them, even when he renounced everything else later in life. In the novel the only character who resembles Tolstoy in his passion for horses and racing is Vronsky.

But as I stumble along in my role as biographer, let me wonder if Tolstoy was as skilled a rider as Vronsky is. In the race in Samara, all the jockeys were young boys. Tolstoy was, like Anna at Vronsky's race, a spectator. Did anyone watch him spectating the way Karenin watched Anna?

> Alexey Alexandrovitch took no interest in the race, and so he did not watch the racers, but fell listlessly to scanning the spectators with his weary eyes. His eyes rested upon Anna.
>
> Her face was white and set. She was obviously seeing nothing and no one but one man. Her hand had convulsively clutched her fan, and she held her breath. He looked at her and hastily turned away, scrutinizing other faces.
>
> "But here's this lady too, and others very much moved as well; it's very natural," Alexey Alexandrovitch told himself. He tried not to look at her, but unconsciously his eyes were drawn to her. He examined that face again, trying not to read what was so plainly written on it, and against his own will, with horror read on it what he did not want to know.
>
> The first fall—Kuzovlev's, at the stream—agitated everyone, but Alexey Alexandrovitch saw distinctly on Anna's pale, triumphant face that the man she was watching had not fallen. When, after Mahotin and Vronsky had cleared the worst barrier, the next officer had been thrown straight on his head at it and fatally injured, and a shudder of horror passed over the whole public, Alexey Alexandrovitch saw that Anna did not even notice it, and had some difficulty in realizing what they were talking of about her. But more and more often, and with greater persistence, he watched her. Anna, wholly engrossed as she was with the race, became aware of her husband's cold eyes fixed upon her from one side.
>
> She glanced round for an instant, looked inquiringly at him, and with a slight frown turned away again. *

---

*   *Anna Karenina*, Part 2, Chapter 28, http://www.literatureproject.com/anna-kareninaanna _62.htm.

We remember, even from the earliest drafts, that Vronsky was not going to win his race. Vronsky's first big disappointment in life is, like Anna's fate, built into the novel. This means that Tolstoy did not discover this scene in the heat of writing the novel, as his contemporaries Dostoevsky and Trollope often did. Instead Tolstoy repeatedly refined this race into another one of the unsurpassable scenes in literature.

❀

As tough a year as 1875 was and would be for Tolstoy, it was a harder year for Sofia. She spent more than two months that summer far from comforts and friends. She remembered: "Around the 15th of August we went home to Yasnaya Polyana, which my brother Stepa and I especially were happy about." Those two, the non–koumiss drinkers, had been "very bored," she recalled (though Stepan never said so in his memoir):

> I recall the difficult journey, the cold and the rain. The carriage was pulled by six horses, while Lev Nikolaevich, the older children, Monsieur Rey, Stepa, and the servants froze and shook on the tarantasses. By the time we were approaching [the town of] Samara, it had already got so dark and dirty that Lev Nikolaevich had to walk the four versts on foot, pointing out the way and keeping us from harm. How we travelled to Syzran' I don't remember, but for some reason we stopped in Syzran' at a rather wretched hostel or simply at someone's house, where there was nowhere we could make do for ourselves properly and the children ended up sleeping on the floor. It was cold, there were no warm clothes, and the children started to cough. [. . .]
>
> It was pretty bad on the steamer to Syzran' too; it was a long voyage—we were beset by rain and fog the whole way, and we felt such a huge relief upon getting home to Yasnaya Polyana. [. . .]*

I don't think Sofia ever forgave Tolstoy for this vacation.

❀

---

*   Tolstaya, *My Life*, 214.

II. Yasnaya Polyana, August–December

The family arrived back at Yasnaya Polyana on August 22 or 23.*

Tolstoy, reinvigorated, immediately got back to work, but not on the novel. He was taking care of business and catching up on correspondence. He anxiously queried Nagornov: "What about our Azbuka business? I'm afraid by your silence that it's bad."[†] But all was better with the *New Azbuka* than Tolstoy could have dreamed possible.

He wrote inviting his brother Sergei to come to see them and hear their summer stories. As a preview, he mentioned, "The harvest in Samara was worse than average, so I again had no profits. I'm content that even so there will not be a loss. I heard about you from Bibikov in outline but the details I don't know. How is your farming business and family doings? In any event, it's soon time to die, which I completely agree with you about."[‡]

Was Tolstoy suddenly glum? Why was Sergei in the dumps? Had Sergei announced, "My problems will be over soon, as it's getting time to die"? There's no saying, but, being brothers, perhaps neither needed to elaborate to the other.

Beyond returning to business, promoting and directing the promotion of the *New Azbuka*, taking on school board duties, and running the estate, Tolstoy seems to have been aggrieved that his return home meant that he was expected to work on *Anna Karenina*. In his letters of August 25 he immediately complained about that task to Strakhov and Fet. First he rather condescendingly complimented Strakhov on his personal unveilings and, as usual with his declarations of intimacy to Strakhov, he became unconscious of his images:

> [. . .] What with this and your last letters [these letters of Strakhov have not survived], you have told me everything you can and wish to say about yourself, and I confess I've learned a great deal that is new.
>
> Above all I learned from your story what I have always guessed, namely that your sympathy for me, and mine for you, is founded on the exceptional affinity of our spiritual lives. I hope that this severance of the umbilical cord, this indifference to one side of life, is only the sign of another umbilical cord through

---

* According to Gusev (*Letopis'*, 445), it was August 22. According to Gusev (*Materials*, 213), it was August 23. Whom are we to trust, Gusev or Gusev? Perhaps the question should be: Whom was *Gusev* to trust, Tolstoy or Tolstoy? In his August 25 letters to Nagornov and Sergei Tolstoy, Tolstoy says they returned "three days ago." Writing to Strakhov on the *same day*, Tolstoy says "two days ago."

† *PSS* 62: 195–196, letter of August 25, 1875.

‡ *PSS* 62: 198, letter of August 25, 1875.

which stronger juices are flowing, and I hope that neither you nor I would want to change places with the people we so envied some 20 or 25 years ago. [. . .]*

What was Tolstoy thinking with all those juices flowing?
He did *not* say such things to his other friends.

> We arrived safely the day before yesterday. I didn't take up my pen for two months and am very pleased with my summer. Now I'm settling down again to dull, commonplace *Anna Karenina* and I pray to God just to give me the strength to get it off my hands as quickly as possible in order to clear a space—I need the leisure very much—not for pedagogical activities, but for others which are taking more and more a hold on me. I love my pedagogical activities just as much, but I want to force myself not to pursue them. [. . .]

R. F. Christian says in a note that the other "activities" he needed space for were "religious writings. Tolstoy began an article on the meaning of religion in November 1875." Tolstoy means, more specifically, the book that came to be called *Confession*, which he had started back in 1874 (see pages 111–112).

After praising the philosopher Vladimir Solov'ev's work, which "stirred up the philosophical ferment in me very much," Tolstoy expressed the hope of seeing Strakhov that year.[†]

He needed Strakhov and enjoyed philosophizing with him, but if we want to be in the company of the family-oriented Tolstoy it's better that we read his letters to Fet. To Fet, on the same day, there was none of the assumption of superiority or would-be spiritual or unconsciously physical affinity, but there were, on the other hand, the horses: "Your horses are recovering on the grass of the steppes. I am grateful to you for both stallions." Tolstoy then told Fet, as he hadn't Strakhov, about Sofia: "The health of my wife is always varying: now better, now worse; but it seems not worse since we've come back." And about the kids: "The children are well. And the new Swiss classics tutor, Monsieur Rey, who came to us before the trip to Samara has been very good ever since as a teacher and master."

But even to Fet he could not resist complaining about *Anna Karenina*: "For two months I haven't stained my hands with ink or my heart with thoughts, and now I'm bearing the boring, vulgar Karenina with only the desire to as soon as possible clear off space for

---

*   Christian, *Tolstoy's Letters*, 280–281, August 25, 1875.
†   Ibid.

myself—leisure for other occupations, but not pedagogical ones, which I love but which I want to abandon. They take up too much of my time."* He missed Samara already ("the flies, uncleanliness, peasants, Bashkirs"†), where everything seemed interesting and important.

Sofia almost immediately felt annoyed by Tolstoy's avoiding the novel; she wrote her sister on August 26: "Levochka is set up to write and goes hunting."‡

Writing is transformative, so perhaps Tolstoy was shaken up and despairing because of what he was discovering in the novel. Anna's hopeless situation, despite her vitality and privileges, had to make him think about the meaning or meaninglessness of life. The contemplation by her and by Levin of the meaning of life and the allure of suicide creates the tension of the novel. Tolstoy's desperate thoughts tormented him, but they also eventually drove the novel forward.

At the end of August, Tolstoy reminded Nagornov again about promoting the *Azbuka*, complaining that nobody knew about it in St. Petersburg. In early September he scolded Nagornov for not taking care of business, asked him for details of all the accounts and reviews, and told him to hire someone to do all the busy work.

In his relations with Strakhov, Tolstoy could be businesslike, direct, without the usual courtesies of friendly correspondence. In his letter of September 6–7, he jumped right in: "I'm answering two of your questions, dear Nikolay Nikolaevich, one minor thing and the other of the most importance."§ The important matter was *seeing* him; Tolstoy would be going nowhere in September except for a week to a session of the district court in the village of Sergievo: "Your criticism is so much needed by me! [. . .] I muddle about in the novel during the morning, but it doesn't *take* and I go hunting."¶

Whether the book was taking or not, Tolstoy continued to think about art, and what art requires of the artist. In a response to Golokhvastov, he reflected on a truth that he had discovered for himself at least as early as a dozen years before when he was teaching peasant children:

> There is nothing worse than communicating to each other one's plans for artistic work. If you could tell in a conversation what you wanted to express

---

*   *PSS* 62: 198–199, letter of August 25, 1875.

†   *PSS* 62: 199.

‡   Gusev, *Materials*, 214.

§   *PSS* 62: 202, letter of September 6–10, 1875.

¶   *PSS* 62: 202.

in your drama, you would not write it. And so I probably couldn't understand what you want to do.[*]

We should remind ourselves of this whenever we encounter Tolstoy's offhand remarks about his novel: nothing he could say about it would change what he wrote. Nothing he said about it was actually the novel. And as he would indeed say when he had finished the novel, the only way to explain the novel would be to quote it in its entirety.

He expressed to Golokhvastov the commonsensical observation he had already made about pedagogy: "Artistic production is the fruit of love. But love without deeds is death. Make the thing of love and we will love what you love."[†] That is, as he wrote in 1862 in "Education and Culture": "If you wish to educate the student by science, love your science and know it, and the students will love both you and the science, and you will educate them; but if you yourself do not love it, the science will have no educational influence, no matter how much you may compel them to learn it."[‡]

He wrote to his brother Sergei in mid-September and asked how Sergei's son Grisha was faring and mentioned that after Sergei's visit, everyone had been sick with whooping cough. It was especially bad for Sofia, he said, as she was pregnant: "I'm also a big part of the time unwell and don't write anything. Yesterday I went out with the dogs and caught 4 hares."[§]

In his next letter to Nagornov, he was pleased that Nagornov had convinced him that taking care of the *Azbuka* business was not too much for him. He mentioned the family's ill health but also, in the postscript, that "The woodcocks have arrived." More hunting!

On September 17, Sofia wrote her sister that Tolstoy "is almost never working, he just hunts and says that 'it's not going.'"[¶] It must have been in the same letter of that date that Sofia mentioned, "Yesterday Levochka went to the Sergievo jury duty, but he is so worried about us that he has sent today a certificate to a doctor and returned home himself."[**]

Gusev writes: "The search for the meaning of life led Tolstoy into a joyous mood when he found satisfactory answers to the agitating questions, but sometimes it caused difficulty

---

[*]   *PSS* 62: 203.

[†]   Ibid.

[‡]   "Education and Culture," in *Tolstoy on Education*, trans. Leo Wiener (Chicago: University of Chicago Press, 1972), 149.

[§]   *PSS* 62: 204, letter of September 15–20, 1875.

[¶]   Gusev, *Materials*, 215.

[**]   *PSS* 62: 203, note 2.

and tormenting depression, despair, and even a complete renunciation of life."* Tolstoy was always trying to catch that clarity in his own life and thoughts that he constantly gives us, his readers, in *Anna Karenina*. His art does for us what he himself was seeking. In his own personal confusion and troubles, he searched for what, as an artist, he created for readers.

At the end of September, Strakhov was at Yasnaya Polyana,† and then or at the beginning of October, Strakhov went to Moscow to see Katkov, who was anxious about Tolstoy's tardiness in delivering *Anna Karenina*. Strakhov wrote Tolstoy: "I convinced him that you want to finish the novel even this year and that I even expected to see the end in the next four issues of the *Russian Herald*. On this he began telling me about some sort of hearsay, that you don't want to publish with him the second half of the novel. I convinced him that I had heard nothing like that from you."‡

Strakhov had gone to see Katkov about his own articles, but the editor, said Strakhov, "spoke only about you. He was agitated that he didn't know how or when *Anna Karenina* would finish, and how he was to place it with the journal."§ Strakhov asked Tolstoy to reassure Katkov.

✳

Gusev and Alexandra Lvovna Tolstaya point us to Sofia's diary of October 12:

> This isolated country life is becoming intolerable. Dismal apathy, indifference to everything, day after day, month after month, year after year—nothing ever changes. I wake up in the morning and just lie there wondering who will get me up, who is waiting for me. The cook is bound to come in, then the nurse [. . .] Then in the evening more darning, with Auntie and Lyovochka playing endless horrible games of patience together. [. . .]
>
> This year, God knows, I have struggled with these shameful feelings of boredom, and have tried, all on my own, to assert my better self, and to reassure myself that it is best for the children, emotionally and physically, to live in the

---

*   Gusev, *Materials,* 215.

†   Gusev, *Letopis'*, 446.

‡   Donskov, *L. N. Tolstoy – N. N. Strakhov*, 219. According to *PSS* 62: 208, Strakhov's letter was written in the period of October 10–17, but in accordance with Donskov (219), the context of the whole letter makes more sense that it was in late September, within a few days after Strakhov's departure from Yasnaya Polyana.

§   Donskov, *L. N. Tolstoy – N. N. Strakhov*, 219.

country, and I have managed to subdue my own selfish feelings, but I then realise to my horror that this turns into a terrifying apathy and a dull animal indifference to everything, which is even harder to struggle against. Besides, I am not on my own, I am tied to Lyovochka and the bonds have grown even tighter with the passing of the years, and I feel it is mainly because of him that I am sinking into this depression. It's painful for me to see him when he is like this, despondent and dejected for days and weeks on end, neither working nor writing, without energy or joy, just as though he had become reconciled to this condition. It is a kind of emotional death, which I deplore in him. Surely it can't go on much longer. It may be vulgar and wrong of me, but I feel oppressed by the terms of our life which he has laid down—by this terrible monotony and solitude which reduce us both to such apathy. [. . .] how *can* I be expected to take sole responsibility [for the children], and how can I help them at all when Lyovochka is in such a dazed and hopeless state that I despair of rousing him? [. . .] my hope is that God will light the spark of life in Lyovochka and he will once more be the person he used to be.*

Sofia's account of Tolstoy's dark mood rubbing off on her is not dramatized in *Anna Karenina*—or anywhere in *Confession*. Had he written about depression in a memoir rather than in a philosophical treatise, Tolstoy would have felt obliged, I think, to mention how his depression affected his loved ones. In *Confession* he writes:

And all this befell me at a time when all around me I had what is considered complete good fortune. I was not yet fifty; I had a good wife who loved me and whom I loved, good children, and a large estate which without much effort on my part improved and increased. I was respected by my relations and acquaintances more than at any previous time. I was praised by others and without much self-deception could consider that my name was famous. And far from being insane or mentally diseased, I enjoyed on the contrary a strength of mind and body such as I have seldom met with among men of my kind; physically I could keep up with the peasants at mowing, and mentally I could work for eight and ten hours at a stretch without experiencing any ill results from such exertion. And in this situation I came to this—that I could not live, and, fearing death, had to employ cunning with myself to avoid taking my own life.†

---

*   *The Diaries of Sophia Tolstoy*, 51–52.

†   *Confession*, Chapter 4, 18–19, http://www.online-literature.com/tolstoy/a-confession/4/.

The depression described in *Confession* had already started in 1875 or earlier, but by the time Tolstoy was writing the epilogue of *Anna Karenina*, he (and Levin) had got beyond it.

Gusev writes: "This was the time of Tolstoy's life in which he in four years remembered in the following way: '. . . I began to find moments of despair, life's end, as if I did not know how I was to live or what I was to do. At the beginning there were only moments in life that gave way to previous habits, but then more and more often, and then at the time that I was writing and finishing my book *Anna Karenina*, the despair reached where I couldn't do anything, but only think, think about the terrible situation in which I found myself.'"* (That quotation is from a draft of *Confession*, where he mentions *Anna Karenina*, but only this once.†)

Gusev then quotes from *Anna Karenina* about Levin's despairing thoughts, but Tolstoy keeps us and himself distant enough from Levin that we are fascinated by the character's situation rather than overwhelmed by it. In *Confession*, on the other hand, Tolstoy *induces* the feeling of depression that he underwent. Levin's pre-marriage depression is plenty affecting, but it's only great fiction; Tolstoy and we are sympathetic observers, but we feel (and know) Levin will pull out of this:

> It was only just at parting that Nikolay kissed him, and said, looking with sudden strangeness and seriousness at his brother:
>
> "Anyway, don't remember evil against me, Kostya!" and his voice quivered. These were the only words that had been spoken sincerely between them. Levin knew that those words meant, "You see, and you know, that I'm in a bad way, and maybe we shall not see each other again." Levin knew this, and the tears gushed from his eyes. He kissed his brother once more, but he could not speak, and knew not what to say.
>
> Three days after his brother's departure, Levin too set off for his foreign tour. Happening to meet Shcherbatsky, Kitty's cousin, in the railway train, Levin greatly astonished him by his depression.
>
> "What's the matter with you?" Shtcherbatsky asked him.
>
> "Oh, nothing; there's not much happiness in life."
>
> "Not much? You come with me to Paris instead of to Mulhausen. You shall see how to be happy."
>
> "No, I've done with it all. It's time I was dead."

---

*   Gusev, *Materials*, 216, [ref: *PSS* 23: 494].

†   *PSS* 23: 494. The novel goes unmentioned in the published edition of *Confession*.

"Well, that's a good one!" said Shtcherbatsky, laughing; "why, I'm only just getting ready to begin."

"Yes, I thought the same not long ago, but now I know I shall soon be dead."

Levin said what he had genuinely been thinking of late. He saw nothing but death or the advance toward death in everything. But his cherished scheme only engrossed him the more. Life had to be gotten through somehow till death did come. Darkness had fallen upon everything for him; but just because of this darkness he felt that the one guiding clue in the darkness was his work, and he clutched it and clung to it with all his strength.[*]

Tolstoy would write or revise this chapter between this fall and its publication in the January 1876 issue.

Gusev then quotes significant lines from the Epilogue (still almost two years away), when Levin is happily married, fulfilled, having achieved the family life he dreamed of:

And Levin, a happy father and husband, in perfect health, was several times so near suicide that he hid the cord that he might not be tempted to hang himself, and was afraid to go out with his gun for fear of shooting himself.[†]

Gusev comments, "It's doubtless that these last lines were autobiographical,"[‡] and quotes from Chapter 4 of *Confession*, in which Tolstoy confesses:

It had come to this, that I, a healthy, fortunate man, felt I could no longer live: some irresistible power impelled me to rid myself one way or other of life. I cannot say I wished to kill myself. The power which drew me away from life was stronger, fuller, and more widespread than any mere wish. It was a force similar to the former striving to live, only in a contrary direction. All my strength drew me away from life. The thought of self-destruction now came to me as naturally as thoughts of how to improve my life had come formerly. And it was so seductive that I had to be cunning with myself lest I should carry it out too hastily. I did not wish to hurry, because I wanted to use all efforts to disentangle the matter. "If I cannot unravel matters, there will always be time," and it was then

---

[*] *Anna Karenina*, Part 3, Chapter 32, http://literatureproject.com/anna-karenina/anna_101.htm.

[†] *Anna Karenina*, Part 8, Chapter 9, http://literatureproject.com/anna-karenina/anna_229.htm.

[‡] Gusev, *Materials*, 216.

that I, a man favoured by fortune, hid a cord from myself lest I should hang myself from the crosspiece of the partition in my room where I undressed alone every evening, and I ceased to go out shooting with a gun lest I should be tempted by so easy a way of ending my life. I did not myself know what I wanted: I feared life, desired to escape from it, yet still hoped something of it.[*]

When Tolstoy later wrote up this autobiographical experience as Levin's experience, the fiction is not as harrowing as it is in *Confession*. In *Confession*, Tolstoy's terror seems quite possibly inescapable, with suicide the most likely option, no matter that we know that the author didn't kill himself.

The truest fictional representation of Tolstoy's depression is Anna's, which affects not just Anna's balance but Vronsky's. (Levin's melancholy only slightly touches his newlywed bride.) Tolstoy's despairing outlook in *Confession* is Anna's.

❋

In late October, perhaps overcoming his "dreary, apathetic state" and fulfilling Strakhov's prompt, Tolstoy wrote Katkov his excuse letter for *Anna Karenina* not being ready. He denied that he didn't want to publish the second part of the novel: "I'm very sorry, esteemed M.N., that the rumors, not having any basis, have disturbed you." The rumors' basis, of course, was Tolstoy's constant grumbling to friends that he was disgusted by the novel and didn't want to write it.

"I'll make use of the opportunity to repeat what I wrote Lyubimov [Katkov's editor in chief]," Tolstoy tried to assure Katkov. (The letter to Lyubimov has not survived.) "I now have only one desire, to finish the novel as soon as possible in order to print it in the *Russian Herald*, but I cannot promise this, as the continuation depends on the capability to work, independent of me, and so I cannot promise."[†]

Katkov could have reasonably exclaimed: "On *whom*, on *what*, does your capability to work depend then?"

Some of Tolstoy's best meditations on art seem to have come when he was not, at the moment, producing it and was thinking about what he needed for it to happen. He now wrote Fet what has become a famous letter about artistic "scaffolding":

---

[*] *Confession*, Chapter 4, http://www.online-literature.com/tolstoy/a-confession/4/.

[†] *PSS* 62: 207–208, letter of October 10–20, 1875.

I haven't written to you for so long, dear Afanasy Afanasich, because I've been unwell myself all this time and have been distressed to watch the illness in the family. Now both they and I are a little better, and I hope—I only hope—to settle down to work.

Our work is a terrible thing. Nobody knows this except us. In order to work it is necessary for the scaffolding to be erected under your feet. And this scaffolding doesn't depend on you. If you start working without scaffolding, you will only waste material and make a mess of the walls and not be able to go on with them. You feel this particularly once the work has begun. You keep thinking—why not go on? And all of a sudden your arms fail you and you sit and wait. This is what I've been doing. But now, I think, the scaffolding has been erected and I'm rolling up my sleeves. [. . .]*

He was blocked and used this image to justify to himself why he hadn't been working. It would in fact be another six weeks before he, his sleeves for a long while rolled up, returned to the scaffolded *Anna Karenina*.

He discusses a book, "a collection of information about the Caucasian mountain tribes [. . .] It contains the legends and poetry of the tribesmen and some remarkable poetic treasures." He wouldn't send the book to Fet yet, because "I'm rereading it on and off." Some of it would be worked into the first draft of *Hadji Murad* about twenty years later. He quoted many lines and remarked, "Marvellous!" Then he quoted some more lines and suggested that Fet could use them in a poem, and Fet did.

His letter to Strakhov, possibly written the same day, continued a variation on the same scaffolding theme:

I haven't written and answered you in a long while, dear Nikolay Nikolaevich, because everything at this time has been in such a bad state—I'm tormented by a sick household, and I myself am sick. I fling myself from one work to another, but I do almost nothing.

Especially at the beginning of the work it's apparent that it's impossible to write on purpose. It seems that's why the beginning is not continuing. You try, you see that the hands don't reach that place where I left the work, and the harder you try, the clearer you see that you're not doing what's necessary

---

*   Christian, *Tolstoy's Letters*, 281, c. October 26, 1875.

but wasting material in vain. And raising the scaffolding depends not on me.

And you sit and wait while under your feet grows this scaffolding.*

On October 26, Tolstoy wrote Nagornov concerning the *Azbuka* business, with the main point being, "I really need the money." He also wanted "On Popular Education" to be sold in "all the bookshops for 15 kopeks apiece." Tolstoy knew prices. He was particular; he directed Nagornov with precision, telling him to follow up with Sokovin, a bookseller who owed Tolstoy money for various editions, including *War and Peace* and even the earlier version of the *Azbuka*.

And then, as usual with Nagornov, at the end of the letter Tolstoy added some family news. All spring and summer it had been illness; Sofia continued to be the worst sufferer: "As soon as the whooping cough began to pass away, a strong neuralgia began in her face."† As soon as that trouble passed away, she had stomach cramps that kept her from sleeping for two days. At the moment, however, there seemed to be a little bit of relief.

But something terrible was looming.

On October 30, because Sofia had peritonitis, their doctor Zakhar'in's assistant, Dr. V. V. Chirkov, came to Yasnaya Polyana. Tolstoy, in a grieved letter that day to Nagornov, wrote: "he did everything that he could."‡ Chirkov operated on Sofia for the peritonitis and relieved her pain, but then she prematurely delivered a girl, Vara, "who," remembered Sofia, "lived for an hour and a half before passing on. [. . .] I was so ill that her death did not upset me."§

Tolstoy wrote again to Nagornov and apologized for not having written with the latest news about Sofia, but "everything was undetermined, and now it seems it can be said that things are getting better. There's no illness and there is appetite, and her strength is increasing."¶

The strain of worry on Tolstoy was terrible, and yet, perhaps with the relief at Sofia's illness passing, it produced in him a bright excited light of discovery. He reflected in a short note to Strakhov: "All this time—2 weeks—I've been looking after a sick wife who gave birth to a stillborn child and has been at death's door. But it's a strange thing—I've never thought with such vigour about the problems which interest me as at this time. I read and reread carefully again the words of Wundt [R. F. Christian's footnote: "Perhaps

---

*   *PSS* 62: 210–211, letter of October 26, 1875.

†   *PSS* 62: 213.

‡   Ibid.

§   Tolstaya, *My Life*, 214. Tolstoy, in the October 30 letter to Nagornov, says the baby lived only a half-hour (see *PSS* 62: 218).

¶   *PSS* 62: 214, letter of November 5–9, 1875.

a reference to two contemporary fragments: *On a Future Life Outside Space and Time*; and *On the Importance of the Christian Religion*"], and understood for the first time the full force of the materialist, but for the first and last time only. Now I rejoice all the more at your plan and challenge you to a correspondence. And so—to a meeting of minds."[†]

Suddenly Tolstoy was engaged by his interest in philosophy, and he could for a moment think outside of the home. In his relationship with Strakhov, Tolstoy could wrestle over philosophical questions while having an opponent he could always defeat. To Strakhov's credit—I don't believe he was as enthusiastic to wrestle as Tolstoy—he was willing to engage and to use his position as confidant and debating partner to occasionally suggest, by the way, that *Anna Karenina* needed its author's attention.

Tolstoy concluded his note to Strakhov with a prima donna's exclamation: "My God, if only someone would finish *A. Karenina* for me! It's unbearably repulsive."

It would be another month before Tolstoy resumed the novel.

※

On November 8 or 9, Tolstoy had to tell his brother, "Don't be mad at me"; he still didn't have the money that he owed Sergei: "I will be in position to give it to you no later than in a month." He continued: "Now onto the business of our life."

> It has been really bad. The simple whooping cough finished very badly. My wife had an inflammation in the peritoneum (as the doctor called it). She gave birth to a six-month-old girl, who died right away, and she herself was near death. [. . .] Generally, I spent two tormenting weeks. Now she's better, but she is still not up. Moreover the whole house is full of masters, governesses and strangers. [. . .] And so I await your decision about the money.[‡]

Who were all those people in the house? The dying "Auntie" Pelageya Il'inishna, Sofia's brother Andrei and her uncle Kostya, G. A. Kolokoltsev, P. F. Samarin and his wife, and "on the most severe day of illness, the Swiss governess from Geneva, Mademoiselle Rey."[§]

---

*   Christian, *Tolstoy's Letters*, 283. Gusev, however, says that it wasn't until November 17 that Tolstoy began "On a Future Life Outside Space and Time." (Gusev, *Materials*, 226.)

†   Christian, *Tolstoy's Letters*, 283, November 8–9, 1875.

‡   *PSS* 62: 216, letter of November 8–9, 1875.

§   *PSS* 62: 216, note 4.

More relaxed, less defensive, Tolstoy also wrote to Fet:

> I received your beautiful verses, particularly "The Eagle." The latter one
> is not as good. [Tolstoy paraphrases two lines of the second poem . . .] I
> received your letter in the terribly severe moments when my wife was near
> death with illness, the inflammation of the peritoneum, and gave birth
> to a premature already practically dead baby girl. Fear, terror, death, the
> merriness of children, food, fuss, doctors, falsity, death, terror. It has been
> terribly heavy. Now she's better, she's not up, but there is no danger. She
> read your letter and is joyful at the thought of seeing you and Olenka on
> the 18th of December.*

On November 9 or 10, he responded to a letter from his brother Sergei, who hadn't
apparently received Tolstoy's previous letter yet. He caught him up, anyway, on Sofia's
health ("almost well," "very weak"). But then he arrived at that inexplicable phenomenon:
"I, as always happens, felt myself absolutely healthy at the time of her illness [. . .]." That
vigor had passed, however, "and now I have settled down and suppose that it's time to die."

> Last night I felt terribly bad; my temples blasted and became terrible. I thought
> to myself, I'm dying, and began to ask for whom this would interest and would
> give pleasure that I die. I sorted this all out and found that everyone would be
> merry or tell stories or pull themselves together, except for my wife and you.

After that depressing and devastating thought, he concluded the letter with a shout of
joy: "What a winter! Three days ago I went out with the dogs and without gunpowder
caught 6 hares."†

What does this mean?

It means that I have given up trying to believe whole-cloth in *Confession* as a *chronicle*,
as a record of his actions. (Yes, "confession" suggests a strict adherence to the truth,
but Tolstoy seems not to have bound himself to everyday, domestic-life "truth" in his
religious and philosophical works. This, for me, reveals why his fiction is truer of the
man than his nonfiction.) In *Confession* he professes: "I, like Sakya Muni, could not
ride out hunting when I knew that old age, suffering, and death exist. My imagination

---

*   *PSS* 62: 216, letter of November 8–9, 1875.

†   *PSS* 62: 218.

was too vivid. Nor could I rejoice in the momentary accidents that for an instant threw pleasure to my lot."[*]

Reading his letters and accounting for his everyday life, we realize that however debilitating Tolstoy's depression was, as profound a despair as he describes it in *Confession*, there were actually, undeniably moments of pleasure, exhilaration, and, of course, hunting. Artistic genius contemporaries of his, among them John Ruskin and Van Gogh, were better at acknowledging the surges and rollbacks of depression and were less inclined to color the entire landscape of a period of their lives in one shade.

✳

The most boring and *perhaps* longest letter that Tolstoy ever wrote is translated in full by R. F. Christian and was written on about November 30 to Strakhov in this long fall period of Tolstoy's *not* working on *Anna Karenina*. It precedes by two weeks his return to writing the novel, but it would be difficult to give the letter any credit for somehow loosening him up for the resumption of his artistic and contractual duty.

The eight-page letter, more than 3,500 words, shows Tolstoy's characteristic philosophical mode, a lecture-like exposition that brooks no interruptions: "The difference between you and me is only an external one. For every thinking man all three questions are inseparably joined into one—'what is my life, what am I?'"[†]

Tolstoy had the impulse here to declaim, and the only person in the world he knew who would listen was Strakhov. But even to patient, devoted, admiring Strakhov, he was rude, scolding Strakhov when he was *sensing* that he was making Strakhov impatient:

> (Please listen to me attentively, don't be angry at this digression and do correct what is not exact, explain what is not clear and refuse what is untrue. This digression is essentially what is called an exposition of method.) I can see the mass of omissions, obscurities and repetitions, as well as the repulsive didactic tone in all that I have written, but I stand by my basic idea about the method of philosophy which I hope you will understand amid all this confusion.[‡]

---

[*]   *Confession*, Chapter 7, http://www.online-literature.com/tolstoy/a-confession/7/.

[†]   Christian, *Tolstoy's Letters*, 283.

[‡]   Christian, *Tolstoy's Letters*, 287.

As usual, Tolstoy nailed himself better than anyone else could: "the repulsive didactic tone." Perfect! But he couldn't stop *that* train; he let it go on and on and on.

Andrew Donskov, the editor of Tolstoy's and Strakhov's letters to each other, reminds us that Strakhov "was often the first to read Tolstoy's new manuscripts."* Together with Tolstoy's insufferable November 30 letter, "Strakhov received the first draft of Tolstoy's *Ispoved'* [*Confession*]—showing that the creation of this work dates not from 1877 as is often considered (some scholars have put it even later), but from a significantly earlier date."†

So?

So this proves *Anna Karenina*'s and *Confession*'s simultaneity and overlappings. And yet . . .

Unlike *Anna Karenina*, it's difficult to read or even dip into *Confession* without being plunged into despair. And in real life, Sofia also suffered in the gloom of her husband's despair:

> Despite Tolstoy's melancholy weighing on her, Sophia found strength to carry on. In her memoir, she recalls, "I was lonesome, working beyond strength . . . while Lev Nikolaevich would often tell me that his life is over, it's time to die, and he can enjoy nothing." Watching Tolstoy struggle with depression, "despondent and dejected for days and weeks on end," she waited patiently and with hope "that God will light the spark of life in Lyovochka and he will be once more the person he used to be."
>
> Sophia hoped he would return to the novel. Although she did not talk to him directly about it, he read this in her eyes. Once, he surprised her by saying: "Don't nag me that I'm not writing, my head is heavy!" To sister Tanya, Sophia explained that she had not said anything: she did not dare.‡

✳

In late November Tolstoy wrote to Nagornov, primarily about business, but he mentioned that "Auntie" Pelageya seemed better. In a follow-up letter, from the beginning of December, he added, "We have woe after woe. As soon as Sonya got righted, Auntie

---

*   Donskov, *L. N. Tolstoy – N. N. Strakhov*, xxxv.

†   Ibid. (In *Materials* [222], Gusev thought the accompanying manuscript of Tolstoy's was "Why I Write." There is a discrepancy here. I trust Donskov, the later editor, that the manuscript was *Confession* rather than the unknown "Why I Write.")

‡   Popoff, *Sophia Tolstoy: A Biography*, 84.

took to her bed, and is suffering and dying. I can't do anything. I don't have the main thing—a peaceful soul.":*

And yet he would have reason to feel financially more secure. According to Gusev, "The *New Azbuka* quickly went into use in people's schools. Already in December 1875 it went into a second printing . . ."[†] So his having put off *Anna Karenina* at times and throwing his energy and heart into revising and promoting the *New Azbuka* had paid off. It had success. The main thing, which he could continue to be satisfied by for the rest of his life, was not the educational debate over how to teach, but that through the *Azbuka* children had good stories as they learned to read and great stories as they became completely adept. He had enriched the dry soil of Russian literacy.

Tolstoy continued to send Nagornov on business errands and continued to send him family news. On December 7 he wrote: "Auntie with each day weakens. We await her death every minute."[‡] He wrote his brother to tell him Auntie's situation, that she "would be very glad to see you, about this there can be no doubt."

He was watching her die, fascinated and maybe appalled: "She's very pitiful. She eats nothing, she lies there, groans from pain in her leg, in her chest, in the heel of her other foot, and then suddenly freshens up and says she's better. But a terrible weakness goes with her. And she doesn't want to die. Only one time she recognized her situation and thought she was about to die. It would be good if you would come [. . .] I received your letter by post and feel guilty before you about the money." Tolstoy's money was only now coming in. "But if you require it, I can get it."[§]

Whether Sergei came to see Auntie or not, we can presume he agreed to wait for the money; nobody ever complained about being shorted by Tolstoy.

Gusev comments: "Family unhappiness unavoidably deprived Tolstoy of peace for work, and only on December 12 was Sofia Andreevna able to write her sister that Lev Nikolaevich 'began working on the novel.'"

Yes, there was Auntie on her death bed, but "family *un*happiness," as Tolstoy himself liked to point out, never deprived him of being able to work. Sofia must have been relieved when she saw that he had gotten back to it. Did he bring her any manuscript? Did he wave the pages for her to see and hope that he could tempt her into copying them?

---

* *PSS* 62: 233.

† Gusev, *Materials*, 208.

‡ *PSS* 62: 233.

§ *PSS* 62: 233, letter of December 10–12, 1875.

Gusev continues: "At the end of the month the work was going very fast, and on December 25 Sofia Andreevna was already informing her sister that Lev Nikolaevich 'had taken up *Anna Karenina* very firmly.'"*

Sometime in the period of December 25–27, Tolstoy wrote an essay, "On the Soul and Its Life in What's Known and Understood by Us of Life," which, despite its impressive title, is as uninteresting as all discussions of the soul.†

Sofia recalled that holiday season:

> On the 28th of December the Golokhvastovs arrived, and, Ol'ga Andreevna read us aloud her historical drama titled *Dve nevesty* {Two brides}. I don't remember the drama, but I recall that Strakhov and Lev Nikolaevich did not like it at all—there was something sham about it.
>
> The Golokhvastovs were dear, clever, and talented people, especially him—he was a real knight when it came to order and decency. But somehow they didn't quite fit in with us. Her Parisian outfits, coquettishness, and her whole outward appearance did not fit in with the simplicity of our family household. They brought the children magnificent gifts, all sorts of books, but when they left, for some reason we began to breathe easier.
>
> Despite the mourning period following Auntie Pelageia Il'inichna's death, there was no stifling the children's fun.‡ [. . .]

Ol'ga Golokhvastova drove Tolstoy up the wall. In *What Is Art?*, completed twenty years later, Tolstoy mocks the kind of literary production that Golokhvastova seems to have indulged in:

> Some forty years ago a stupid but highly cultured—*ayant beaucoup d'acquis*—lady (since deceased) asked me to listen to a novel she had written. It began with a heroine who, in a poetic white dress and with poetically flowing hair, was reading poetry near some water in a poetic wood. The scene was in Russia, but suddenly from behind the bushes the hero appears, wearing a hat with a feather *à la Guillaume Tell* (the book specially mentioned this) and accompanied by two poetical white dogs. The authoress deemed all this highly poetic, and it might have passed muster if only it had not been necessary for the hero to speak. But as soon as the

---

* Gusev, *Materials*, 229–230.

† *PSS* 17: 340–352.

‡ Tolstaya, *My Life*, 217.

gentleman in the hat *à la Guillaume Tell* began to converse with the maiden in the white dress it became obvious that the authoress had nothing to say, but had merely been moved by poetic memories of other works and imagined that by ringing the changes on those memories she could produce an artistic impression.

Just as we'll see Vronsky thinking he can make art by imitating the manner of other painters, Golokhvastova communicated other authors' affectations. Tolstoy explains what's wrong with imitative, secondhand art:

> But an artistic impression, that is to say, infection, is only received when an author has in the manner peculiar to himself experienced the feeling which he transmits, and not when he passes on another man's feeling previously transmitted to him. Such poetry from poetry cannot infect people, it can only simulate a work of art, and even that only to people of perverted aesthetic taste. The lady in question being very stupid and devoid of talent, it was at once apparent how the case stood; but when such borrowing is resorted to by people who are erudite and talented and have cultivated the technique of their art, we get those borrowings from the Greek, the antique, the Christian, or mythological world, which have become so numerous, and which, particularly in our day, continue to increase and multiply and are accepted by the public as works of art if only the borrowings are well mounted by means of the technique of the particular art to which they belong.[*]

I take it that Tolstoy, out of consideration for his former friends, deliberately misdated the memory to the late 1850s. Ol'ga Golokhvastova had died in 1894.[†]

---

[*] *What Is Art? and Essays on Art,* The World's Classics edition, trans. Aylmer Maude (London: Oxford University Press, 1950), 182–183.

[†] Explaining more comically (perhaps) and certainly with more disgust, Tolstoy describes the effect of Vronsky's painting on Mikhailov: "He knew that Vronsky could not be prevented from amusing himself with painting; he knew that he and all dilettanti had a perfect right to paint what they liked, but it was distasteful to him. A man could not be prevented from making himself a big wax doll, and kissing it. But if the man were to come with the doll and sit before a man in love, and begin caressing his doll as the lover caressed the woman he loved, it would be distasteful to the lover. Just such a distasteful sensation was what Mihailov felt at the sight of Vronsky's painting: he felt it both ludicrous and irritating, both pitiable and offensive." Part 6, Chapter 13, http://www.literatureproject.com/anna-karenina/anna_137.htm.

9

The Serialization of *Anna Karenina* Resumes: January–May 1876

❋

T
olstoy was in lecture mode again in his New Year's letter to Strakhov and dis-
coursed upon philosophical and scientific ideas. He also mentioned, as if by
the way: "You write about spiritism, and I've just written about that. My article
is ready."*

I thought that I had read everything Tolstoy had written during these *Anna Karenina*
years, so I looked for this article. Frustrated, unable to track it down, I returned to the
Jubilee Edition and read the letter's footnote: "The article on spiritism was not written;
by the word 'ready' Tolstoy apparently meant to say that the article was completely
thought-through and it only remained for him to write it." †

In a manner characteristic of freelance writers and college freshmen, our hero was
lying. So why does his deception about it please me? Perhaps Tolstoy had only goaded
himself into competing with his friend. *Oh, yeah?* You're *writing an article about spiritism?
Well,* I *have one in the works too!* Perhaps a potential article by Tolstoy is more interesting
than what Strakhov actually wrote? Or, perhaps, any unwritten article about spiritism is
better than one that exists?

Tolstoy asked Strakhov to send him inexpensive editions of David Hume and Francis
Bacon, preferably not in Russian ("the worst of all"). He put off as usual any mention of

---

*   *PSS* 62: 235.

†   *PSS* 62: 237, footnote 2.

his novel until the end: "About *Anna Karenina*, I'll write nothing to you; and I will not write. If it comes out, you will surely read it through."*

In his letter to Nagornov, he thanked him for his accounting of the book sales in 1875 and said that he would like to visit him and Varya, but he had a strong cold: "But mainly, after the misery of the first half of the winter now, thank God, I'm working well and don't want to lose any time, which I have so little remaining."† He had thirty-eight years to live; or did he mean he was trying to honor the publishing deadlines? He seemed surprised he was "working well," so either way it was sensible that he wanted to continue striking while the iron was hot.

Katkov, meanwhile, had announced in his December issue the resumption of *Anna Karenina* in the January issue (to remind ourselves again: all the issues came out about four weeks into, or just beyond the date of, the publication month), but he and Tolstoy had not been in contact about it.

Tolstoy answered his sister-in-law Tatyana's January 11 letter, expressing his happiness "at the thought we'll be together as of old, spending the summer if it all turns out. The familiar joys are ten times a greater joy for us old ones."‡ As a matter of fact, that summer he would complain about the visitors and the full house, and we know, from *Anna Karenina*, that for Levin, his wife's family could upend his longstanding domestic arrangements.

He dashed off a quick note to Strakhov and mentioned, "My A Karenina is getting on. I'm not publishing it only because I have no news from the *Russ Hera*."§ Did this remark get back to Katkov? ("No news from *me*?" the editor could have exclaimed.) Tolstoy also nudged Strakhov to ask the booksellers about the *New Azbuka* and his "On Popular Education" booklet.

In his letter to Nagornov at the end of January, he took care of publishing business concerning reprintings of *War and Peace* and *Childhood*.⁵ He was quite actively involved in the publishing of his work, but in a few years he would leave it all to Sofia to take care of.

He also wrote to his sister Maria:

> I wanted to write you at length, dear friend Mashenka, but Sonya wrote everything. The only thing she didn't write is that she herself is sick; and that

---

*   *PSS* 62: 237.

†   *PSS* 62: 238, letter of January 3–4, 1876.

‡   *PSS* 62: 240, letter of January 17, 1876.

§   *PSS* 62: 241, letter of January 24–25, 1876.

⁵   *PSS* 62: 241–242.

for me at least, is the main change in our life, that from a healthy, energetic housewife, she is making herself a sick woman, or making herself worse. And generally we've changed a lot. We're gradually walking off the scene, but the children remain. For a while the children have been good. One thing we haven't changed is love for you. I feel this, having received your letter. [. . .] Losing Auntie was very hard for me—much more than you think and that I would've thought. How good it will be to see you. [. . .] I don't count this a letter, so I'll write you another one. Be angry, don't be angry, be annoyed at me, but know that no one more firmly loves you than we do.[*]

It seems that *Anna Karenina* shows us, through the siblings Stiva and Anna, evidence of the relationship between the siblings Lev and Maria. Tolstoy and Stiva were older than their sisters, and both treated their sisters with respect and love. There is no record of the harsh moralist Tolstoy ever expressing contempt for Maria's having had a child out of wedlock (of course, so had he before his marriage and so had brother Sergei), and in the novel Stiva is Anna's unwavering champion throughout her life.

It turns out, though, that Tolstoy's forty-six-year-old sister Maria was something like Anna, just one generation older.

Maria Nikolaevna Tolstaya was born March 1, 1830, at Yasnaya Polyana, when Lev was one and a half. Tolstoy's mother died August 4, 1830. I had long imagined, due to ignorance or inattention, that her death was connected with Maria's birth, but it wasn't. The Tolstoy children's mother died from falling off a swing, hitting her head and having an "inflammation of the brain."

Maria married at sixteen or seventeen and lived at her husband Valerian Petrovich Tolstoy's estate. He was a distant cousin and much older. Ivan Turgenev was Maria and Valerian's neighbor; Turgenev became attracted to her and dedicated a story to her. She had three children with her husband but was so unhappy that she left him in 1857. In Europe she met a Swede with whom she had a daughter, Elena, in 1863. When Maria's husband died in 1865, the Swede didn't marry her after all, and she continued raising her daughter abroad. Tatyana (Bers) Kuzminskaya's account of Maria's life is wonderfully opinionated and vivid:

Exceedingly spoiled from early childhood by her aunts [. . .] she was contrary and headstrong, but had a generous heart and an original mind. Her candid

---

[*]   *PSS* 62: 243. The editors guess the date as sometime in January.

religious faith was never clouded with doubts and helped her to bear many unhappy situations. Her married life was unhappy; the aunties had married her off when she was sixteen years old. She told me she was very "babyish" and didn't care whom she married. [. . .]

Valerian Petrovich led a very immoral life and was unfaithful to his wife whenever the occasion permitted. His mother, who was very fond of Marya Nikolayevna, shielded her from unpleasantness as much as she could and always tried to conceal matters from her. But after her death, this was no longer possible: Marya Nikolayevna, realizing what had been going on, felt so embittered and lonely that Leo and Sergey Nikolayevich persuaded her to leave her husband. They brought her and the children to Pirogovo where a house had been built on the opposite bank of the river.

Years later, when Leo Nikolayevich had changed his views on life and people, he said: "I always reproach myself for one thing—that I persuaded Mashenka to leave her husband and be separated from him for good. That is wrong. Whom God has joined together, let no man put asunder. My sister ought to have borne patiently everything God visited upon her."

I argued with him, saying that an immoral husband and father caused nothing but harm to his family.[*]

❋

On February 2, the January 1876 issue of the *Russian Herald* came out; it contained Part 3, Chapters 11–28, which correspond to the book publication's Chapters 13–32.[†] For Tolstoy, chapter breaks are sometimes superficial and sometimes indicate no change of scene or time; other times, the new chapters force us to completely reorient ourselves: life, he suggests, has been continuously running elsewhere. This new installment begins with a big changeover.

---

[*] Tatyana A. Kuzminskaya, *Tolstoy as I Knew Him: My Life at Home and at Yasnaya Polyana* (New York: Macmillan, 1948), 333–334. See also "Exhibition Devoted to Leo Tolstoy's Sister Mariya Tolstaya," Yasnaya Polyana website, http://ypmuseum.ru/en/2011-04-13-17-30 -44/2011-04-14-19-34-40/1021-13-02-2013.html and *L. N. Tolstoi: Entsiklopediya* (Moscow: Prosveshchenie, 2009), 309–310, 315.

[†] William Mills Todd III, "V. N. Golitsyn Reads *Anna Karenina*: How One of Karenin's Colleagues Responded to the Novel," in *Reading in Russia*, ed. Damiano Rebecchini and Raffaella Vassena (Milan: Ledizioni, 2014), 189–200.

If I had been as big a fan of *Anna Karenina* then as I am now, I would have reread the previous installments in preparation for this new one. I would have finished that rereading all the way through Part 3, Chapter 10 (Chapter 12 in the book), where Levin has had a literal and figurative vision of Kitty. I wonder how long it took Tolstoy to decide that he would let himself get away with presenting this improbable coincidence:

Forty paces from him a carriage with four horses harnessed abreast was driving toward him along the grassy road on which he was walking. The shaft-horses were tilted against the shafts by the ruts, but the dexterous driver sitting on the box held the shaft over the ruts, so that the wheels ran on the smooth part of the road.

This was all Levin noticed, and without wondering who it could be, he gazed absently at the coach.

In the coach was an old lady dozing in one corner, and at the window, evidently only just awake, sat a young girl holding in both hands the ribbons of a white cap. With a face full of light and thought, full of a subtle, complex inner life, that was remote from Levin, she was gazing beyond him at the glow of the sunrise.

At the very instant when this apparition was vanishing, the truthful eyes glanced at him. She recognized him, and her face lighted up with wondering delight.

He could not be mistaken. There were no other eyes like those in the world. There was only one creature in the world that could concentrate for him all the brightness and meaning of life. It was she. It was Kitty. He understood that she was driving to Ergushovo from the railway station. And everything that had been stirring Levin during that sleepless night, all the resolutions he had made, all vanished at once. He recalled with horror his dreams of marrying a peasant girl. There only, in the carriage that had crossed over to the other side of the road, and was rapidly disappearing, there only could he find the solution of the riddle of his life, which had weighed so agonizingly upon him of late.

She did not look out again. The sound of the carriage-springs was no longer audible, the bells could scarcely be heard. The barking of dogs showed the carriage had reached the village, and all that was left was the empty fields all round, the village in front, and he himself isolated and apart from it all, wandering lonely along the deserted highroad.

He glanced at the sky, expecting to find there the cloud shell he had been admiring and taking as the symbol of the ideas and feelings of that night. There was nothing in the sky in the least like a shell. There, in the remote heights above, a mysterious change had been accomplished. There was no trace of shell, and there was stretched over fully half the sky an even cover of tiny and ever tinier cloudlets. The sky had grown blue and bright; and with the same softness, but with the same remoteness, it met his questioning gaze.

"No," he said to himself, "however good that life of simplicity and toil may be, I cannot go back to it. I love *her*."*

We would have originally read that last chapter on May 2, 1875, exactly eight months before. We would have guessed then that *Levin and Kitty are going to get married*. There is no real dramatic tension about that; Tolstoy will execute that romance the way a master carpenter will carry out an order for a casket.

Tolstoy resumes the novel in Part 3 in a different mood, time, and place, catching us up on poor Karenin, whose secret vulnerability are the tears of women and children. Tolstoy's change of scenes are so vivid and captivating, we hardly blink, even if we have to wonder for a moment, "Who? What's this?"

Tolstoy knows that we'll catch on.

In Constance Garnett's 1901 translation, these seventeen chapters in the January 1876 installment of the novel cover eighty pages (in twenty chapters). Among the events:

- Now that he knows the truth of Anna's adultery, Karenin settles down and is satisfied with his own behavior in response.
- Anna regrets, at first, having told Karenin the truth.
- Vronsky sees prospects for a political career.
- Anna visits Betsy's gathering of frivolous women.
- Anna and Karenin meet to discuss their living arrangements.
- Levin takes a short trip in which he discusses ideas with his friend Sviazhsky, but Sviazhsky is leery of being caught up in* Levin's arguments about land and the peasantry.

A hundred and forty years ago, whoever I might have been, I would have read the January installment through in one excited sitting and then have had to end by pausing with Levin, gloomy after having hosted his sick brother Nikolai at the estate, as he (Levin)

---

* *Anna Karenina*, Part 3, Chapter 12, http://literatureproject.com/anna-karenina/anna_81.htm.

is about to head off to Europe. Tolstoy dramatizes Levin's plight from enough distance so that, despite Levin's low spirits, we cannot be too anxious about him. (In Chapter 8, above, Gusev discusses this scene in relation to *Confession*.)

In Part 3, Chapter 13, I paused over this passage about Karenin:

> "No honor, no heart, no religion; a corrupt woman. I always knew it and always saw it, though I tried to deceive myself to spare her," he said to himself. And it actually seemed to him that he always had seen it: he recalled incidents of their past life, in which he had never seen anything wrong before—now these incidents proved clearly that she had always been a corrupt woman.*

Who could blame Karenin for renouncing and defaming his wife Anna here? He has just dropped her off at home after she has told him that she is Vronsky's lover. Nobody has to think well of a spouse in such circumstances.

But I noted this moment because I realized I keep wishing that Tolstoy had told us more incidents of "their past life." Why do we have to know so little? Is a *Life of Johnson*–sized and –detailed biography of Anna what I really want? That is . . .

Would I like to know about her birth and her habits as a toddler? Her first words, her childhood sayings? What her mother and father were like? From which parent did she get her beauty and from which her energy? Who taught her English and French? What were she and her brother Stiva like as children together? How old were they when their parents died? How did she react? How did the aunt who then raised them assess little Stiva and Anna? What did her voice sound like as a girl? Did she play an instrument? Did Anna sing? What exactly happened that made her aunt feel that Karenin could be coerced into marrying Anna?

Would I really want to know *everything*, as if we were in a 21st-century novel? Why would I be interested in what her first time in bed with Karenin was like? Was it as ghastly as her and Vronsky's first time?

Does my fascination with brilliant, desperately suicidal Anna have limits?

Would I really want to know about Anna's amazement when she gave birth to Seryozha? Did nine years of married life with Karenin seem possible because she so loved their child?

Would I really like to know all those thousands of details that we think we know about ourselves, but about Anna?

Of course!

---

* *Anna Karenina*, Part 3, Chapter 13, http://literatureproject.com/anna-karenina/anna_82.htm.

We can say for Tolstoy that he makes it possible to imagine that such details (facts) could be known because they must have happened, as in life. This is his highest, finest morality—showing us again and again that no one is a walk-on, a bit player; everyone exists—seems to exist—beyond the confines of the novel, beyond their author's presentation of them. We know ourselves in and by the moment and almost everyone we meet in his fiction seems to exist in that same way. The characters don't know they're in a novel and almost never behave as if they are. They think they exist in three dimensions, with their own minds, feelings, and bodies—and we, our moral senses sharpened by Tolstoy's, take for granted that they do.

True enough, Tolstoy didn't know all the details because he hadn't thought of them or written them all down. *Oh, but he could have.*

Do I want to know what Anna wrote in her unhappy, idle-time children's novel in Part 7, Chapter 10?

I do! I want to pry that leather-bound manuscript from her hand and read it. One summer twenty years ago I spent way too long trying to figure out what it would have been about. (That is, I *wrote* Anna's children's novel, much to the embarrassment of some of my friends who read it.) And what were her writing routines? In the morning, like her creator, with a big glass of tea? In the long society-less afternoons? Did she revise extensively, as Tolstoy did? Did she (she could have) page through Tolstoy's *Azbuka* to find the right tone and vocabulary? He had just revised and published that reading primer to great acclaim before he took on the serialization of *Anna Karenina* in 1875. Wouldn't many of the people in her circle have read *War and Peace*? She was a big reader; I think that she would have read *War and Peace*—if Tolstoy could've imagined it. Wouldn't reading that novel have made Anna conscious of herself in a way that Tolstoy's sister-in-law Tatyana did in fact become conscious of herself through reading about Natasha in *War and Peace*?

We see in drafts of the novel the transformation of scenes and characters; we see pieces of Tolstoy's sudden or steady inventions and his abandonment of perfectly good or inert scenes. But there is absolutely no evidence of how, why, or exactly when a coarse, head-of-fluff flirt in the earliest drafts became the elegant, hyper-conscious Anna. I don't believe in miracles, but that was a miracle.

We readers can't invent the unknown details of *Anna Karenina*, because we're not Tolstoy, but he doesn't seem to have invented them so much as to have discovered them, and then dug them out of the earth with his pen's imagination.

I could do with more Anna. For me, the greatest book that doesn't exist is *Life of Karenina*.

Having finished reading the January issue back on February 2, 1876, I would have wanted to talk about what I had just read. I would have encouraged my friends and my wife to read it. And then I would have proceeded with my life and daydreamed about Anna in anticipation of the next month's issue. Probably I would not have been wondering about Tolstoy at home at Yasnaya Polyana refining the writing, weighing anew each scene and moment, though that was indeed what was preoccupying him.

In the midst of revising the February issue's installment, Tolstoy wrote to request Strakhov's response to his last letter's (dull) philosophizing. He added, only at the end, as if by the way: "I'm very busy with Karenina. The first part of the book is dry and, it seems, poor, but now I'm sending the corrections of the second installment and it, I know, is good."* The editors of the Jubilee Edition say the "dry and . . . poor . . . first part" that Tolstoy had in mind were the January chapters just published.† The "good" part, to him, is Part 4, Chapters 1–17,‡ which starts with the awkwardness of Anna's home arrangement: that is, still living with Karenin but seeing Vronsky on the side.

Tolstoy's next two bits of correspondence are to Sofia, but vaguely dated. The first is a postscript to their daughter Tanya's letter to Sofia when Sofia was in Moscow for a wedding. It's an unusual situation—Tolstoy home, Sofia away. This was one of the few times in their married life so far that she was away while he was home with the children. "I received your telegram and I'm very glad," he wrote. "I slept downstairs and can't understand how I lived alone. Please don't hurry—stay even a few more days if you're happy, but, mainly, don't worry. The more money you spend on yourself the better. The children and teachers are fine, as you see.

"I was occupied this morning.

"I envy you that you see them together—groom and bride [. . .] I'm glad I won't be at their wedding or would cry all over the place. I'm going to eat blini."§

The Jubilee editors narrowed down their guess for the next letter, this one from Tolstoy in Moscow to Sofia in Yasnaya Polyana, to either January or February. Let's say it's February. He wrote her from the Nagornovs' about his day and how he hadn't slept. He had gone to the printer's for galleys and had sat with Varya Nagornova while doing corrections of that installment and then he went to eat at the D'yakovs'. Then he met with Katkov,

---

*   *PSS* 62: 247, letter of February 14–15, 1876.

†   I wish I could design a chart illustrating "Tolstoy's Assessments of *Anna Karenina*." The categories are: Good, Bad, Disgusting. Almost all of his assessments fall into the second and third categories.

‡   In the February issue of the *Russian Herald*, what became the *book*'s 17 chapters were divided into 15.

§   *PSS* 83: 221, letter of February 9–15,1876.

with whom he didn't—he seemed to be confessing—speak about the money. Finally, in closing, he mentioned seeing the tailor Ayet to order a special coat.*

What is there to say about Tolstoy's tailor, Philippe Ayet? Why would anyone care about him?

I don't know why, but I do care, and this little shopping trip sheds light on both Sofia and Tolstoy. Sofia noted: "Ayet was the best French tailor in Moscow. L.N. at home in the country wore blouses, big gray flannels, or coarse unwhitened linen, which I myself sewed. When L.N. went to the city, he wore very elegant clothes from the best tailors. I've preserved ever since [in 1919] a frock-coat from Ayet and a blackbear coat and many other clothes."†

Sofia saved his clothes! Lest we imagine Tolstoy always in homemade peasant-blouses and boots, she reminds us that he had a long period of appreciating fine clothes.

Of the four surviving photographs of Tolstoy during his *Anna Karenina* years two show him one day in 1876 (either now in midwinter or late in the fall) posing in a fine coat, which I'm guessing is the one Ayet made for him:

Tolstoy in 1876‡

✳

*   *PSS* 83: 222.

†   *PSS* 83: 223, footnote 7.

‡   Tolstoy, 1876, http://tolstoy.ru/media/photos/index.php?df=1846&dt=1876&q=&page=5.

On February 21 Aleksei P. Bobrinsky and the Tula governor Sergei P. Ushakov came to Yasnaya Polyana to talk religion with Tolstoy. On the same day, he wrote his brother Sergei:

> [. . .] The longer you live, the less free time. Or you get sick, or family duties, or writing, which I started up, but I'm afraid that I can't succeed in finishing this year, despite that it often disgusts me.*

What is it exactly about *Anna Karenina* that disgusts him, though? The characters? The characters who, he would say later, seemed more real to him than actual people? Was it the burden of writing a compelling novel for those same sorts of people that he was disgustedly writing about? It's a "gloomy" time:

> I myself this winter am healthier than before and better than the others. Whooping cough even now leaves its traces as Seryozha, Lelya, and Sonya cough. Sonya is very weakened in health and I am beginning to be seriously afraid for her. [. . .] A week ago she was in Moscow. [. . .] and there the doctors found her unwell. I told nobody about this but I involuntarily tell you that I am afraid. In general this winter for me has been morally very heavy; and the death of Auntie left me terribly heavy memories that I can't write in a letter. *Time to die*—this is not true; but it's true that there's nothing more left in life than to die. This is what I ceaselessly feel. [. . .]

He had used the phrase "time to die" twice in 1875 to Sergei, and his creation Levin has used it, too.[†] In the coming summer he would use the phrase "we'll soon die" in his correspondence to Strakhov.[‡] In *Confession*, he has no hesitation about recounting his unnerving attraction to suicide; in his letters, however, to sensitive and loving correspondents, it seems that "time to die" was the closest he could come to suggesting his thoughts of suicide.

He told Sergei that he had the money, that however much of the debt Sergei needed now, he would get now, but "If you're not coming to us this month, in March I'll bring you all the money. But now, come or write, but write everything in detail, about yourself

---

*   *PSS* 62: 247–248, letter of February 21, 1876.

†   *PSS* 62: 198, letter of August 25, 1875. *PSS* 62: 218, letter of November 9–10, 1875.

‡   *PSS* 62: 282, letter of July 31, 1876.

and your family. [. . .] Write everything that comes in your head, and I will already completely understand it."[*]

The connection between the brothers, wherein they understand by the slightest utterance what the other is feeling, is similar to that between Konstantin Levin and his dying brother Nikolay in a scene that Tolstoy had only recently written into the novel:

> He felt that if they had both not kept up appearances, but had spoken, as it is called, from the heart—that is to say, had said only just what they were thinking and feeling—they would simply have looked into each other's faces, and Konstantin could only have said, "You're dying, you're dying," and Nikolay could only have answered, "I know I'm dying, but I'm afraid, I'm afraid, I'm afraid!" And they could have said nothing more, if they had said only what was in their hearts. But life like that was impossible, and so Konstantin tried to do what he had been trying to do all his life, and never could learn to do, though, as far as he could observe, many people knew so well how to do it, and without it there was no living at all. He tried to say what he was not thinking, but he felt continually that it had a ring of falsehood, that his brother detected him in it, and was exasperated at it.[†]

There's no use lying to a brother.

To return for a moment to Tolstoy's letter to Sergei: "Rey's good for us but his sister is bad. Sonya can't stand her and I'm afraid it's going to wreck things with the brother."[‡]

In *My Life*, Sofia writes: "During my illness {Jules Rey's sister} Mademoiselle Rey arrived {from Switzerland}. She was fair-haired, short of stature, round-shouldered, dressed in a black lutestring apron, and looked more like a servant than a governess. Her voice was smooth-tongued, her words were flattering, and her mannerisms were catlike. I did not take to her right from the start."[§] A dozen pages later, Sofia called her "repulsive."[¶] According to the Jubilee editors, who date a Sofia letter on this topic as January–February: "Mademoiselle Rey lived with her brother at Yasnaya Polyana from November 1875 to

---

[*]   *PSS* 62: 247–248, letter of February 21, 1876.

[†]   *Anna Karenina*, Part 3, Chapter 32, http://literatureproject.com/anna-karenina/anna_101.htm.

[‡]   *PSS* 62: 248, letter of February 21, 1876.

[§]   Tolstaya, *My Life*, 215.

[¶]   Tolstaya, *My Life*, 228.

September 1876."* The Tolstoys were worrying about firing her; that is, if they fired her, would her brother leave, too? (They did, but he didn't.) As a replacement-in-waiting they hired Annie Phillips, a nineteen-year-old English woman.† Oh, would that we could discover that Miss Phillips wrote detailed letters to England about her new home! While we're wishing, would that she were practically a Jane Austen or Anthony Trollope heroine who went to Russia for her financially desperate family, and in trepidation and curiosity noticed everything and wrote it all down. How bewildering would the Tolstoy family have been to a Victorian girl? What would she have said of this couple? Would she have explained to her parents that the father of the family seemed to be a famous literary man? (There is a novel-in-waiting or a Netflix series here: *Annie Phillips: Governess to the Tolstoy Family*.)

Would Tolstoy have looked her over and wondered if his rakish Stiva would have made a play for her? Did Sofia make sure Miss Phillips was *not* beautiful? In this year's April installment of the novel, Anna makes a mistake in Italy by hiring a beautiful local woman to mind her baby Annie:

> "Here she is," she added, looking out of the window at the handsome Italian nurse, who was carrying the child out into the garden, and immediately glancing unnoticed at Vronsky. The handsome nurse, from whom Vronsky was painting a head for his picture, was the one hidden grief in Anna's life. He painted with her as his model, admired her beauty and medievalism, and Anna dared not confess to herself that she was afraid of becoming jealous of this nurse, and was for that reason particularly gracious and condescending both to her and her little son.‡

I'll bet Sofia didn't ever make that mistake. But wait . . . A note by the Jubilee editors about the next letter to Sofia, of unknown date (January or February), says Jules Rey was fired in January 1878 for "carrying on an amour with Annie." Rey was about thirty by that time. Sofia wrote that Rey "had become a hopeless inebriate."§ Sofia recalled that Annie Phillips was "a very dear young Englishwoman [. . .] who eventually got involved

---

*　*PSS* 83: 223.

†　Tolstaya, *My Life,* 216.

‡　*Anna Karenina,* Part 5, Chapter 9, http://literatureproject.com/anna-karenina/anna _133.htm.

§　Tolstaya, *My Life,* 243.

in a romantic relationship with the Monsieur Rey, although nothing ever came of it."* Sofia remembered a skating incident in 1876, where her son Lev fell through the ice, and that Annie was "flirting" at the time with Rey and didn't notice, though fortunately the gardener Semen did and rescued the boy.† (Annie never wrote a novel or memoir of her Tolstoy time, but she did meet "an English railway technician in Tula" and married him in 1880. The next new Englishwoman the Tolstoys hired, Lizzie Ford, was a "silly, doll-like and unhelpful person."‡)

On this busy February 21, visiting with friends and writing letters, Tolstoy thanked Prince S. S. Urussov for a letter regarding Tolstoy's "religious doubts," which doubts Tolstoy didn't want to write about now, as they were not as doubtful as usual. He appreciated that Urussov hadn't tried to "prove" why Tolstoy should believe.§

❋

The February issue of the *Russian Herald* was published on February 29.

Finally!

We cancel any appointments for the afternoon and evening and sit and read Part 4, Chapters 1–15 (those 15 will be 17 chapters in the book) . . .

The Karenins are living together in St. Petersburg with a compromise that Anna not see Vronsky at the house. Anna's two men encounter each other one evening, Vronsky arriving when Karenin is leaving the house. Because of a nightmare, Anna predicts to Vronsky that she will soon die in childbirth. Karenin sees a lawyer about the legal procedures of a divorce. Karenin, on his way to investigate a provincial governmental matter, goes to Moscow, where Oblonsky pulls him into the dinner party that he is hosting. It is at this party that Levin and Kitty re-meet and seal their love. Dolly learns from Karenin that he means to divorce Anna. She tries to dissuade him from this. Levin, now engaged to be married, is ecstatic and has a sleepless but revelatory night. He meets with Kitty's parents. Then Levin has Kitty read his diaries, which are apparently full of unimaginably shameful details of his sexual life; this knowledge distresses her, but his conscience is cleared. Tolstoy jumps us back to Karenin; he receives Anna's telegram announcing her impending death; he takes the train to Petersburg and hopes that she is in fact going

---

*   Tolstaya, *My Life*, 223.

†   Tolstaya, *My Life*, 230.

‡   Tolstaya, *My Life*, 281.

§   *PSS* 62: 248–249.

to die. She seems to be dying as a result of an infection during childbirth; she begs his forgiveness and insists he forgive the shamed, pitiful Vronsky: Karenin does so.

I used to think that Sofia's misery the past November and the miserable death of the infant daughter, Vara (Varvara), had given Tolstoy the idea of presenting Anna's false premonition of death in childbirth, but Sofia's fear and agonizing illness dated from at least five years before, and Tolstoy, we have seen, had planned in early outlines of the novel for Anna to have a premature premonition of dying in childbirth.

While such a premonition makes sense with Dolly, an experienced mother who does in the course of the novel lose a baby, it has never seemed to me to fit Anna, that is, the Anna we know, in contrast to Tolstoy's original conception of her.

An impressive group that includes Dostoevsky, Fet, and Strakhov thought that the scene of forgiveness at her prematurely foreseen death was *great*. Fet compared it to an operatic trio. Strakhov thought that it was "so good and strong." Why did Dostoevsky admire the scene? He had grown bored, he wrote, with Levin, but then . . .

> [. . .] the scene of the heroine's death (later she recovers) explained to me the essential part of the author's design. In the very center of that petty and inso-lent life there appeared a great and eternal living truth, at once illuminating everything. These petty, insignificant and deceitful beings suddenly became genuine and truthful people, worthy of being called men, solely because of a natural law, the law of human death. Their shell vanished, and truth alone appeared. The last ones developed into the first, while the first ones (Vronsky) all of a sudden became the last, losing their halo in humiliation; but having been humbled, they became infinitely better, worthier, more truthful than when they were the first and the eminent. Hatred and deceit began to speak in terms of forgiveness and love. . . . these people began to resemble genuine human beings! There proved to be no guilty ones; they all accused themselves.[*]

Who am I to argue with Dostoevsky? I'll just offer up my own two kopecks: For me, a worshiper at the temple of *Anna Karenina*, Chapter 17 of Part 4 is the most artificial scene in the novel. It seems to me that Tolstoy is cobbling together with plastic beads and Elmer's glue a tableau that he saw on a stage. Or take out my artistic evaluation of

---

[*] F. M. Dostoievsky [sic], *The Diary of a Writer*, trans. Boris Brasol (New York: George Braziller, 1954). (See "Chapter II, 1, One of the Principal Contemporaneous," February 1877, 610–611.)

it. Let's say instead that this scene is where I don't like or recognize the Anna that he has conjured up for us.

We'll backtrack over the scene. Karenin has returned home:

> With a sense of weariness and uncleanness from the night spent in the train, in the early fog of Petersburg Alexey Alexandrovitch drove through the deserted Nevsky and stared straight before him, not thinking of what was awaiting him. He could not think about it, because in picturing what would happen, he could not drive away the reflection that her death would at once remove all the difficulty of his position. Bakers, closed shops, night-cabmen, porters sweeping the pavements flashed past his eyes, and he watched it all, trying to smother the thought of what was awaiting him, and what he dared not hope for, and yet was hoping for. He drove up to the steps. A sledge and a carriage with the coachman asleep stood at the entrance. As he went into the entry, Alexey Alexandrovitch, as it were, got out his resolution from the remotest corner of his brain, and mastered it thoroughly. Its meaning ran: "If it's a trick, then calm contempt and departure. If truth, do what is proper."*

I feel as reluctant to enter this scene as Karenin is. I anticipate the melodrama. Karenin asks a servant after Anna; he hears that she's alive and has given birth. Vronsky's coat is hanging on the hatstand.

Is my distaste the result of Anna and Vronsky being melodramatic?

> At the table, sitting sideways in a low chair, was Vronsky, his face hidden in his hands, weeping. He jumped up at the doctor's voice, took his hands from his face, and saw Alexey Alexandrovitch. Seeing the husband, he was so overwhelmed that he sat down again, drawing his head down to his shoulders, as if he wanted to disappear; but he made an effort over himself, got up, and said:
> "She is dying. The doctors say there is no hope. I am entirely in your power, only let me be here . . . though I am at your disposal. I . . ."
> Alexey Alexandrovitch, seeing Vronsky's tears, felt a rush of that nervous emotion always produced in him by the sight of other people's suffering, and

---

*   *Anna Karenina,* Part 4, Chapter 17, http://www.literatureproject.com/anna-karenina /anna_118.htm.

turning away his face, he moved hurriedly to the door, without hearing the rest of his words. From the bedroom came the sound of Anna's voice saying something. Her voice was lively, eager, with exceedingly distinct intonations. Alexey Alexandrovitch went into the bedroom, and went up to the bed. She was lying turned with her face toward him. Her cheeks were flushed crimson, her eyes glittered, her little white hands thrust out from the sleeves of her dressing gown were playing with the quilt, twisting it about. It seemed as though she were not only well and blooming, but in the happiest frame of mind. She was talking rapidly, musically, and with exceptionally correct articulation and expressive intonation. [It seems to me that Tolstoy is stage-managing: whispering unconvincing directions and words to an actress playing Anna.]

"For Alexey—I am speaking of Alexey Alexandrovitch (what a strange and awful thing that both are Alexey, isn't it?)—Alexey would not refuse me. I should forget, he would forgive. . . . But why doesn't he come? He's so good he doesn't know himself how good he is. Ah, my God, what agony! Give me some water, quick! Oh, that will be bad for her, my little girl! Oh, very well then, give her to a nurse. Yes, I agree, it's better in fact. He'll be coming; it will hurt him to see her. Give her to the nurse."

"Anna Arkadyevna, he has come. Here he is!" said the midwife, trying to attract her attention to Alexey Alexandrovitch.

"Oh, what nonsense!" Anna went on, not seeing her husband. "No, give her to me; give me my little one! He has not come yet. You say he won't forgive me, because you don't know him. No one knows him. I'm the only one, and it was hard for me even. His eyes I ought to know—Seryozha has just the same eyes—and I can't bear to see them because of it. Has Seryozha had his dinner? I know everyone will forget him. He would not forget. Seryozha must be moved into the corner room, and Mariette must be asked to sleep with him."

All of a sudden she shrank back, was silent; and in terror, as though expecting a blow, as though to defend herself, she raised her hands to her face. She had seen her husband.

"No, no!" she began. "I am not afraid of him; I am afraid of death. Alexey, come here. I am in a hurry, because I've no time, I've not long left to live; the fever will begin directly and I shall understand nothing more. Now I understand, I understand it all, I see it all!"

Alexey Alexandrovitch's wrinkled face wore an expression of agony; he took her by the hand and tried to say something, but he could not utter it; his lower lip quivered, but he still went on struggling with his emotion, and only now and then glanced at her. And each time he glanced at her, he saw her eyes gazing at him with such passionate and triumphant tenderness as he had never seen in them.

"Wait a minute, you don't know . . . stay a little, stay! . . ." She stopped, as though collecting her ideas. "Yes," she began; "yes, yes, yes. This is what I wanted to say. Don't be surprised at me. I'm still the same. . . . But there is another woman in me, I'm afraid of her: she loved that man, and I tried to hate you, and could not forget about her that used to be. I'm not that woman. Now I'm my real self, all myself. I'm dying now, I know I shall die, ask him. Even now I feel—see here, the weights on my feet, on my hands, on my fingers. My fingers—see how huge they are! But this will soon all be over. . . . Only one thing I want: forgive me, forgive me quite. I'm terrible, but my nurse used to tell me; the holy martyr—what was her name? She was worse. And I'll go to Rome; there's a wilderness, and there I shall be no trouble to any one, only I'll take Seryozha and the little one. . . . No, you can't forgive me! I know, it can't be forgiven! No, no, go away, you're too good!" She held his hand in one burning hand, while she pushed him away with the other. *

The original, insincere, melodramatic Anna could have said all that as could any raving drama queen. "Now I'm my real self" is the most blasphemous statement in the book. *She is not!* When Tolstoy first imagined this event, it was the original Anna that he had in mind and he despised her, but for some reason he was quite moved by it: "The scene, describing the reconciliation of Karenin with Udashev [Vronsky] by the bed of the dying wife, which, doubtless, Tolstoy gave a lot of meaning to and was writing it, perhaps, 'with tears in his eyes,' was written straight off and, without essential changes, it reached the finished text," writes Gusev. †

Coming to the now ill-fitting material while writing for the serial deadline, Tolstoy's artistic vision was not alert to the new, real Anna. I reject or don't want to accept that Anna is melodramatic. (Yes, I know she will throw herself under a train, I know!) But

---

*   *Anna Karenina,* Part 4, Chapter 17, http://www.literatureproject.com/anna-karenina/anna _118.htm.

†   Gusev, *Materials,* 288.

this scene of Anna's delirium, recognizing and not recognizing Karenin, babbling about Karenin's goodness and forgiveness, and next her insisting on her two Alexeis to shake hands and forgive each other! I don't like it. *We know that for now she's not going to die;* I get the feeling, in spite of the doctor's insistence that she'll die, that everyone knows she's not going to die and that they're all playacting. Tolstoy did not believe in doctors' evaluations, he said, and yet he hung on their words anyway: "The doctors said that it was puerperal fever, and that it was ninety-nine chances in a hundred it would end in death."* "Ninety-nine chances in a hundred" was not a scientific estimate based on studies conducted by the Russian Medical Association. At best, it meant the doctors were guessing she would die; they were only admitting that they couldn't help her. It's *La Traviata*, except that no one is singing beautifully, *and Anna doesn't die*! I can't recall my first response to this chapter, but I cannot read it anymore without feeling embarrassed.

Anna Karenina, in a novel named after her, *cannot* die yet.

In 1871, when Sofia was suffering the same childbirth infection, Sofia *could* have died (Tolstoy heard back then the doctors' assessment of there being a "one percent chance" of her survival), and Tolstoy was in real agony. By 1876 they knew death close up, losing three children in the last two years. Death was no stranger to either of them. Here, in the novel, however, everyone's just pretending.

✳

While Tolstoy never expressed admiration for *Anna Karenina* and never asked anyone to admire it, he didn't mind continually expressing his bewilderment at the lack of admiration of the *Azbuka*. On February 29, he replied to the children's book author Evgeniy V. Lvov: "[Your letter] gave me great pleasure, dear Prince, and also made me sad. It gave me pleasure because you appreciated the form of my stories for the people, but it also made me sad because in the 5 years, I think it is, since these stories came out, you have never come across them and, like the public, you considered me either a speculator, writing for the people for money, or a 50-year-old fool talking about something he knows nothing about. I fought against German pedagogy precisely because I have devoted a big part of my life to this matter, because I know how the people and the people's children think and because I know how to talk to them, and this knowledge did not fall out of the sky because I have talent (a most foolish, nonsensical word), but because I acquired this knowledge by

---

*   *Anna Karenina,* Part 4, Chapter 17, http://www.literatureproject.com/anna-karenina/anna _118.htm.

love and hard work. The stories and fables written in the booklets are what has been sifted out from a quantity of adapted stories 20 times as great, and each of them was revised by me as many as 10 times, and cost me more hard work than any passage in any of my writings. The *Primer* cost me even more hard work. I have been praised for everything I have written, but not a single word which is not abusive has been said in print about the one really good and useful thing that I have done, the *Primer* and these booklets. You read them and appreciated them because you write yourself, and want to write, and because you have taste and feeling. But anyone with taste and feeling reading these booklets could say: 'Yes, all right, simple and clear, but in places bad and false.' And anyone who read them and said this would be absolutely right. But if anyone tries to write stories like these he will see how hard to come by these negative virtues are, which consist merely in a thing being simple and clear and having nothing superfluous or false about it."*

Was Tolstoy dissatisfied with *Anna Karenina* because it wasn't simple or clear enough? No one has ever criticized the novel as difficult or obscure. But perhaps he wasn't reconciling what he had achieved by hard work in the *Azbuka* with what was necessarily more complex and difficult: the problems dramatized in *Anna Karenina* of how to live, why to live, and, finally, how to survive one's suicidal thoughts.

On the same day as his letter to Lvov or the day after, March 1, Tolstoy followed up with Nagornov on the marketing strategy concerning *Childhood* and *War and Peace*. When the business planning was complete, Tolstoy moved on to family news. Sofia "continues sick" and that night was so sick that they telegraphed for Dr. Chirkov—but when Sofia was better in the morning, they telegraphed again to Dr. Chirkov that they didn't need him after all, but now, that day, they didn't know if he had got the second telegram or if he was about to arrive.†

Tolstoy was impulsive in his use of the new technology, and in *Anna Karenina* Dolly kvetches that Stiva loves to telegraph. Anna also sends hasty telegrams.

In a letter to Fet, Tolstoy mentioned that because of Sofia's poor health, ranging from fever to migraines to pain in the stomach, he had no "peace of mind, which I especially need now for work. The end of winter and the beginning of spring are always my more productive times, and it's necessary to finish this sickening to me novel."‡ He jokingly wished Fet a pain in the tooth that would take him to Moscow so that Tolstoy could see him. For perhaps the first time in a few years of letters to Fet, Tolstoy didn't mention horses.

---

*   Christian, *Tolstoy's Letters*, 291–292.

†   *PSS* 62: 253, letter of March 1, 1876.

‡   *PSS* 62: 253, letter of February 29–March 1, 1876.

Dostoevsky found something annoying about Tolstoy's men being so smitten with horses and wrote in an essay: "characters, such as Vronsky (one of the heroes of the romance), who can speak of nothing but horses, and who is even unable to find a subject for conversation other than horses, are, of course, curious from the standpoint of ascertaining their type, but very monotonous and confined to a certain taste only. . . ."[*]

Fet answered Tolstoy: "If I hold back from sending a letter to you, dear Lev Nikolaevich, it's to spare Katkov, the public and myself. When someone builds such a splendid cathedral as your novel, the sins get pulled under the elbow."[†]

This late winter, Tolstoy was anxious that Alexandrine Tolstaya had not written him in a while; he sensed or feared that he had done something wrong or had offended her and he asked her to reassure him by writing him back. "My life," he explained, "goes on as of old, only with new losses. I wrote you about the death of Auntie Ergol'skaya; since then I have buried three young children and the relative-aunt Yushkova, who lived lately with us."[‡]

Sofia, in the "New Projects" chapter of *My Life*, remembered, "While Lev Nikolaevich continued work on *Anna Karenina*, his imagination was already exploring new themes, new images, and the germ of a new novel was sprouting in his thought, which he told me about in the following words, uttered on the 3rd of March 1876":

> "For the work to be good, {the author} must love its basic underlying thought. In *Anna Karenina* I loved the thought of *family*. In *War and Peace* I loved the thought of *the people* (in the sense of *all* the Russian people). And now I have the clear feeling that I shall love the thought of the Russian people in the sense of the power of conquering {new lands} (migration)."
>
> And Lev Nikolaevich wanted to write a story about a cultured person who rejected the life of his own milieu and went off with migrants to new places. Lev Nikolaevich was always fascinated by this life in new places, this populist appeal of the life of a Robinson Crusoe. [. . .][§]

---

[*]   Dostoievsky [sic], *The Diary of a Writer*, 610.

[†]   This is how I understand the expression "the sins get pulled under the elbow": *When you are doing something great, the little faults are forgotten. PSS* 62: 254, letter of March 8, 1876.

[‡]   Regarding the "relative-aunt," Tolstoy's "Auntie" helped raise him; she was his father's second cousin. Andrew Donskov, *Tolstoy and Tolstaya: A Portrait of a Life in Letters* (Ottawa: University of Ottawa, 2017), 412. *PSS* 62: 254, letter of March 1, 1876.

[§]   Tolstaya, *My Life*, 222.

Sofia didn't notice, it seems to me, that through his Robinson Crusoe fantasy her husband was describing his own unfulfilled dream of leaving home and her. He seems never to have extinguished this desire.

> After conceiving this story about the migrants, Lev Nikolaevich spent a good deal of time walking along the high road, talking to the local populace and, as always, recording in his notebooks anything that seemed interesting to him in the stories told to him. Or he would simply jot down many of the folk idioms he heard from passing pilgrims, travelers, or peasants on their way to and from work in various parts of Russia and speaking the dialects of the area whence they hailed.
>
> "I toss all that into a drawer in my mind and select from it what I need for my writing," Lev Nikolaevich told me.

Tolstoy's notebooks from this time do not exist, and he didn't record folk idioms and stories in his diaries. Did he have a scrap pile of "jottings" from this time that Sofia was unable to squirrel away and preserve for us? (No, not that I have discovered.) Was Sofia misremembering or confused about there being actual notebooks? She quotes him *saying* "a drawer in my mind," which is similar to the way in *Anna Karenina* Mikhailov takes note of people's faces and then, as he sketches, selects what he needs for his paintings:

> He walked rapidly to the door of his studio, and in spite of his excitement he was struck by the soft light on Anna's figure as she stood in the shade of the entrance listening to Golenishtchev, who was eagerly telling her something, while she evidently wanted to look round at the artist. He was himself unconscious how, as he approached them, he seized on this impression and absorbed it, as he had the chin of the shopkeeper who had sold him the cigars, and put it away somewhere to be brought out when he wanted it. [*]

But back to the travelers that Sofia remembered Tolstoy encountering near Yasnaya Polyana: they made him think about the Russian people's "union of friendship," how the pilgrims could travel everywhere and be provided for.

---

[*] *Anna Karenina,* Part 5, Chapter 10, http://www.literatureproject.com/anna-karenina/anna _134.htm.

If you, too, want to be included in this union of friendship, Lev Nikolaevich reasoned with himself, *you have to confess the same faith as the people.* He spoke about this with me as well, and began seeking truth and religion in carrying out *all* the rituals of the Orthodox Church. I would emphasize that in 1876 this was still just a faint stirring in Lev Nikolaevich's heart, which did not reach its full development until 1877, and by 1878 had already begun to give way to denial.[*]

I am often skeptical of Sofia's accounts, but I completely trust her on this. She was there with him every day and studied his moods; this was one of those dark periods about which he wrote in *Confession*. Sofia recalled:

> [. . .] When Lev Nikolaevich wasn't busy writing, he would play the piano for four to six hours a day, or spend his time out hunting. It seemed as though he was trying at any cost to forget about himself, to avoid thinking about the emptiness of his life and his desire to end it.[†]

In "Family Life," her next chapter, Sofia took a long but forgetful view: "We had very few visitors at the beginning of 1876, and I can't recall any details of our life during that period."[‡]

She may not have recalled that in the beginning of March she wrote her sister Tatyana that Tolstoy was preparing the chapters for the March issue, and yet he was also so worried about her health that it prevented him from working.

❊

Tolstoy could expect regular responses from Strakhov, so when he didn't receive them, he grew anxious. He wrote Strakhov in early March: "You can't imagine how much I desire to know your opinion on what I wrote you in the last letter and with what conviction in the firmness of my position I await you and desire a strong attack in order to show my firmness."[§] These philosophical debates continued being for him a kind of exercise, like fencing or chess. He didn't even mention *Anna Karenina*.

---

[*]   Tolstaya, *My Life*, 222–223.

[†]   Tolstaya, *My Life*, 223.

[‡]   Ibid.

[§]   *PSS* 62: 255, letter of March 8–9, 1876.

He wrote Alexandrine again, apparently in answer to a March 6 letter from her, and explained the winter's unhappinesses:

> My children died like this: after 5 living (merciful God), the 6th was a strong boy, who my wife loved very much, Petya. At a year he got sick one night, and in the morning, as soon as my wife left him, they called to me that he had died—the croup. The other after him, a charming baby (already at a few months it was seen he had a miraculously sweet nature), also at a year old. He got sick with water on the brain. And ever since it's very painful to remember that terrible week of his dying. This winter my wife was near death with illness. She had whooping cough. But she was pregnant. She was near death and prematurely gave birth to a daughter, who lived only a few hours and who was terribly pitied only later when her mother was out of danger. My wife hadn't even got up (she couldn't for six weeks), when the fresh, lively old woman, Auntie Pelageya Il'inishna, who only in that year came from a monastery to live with us, lay down and in terrible torment passed on. Strange to say, but this death of an old eighty-year-old acted on me like no other death acted. It made me so sad to lose her, so sad, the last memories about the past generation of my father, mother, sad for her suffering, but in this death was something else that I can't describe to you and I'll tell you sometime. Not an hour passes that I don't think about her.[*]

He was in a low mood and even seemed to blame his novel's heroine for disappointing him: "My Anna has become a bore, insipid as a bitter radish. I have to worry along with her as one would with an ill-natured pupil; but do not speak ill of her or, if you must, do it with *ménagement*, for after all I have adopted her."[†]

This was a rare expression of paternal feeling in Tolstoy in regard to a character. As a narrator or author he wasn't inclined to express fondness or sympathy for characters, as Trollope so regularly does. Tolstoy here seemed to be amusing himself with the idea that his Anna was acting out.

When he wrote Fet, he asked for family news and told him his own. Then he wanted to know if Fet had a stallion with Arabian blood, not too expensive, to mate with Tolstoy's Kirgiz mares, and maybe he could also buy some mares "for recreation."

How many horses does a man need?

---

[*] *PSS* 62: 256–257, letter of March 8–12, 1876.

[†] Tolstoy, *Tolstoy: A Life of My Father*, 213.

Tolstoy had the same kind of appetite for horses as a particular kind of 20th-century American might have had for cars. *One can't have too many!*

He returned to the topic of his wife's health: "We're as of old. My wife became worse but is now tolerable." And finally to *Anna Karenina*: "I still dream of finishing the novel by summer, but I'm beginning to doubt that."* It was already mid-March.

The darkness Tolstoy was living in seems, in *Confession*, to cover 1875 and this year of 1876 and then 1877. But at this moment in March, despite his blues, he was busy, and he was eager to hear from friends. He still had so many interests. He was not a monomaniac, though his nonfictional writings, so powerfully focused, can make it seem as if he was. *Confession* is a peculiar and disturbing book because of its relentless focus.

Meanwhile, Sofia was "again becoming ill."† A new grief came. Sofia recalled that "on the 17th I had {another} miscarriage, which I soon recovered from." For a year she would not become pregnant again. (Or at least she would not have another baby until December of 1877.) Tolstoy, meanwhile, was trying to balance himself, doing something repetitious, rhythmical, while unintentionally driving that repetition into the brains of his wife and children. Sofia recalled: "I got terribly tired of listening to Lev Nikolaevich's practicing on the piano."

> His scales and exercises would go on for hours. I recall he learnt to play a Weber sonata, which greatly appealed to me. His musical accomplishments gave him cheer and distracted him from his more weighty thoughts.‡

Sofia wrote her sister Tatyana on March 17: "Have you read *Karenina*? The January issue is not very good, but the February one, to me, is *miraculous*, and now Levochka, without a break, sits over the March issue and it's still not ready. However, soon it will be ready. Katkov showers us with telegrams and letters."§

Although behind schedule himself and feeling pestered by Katkov for his promised installment of the novel, Tolstoy wrote Golokhvastov to scold *him* about procrastinating:

> Thank you, dear Pavel Dmitrich, for remembering me—the only unfortunate thing is that you send me bad news about yourself—firstly the fact, as I see,

---

*   *PSS* 62: 258, letter of March 12–15, 1876.

†   *PSS* 62: 255.

‡   Tolstaya, *My Life*, 223.

§   Gusev, *Letopis'*, 453.

that you are not working, that you are not up to your eyes in work. That's the only real way. I don't even want to know what you ought to be working at. That doesn't matter. I only know that there are things which you know and others don't—poetic or philological, scientific or artistic—and that only you ought to express these things, and that in order to do so you must immerse yourself up to your eyes in work. And you are not doing so, and that's bad.*

Considering that Golokhvastov must have known how much Tolstoy had been dragging his feet while writing *Anna Karenina*, this was rather rich. His own procrastinating thoughts having drifted to the location where Golokhvastov was goofing off annoyed Tolstoy further:

Secondly, the fact that you are living abroad, and in Italy. You wouldn't believe that I would rather live in Mamadysh [R. F. Christian notes: "A small town in the Kazan province used by Tolstoy to mean any provincial backwater"] than in Venice, Rome, or Naples; these towns and the life in them have such a conventional, and invariably identical, grandeur and elegance for everyone else, but such vulgarity for me, that it makes me sick to think about them, and it's unbearable to read about them (Strakhov recently sent me his article about Italy and art).

Tolstoy's annoyance with the thought of Italy worked fortunately like a grain of sand in an oyster and seemed to have helped him produce for the April issue (published on April 29) the pearl of Mikhailov, the Russian artist in Italy who, with contempt in his heart and on his face for these Russian aristocrats touring Europe, paints Anna's portrait. Tolstoy's rant to Golokhvastov continued:

But worst of all is the fact that Olga Andreyevna [Golokhvastov's wife] is ill. There can be no situation more awful for a husband's health than the illness of his wife. I have experienced this condition this year and continue to experience it. My wife has been dangerously ill. All winter she was sick and weak and now she is in bed again, and you tremble every moment lest the situation should get worse. This situation is particularly painful for me because I don't believe in doctors or in medicine, or in the fact that human remedies can make a scrap of

---

* Christian, *Tolstoy's Letters*, 292–293, March 17–20, 1876.

difference to a person's state of health, that is to his life. Owing to this conviction which I can't alter, I call in all the doctors, follow their prescriptions and can't make any plans. It's very likely that we shall go abroad soon, and probably to Italy, which is so repulsive to me, but less so than Germany. In Europe it seems to me that I could only live in England, but people go away from there for their health, and there's no point in going there. Generally speaking my wife's illness, the death of my aunt who died at our house this winter, and the death of our newly born little girl all made this winter very hard for me. The only comforts are the children who, thank goodness, are growing up nicely, and my work in which I'm immersed up to my eyes.

He was, he claimed, "immersed"—and was annoyed that Golokhvastov wasn't.

Tolstoy was continuing to describe what seemed to be his odd relationship to doctors and treatment. He didn't like doctors or "believe in" them, but he decided he had to do what they said. Doctors were the only experts he regularly deferred to and perhaps he resented them for that. (It's a shame Tolstoy didn't ever study medicine, or even, as Chekhov pointed out in response to Tolstoy's fumings about sex in *The Kreutzer Sonata*, read up on human physiology.*)

Tolstoy closed his letter by scolding Golokhvastov once more ("You don't have the first comfort [children], but you must provide yourself with the second") and by wishing Golokhvastov's wife "good health, for her sake as well as for your own."†

---

* "As you read [*The Kreutzer Sonata*], you can barely keep from shouting, 'That's true!' or 'That's ridiculous!' True, it has some very irritating faults. Besides the ones you listed [Simon Karlinsky's editorial note tells us that Alexei Pleshcheyev, Chekhov's letter's recipient, had called Tolstoy's novella "paradoxical, one-sided, extraordinary and possibly false"], there is one that I am unwilling to pardon the author, namely the audacity with which Tolstoy treats topics about which he knows nothing and which out of obstinacy he does not wish to understand. For example, his opinions on syphilis, foundling homes, women's revulsion for sexual intercourse, and so on are not only debatable; they expose him as an ignorant man who has never at any point in his long life taken the trouble to read two or three books written by specialists. Nevertheless, these faults are as easily dispersed as feathers in the wind; the worth of the work is such that they simply pass unnoticed. And, if you do notice them, the only result is that you find yourself annoyed it has not escaped the fate of all human works, all of which are imperfect and tainted." *Anton Chekhov's Life and Thought: Selected Letters and Commentary*, selected by Simon Karlinsky, trans. Michael Henry Heim and Karlinsky (Berkeley: University of California Press, 1973), 155–157.

† Christian, *Tolstoy's Letters*, 293.

He received a letter from Alexandrine now in which she fretted: "It was rumored here that Anna will kill herself on the railroad tracks. I do not want to believe that. You are incapable of such vulgarity."[*]

No, *Alexandrine* (who sounds here like Karenin's friend Lidia), it's not because of vulgarity that Anna kills herself. Or if we don't want to bicker over that point with her, let's retreat to the original idea and plan of the novel. While Tolstoy famously said he didn't know that Vronsky was going to shoot himself until Vronsky did so, we know that he knew from the start that Anna was going to kill herself. I sympathize with Alexandrine not wanting Anna to kill herself. It's shocking, but that's where Anna was headed. That's why it's disturbing. On the other hand, if Vronsky had managed to kill himself with that shot to his chest, we would've shaken our heads and muttered: "What an idiot!"

Sometime in the third week of March, Tolstoy wrote Alexandrine, but not in answer to her protest over Anna's rumored death. He apologized for having sent to her, perhaps accidentally on purpose, a letter to Urusov about belief. "Thank you very much for praying for me. Although I'm unable to believe in the efficacy of prayer, I'm glad, because this proves your affection for me and because, although I don't believe, I can't say for sure that it's useless. And perhaps it's even true. In any case I know that the more I think, the less I'm able to believe, and that if I come to do so, it will be by a miracle. So please don't try to persuade me. There's no question but that I think ceaselessly about the problems of the meaning of life and death, and think just as seriously as it's possible to think. There's no question either but that I desire with all my heart to find solutions to the problems tormenting me, and don't find them in philosophy; but it seems to me impossible that I could believe."[†]

Soon he *would* believe.

We know from *Confession* how unhappy he was. We know that he wanted relief, however it could come. He was suffering, but he knew that he had to figure it out from inside—or by "miracle."

We find out a lot from Tolstoy's letters about his life and thoughts, but the best we can sometimes do with his letters to Alexandrine is wince, as we might at Karenin's conversations with Lidia. We know that in the earliest drafts of *Anna Karenina* Karenin had a sister; she was a confidante and friend. Karenin needed a sister like *Tolstoy's* sister.

In the second half of March, Maria wrote her brother about her suicidal thoughts and about the circumstances that she shared with Anna Karenina:

---

[*]   Eikhenbaum, *Tolstoi in the Seventies*, 121.

[†]   Christian, *Tolstoy's Letters*, 294, March 20–23, 1876.

Sweet dear Levochka, I'm so annoyed with myself that it's to write to you on business; I didn't answer Sonya's letter and your note, because I could not write anyone, I positively could not. I'm in such a disgusting moral situation, the loneliness is so terrible for me, with constant worry that like a sword hangs over me and about which I think day and night, so that I've never been so scared. Thoughts about suicide have begun chasing me, and positively pursue me so relentlessly that this has become a kind of sickness or insanity. Don't think that anything unusual happened, but simply nothing sticks, nothing comes of it; it's only that I think—I built it all again anew, it's not that, everything is not right—I don't know, I positively don't know. I thought about traveling to Russia and living there in the winter, as much as health allowed, but it would be necessary again for *her* [Maria's out-of-wedlock daughter Elena*] to return, but to where—again I don't know. I tried to take her myself—I can't, but then I make myself so wild from everything and I spin around, I cannot give up my daughter to a stranger . . . [. . .] I haven't seen that a woman of our circle, if she was not with a middle-brow, take to herself an unlawful child and alone, without support, be able to have enough courage to say: "Here, be curious, this is my unlawful child," I can't, and the other way out, like the death of one of us, I can't see.

You see what I can't write to anybody. I wait with impatience for when I will receive the money, and right away I'll go to Russia; more than anything I want to see you. Your postscript touched me to tears, how if I want to live with you and help Sonya and share her concerns and relieve your soul, but no, *my cross* won't allow it.

God, if all the Anna Kareninas knew what awaited them, how they would run from momentary pleasures that never were and can't be pleasures, because all that is unlawful can never be happy. [. . .]

---

* Elena Sergeevna Tolstaya (1863–1942). (See also *PSS* 83: 531.) Maria Tolstaya returned for visits to Yasnaya Polyana and to her own estate, Pokrovskoye, but did not visit Russia with her illegitimate daughter until Elena turned eighteen, at which time she brought her there and introduced her as her ward. Maria eventually became a nun. When Tolstoy left Sofia in 1910, he tried to go see Maria in her convent, but he died on the way. Tolstoy's son Sergei says, "She lived for a time at Yasnaya Polyana, though my mother never approved of it. Aunt Masha was always restless and never seemed to settle down anywhere." (*Tolstoy Remembered by His Son*, 157.) Sofia did not in *My Life* or her diaries express disapproval of Maria or her visits.

The answer to all the difficult situations in life is in the New Testament. If I had read it more often, when I was undeservedly unhappy with my husband, then I would have understood that it was a cross that He had sent me [. . .].*

Concerning his own sister, Tolstoy was Stiva: tactful, sympathetic, helpful. His friends and family seemed to associate Tolstoy only with Levin's character, but he was also partly like Stiva and sometimes, unfortunately, like Karenin and sometimes, to his own terror, very much like Anna.

✳

On March 31, *Russian Herald* subscribers began receiving the March issue with Part 4, Chapters 18 to 23 (the book chapters), and Part 5, Chapters 1–6.

Let's imagine reading those chapters ourselves.

Following the melodramatic fake-death-of-Anna episode that concluded the February issue (Part 4, Chapter 17 in the book), Vronsky goes home and, in a fit of humiliation, shoots himself in the chest. His brother's wife, Varya, takes charge of his recovery. With Anna ill and Vronsky wounded, Karenin finds himself the master of the house again and more or less takes charge of Anna and Vronsky's baby. Anna comes back to herself; she obviously still loves Vronsky and can't love Karenin. Everyone sees that their life together is unbearable for them both. In Part 4, Chapter 21, Stiva visits Anna and sees that she needs to divorce Karenin.

Someone could write a book on "Stiva's smile." Anna is so very low that she thinks she couldn't feel worse. She sees death as a way out, but Stiva won't let her express that thought:

"I have heard it said that women love men even for their vices," Anna began suddenly, "but I hate him for his virtues. I can't live with him. Do you understand? The sight of him has a physical effect on me, it makes me beside myself. I can't, I can't live with him. What am I to do? I have been unhappy, and used to think one couldn't be more unhappy, but the awful state of things I am going through now, I could never have conceived. Would you believe it,

---

* *Perepiski Russkikh Pisateley: Perepiska L. N. Tolstogo s sestroy i brat'yami* (Moscow: Khudozhestvennaya Literatura, 1990), 352–353, letter of March 1876.

that knowing he's a good man, a splendid man, that I'm not worth his little finger, still I hate him. I hate him for his generosity. And there's nothing left for me but . . ."

She would have said death, but Stepan Arkadyevitch would not let her finish.

"You are ill and overwrought," he said; "believe me, you're exaggerating dreadfully. There's nothing so terrible in it."

And Stepan Arkadyevitch smiled. No one else in Stepan Arkadyevitch's place, having to do with such despair, would have ventured to smile (the smile would have seemed brutal); but in his smile there was so much of sweetness and almost feminine tenderness that his smile did not wound, but softened and soothed. His gentle, soothing words and smiles were as soothing and softening as almond oil. And Anna soon felt this.[*]

It's as if Tolstoy himself was charmed by Stiva. Anna, however, is not awed or amazed by or reflective about Stiva's grace; she takes it as characteristic of her brother:

"No, Stiva," she said, "I'm lost, lost! worse than lost! I can't say yet that all is over; on the contrary, I feel that it's not over. I'm an overstrained string that must snap. But it's not ended yet . . . and it will have a fearful end."

"No matter, we must let the string be loosened, little by little. There's no position from which there is no way of escape."

"I have thought, and thought. Only one . . ."

Again he knew from her terrified eyes that this one way of escape in her thought was death, and he would not let her say it.[†]

Her brother listens to her! He doesn't miss a trick. He uses the image she spoke and undoes it. We're as chilled and frightened and anxious as he is—we fear or know that she's the taut string that is indeed going to snap.

Stiva, just as Tolstoy did for his sister Maria more than ten years before, offers to negotiate for the divorce. Tolstoy had not been able to persuade his ornery brother-in-law, but smooth Stiva manages to talk Karenin into it. In the last chapter of Part 4, Vronsky

---

[*]   *Anna Karenina,* Part 4, Chapter 21, http://www.literatureproject.com/anna-karenina/anna_122.htm.

[†]   Ibid.

goes to Anna and they agree, even without a divorce, to go to Italy. The only regret that Anna feels is leaving Seryozha behind.

Part 5 resumes with the planning for Levin and Kitty's wedding. Levin finds that there are details large and small that he needs to take care of. Giddy with happiness on his wedding day, Levin spends time with his friends and half-brother, but then he panics and goes to Kitty to be reassured that she really loves him. Later that day, Levin is late for the wedding; he and Stiva have to wait at his hotel for his proper clothes to be found by his servant, who has packed them to send them ahead. The last three chapters cover the wedding.

I remember this wedding more vividly than my own, but my familiarity with Kitty and Levin's has made it boring. I now consider the wedding scene as Tolstoy's gift to Sofia for having copied and recopied so many drafts of this novel's many chapters.

"So, Mr. Biographer," you might say, "maybe don't read the wedding parts again! Why crab about it? Tolstoy didn't mean anybody to read the book compulsively!"

"True, but why then does so much else hold up? Why is nothing and no one else, except maybe Varenka and Kozneshev, consistently boring to me now? How can the rest of the novel hold up so well, like new!, over repeated readings?"

I'll attempt to answer those questions.

A couple of decades ago, when I allowed myself to acknowledge that the wedding was boring, I realized that I was much more curious about what Anna's wedding had been like. I'm still more interested in anything about Anna than I am in whatever Tolstoy seems to be presenting as normal and good in Kitty and Levin, the contrasting couple. And, anyway, the more I learned about Tolstoy and Sofia's wedding and marriage, the less I believed in the rosiness of Levin and Kitty's wedding. In the novel, the wedding is a set-piece, a functional piece, but it doesn't *matter*. Of course I'm aware that many readers love it! The image of Levin and Kitty standing there in the formal Russian wedding makes them swoon. I used to like it, too.

Anyway, try this experiment: read the whole novel twenty-five times and see if the wedding doesn't begin to dull on you.

If it's still good, you win.

✳

In *My Life*, Sofia describes the "Beginning of Lev Nikolaevich's Moral Transformation." Though seemingly attuned to everything going on in him and with her children, she couldn't pin down a moment or incident that precipitated a real change in him:

"In 1876 this need for faith was only dimly awakened in Lev Nikolaevich. I don't remember—indeed, it would be hard to trace—just when he suddenly came out and started fervently professing his Orthodox faith with all its rituals.

"It is my opinion that Lev Nikolaevich always had a faith in God in his soul. But this quick transformation to ecclesiastical Orthodoxy somehow escaped me."[*]

This seems a brilliant and modest summation of her husband's "moral transformation." She must have been aware of the biographical speculation about it, and here, as the primary witness, she confesses that on the one hand the change was unnoticeable and yet one day there it was, full-blown, with Tolstoy trying to conform his behavior and thinking to Orthodoxy.

To his sister-in-law Tatyana, Tolstoy wrote in early April:

> I'm writing you, my dear friend Tanya, a few words just to express my offended feelings because of your stupid and indecent words about me: that I won't be able to stand your visit. Truly, this was offensive to me and very unpleasant. I love you and Sasha and your children and the older I get the more I value my attachments, and the thought that you will be with us is one of those thoughts that, you know, you remember: "Uh, what is this that will be pleasant? Right, the Kuzminskiys will be here."[†]

He was saying all the right things, but if he was as depressed as *Confession* presents him to have been, was he only hoping that he would feel up to it?

Or do we simply call into question again the "truth" of *Confession*? In it, he does not discuss or dramatize domestic life, so perhaps that explains how his coloring of his thoughts is unnaturally consistent and dark. We know that he was involved in family life during the period described in *Confession*; we know he was also writing the novel, and that he was an active father, occasionally minding the children on his own, and that he was a sportsman frequently hunting, and a businessman intently wheeling and dealing about publications and horses. So *Confession*, variously dated by Tolstoy himself, has to be given fluctuating weight as a documentary record. As a chronicle of his experience, it is less vivid and revealing than Anna's whirling tumble into despair. On the other hand, it continuously shows how familiar her despair was to him.

---

[*]   Tolstaya, *My Life*, 221.

[†]   *PSS* 62: 262, letter of early April 1876.

On April 6, Sofia wrote her uncle Kostya that the novel "seems to have stopped."[*] Indeed, it was stopped in its tracks. Tolstoy would not get working on it again for more than seven months.

What killed its momentum?

Gusev points us to an April 8 letter from Strakhov to Tolstoy: "Just as earlier Strakhov wrote Tolstoy more than once that he placed his artistic productions higher than his pedagogical articles, now he writes Tolstoy that he places his artistic productions immeasurably higher than his philosophical discourses."[†] Most of Strakhov's letter is a discussion of philosophers, among them Schopenhauer and Hegel. But as Strakhov was arguing with Tolstoy, he was also trying to cajole Tolstoy back to the most important matter at hand, *Anna Karenina*:

> I am most convinced that the results that you get [from writing philosophy] will be a hundred times poorer than what is contained in your artistic productions. Judge, for example, whether what I can see spread through your work is not endlessly higher than what Schopenhauer or Hegel—or anyone else you like—says about life.[‡]

That is, philosophy doesn't hold a candle to Tolstoy's art. Is it possible that anyone would disagree with Strakhov's assessment?

One trouble with Tolstoy's essays and discourses is that in the midst of them *Tolstoy* seems to think they're more important, more true than his art. They're consistent but rigged, as they argue but they don't discover. Expository prose brought out Tolstoy's tendency of emphatically agreeing with himself. In his artistic productions, on the other hand, his sympathy and engagement with the imagined people and situations couldn't be settled as an argument could; writing fiction induced his deepest attention and feeling.

In his final paragraph Strakhov pointed out the unprecedentedness of the novel:

> *Anna Karenina* raises such excitement and such bitterness, which I don't remember in literature.[§]

---

[*]   Gusev, *Letopis'*, 454.

[†]   Gusev, *Materials*, 288.

[‡]   Donskov, *L. N. Tolstoy – N. N. Strakhov,* April 8, 1876, http://feb-web.ru/feb/tolstoy/texts /selectpe/ts6/ts62256-.htm.

[§]   Donskov, *L. N. Tolstoy – N. N. Strakhov,* 256, http://feb-web.ru/feb/tolstoy/texts/selectpe /ts6/ts62256-.htm.

It doesn't seem that Tolstoy had received Strakhov's April 8 letter when he wrote Strakhov on April 8–9; he was out of sorts with the novel and seemed annoyed with Strakhov himself:

Thank you, dear Nikolay Nikolayevich, for sending Grigoryev [that is, a book on the late poet and critic A. A. Grigoryev that Strakhov had edited and introduced]. I read the introduction but—don't be angry with me—I feel that I could never read it all through if I were incarcerated in a dungeon. This is not because I don't appreciate Grigoryev—on the contrary—but because criticism is to me the most boring of all things in the world. In clever art criticism everything is the truth, but not the *whole* truth, and art is only art because it is *whole.*

I feel with alarm that my summer condition is coming on: I'm disgusted with what I've written, and now there are the proofs for the April issue and I'm afraid I shan't have the strength to correct them. Everything in them is bad, everything needs to be revised and revised—everything that's been printed—and I need to cross it all out and throw it away and disown it and say, "I'm sorry, I won't do it again," and try to write something new, something not so clumsy and neither one thing nor the other. This is the condition I'm in now, and it's very pleasant. [. . .] And don't praise my novel. Pascal made himself a belt of nails which he pressed his elbows against every time he felt that praise gave him pleasure. I need to make a belt like that. Be a true friend to me: either write nothing about my novel or only write and tell me everything that's bad about it. And if it's true, as I suspect, that I'm getting feeble, please write and tell me.

Our vile literary profession is corrupting. Every writer has his own atmosphere of flatterers which he carefully surrounds himself with, and he can have no idea of his own importance or the time of his decline. I wouldn't like to lose my way and have to turn back further on. Please help me in this.

[P.S.] And don't be inhibited by the idea that your stern criticism might upset the work of a man who has talent. Far better to stop at *War and Peace* than to write *The Watch* [by Turgenev], etc.[*]

He really let himself out to Strakhov about the novel—he could always complain at length to him and press Strakhov and get a response; he didn't have to be jolly, as he usually

---

[*] Christian, *Tolstoy's Letters,* 295, April 8–9, 1876.

chose to be with Fet. He told Strakhov, his best reader, not to flatter him. This letter is just one more example of their interchange throughout the writing of the novel—Strakhov praising, Tolstoy disparaging the work.

Tolstoy was in Moscow sometime in the period of April 9–13. Perhaps he was proofreading those April galleys, perhaps he was visiting friends. There are no details of his activities.

Back at Yasnaya Polyana, he responded defensively to Alexandrine's March 28 letter questioning him about his beliefs:

> You say you don't know what I believe in. Strange and terrible to say: not in anything that religion teaches us; but at the same time I not only hate and despise disbelief, but I can see no possibility of living, and still less of dying, without faith. And I'm building up for myself little by little my religious beliefs, but although they are all firm, they are very undefined and uncomforting. When questioned by the mind, they answer well; but when the heart aches and seeks an answer, they provide no support or comfort. With the demands of my mind and the answers given by the Christian religion, I find myself in the position, as it were, of two hands endeavouring to clasp each other while the fingers resist. I long to do it, but the more I try, the worse it is; and at the same time I know that it's possible, that the one is made for the other [. . .]*

The search that he describes in *Confession* seems to have been going on now; he was terrified, but this confession was as far as he could go with a friend in describing his situation. In *Confession* Tolstoy plunges deeper and more terrifyingly into his state of mind. Here, for example, from Part 5:

> "But perhaps I have overlooked something, or misunderstood something?" said I to myself several times. "It cannot be that this condition of despair is natural to man!" And I sought for an explanation of these problems in all the branches of knowledge acquired by men. I sought painfully and long, not from idle curiosity or listlessly, but painfully and persistently day and night—sought as a perishing man seeks for safety—and I found nothing.
>
> I sought in all the sciences, but far from finding what I wanted, became convinced that all who like myself had sought in knowledge for the meaning

---

* Christian, *Tolstoy's Letters*, April 15–17?, 1876, 296.

of life had found nothing. And not only had they found nothing, but they had plainly acknowledged that the very thing which made me despair—namely the senselessness of life—is the one indubitable thing man can know.*

Tolstoy dramatizes in *Confession* the feeling in a way that keeps us inside that despair and doesn't comfort us with the thought that it is all going to be okay.

At the same time in real life, he had the real comfort and hope of thinking about horses, which kind of idle activity he belittles in *Confession*. But these thoughts *really did engage him*. Thus Tolstoy falsified his own life, and we biographers falsify it if we decide that his craze for horses doesn't really count.

The despairing philosopher still got a thrill out of horses.

He wrote Fet (about a week after his letter to Alexandrine) to ask him to send him the coveted stallion to Nikol'skoe. He wrote that he was grateful for the Fets' visit in mid-April and for their conversations, which he was still "chewing over."† There are no details, but by his letter later in the month to Fet, it seems that they discussed his difficulties in finding the purpose of life.

Strakhov in the meantime tried to buck up Tolstoy, reminding him:

> We all have our woes. Yours, esteemed and envied Lev Nikolaevich—meanwhile—the torment of childbirth. You're losing your usual coldbloodedness, and, it seems, you desire from me the advice to stop the publication of Anna Karenina and leave in the most cruel confusion thousands of readers, those who wait for and are always asking how this is going to end. Are you really going to fall into humiliation that you make a few mistakes, that the bride had to leave after the groom, that after the wedding they had to bow to the icon, and something else. All the same, the wedding description with all its spirit and color appears in our literature for the first time.‡

Tolstoy was chagrined by a couple of mistakes of fact about the fictional wedding ceremony; he fixed those errors for the book publication. He didn't grant himself artistic license about these kinds of facts.

---

*   *Confession,* Chapter 5, http://www.online-literature.com/tolstoy/a-confession/5/.

†   *PSS* 62: 267–268, letter of April 20–23?, 1876.

‡   In Donskov's edition (*L. N. Tolstoy – N. N. Strakhov,* 264), dated as "the second half of April," http://feb-web.ru/feb/tolstoy/texts/selectpe/ts6/ts62264-.htm.

Then Strakhov, having properly girded himself, accepted Tolstoy's challenge:

> So, fine—I'll criticize your novel to you. The primary deficiency—the cold-
> ness of the writing, so to say the cold tone of the narration. That which, strictly
> speaking, is called tone is not yours, but the whole current of the narration
> *I could hear* the coldness. But apparently this is only for me, a person who is
> reading it who can almost hear your voice.[*]

Tolstoy's usual narrative mode—the detached omniscient voice—was a deliberate
artistic choice, but Strakhov reacted to what he called its coldness and regretted its not
having Tolstoy's warmth—Tolstoy's actual speaking voice. Is it that Tolstoy as a writer of
this novel couldn't have proceeded with a warm, connected voice (in the manner of, for
example, Dickens, Hugo, or Trollope)? I think Tolstoy had to detach himself emotionally. But Strakhov was bothered by the tone that readers ever since have been impressed
by—that clarity and assuredness of an unseen, irrefutable god-artist. Tolstoy made most
scenes seem as if they belong to the characters and not to their creator.

Strakhov's letter is one of the most provocative and *penetrating* (that word is appro-
priate here) responses to the novel ever written—and it was composed to its author:

> Because—or as a consequence—the descriptions of the strongest scenes are
> somewhat dry. After them, one involuntarily asks for language somewhat
> revealing or thoughtful words, but you choose not to give those understanding
> and quietening sounds that usually conclude the finale in music. Further—the
> funny parts are not very merry, but if one laughs, ones laughs terribly.[†]

Strakhov was unhappily affected by the strictness, or the withholdingness, but he was
accurately describing Tolstoy's way. He didn't favor it, but he noticed it. As for "the funny
parts," the funniest for me is when the calculating lawyer, whose chairs are moth-ridden,
interviews Karenin:

> "Won't you sit down?" He indicated an armchair at a writing table covered
> with papers. He sat down himself, and, rubbing his little hands with short

---

[*]   Donskov, *L. N. Tolstoy – N. N. Strakhov*, http://feb-web.ru/feb/tolstoy/texts/selectpe/ts6
        /ts62264-.htm.

[†]   Ibid.

fingers covered with white hairs, he bent his head on one side. But as soon as he was settled in this position a moth flew over the table. The lawyer, with a swiftness that could never have been expected of him, opened his hands, caught the moth, and resumed his former attitude.*

I acknowledge there are scenes where Tolstoy is sarcastically presenting the aristocrats and that he may have imagined that they were funny, but because those portrayals are colored by his prejudices and not by his love or interest, the characters appear flat. He was superior to those contemptible aristocrats . . . and even Tolstoy couldn't create living characters if he felt superior to them. He did not identify with them, not at all the way Dickens so delightedly identified with his comic and sometimes wicked characters.

Further words from Strakhov:

> I follow you and see all the reluctance, all the struggle with which you, the great master, do this work; and all the same it brings out what has to be brought out by a great master: everything is true, everything lives, everything is deep. Vronsky for you is the most difficult, Oblonsky easiest of all, but the figure of Vronsky is still unrooted. Having read through the last part, I took it up again and read it from the beginning. The suicide of Vronsky, his meeting with Karenin—how good and strong!†

As loyal and respectful as Strakhov was, he couldn't let Tolstoy accuse him here of overpraising him about *Anna Karenina* or saying anything false or flattering. Another of Strakhov's observations helps us imagine the pleasure and excitement of awaiting a new installment of this novel:

> But here I said everything that I was able to; I said directly that in it nothing is hidden, nothing is exaggerated. *War and Peace* in my eyes (I'm convinced in yours too) grows with each year; I'm convinced that this is happening with *Anna Karenina*, and that for a long long time readers will

---

*   *Anna Karenina,* Part 4, Chapter 5, http://www.literatureproject.com/anna-karenina/anna _106.htm.

†   Donskov, *L. N. Tolstoy – N. N. Strakhov,* 264, http://feb-web.ru/feb/tolstoy/texts/selectpe /ts6/ts62264-.htm.

remember about the time when they impatiently awaited the issue of the *Russian Herald*, just as I cannot forget the time of the appearance of *War and Peace*.*

Strakhov was right: readers of his time would or should one day have remembered their excited experience of waiting for the next installment of *Anna Karenina*. But that's true for us, too, reading it *after* its time. If we're really taking it in, we do so as eager, anxious readers. Then, as today, we feel: A stupendous work of art is happening before my eyes! In April 1876, maybe a few thousand Russians realized that this was a memorable time. But it can also happen when we read or reread *Anna Karenina* now.

Strakhov began winding up the letter:

> I ask you to write me how you find my judgments. [Tolstoy immediately did so.] I keep thinking over Karenin. I'm afraid I'm completely mistaken in thoughts of details, and in understanding of the technique I'm always weak. And so I wrote you only about the general pieces. But apparently you—I'm convinced—are at a low point because you're struggling with the technique and are weary.†

Tolstoy must have irritatedly exclaimed, "Technique? *Technique?*" He had just written and proofread the scenes involving Mikhailov:

> "Yes, there's a wonderful mastery!" said Vronsky. "How those figures in the background stand out! There you have technique," he said, addressing Golenishtchev, alluding to a conversation between them about Vronsky's despair of attaining this technique.
>
> "Yes, yes, marvelous!" Golenishtchev and Anna assented. In spite of the excited condition in which he was, the sentence about technique had sent a pang to Mihailov's heart, and looking angrily at Vronsky he suddenly scowled. He had often heard this word technique, and was utterly unable to understand what was understood by it. He knew that by this term was understood

---

* Donskov, *L. N. Tolstoy – N. N. Strakhov*, http://feb-web.ru/feb/tolstoy/texts/selectpe /ts6/ts62264-.htm.

† Donskov, *L. N. Tolstoy – N. N. Strakhov*, 264, http://feb-web.ru/feb/tolstoy/texts/selectpe /ts6/ts62264-.htm.

a mechanical facility for painting or drawing, entirely apart from its subject. He had noticed often that even in actual praise technique was opposed to essential quality, as though one could paint well something that was bad. He knew that a great deal of attention and care was necessary in taking off the coverings, to avoid injuring the creation itself, and to take off all the coverings; but there was no art of painting—no technique of any sort—about it. If to a little child or to his cook were revealed what he saw, it or she would have been able to peel the wrappings off what was seen. And the most experienced and adroit painter could not by mere mechanical facility paint anything if the lines of the subject were not revealed to him first. Besides, he saw that if it came to talking about technique, it was impossible to praise him for it. In all he had painted and repainted he saw faults that hurt his eyes, coming from want of care in taking off the wrappings—faults he could not correct now without spoiling the whole. And in almost all the figures and faces he saw, too, remnants of the wrappings not perfectly removed that spoiled the picture.[*]

After all, Tolstoy didn't let loose at Strakhov with Mikhailov's irritation, but in less than two weeks Strakhov would read this chapter for himself.

As Strakhov concluded the end of his long, difficult but admiring letter, he seemed to sigh:

Well, what will be, will be! I would be glad to help you, but I don't know with what? I say only that you drove me into agitation, as if I had to write the end of the novel. That you would fail in the effort—this I'm not afraid of; but that you would delay the end of the novel—this perhaps comes from you.

[P.S.] *Art is the everything*, you write; and just so thinks Ap. Grigoryev, and he so thinks only. It's possible to say that his book was written *against criticism*.[†]

Strakhov even conceded Tolstoy that point—that Strakhov need not have written the introductory essay to Grigoryev's book, an introduction Tolstoy couldn't bring himself to finish reading.

---

[*]   *Anna Karenina,* Part 5, Chapter 11, http://www.literatureproject.com/anna-karenina anna_135.htm.

[†]   Donskov, *L. N. Tolstoy – N. N. Strakhov,* 265, http://feb-web.ru/feb/tolstoy/texts/selectpe/ts6 /ts62264-.htm.

Tolstoy, however, would concede almost nothing to his friend.

There are great critics—Tolstoy himself, D. H. Lawrence, Ezra Pound, Virginia Woolf, Anne Carson—who can sometimes seem to say more than the author himself wanted to say, but Strakhov, as well as anybody has, presented a living response to *Anna Karenina*. And why shouldn't he have? Strakhov was excitedly, intelligently reading the novel in its stages, watching its development. He had the best seat in the house and he made responsive, fine judgments. He wasn't even trying to do what Tolstoy and Lawrence do as critics—express the essence of what the author wanted to say. Strakhov did better than any of the rest of us mortals could do as critics, and Tolstoy became annoyed because Strakhov's primary point was right, *that this was a brilliant, unprecedented novel,* and this meant that Tolstoy had to go on with the hard work.

Tolstoy responded to Strakhov's letter with his own long letter on April 23 (and post-scripted on April 26):

> You write: do you understand my novel correctly, and what do I think about your opinions? Of course you understand it correctly. Of course your understanding heartens me beyond words; but not everyone is bound to understand it as you do.

Tolstoy had the bad habit of having to correct Strakhov. Even if Strakhov was right, he had to be checked and his opinion picked through:

> Perhaps you are only an amateur at these things, just as I am. Just like one of our Tula pigeon-fanciers. He rates a tumble-pigeon very highly, but whether the pigeon has any real merits is another question. Besides, the likes of us, as you know, are constantly leaping without any transition from despondency and self-abasement to inordinate pride.

Quite true, as far as despondency and self-abasement go, *for Tolstoy.*

As for Strakhov's correct assessment of *Anna Karenina*, oh, please! Strakhov was no pigeon-fancier. Tolstoy was teasing, a little, and trying to restrain his own pride, but he also just wanted to undercut Strakhov, his friend, supporter, and admirer, and keep him in his place. I'm offended for poor earnest Strakhov:

> I say this because your opinion about my novel is true, but it isn't everything—i.e., everything is true, but what you said doesn't express every-thing I wanted to say.

Our most esteemed Lev Nikolaevich, did Strakhov ever claim that he had?

> For example, you speak about two sorts of people. I always feel this—I know—but I didn't intend it so. But when you say it, I know that it's one of the truths that can be said. But if I were to try to say in words everything that I intended to express in my novel, I would have to write the same novel I wrote from the beginning. And if short-sighted critics think that I only wanted to describe the things that I like, what Oblonsky has for dinner or what Karenina's shoulders are like, they are mistaken. In everything, or nearly everything I have written, I have been guided by the need to gather together ideas which for the purpose of self-expression were interconnected; but every idea expressed separately in words loses its meaning and is terribly impoverished when taken by itself out of the connection in which it occurs. The connection itself is made up, I think, not by the idea, but by something else, and it is impossible to express the basis of this connection directly in words. It can only be expressed indirectly—by words describing characters, actions and situation.
>
> You know all this better than I do, but it has been occupying my attention recently. For me, one of the most manifest proofs of this was Vronsky's suicide which you liked. This had never been so clear to me before. The chapter about how Vronsky accepted his role after meeting the husband had been written by me a long time ago. I began to correct it, and quite unexpectedly for me, but unmistakably, Vronsky went and shot himself. And now it turns out that this was organically necessary for what comes afterward.

This, about Vronsky's attempted suicide, is one of the only times Tolstoy discussed an artistic moment of decision. Tolstoy said all sorts of general things in retrospect, but the Vronsky incident is one that we would not have known if he hadn't told us:

> That's why such a nice clever man as Grigoryev interests me very little. It's true that if there were no criticism at all, then Grigoryev and you who understand art would be redundant. But now indeed when 9/10 of everything printed is criticism, people are needed for the criticism of art who can show the pointlessness of looking for ideas in a work of art and can steadfastly guide readers through that endless labyrinth of connections which is the essence of art, and toward those laws that serve as the basis of these connections.

And if critics already understand and can express in a newspaper article what I wanted to say, I congratulate them and can boldly assure them *qu'ils savent plus long que moi* [that they know further than I].

I'm very, very grateful to you. When I read through my last dejected and humble letter, I realised that I was really asking for praise and that you had sent it to me. And your praise—sincere, I know, although, I'm afraid, too partial—is very, very dear to me.

I'm very annoyed that I made mistakes over the wedding, especially as I love that chapter.

I'm afraid there may also be mistakes over the special subject which I touch on in the part which will come out now in April. [R. F. Christian footnotes this: "Presumably the chapters in Mikhaylov's studio on the subject of art."] Please write and tell me if you or other people find any.

You are right that *War and Peace* grows in *my* eyes. I have a strange feeling of joy when people remind me of something from it as Istomin did recently (he'll be staying with you), but it's strange, I remember very few passages from it, and the rest I forget.

Goodbye; a thousand thanks once more. I still hope to finish. But I shall hardly have the strength. In summer I often feel the physical impossibility of writing.

The postscript:

I wrote this letter several days ago and didn't want to send it—so obtrusive was my author's flattered vanity. But I've just written 7 letters and needed to write to you again, and decided to send this.

Murder will out, and you know me through and through.*

Yes, Strakhov knew Tolstoy and his art and also saw his weaknesses—and still loved the novel and the man.

Tolstoy's other important friend of the period, Fet, was meanwhile experiencing something of the existential despair that was also overwhelming Tolstoy. Tolstoy wrote:

[. . .] I thank you for your idea of calling me to see you pass away, when you thought that the end was near. I will do the same, when I get ready to

* Christian, *Tolstoy's Letters*, 296–297, April 23 and 26, 1876.

go there, if I shall have enough strength to think. I would need no one so much at that moment as you and my brother. Before death the communion with men who in this life look beyond its confines is dear and joyous; and you and those rare, real men whom I have met on a close footing in life, in spite of their wholesome relation to life, always stand on the very brink and see life clearly, for the very reason that they look, now into Nirvana, into unlimitedness, into the unknown, now into sansara, and this looking into Nirvana strengthens their vision. But worldly people, no matter how much they may speak of God, are disagreeable to men of our calibre and [it] must be painful in the time of death, because they do not see what we see, namely, that God [is] more indefinite, more distant, but higher and more indubitable, as it says in that article.*

The God of Sabaoth and his son, the God of the priests, is just as little and ugly and impossible a God—indeed far more impossible—than a God of the flies would be for the priests, if the flies imagined him to be a huge fly only concerned with the well-being and improvement of the flies.†

Tolstoy hadn't yet figured out how or *if* he was going to live. Fet and he were depressed and seeing only death:

You are ill and you think about death, while I am well, and never cease to think about the same thing and to prepare for it. Let's see who will be first.‡ But various imperceptible facts suddenly revealed to me how deeply akin to mine is your nature—your soul (especially in relation to death), and I suddenly came to appreciate our relationship and began to value it far more than before. [. . .] I have tried to express much of what I thought in the last chapter of the April issue of the *Russian Herald*. [That is, the death of Levin's brother Nikolai.] §

---

*   *The Complete Works of Count Tolstoy*, Volume 24, trans. Leo Wiener (London: J.M. Dent, 1905), 262–263.

†   Christian, *Tolstoy's Letters*, 298, April 28–29, 1876.

‡   Fet died in 1892, eighteen years before Tolstoy.

§   Christian, *Tolstoy's Letters*, 298.

So even though he was despairing of his life, he had a kindred spirit in Fet. And even though death was waiting for them . . . there were, for now, horses! In the postscript Tolstoy noted, quite businesslike:

> Thanks very much for sending Hamlet. I'll be waiting.[*]

"Hamlet"? To buy or not to buy, that had been the question of the stallion that Fet had recently sold to Tolstoy. (Did Fet name him before or during his bout of despair?)

Gusev points out that *Levin*'s attraction to philosophy doesn't last very long; it's like an intoxicant or frame of mind that can't survive a return to everyday life:

> Tolstoy's own philosophy, laid out in a letter to Strakhov, pleased him, apparently, not for long. In *Anna Karenina* he narrated that Levin, "At one time, reading Schopenhauer [. . .] put in place of his *will* the word *love*, and for a couple of days this new philosophy charmed him, till he removed a little away from it. But then, when he turned from life itself to glance at it again, it fell away too, and proved to be the same muslin garment with no warmth in it."[†]

Tolstoy could not suppress himself before anybody or before almost any idea for very long. He was always going his own way. He lit up problems, resolved them, then re-resolved them and encountered new problems; and meanwhile, somehow, he was creating glorious work.

Somewhere near the time of the long, wrung-out letters to Strakhov and Fet in late April, Sofia went to Moscow with daughter Tanya to buy hats and shoes. From Yasnaya Polyana, Tolstoy communicated to Sofia not the state of his soul but the state of the family:

> Istomin came at 3 o'clock; when I only wanted to go horseback riding. He's very sweet [. . .].
>
> The children went for a walk, but warmly dressed and not freezing. The governesses are very careful. Everyone carries himself well. Rey with Istomin

---

[*]   *PSS* 62: 273.

[†]   Gusev, *Materials*, 238. (*Anna Karenina,* Part 8, Chapter 9, http://www.literatureproject.com /anna-karenina/anna_229.htm.)

played chess. Ilyusha without Tanya slept on the couch. I was with Istomin in the carriage and shot a lot, but didn't kill anything. Bewitching snipes.

So, despite his worries expressed in *Confession* of turning the gun on himself, he again and again went hunting! And he worried not for himself but for Sofia:

I'm afraid for you that in this cold you'll get a cold. Please remember that purchases are very important, but your health is more. [. . .] Farewell, darling. Without Tanya at the table it's terribly empty. I kiss you, Tanichka. I'm bored without you.*

He was depressed, contemplating the end of life, ruing the lack of salvation in writing, yet for all that, he was still in his inconsistency human, and did go hunting, and did take note of expenses, and did miss his daughter!

Anna Karenina is smarter than and truer than his convictions, than his philosophy, than Schopenhauer.

A favorite daughter not being at the table matters. Horses matter.

❋

The April issue of the *Russian Herald,* Chapters 7–19 of Part 5, was published on April 29 (they were numbered Chapters 7–20 in the book). Tolstoy began the new installment by rolling up three months of events of Anna's life in a summary. Tolstoy makes life in its moment-by-moment experience completely vivid, but in his long-view summary he and we are emotionally distant. Weary apparently of trying to interest himself in the details of Anna's daily life, Tolstoy had become quite cynical about what she was up to. From Chapter 8:

The thought of her husband's unhappiness did not poison her happiness. On one side that memory was too awful to be thought of. On the other side her husband's unhappiness had given her too much happiness to be regretted. The memory of all that had happened after her illness: her reconciliation with her husband, its breakdown, the news of Vronsky's wound, his visit, the preparations for divorce, the departure from her husband's house, the parting from

---

*   *PSS* 83: 223–224, letter of April 1876.

her son—all that seemed to her like a delirious dream, from which she had waked up alone with Vronsky abroad.*

All those weeks in Europe boxed up as a "delirious dream." Tolstoy had no sympathy for or imagination about Anna's life on the lam. Her experience before and during Italy does not demonstrate artistic development of her character but Tolstoy's evasion of artistic engagement.

In the second paragraph, Tolstoy grouses:

But, however sincerely Anna had meant to suffer, she was not suffering.

This analysis by Tolstoy is on a par with that of the society gossips in the novel. But we sympathetic readers know that this woman is going to suffer. Tolstoy has given us her thoughts and conscience and guilt—and yet at this moment and in this installment of the novel, as the omniscient author, he begrudges her the little time that she has when she's happy. He won't let us readers appreciate these few fulfilled moments in her life. She will soon be crippled by suffering. Even knowing what she has in store, Tolstoy at this moment allows her nothing—she is on trial and has been found guilty for being happy.

And then there is Tolstoy's offhand summation:

Separation from the son she loved—even that did not cause her anguish in these early days. The baby girl—*his* child—was so sweet, and had so won Anna's heart, since she was all that was left her, that Anna rarely thought of her son.

Just because Tolstoy writes that she "rarely thought of her son" doesn't mean she isn't thinking a lot about her son. She is still herself, just as Pushkin's heroine Tatyana in *Eugene Onegin* is *herself* when she, to Pushkin's surprise in the love story's conclusion, turns down the attractive but cocky hero. Tolstoy suppresses Anna here; but we know that the Anna he has created would continually think about Seryozha.

Then Tolstoy tries to settle this "unrooted" Vronsky person. We still don't know Vronsky the way that we know almost all the other characters. With Vronsky, Tolstoy

---

* *Anna Karenina*, Part 5, Chapter 8, http://www.literatureproject.com/anna-karenina/anna _132.htm/.

shows us that what he has done to create Anna and Levin is not easy. Vronsky is a hodge-podge. Tolstoy sometimes has a bead on him, and sometimes he doesn't, like now:

> All the traits of his character, which she learned to know better and better, were unutterably dear to her. His appearance, changed by his civilian dress, was as fascinating to her as though she were some young girl in love. In everything he said, thought, and did, she saw something particularly noble and elevated. Her adoration of him alarmed her indeed; she sought and could not find in him anything not fine.

Tolstoy couldn't or didn't want to show the development of Anna's feelings. Instead, he informs us that Anna can see the magic in Vronsky. But her vision doesn't create Vronsky's character for us. Tolstoy is already checked out, disengaged from the runaway couple. Look at the vagueness of "*all* the traits," "*better* and *better*," "*everything* he said, thought, and did," "she saw *something* particularly noble."

But then, suddenly, *something* happens: Tolstoy's real interest (and ours, too, of course—can we ever not become interested when he gets interested?) is piqued by Vronsky's new hobby of painting. While he is making short work of Vronsky's intelligence and artistic feeling, Tolstoy now has a real subject, one that will occupy him and us for quite a while—all the way through Levin's encounter with Anna's portrait. Vronsky, we discover, "had a ready appreciation of art, and probably, with a taste for imitating art, he supposed himself to have the real thing essential for an artist, and after hesitating for some time which style of painting to select—religious, historical, realistic, or genre painting—he set to work to paint."

> He appreciated all kinds, and could have felt inspired by any one of them; but he had no conception of the possibility of knowing nothing at all of any school of painting, and of being inspired directly by what is within the soul, without caring whether what is painted will belong to any recognized school. Since he knew nothing of this, and drew his inspiration, not directly from life, but indirectly from life embodied in art, his inspiration came very quickly and easily, and as quickly and easily came his success in painting something very similar to the sort of painting he was trying to imitate.[*]

---

*   *Anna Karenina*, Part 5, Chapter 8, http://www.literatureproject.com/anna-karenina/anna _132.htm.

Vronsky is inspired by the inspiration that the artists he imitates have actually had. That's why painting is so easy for the former army captain.

Not so easy was writing this *Anna Karenina*, "inspired directly by what is within the soul."

To continue with the April 1876 issue, Chapters 9–13 bring us to Tolstoy's most self-revealing portrait of an artist (a portrait-artist at that). Mikhailov, the Russian painter living in Italy, comes from an unprivileged background but was given an opportunity for education and he flourished. His background does not connect him to Tolstoy; his artistic sensibility, however, is Tolstoy's. He is serious, he is driven; he is aware of the accidents that help him see and evoke the essential life in his subjects. His past work is *past*. The work that enlivens him and torments him is what he's working on now. But when these Russians—Anna, Vronsky, and a friend of Vronsky's—come to look at his paintings, he has to stop working; while he observes them observing his work, he cares what they think, but, like Tolstoy, once his head is clear and their presence removed, he doesn't care at all.

Mikhailov (*Mihailov* in Garnett's spelling) is a portrait of the author who was creating him. Mikhailov paints the portrait of Anna that is the imaginary visual equivalent of Tolstoy's literary creation of her.

It's almost only in this installment where Anna's light is not the brightest of all the characters; she is outshone by the cranky artist. While Anna is the subject of Mikhailov's attention and revelation, Mikhailov is the focus of Tolstoy's. Only later, in Part 7, in an installment a year away, as Levin gazes at Mikhailov's portrait of her, will we understand what Tolstoy saw as his own accomplishment of creating Anna's character.

In Chapter 14, Tolstoy transports us from Italy back to Russia and to Levin's surprised experiences of marriage:

> Altogether their honeymoon—that is to say, the month after their wedding—from which from tradition Levin expected so much, was not merely not a time of sweetness, but remained in the memories of both as the bitterest and most humiliating period in their lives. They both alike tried in later life to blot out from their memories all the monstrous, shameful incidents of that morbid period, when both were rarely in a normal frame of mind, both were rarely quite themselves.[*]

---

[*]   *Anna Karenina*, Part 5, Chapter 14, http://www.literatureproject.com/anna-karenina/anna _138.htm.

As he depicted Levin and Kitty flinching in remembrance of those "monstrous, shameful incidents," I believe that Tolstoy was guiltily remembering his and Sofia's honeymoon.

Three months after the wedding, Levin and Kitty go to Levin's estate. Levin tries to get back to his book about Russian agriculture and to his farming routines, but he keeps discovering surprises about what his married life entails. They hear from Levin's dissipated brother Nikolai, who is living with a prostitute and suffering a fatal illness in a hotel in a "provincial town"; Levin argues against Kitty's desire to go with him to minister to Nikolai. To his surprise, despite his being sure that he is right and that he's the acknowledged decision-maker in the couple, Kitty wins the argument. They arrive at the hotel, and it's Levin rather than Kitty who is discombobulated. Nikolai is difficult and unhappy, but Kitty is tactful and helpful and charms him. Levin is confused and can't see anything straight, while Kitty understands that death is on the doorstep. In Chapter 20, Nikolai dies and Kitty finds out that she's pregnant.

There is quite a contrast between the halves of this installment. As he was writing the April chapters Tolstoy seemed to anticipate that there would not be another installment for several months, that he was quitting for the summer. He had wrapped up Anna and Vronsky's time abroad rather tightly and had concluded Kitty and Levin's early period of marriage with the finality of death and the promise of birth.

Did Katkov and the subscribers to the *Russian Herald* know by now that Tolstoy's summer vacations began in April?

Strakhov wrote Tolstoy on May 8:

> In the last, April installment, I as usual read it through twice in a row. It seems to me that in general in the last three installments you were going at your full strength. What originality! The descriptions of the wedding, the confession, death, visiting the artist, the first jealousy—all these and so many other things of the ordinary kind that the high romantics neglect and all are looking for something more miraculous and important—this topic is obviously described by you *for the first time,* and by your descriptions they exist in narratives of somehow so simple and so good people, and here are seen with the full light of the artist.˙

---

* Donskov, *L. N. Tolstoy – N. N. Strakhov,* 270, May 8, 1876, http://feb-web.ru/feb/tolstoy /texts/selectpe/ts6/ts62270-.htm.

Strakhov's ecstatic response provoked a rare instance of Tolstoy feeling good about the novel. "I received your two letters, dear Nikolai Nikolaevich," he wrote Strakhov, "and sigh with joyful excitement reading them."[*]

Then Tolstoy made light of the praise, again with the pigeon-peddler analogy: "Even if the pigeon-seller knows that the pigeon is worth just 10 kopecks, he is all the same glad that such a hunter values the tumbler-pigeon at 100 rubles."[†] He mentions that there would not be a May installment but that he was dreaming of resuming publication in June. (No prophetic dream there. He missed that hopeful date by six months.) In the postscript, he asked Strakhov to lend him a book or two on pedagogy: "About general education, of the Ushinskiy anthropological kind, the newest, and artificial, as much as possible not stupid. Such books that A. A. Karenin would study in starting the education of the son left on his hands."[‡] Tolstoy needed to read the books that a fictional character would read, and Strakhov, the perfect assistant, would know what they were.

This bit of research led to the following passage in Chapter 24 of Part 5 (seven months later):

> When Alexey Alexandrovitch with Lidia Ivanovna's help had been brought back anew to life and activity, he felt it his duty to undertake the education of the son left on his hands. Having never before taken any interest in educational questions, Alexey Alexandrovitch devoted some time to the theoretical study of the subject. After reading several books on anthropology, education, and didactics, Alexey Alexandrovitch drew up a plan of education, and engaging the best tutor in Petersburg to superintend it, he set to work, and the subject continually absorbed him.[§]

※

Tolstoy wrote Fet that he had been meaning to write him for five days; he had received Hamlet the horse, so "Where do I send the money?" He explained that they had "begun

---

[*]   Donskov, *L. N. Tolstoy – N. N. Strakhov,* 272, May 17–18, 1876, http://feb-web.ru/feb/tolstoy /texts/selectpe/ts6/ts62272-.htm.

[†]   Ibid.

[‡]   Ibid.

[§]   *Anna Karenina,* Part 5, Chapter 24, http://www.literatureproject.com/anna-karenina /anna_148.htm.

spring-summer life, and the house is full of guests and bustling. This summer life for me is exactly like a dream; something remains from my real winter life, but more some sort of vision, now pleasant, now unpleasant, from some pointlessness, not guided by the common judgment of the world." As for the crops at Yasnaya Polyana and the region, "What a terrible summer. It's terrible and pitiful for us to look at the forest, especially at the young shoots that have grown. Everything is destroyed. The buyers have already started to trade the wheat. It's apparent it will be a bad year."*

That being said, he asked Fet about three more stallions that he would like to buy. Whatever could raise his spirits was what he wanted.

He wrote and told Golokhvastov, who (to Tolstoy's satisfaction) had returned to Russia, that he was now interested in Sofia going abroad for the "waters." Sofia, however, didn't want to because her sister Tatyana was coming, so Tolstoy would be taking Sofia to a Moscow doctor "in two weeks," and in the early part of June he would be going to the Voronezh district. He invited the Golokhvastovs to Yasnaya Polyana anytime, except not right then while everything was so undetermined. "I wrote you in Venice and wrote that I was very glad about the finishing of your work. Unfortunately, I can't say that about the work of Ol'ga Andreevna [Golokhvastov's wife, the romance author]; I feel that I have unfounded prejudice against drama—historical and in verse—and in this matter there's no judging."† He did, however, cringe and indeed judge it, both at the time and slightly disguised in *What Is Art?*

On or about the same day as his letter to Strakhov, he wrote to Fet about his full house and how he felt "low and dull-witted."‡

---

*   *PSS* 62: 273–274.

†   *PSS* 62: 275, letter of May 16, 1876.

‡   *PSS* 62: 277, letter of May 17–18, 1876.

ABOVE: Sofia Tolstaya was twenty-four years old in 1866, when this photograph was taken in Tula with her and Tolstoy's first two children, Sergei (Seryozha, born in 1863) and Tanya (1865). LEFT: In 1871 Sofia nearly died from puerperal fever, contracted with the birth of her daughter Maria. In order to get relief from cold compresses, Sofia had to shave her head, which she covered here with a scarf. Anna Karenina would also almost fatally succumb to puerperal fever.

ABOVE LEFT: The house at Yasnaya Polyana, Tolstoy's mother's estate, which he inherited. ABOVE CENTER: Tolstoy's first four children in a photographic studio in Tula in 1870. From left to right: Ilya, Lev, Tanya, and Seryozha. ABOVE RIGHT: Maria Tolstaya, the Tolstoys' second daughter (1871–1906), in 1874. Her birth nearly proved fatal to her mother. BELOW: The house at Yasnaya Polyana was nationalized by the USSR in 1919 and soon became an official cultural attraction. In modern times, it remains a popular year-round tourist site.

ABOVE LEFT: Seryozha Tolstoy was fourteen or fifteen when this photo was taken in 1878. ABOVE RIGHT: Daughter Tanya, c. 1884. BELOW: This is artwork by Konstantin Pechurichko (b. 1931) of the Patrovka steppe and the sharp Shishka hill, imagined by him at about the time in the 1870s when Tolstoy had a farmhouse here.

ABOVE LEFT: The Patrovka historian Valentina Petrovna Salazkina at the site-marker of Tolstoy's farmhouse in 1873. The Shishka is the sharper of the hills in the background. Tolstoy loved strolling "like Adam" over the steppe. ABOVE RIGHT: The site-marker of Tolstoy's second Patrovka farmhouse. BELOW LEFT: The title page of the first book edition of *Anna Karenina* in January of 1878. It reads Anna Karenina / Novel / Count / L. N. Tolstoy / In Eight Parts / Volume the First. BELOW CENTER: Tolstoy's sister-in-law, Tatyana Kuzminskaya (1846–1925), when she was still Tatyana Andreevna Bers, in 1864. Sofia's lively younger sister inspired Tolstoy's creation of Natasha in *War and Peace*. BELOW RIGHT: Tolstoy's close relative Alexandrine Tolstaya (1817–1904), one of his lifelong confidants, photographed here in the 1860s.

TOP LEFT: Tatyana Kuzminskaya, Tolstoy's sister-in-law, in 1872, in Tiflis (present day Tbilisi), where her husband was a Russian government official. TOP CENTER: Tolstoy's brother-in-law Stepan Bers (1855–1910) in about 1870. He sometimes served as Tolstoy's traveling companion; sometimes he helped his sister with her children when Tolstoy was away. TOP RIGHT: Mikhail Katkov (1818–1887), c. 1866, was the publisher of the *Russian Herald*'s serialization of *Anna Karenina*. BOTTOM LEFT: Afanasy Fet (1828–1894). The poet was one of Tolstoy's closest friends in the 1870s. They discussed literature, family life, God, and, most enthusiastically, horses. BOTTOM RIGHT: Tolstoy's daughter Tanya Sukhotina-Tolstaya and her first and only child, her daughter Tatiana, in 1905.

TOP LEFT: A manuscript page of a first draft of *Anna Karenina*. Tolstoy wrote by day and Sofia happily but wearily recopied by night, leaving a large margin for him to write his revisions. She then recopied and again left him a margin to insert revisions. And so on and so on, until Tolstoy finally sent off the serial installments of the novel. TOP RIGHT: This caricature of Tolstoy in a popular periodical was based on the 1876 photograph below. Though copies of *Anna Karenina* are part of the heap of books, the boys seem more inspired by *Boina i Mir* (*War and Peace*). BOTTOM LEFT: A galley of *Anna Karenina* with Tolstoy's rewriting of the entire page. Tolstoy revised many passages in this manner. BELOW: An image of Tolstoy in 1876 that was caricatured above.

TOP LEFT: Tatyana Kuzminskaya, Tolstoy's sister-in-law, in 1872, in Tiflis (present day Tbilisi), where her husband was a Russian government official. TOP CENTER: Tolstoy's brother-in-law Stepan Bers (1855–1910) in about 1870. He sometimes served as Tolstoy's traveling companion; sometimes he helped his sister with her children when Tolstoy was away. TOP RIGHT: Mikhail Katkov (1818–1887), c. 1866, was the publisher of the *Russian Herald*'s serialization of *Anna Karenina*. BOTTOM LEFT: Afanasy Fet (1828–1894). The poet was one of Tolstoy's closest friends in the 1870s. They discussed literature, family life, God, and, most enthusiastically, horses. BOTTOM RIGHT: Tolstoy's daughter Tanya Sukhotina-Tolstaya and her first and only child, her daughter Tatiana, in 1905.

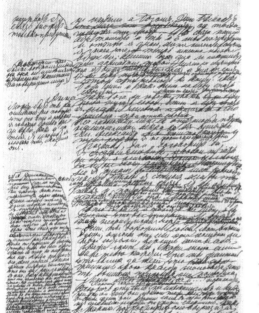

TOP LEFT: A manuscript page of a first draft of *Anna Karenina*. Tolstoy wrote by day and Sofia happily but wearily recopied by night, leaving a large margin for him to write his revisions. She then recopied and again left him a margin to insert revisions. And so on and so on, until Tolstoy finally sent off the serial installments of the novel. TOP RIGHT: This caricature of Tolstoy in a popular periodical was based on the 1876 photograph below. Though copies of *Anna Karenina* are part of the heap of books, the boys seem more inspired by *Boina i Mir* (*War and Peace*). BOTTOM LEFT: A galley of *Anna Karenina* with Tolstoy's rewriting of the entire page. Tolstoy revised many passages in this manner. BELOW: An image of Tolstoy in 1876 that was caricatured above.

Though we never see Mikhailov's painting of Anna that awes everyone who sees it, readers and artists have been illustrating the novel in their imaginations and on paper ever since. These are three from the Soviet era: TOP RIGHT: By Mikhail Ksenofontovich Sokolov (1946): Anna at Vronsky's horse race. BOTTOM LEFT: By Aram Vramshapu Vanetsian: From Part 5, Anna enters her husband's house to see her beloved son Seryozha on his ninth birthday. BOTTOM RIGHT: By Konstantin Ivanovich Rudakov (1940): From Part 1 of the novel: At the train station in St. Petersburg, Anna introduces Captain Vronsky to her husband Karenin, who has come to greet her on her return from Moscow.

LEFT: Nikolai Gusev was Tolstoy's secretary for part of the last decade of Tolstoy's life. He became a biographer and his books chronicling Tolstoy's daily life and work have been the most prominent scholarly sources for this book. CENTER: Sophia Tolstoy's "Anna Karenina" ring. BOTTOM: Tolstoy's grave on the grounds of Yasnaya Polyana. It sits on a rise above one of Tolstoy's favorite groves.

10

From Idle to Full Steam Ahead: June–December 1876

※

At the beginning of June, Tolstoy and Sofia were in Moscow to see a doctor about her health,* and on June 6, Sofia's sister Tatyana arrived in Yasnaya Polyana for the summer. She and her children stayed almost three months.

Tolstoy wrote both Strakhov and Fet. "A beautiful summer has come," he told Strakhov, "and I love it and I wander around and can't understand how I wrote in the winter."[†] Similarly to Fet: "This summer something has strongly happened to me, and if I were you, I would only write verses. Everything's very beautiful this year."[‡]

But it was only to Fet (to whom he was sending the payment for Hamlet) that he mentioned a family matter: "Three days ago from abroad my sister Maria Nikolaevna came, whom I hadn't seen in 3 years, and I'm very glad to see her." Fet, I presume, knew Maria's story, while Strakhov, a more recent friend, may not have.

But where was *Anna Karenina*? Where was Anna? It and she seem to have gone on vacation.

Tolstoy wrote Strakhov about how pleased he was that Strakhov would visit. Tolstoy warned him that he would be going various places on magistrate duties within three hours away, so when Strakhov arrived in July, he was to telegraph him and Tolstoy would hustle

---

*   Gusev, *Letopis'*, 459.

†   *PSS* 62: 278, letter of June 7–8, 1876.

‡   Ibid.

back: "I'm not saying that right now I have especially much to tell you, because I always have a whole world of thoughts which I know only you understand, and a whole world not of questions but of topics about which I need to know your views." Meanwhile, "My wife's health this summer is fair, but not good; this is my only but large misery."[*]

It was a light summer for letter-writing, although when he had been in Samara two of the last three summers, it had been even lighter.

His next two surviving letters, nearly a month later, went to Fet.

He wanted to see Fet and travel with him; it would be best in the first half of August. Then Tolstoy inquired about three stallions, followed by news of Sofia: "My wife's health (I'm afraid even to believe in this happiness) in the middle of summer became significantly better, and about our trip abroad, which was already decided on, we have begun to speak doubtfully." Tolstoy had plans now for going to Samara in September with his nephew, Maria's twenty-five-year-old son, Nikolai, and he invited Fet and Fet's brother to join him and D'yakov "to see the Kirgiz and their horses."[†] Strakhov's July visit, he told Fet, was spent philosophizing to weariness, and he was constantly remembering and bringing up *him*, Fet. The main thing now on Tolstoy's mind seems to have been Samara. That trip, from September 3 to September 20, would end up including only Tolstoy and his nephew.

On July 28, Tolstoy arranged through a short note to go see Fet on the 12th of August. He remarked, by the way, that nobody understood anything about the Herzegovina and Serbian war, and "it's impossible to understand anything" about it.[‡]

This was the summer of dueling friendships.

If he was more confidential to Fet in the letters, he was more exuberantly affectionate to Strakhov. In the July 31 letter to Strakhov, he said, "I'm afraid I don't love making plans," and immediately made plans that he would see *Strakhov* instead of Fet if the time that Strakhov had would be conflicting with the plans he had made with Fet. He also asked if Strakhov still wanted to go to the Optina Monastery. (At this point, Tolstoy thought he was leaving for Samara on the 25th of August, but a surprise wedding would keep him around until September.)

Weary with the planning and contingency arrangements, Tolstoy sighed to Strakhov: "Now we'll soon die. But in that world it's still unknown what our relations will become. You shortly but so well described your life[§] that I became envious.—If only you instead

---

[*]   *PSS* 62: 279, letter of June 22–23, 1876.

[†]   *PSS* 62: 281, letter of July 21, 1876.

[‡]   Ibid.

[§]   The letter containing this description hasn't been found.

of reading Anna Kar would finish it and save me from this Damocles torture." Again with the teasing of Strakhov that Strakhov finish the novel for him! "Yesterday I tried to do it, but I without fail want to force myself to work."* There's nothing to show that Tolstoy did any work on it.

I try to imagine him trudging to his desk. Was he reluctant to sit down at it? Trollope, over in London, believed inspiration for novel-writing came from gluing one's bottom to the chair every morning. Did Tolstoy open a folder of drafts? Did he reread a page or two and give up? Did he write a sentence off the top of his head to see if it would spark a new chapter?

In Tolstoy's second to last (known) letter before his trip to Samara, he regretted that Fet wouldn't sell him the horse Favorita, but in the meantime he would like to buy Gunib.† With all the horse-dealing with Fet, it's surprising that there never seems to have been a dispute or misunderstanding about money or the quality of a horse. When Tolstoy's passion for buying horses cooled in the 1880s, though, their friendship seems to have cooled off, too.

The last surviving letter of the summer went to Tolstoy's brother Sergei: "After the parted guests and commotion, our usual life has restarted." He asked Sergei to send him two female dogs to take with him to Samara.

Despite her shaky health, Sofia probably enjoyed that summer of 1876 more than Tolstoy. He was raring to get away now as soon as possible, although his five letters to her during this trip September 4–20 reveal him as a loving husband and father. He knew that she loved him; he told her details that only a loving wife could care about. He was happy to be away but anxious because he was away. He was free of home and responsibilities; his imagination glowed with nostalgia.

On Saturday, the 4th, at noon, he wrote from a steamer on the Volga. Before leaving Moscow, he and his nephew Nikolai went and said farewell to Nikolai's mother, Maria Tolstaya, and then they left from the Nizhegorod station, which station Anna Karenina also leaves from, before she gets out at her stop and kills herself. "Even though we took places in second-class, we slept excellently." At Nizhegorod, there was a mix-up before they could get on a ship: "I didn't write from Nizhe from all the confusion; but I not only remembered but thought and think of you every minute [. . .]"‡

His letters were loving and considerate:

---

*   *PSS* 62: 282.

†   *PSS* 62: 284, letter of August 27–28, 1876.

‡   *PSS* 83: 225–226, letter of September 4, 1876.

> I know that you're downcast and suffering, but I see that strength which you
> have in yourself to not bother me and, if it's possible, I love you even more for
> this. [. . .] My plan, despite being very undetermined, is this: when I get to
> Samara, find Bull and ask him to bring me to Buzuluk; from there I'll go to the
> farm, and if possible, from Buzuluk go as far as Orenburg [. . .]

If there was enough money, he would get a couple of men to help him drive the horses. His postscript: "I kiss all the children and ahead of time thank them for listening to you and trying to be happy." (The children in September 1876: Sergei, Tanya, Ilya, Lev, and Maria.)

The next day, September 5, now in Kazan, he wrote Sofia again: "Weather superb, health good. You're probably mushroom-hunting. Please don't ride on Sharik." Sharik was one of the Kirgiz horses. Was it too spirited, too unpredictable?

Again he announced to Sofia a plan: to have a local man help him buy horses in Orenburg. He would try not to be gone two weeks. "Kazan excites in me my memories of unpleasant sadness. Oh, if only you and the children, mainly you, were well and at peace." He sent kisses to her and to the children. His postscript contained a realization that seemed to have surprised Tolstoy himself: "It's as if I very much want to write."[*] This unexpected stirring petered out. He didn't start writing *Anna Karenina* again until the end of November.

While Tolstoy was gone, Sofia's brother Stepan helped her before his return to law school in St. Petersburg. In her memoir, Sofia narrated Tolstoy's September adventure in her own way:

> On the 3rd of September of that year, 1876, my sister left us once again to
> go back to the Caucasus with her whole family, and Lev Nikolaevich made
> plans to go to Samara and Orenburg. He thought of using our Samara estate
> to raise English purebred horses, which he had already bought, along with
> Kirghiz steppe horses, which he intended to purchase presently in Orenburg.
>
> Crossing these two breeds—English and Kirghiz—was aimed at developing
> a special type of horse at our Samara stud-farm. And Lev Nikolaevich got it
> started, to be sure, but like all his ventures in life, this one, too, as they say,
> came to nought. The best stallion purchased was drowned along the way by
> the peasant set to fetch it, or at least that is what he said, but I didn't believe

---

*   *PSS* 83: 228.

him. He simply sold it. Other horses had died, and I can't recall now exactly
how Lev Nikolaevich got out of this business.[*]

As she wrote her memoir, much of it after her husband's death in 1910, Sofia was not
only a proud widow, who more than anyone else helped preserve the work of the world-
famous author, she was also a wife who knew her husband's faults ("like all his ventures
in life, this one . . . came to nought") and was open about it.

She remembered that he "wrote me touching letters on his trip," and she offered quotations from a couple of them:

> "I think that since I am terribly in love {with you}, I am transported back into the
> past—Pokrovskoe, that lilac dress, that sense of sweetness, and my heart pounds."
>
> And again:
>
> "Every minute on this trip I think about you tenderly and am ready to fill
> my letter with tender words."
>
> And again:
>
> "I take such delight in the feeling I have for you, and for your existence
> in the world."[†]

Was she shy to quote more? He did write more, so I don't know why she pared and
paraphrased. I suspect that she did not want her readers to grant him some additional
points on the husband chart. He wrote her on September 7 from the ship on the Volga,
and in it made that last declaration about his "delight":

> I write this letter on the 7th at 2 in the afternoon, still on ship, and I'll post it
> in a box in Samara, where we'll be, God willing, at 7 this evening. [. . .] My
> runny nose has passed, and thanks to grapes and watermelon, my stomach [is
> better?], and so my state of mind is in order. I hope that I'll write often and
> that I, even just once, receive letters, and I will know about you in various
> periods. You so frightened me, reluctant to let me go, that it seems I am afraid
> more than before for all of you, and mainly for you alone. [No particular
> details about his farewell are provided by either Tolstoy or Sofia, but we might
> remember this awkward, disturbing departure when we get to the February

---

[*]   Tolstaya, *My Life*, 226.

[†]   Ibid.

1877 installment of *Anna Karenina* wherein "there had been almost a quarrel between Vronsky and Anna over this proposed expedition."*]

Sometimes when writing you, I don't say anything about my feelings, because at the moment when I was writing I was not in such a situation, but [the *italics* of what follows are the phrases Sofia chose to quote in her memoir] *on this trip I think about you tenderly and I am ready to fill my letter with tender words.* Farewell, sweet darling. *I take such delight in the feeling I have for you, and for your existence in the world.*

If only you were healthy, and so as you are. From Orenburg I'll telegraph you.†

He wrote her a short note that evening, "As promised, I write you two words from Samara." He had found Bull and they were leaving on the train for Orenburg right away.‡

Sofia also wrote him, on September 7, a good newsy letter regarding the fine weather and Jules Rey's hunting.§

Is it possible that she did not sense her husband's depression? And if she didn't, what does that mean about that dark cloud that by his own account never left him? Does it mean that when we're depressed, we see the dismal weather everywhere, but others, even those who love us, can't see the clouds socking us in?

In her memoir she recalled:

At that time nothing had yet ruined our happiness and love. We were of one mind and agreed on everything: the raising of the children, life in the country, all our beliefs—about religion, about life. [Such declarations as this, which she makes throughout *My Life*, remind us to be skeptical about her scrupulousness. Even when they were happy, they almost never seemed of one mind. Perhaps it was simply that the disputes seemed mild to her compared to those ahead?] If Lev Nikolaevich entertained any doubts or questions in his heart, they didn't interfere with our lives, and Lev Nikolaevich treated us with love and compassion and he himself became ever better and more meek. Our approach to the raising of our children, too, was the same. Lev Nikolaevich decided we

---

*   *Anna Karenina,* Part 6, Chapter 25, http://www.literatureproject.com/anna-karenina/anna _182.htm.

†   *PSS* 83: 229–230, letter of September 7, 1876.

‡   *PSS* 83: 230, letter of September 7, 1876.

§   *PSS* 83: 229, footnote 6.

would prepare Serezha at home for university entrance and then, when he got in, we would all go live in Moscow.

"By that time Tanja will have grown up, and we'll have to help her with her coming out," Lev Nikolaevich added, and I agreed, and everything went along nice and smoothly in our family. [Our sympathy for her nostalgia does not require us to *believe* her.]

It would be quite a different story when {later} he turned away from the church, his family and duties all at once, and began to malign everything on the basis of his new faith—his new views on life—meanwhile explaining it all away by citing Christianity and its principles!

But about that later.

Back then in 1876 it was hard for us to part and to break, even temporarily, that tie which so lovingly bound us all together; to the point where any separation, even a short one, was effected only with great effort. [Well, the "effort" to get away was all his. See Sofia's September 15, 1876, diary below.]*

She said that he was going to stop over in Kazan, "but he was still haunted by certain past memories which caused him nothing but anguish, as he himself wrote me." What exactly haunted him? If she knew, she never said what he meant (in his September 5 letter) by "memories of unpleasant sadness."

She recalled:

> They [i.e., Lev and his nephew Nikolai] informed us that while the railway didn't officially go as far as Orenburg just yet, they wangled permission to travel on a service (or workers') train. Somewhere at the station Nikolen'ka started to head over to the other side, which necessitated climbing under a railway carriage. No sooner had he crawled under the train than the train began to move, and Nikolen'ka just barely managed to get out of the way in time, which was a bad fright for both of them.

Crawling under the train! Can we help fearfully thinking of Anna?

He telegraphed Sofia from Orenburg that he was well (not mentioning Nikolai's near accident on the train track) but had been delayed two days.†

---

*   Tolstaya, *My Life*, 226.

†   *PSS* 83: 231, letter of September 12, 1876.

Sofia resumes the story:

> In Orenburg Lev Nikolaevich got together with his old acquaintance and army
> chum, now the governor-general of the Orenburg Territory, Kryzhanovskij,
> which was very pleasant for him. Overall, he found the trip quite successful.
> He had purchased some steppe horses there and sent them to his Samara estate,
> still dreaming of instituting a new breed of horses.[*]

Sofia wrote in her diary only three times that year and those three entries occur during
Tolstoy's absence; they start on September 15 and end September 18. Sofia unselfcon-
sciously poured out her complaints. In writing her memoir, she was variously motivated
and skipped over some of the diary's raw details, if she even looked at them at all. Perhaps
she was unhappy with what they revealed:

> We live in such isolation, and here I am again with my silent friend, my diary.
> I intend to write it every day without fail from now on. Lyovochka went off to
> Samara, and from there to Orenburg, a town he had always wanted to visit.
> I got a telegram from him there. I miss him a lot and worry even more. I try
> to tell myself I am pleased he is enjoying himself, but it isn't true. I am hurt
> that he has torn himself away from me just when we were getting along so
> well and were such good friends, and has sentenced me to two sad, anxious
> weeks without him.[†]

Her diary catches her conflicted feelings: *Why should he go away if he's happy? Why does
he need to chase down exotic horses?*[‡]

Why wasn't Sofia enough for Tolstoy; *why isn't Anna enough for Vronsky?*

Why do these men find themselves happy and relieved to be away from their loving
partners?

Sofia described in the second paragraph of that first entry her poor health and her
impatience with the children.

---

[*]   Tolstaya, *My Life*, 227.

[†]   *The Diaries of Sophia Tolstoy*, 52–53.

[‡]   Tolstoy eventually had about 400 horses on his Samara farmland, but by the mid-1880s they
       were almost all gone—escaped, stolen, or dead. (See Donskov, *L. N. Tolstoy – N. N. Strakhov*,
       282, http://feb-web.ru/feb/tolstoy/texts/selectpe/ts6/ts62282-.htm.)

She announced in her diary on September 17 (she right away had missed a day) that it was her name day:

One more day has passed without Lyovochka, or so much as a word from him. This morning I got up feeling lazy and unwell, plagued by minor worries. The children went off with Styopa [Sofia's brother Stepan] to fly the kite, and ran back, red-faced and excited to beg me to go and watch. But I didn't go, for I had ordered all Lyovochka's papers to be fetched out of the gun-closet and was immersed in the world of his novels and diaries.

In those thousands of pages written by the person she regarded as the supreme author in the world, there was something she wanted to find out:

I was very excited, and experienced a wealth of impressions. But I realised I could never write that biography of him as I had intended, for I could never be impartial; I avidly search his diaries for any reference to love, and am so tormented by jealousy that I can no longer see anything clearly. I shall try to do it, though. I am afraid of my resentment of Lyovochka for leaving me just when I loved him so much, but in my soul I blame him constantly for causing me so much worry and misery. It seems odd that although he is always so anxious that I should not fall ill, he should torture me by going away at a time when my health was so poor. I now cannot sleep for worry and eat practically nothing. [. . .] God help me survive, perhaps for several more days. "What is he punishing me for?" I keep asking myself. "Why, for loving him so much." And now all my happiness is in pieces, and I feel very bitter that my good humour and my spontaneous loving feelings have once again been crushed.*

Her anxiety ("What is he punishing me for?") was on a par with Anna's when Vronsky goes away to the elections, but Sofia would in fact dabble at writing up a short biography for the next few years. The Tolstoys' daughter Alexandra Lvovna Tolstaya's biography of him is impressive for how moderately toned and *impartial* it is. Sofia knew herself well enough to know that she could not write like that. (A few years before, when Tolstoy was on the steppe in July, he wrote and told her, with fondness, that he couldn't read her letters without crying: "I tremble all over, and my heart beats {fast}. And you write

---

* *The Diaries of Sofia Tolstoy*, 53.

whatever comes into your head, while for me *every word* is significant [. . .]."*) She let herself remember as the memories returned and as she created those memories. She didn't trouble herself to check all her own materials for facts or to review her own diaries for her actual contemporary responses.

The next day's diary: "I had a telegram from him in Syzran today saying he will be home the day after tomorrow in the morning. I suddenly felt more cheerful, and the house was all happiness and light, the children's lessons went well, and they were adorable. [. . .] My heart leaps when I think that the day after tomorrow Lyovochka will be coming back, lighting up the house."† (He also sent a telegram from Syzran on the 17th, announcing that he was shipping the horses.)

In her memoir, Sofia gilds the page:

> Lev Nikolaevich returned home in two-and-a-half weeks, more in love {with me} than ever and feeling completely refreshed in his soul.‡

As she was writing that sentence, probably decades after the event, I imagine she simply wanted to believe that he had been more in love with her than ever. If Tolstoy had actually told her so, she would have happily declared it in her diary that he had. She acknowledged that his adoring love for her was going to end very soon, so perhaps she needed to convince herself that the perverse downturn of his feelings happened at love's very height.

As usual on his return from trips, Tolstoy wrote his friends, but he was deflated, despite Sofia's recollected impression that he was "completely refreshed in his soul."

Tolstoy told Golokhvastov, "After an extended and wearying trip, I'm tired and not fully well. It's my intention to sit at home, not leaving, and make up for the lost time of summer—that is, heartily work a lot. My wife was only waiting for my return and in a few days, that is, around the 27th, leaves for Moscow for a few days to look for and choose a governess for our daughters. Small children, small worries, big children . . ."§

He wrote to tell Strakhov only that he was back home and that indeed all was well with him and the family.⁵ To Fet, however, on the same day or so, he confessed: "I returned well, but became terrible, and having arrived got a cold and I lie at home in low spirits

---

*   Donskov, *Tolstoy and Tolstaya*, 63, July 16–17, 1871.

†   *The Diaries of Sofia Tolstoy*, 54, September 18, 1876.

‡   Tolstaya, *My Life*, 226.

§   *PSS* 62: 285, letter of September 25–27, 1876.

⁵   *PSS* 62: 286, letter of September 26–27, 1876.

with no strength to do anything. My trip was very interesting. I took a rest from all that Serbian thoughtlessness."* (Tolstoy was referring to the nationalistic rallying for Russian intervention in the war in Serbia; that intervention would lead to Vronsky's grief-inspired participation in it in 1877.) As for the horse Gunib, Tolstoy paid one hundred rubles to an office in Fet's name.

Over the next three weeks there are no extant letters, but we know that Tolstoy could not get himself back to writing—and completing—*Anna Karenina*. Sofia complained on October 10 about this to her sister Tatyana that he "still hasn't taken up the writing . . . he reads a lot and takes walks, and thinks, and gathers himself to write."†

We remember that he wanted to read the books that Karenin would have read in order to educate Seryozha, but otherwise it's hard to see how reading could help him with the novel. Or is it that reading helped him turn the inner wheels?

Sofia remembered that his "main activity this winter was still the writing of *Anna Karenina*, and somewhere I have recorded that in October [not true, according to her own diary, as she recorded there that he didn't start writing again until mid-November] he wrote the chapter about Aleksej Aleksandrovich Karenin's relationship to Lidija Ivanovna [she names this detail in her November 20 diary entry]. I recall how pleased he was at the humour he had infused into their relationship. I also recall the affection with which he wrote the scene of Anna Karenina's meeting with her child, and I wept as I transcribed this chapter."‡

What this memory proves again, unfortunately, is that she wrote at least some parts of *My Life* without even opening her own diary, and specifically that she hadn't even reread the small special section that she had dedicated to Tolstoy's writing activities. She ignored or couldn't find the world's best source, her own "somewhere I have recorded" diary.

Let me try to forgive her carelessness, just as I will need to be forgiven many more offenses and carelessnesses in this biographical study.

So what did Tolstoy think or say when Sofia told him that she had cried transcribing that tearful scene of Anna and Seryozha's last reunion? She was at liberty to tell him so, even if there were times that he ignored her suggestions and regrets. She loved this transcribing job, despite that recopying had given her a pain in the right shoulder the previous year. While Strakhov was the first reader of the complete book, she was the first reader of most of the drafts. She took in the novel through her head, heart, and hand.

---

*   *PSS* 62: 286–287, letter of September 27?, 1876.

†   Gusev, *Materials,* 298, letter of end of September 1876.

‡   Tolstaya, *My Life,* 229.

In her "The Teachers' Seminary" chapter, Sofia recalled: "In our Tula [. . .] Lev Niko-laevich wanted to found a university *in bast shoes*, as he himself put it. The future teachers trained in this seminary were not to leave the peasant milieu—they were to spend their summers ploughing, sowing, cutting grain, etc., and to teach and work on their own further self-education in the wintertime. But this was a dream, one of many which Lev Nikolaevich had in various areas of life."[*]

In mid-October, Tolstoy was preparing rooms and furniture for these courses and had found a teacher who had graduated from a university.[†] (This project was refused funding by the Tula government on December 12, but by then his heart for it seems to have disappeared anyway.)

He resumed correspondence by writing a note to Fet; he praised a new verse by Fet ("I retold it twice and each time my voice broke off from tears"), and took care of some horse business, and reaffirmed their friendship: "It's amazing how closely we're related by mind and heart."[‡]

In "The Blind Woman and a Trip to Moscow," Sofia recalled how Tolstoy had ordered for her "a black velvet cloak to be made out of the light kidskin material which Lev Niko-laevich had brought me back from Orenburg. I wrote my sister that covering the cloak with velvet was something *Levochka insisted on*, even though this year we had significant losses [. . .] and the only income we had was from Lev Nikolaevich's writings."[§] Sometime in late October, Tolstoy asked Nagornov to go "if you have my money" and pay "Madam Reno on Nikitskiy Boulevard," and have the coat sent.[ⁱ] The coat must not have been sent, because Sofia later wrote that Tolstoy had to go to Moscow himself to get it.

Tolstoy heard from Strakhov: "I imagine that you're now busy with the end of *Anna Karenina* or even some other thing just as serious and very important."[**] We know that discreet and tactful Strakhov did not believe that there was anything in the world that Tolstoy could be writing or working on as "serious" or "important" as *Anna Karenina*. Strakhov went on:

---

* Tolstaya, *My Life*, 228.

† Gusev, *Letopis'*, 460.

‡ *PSS* 62: 287, letter of October 17–18, 1876.

§ Tolstaya, *My Life*, 228.

ⁱ *PSS* 62: 288, letter of late October 1876.

** Donskov, *L. N. Tolstoy – N. N. Strakhov*, 287, November 4, 1876, http://feb-web.ru/feb/tolstoy/texts/selectpe/ts6/ts62287-.htm.

About Anna Karenina the talk here doesn't stop. Everyone waits and scolds you. I admit I firmly hoped that it would appear in the Oct installment; yesterday I found out that it's not. What does this mean? Is Katkov being cunning? He expressed the opinion to me that now there is no counting on finishing the novel this year, that it would be better to put off the end to the next.[*]

According to the Jubilee edition, Tolstoy was in Moscow November 8–10,[†] though Sofia placed him there just a bit later:

Lev Nikolaevich first gave me money for the cloak, as well as the clothing and shoes for me and the children I had obtained in Moscow, and then later, on the 11th of November, he himself went to Moscow for the same purpose. He bought himself a black bearskin fur coat for 450 rubles, and ordered shoes and other clothing. Lev Nikolaevich was buying his clothes then from the best Moscow tailor, Ayet, saying he had no time to deal with poor tailors, with all the measuring, re-sewing, etc., and how it was much more profitable to have clothes made by a good tailor, since they will last much longer.[‡]

Л. Н. Толстой.
1876 г.

---

[*]   Donskov, *L. N. Tolstoy – N. N. Strakhov*, 287.

[†]   *PSS* 62: 288, footnote 1.

[‡]   Tolstaya, *My Life*, 230.

Sofia continued her recollection (and now contradicting her own earlier statement that he began writing again in October):

> After returning from Moscow Lev Nikolaevich was restless for a while and kept saying: "My mind's asleep." But then all at once something seemed to blossom forth in him, and he began writing feverishly. Once he said to me:
>
> "I was looking at the white silk band on the sleeve of my dressing gown, which is very beautiful. I thought about how people are led to think up all sorts of patterns, embroideries and trimmings . . . A whole world in a woman's life. And I realised that that could be something lovable . . . And, of course, right now my thoughts are on my novel, *Anna Karenina*. And this gave me a whole chapter, where Anna, as a lonely woman, is bored, since all the women have rejected her."*

An interesting statement, and one that has often been quoted. But it cannot have been taken down verbatim. That is, he would not have had to explain to Sofia which novel he was referring to. Again, Sofia did not fuss about exactitude, though this time there is no diary entry concerning it to contradict her.

Gusev believes that "Tolstoy's bad mood was even intensified by the political situation taking shape in the country."† Granted, the political situation affected his mood; but while he in fact said it inspired his trip ("I went to Moscow to find out about the war"‡), we also know he went *shopping*.

Tolstoy's response to Strakhov's last two letters (October 12 and November 4) was written November 12–13:

> You are a true friend, dear Nikolay Nikolaevich. Despite my silence and the silence on your important letter, you all the same gladden me with your letters. I cannot express how grateful I am to you for the last, not deserved by me, of your letters. In order to explain and justify my silence I ought to speak about myself.
>
> Having come from Samara and Orenburg now two months ago (I had a miraculous trip), I thought that I would take up my work, finish the work given me—finishing the novel—and take up a new thing; and suddenly

---

*   Tolstaya, *My Life*, 230.

†   Gusev, *Materials*, 242.

‡   *PSS* 62: 288, letter of November 12, 1876.

instead of all this, ever since I have done nothing.* I am spiritually asleep and cannot wake up. Ill health, depressed.† Despair for my powers. What fate has predestined for me, I do not know, but to live through my life without respect for it—and respect for it comes to me only through work of a certain kind—is agonizing.‡ [. . .]

The last question of yours in our philosophical exchange was: what is evil? I am able to answer that for myself. I am going to explain this answer and will give it to you another time, I hope at Christmas.§

He also wrote Fet, regretting their missed connection in Moscow, and added, "Pity me two things. (1) A son of bitch driver in Samara drove the stallions almost 15 miles and wanting to take a shortcut, he got Gunib drowned in a marsh. [Perhaps Sofia did not tell him of her suspicions about the driver?] (2) I sleep and cannot write. I despise myself for my idleness and can't get myself to take up other business."¶

He answered Ya. P. Polonskiy, "an old acquaintance," granting permission to a woman Polonskiy knew who had translated Tolstoy's 1859 novella *Family Happiness* into French: "I'm often addressed in letters by translators, and as I don't understand why it [my permission] is needed, I never answer."** (While contemporary French and English novels were being translated and published in the *Russian Herald*, Dostoevsky and Tolstoy were still unknown except by hearsay in France and England.) Tolstoy mentioned that for sixteen years he hadn't been in St. Petersburg, where Polonskiy was, and hoped never to be there again. (He in fact went again.)

Tolstoy's next letter to Strakhov was unusually cheerful as, to Tolstoy's relief and ours, he had resumed, finally, *Anna Karenina*:

I've come to life a little, dear Nikolay Nikolaich, and have stopped despising myself, and so I feel like writing to you. "That's a true friend," I couldn't help

---

*   *PSS* 62: 290, letter of November 12–13, 1876.

†   *PSS* 62: 290. [The first two sentences are my translation; they're followed by Albert Kaspin's in Eikhenbaum's book.]

‡   Eikhenbaum, *Tolstoi in the Seventies*, 122.

§   R. F. Christian omits the beginning and end of this letter. Hence, my patchwork translation. *PSS* 62: 290–291.

¶   *PSS* 62: 288–289, letter of November 12, 1876.

** *PSS* 62: 292, letter of November 17–18, 1876.

saying to myself when I saw your handwriting on your last letter enclosing Polonsky's. [. . .]

Literature is a terrible abomination, except for its highest manifestations— true scholarly work without any bias, philosophical impartiality of thought and artistic creativity which, I flatter myself with proud hope, has descended on me these last few days. [. . .]

While his definition is cranky ("Literature is a terrible abomination, except for its highest manifestations"), it is also a recognition—for once—of what he was doing in *Anna Karenina,* obviously one of literature's "highest manifestations," though he only gives himself credit for the little he had most recently written. Meanwhile . . .

What do you say about Christmas? I shall await your reply anxiously. Only you will have to get up on a chair and decorate the Christmas tree and tie ribbons on to sweets.

It seems we can't avoid the Golokhvastovs, and my wife has invited them [. . .] to come for Christmas. [. . .] He's nice, but she's intolerable; she is literature and a bit of *The Citizen* [for which publication Strakhov was writing], only without the Christianity. [. . .]*

We can imagine Tolstoy grumbling to himself in anticipation of Ol'ga Golokhvastova's visit and wonder how he was going to manage to talk civilly with her.

In "Various Notes for Future Reference," dated November 20 but remembered in her memoir as October, Sofia wrote:

All this autumn he kept saying, "My brain is asleep." But suddenly, about a week ago, something within him seemed to blossom and he started working cheerfully again—and he seems quite satisfied with his efforts, too. He silently sat down at this desk this morning, without even drinking his coffee, and wrote and wrote for more than an hour, revising the chapter dealing with Anna's arrival in St. Petersburg and Aleks. Aleks.'s relations with Lidia Ivanovna.†

---

*   Christian, *Tolstoy's Letters,* 299–300, November 17–18, 1876.

†   *The Diaries of Sofia Tolstoy,* 849, November 20, 1876.

The next day, this time in the section of her diary titled "Notes on Remarks Made by L. N. Tolstoy on His Writing," Sofia wrote:

> He came up to me and said: "This bit of writing is so tedious!"
>
> "Why?" I asked.
>
> "Well, you see, I've said that Vronsky and Anna were staying in the same hotel room, but that's not possible. In St. Petersburg at least, they'd have to take rooms on different floors. So as you see, this means that all the scenes and conversations will have to take place in two separate places, and all the various visitors will have to see them separately. So it will all have to be altered."[*]

This discussion with Sofia about his resolving of a scene is a rare occurrence. But little mistakes like this particularly vexed Tolstoy. We remember that Strakhov had to mollify him after Tolstoy got frustrated with two little errors in the depiction of Levin and Kitty's wedding.

Strakhov was Tolstoy's and our man on the ground, reporting live for now from St. Petersburg on November 28, but gratefully accepting Tolstoy's invitation to spend Christmas at Yasnaya Polyana. Tolstoy's state of mind alarmed him:

> Your first letter saddened me, the second didn't at all console me. What agitation is in you! From an abstract point of view I ought to have been gladdened because this agitation of effort promises good fruit. But, knowing your delicate constitution, I understand that you are in a moment of depression, and this situation torments me. Really, while a person lives he cannot be at peace? You, famous, independent, surrounded by a charming family and even having perfected work that will forever remain great—how can you speak about the moments when your life is not worth respect? Such moments cannot be, ought not to be. And in good moments you yourself, of course, feel how little basis your woe has in your bad moments.[†]

Tolstoy's note in reply to these generous, kind words was unusually reassuring: he reconfirmed Strakhov's visit over Christmas and New Year, despite the presence of others:

---

[*]   *The Diaries of Sofia Tolstoy*, 849, November 21, 1876.

[†]   Donskov, *L. N. Tolstoy – N. N. Strakhov*, 295, November 28, 1876, http://feb-web.ru/feb /tolstoy/texts/selectpe/ts6/ts62295-.htm.

"Your barrel of honey won't be spoiled for me by a spoonful of Golokhvastovs. [. . .] I, thank God, have been working already for some time and so—have a calm spirit."[*]

He also wrote Fet, for the most part about a poem of Fet's, which was "quite exceptionally good," and about Alexei Tolstoy's poems, which were "terrible. I opened him in various places, each worse than the last. For example, a picture of night: 'the steps do not creak in the vestibule.' Why not have said: 'the pigs do not grunt in the pig-sty'? And all in the same vein."[†]

Sofia wrote her sister Tatyana: "We're writing *Anna Karenina* finally now, that is, without interruption. Levochka, enlivened and focused, each day adds a new chapter. I with effort recopy, and now even under this letter lie ready pages of a new chapter, which he wrote yesterday. Katkov telegraphed three days ago, begging to be sent some chapters for the December issue, and Levochka himself is bringing the novel in a few days to Moscow."[‡]

Note the "*We*'re writing": Sofia was happy. The use of "we" was her habit when Tolstoy was writing and she was helping him. Through her recopying of it each night, she was making it easier for him to continue. This month of work would be, it seems, Tolstoy's only pleasant memory of writing *Anna Karenina*:

On June 25, 1902, Sergei Yakovlevich Elpat'evskiy accompanied Tolstoy, leaving Crimea:

> "Lev Nikolaevich asked me about the business with which I was much occupied at the time—about the system in Crimea for the poor visiting tubercular people—and excitedly spoke his feelings about this business and then suddenly unexpectedly asked: 'How old are you?' I answered forty-eight. To my amazement, his face right away became serious, even severe—and I can't find another phrase—and with an envious glance, turning away, moodily said: "Forty-eight! . . . The best time of my work . . . I never so worked like that." [. . .] "I was writing *Anna Karenina*."[§]

Well? Secondhand testimony, twenty-five years after the fact . . . We can hope that it's true.

---

[*]   *PSS* 62: 294, letter of December 5–6, 1876.

[†]   Christian, *Tolstoy's Letters,* 301, December 6–7, 1876.

[‡]   Donskov, *L. N. Tolstoy – N. N. Strakhov,* December 9, 1876, http://feb-web.ru/feb/tolstoy/texts/selectpe/ts6/ts62297-.htm.

[§]   Gusev, *Materials,* 245.

On or about December 10, he wrote to Fet to say that he would soon be in Moscow and would stay at the Paris Hotel on purpose in order to see him there. He mentioned: "My work goes well and is almost ready for the journal."

He continued in this satisfied mood and wrote his brother: "The largest of all of my writings was delayed for me, which is going successfully for me. I was unable to get going for a long time, but now it goes and it's a very joyful feeling."[*] He also invited Sergei and his wife and twelve-year-old daughter for Christmas.

Glad to be making progress with the book, Tolstoy was clear of his depression, it seems, and looking forward to hosting the Christmas festivities.

The chapters from Part 6 that Sofia had copied she dated December 9 and 10. This means Part 5 was finished. Was it now packed and carried by Tolstoy when he went to Moscow? In Moscow, in the middle of December, he met the composer Pyotr Ilyich Tchaikovsky, who was twelve years his junior. Tchaikovsky admired Tolstoy so much that he had asked the head of the Moscow Conservatory, Nikolai Rubinstein, to set up a quartet ensemble in Tolstoy's honor.

Tchaikovsky remembered, "Maybe there was never a time in my life I was so flattered and touched in my authorial self-love as when L. N. Tolstoy, listening to the Andante of my first quartet and sitting beside me, filled up with tears."[†]

Having returned to Yasnaya Polyana, Tolstoy wrote Tchaikovsky a lively letter:

> I am sending you the songs, dear Pyotr Ilich. I have looked through them again. They will be a wonderful treasure in your hands. But for goodness sake, work them up and use them in a Mozart-Haydn style, and not in a Beethoven-Schumann-Berlioz artificial style, striving for the unexpected. How much I left unsaid to you! I really said nothing of what I meant to say.

Imagine that, *Tolstoy* tongue-tied.

> There was simply no time. I did enjoy myself. Indeed this last visit of mine to Moscow will remain one of my best memories.
>
> I have never received such a valuable reward for my literary works as that wonderful evening. And what a nice man Rubinstein is! [. . .]

---

[*]   *PSS* 62: 296, letter of December 7–15, 1876.

[†]   Gusev, *Materials*, 247. In the *Letopis'* (464), Gusev says Tchaikovsky wrote this memory in his diary on July 1, 1886.

I haven't looked through your pieces yet [R. F. Christian footnotes this: "Tchaikovsky presented Tolstoy with some of his own compositions"], but when I settle down to them, I will give you my opinion—whether you need it or not—and give it boldly, because I have grown to love your talent. [. . .]*

Tolstoy was not daunted by a genius in another artistic genre. Tchaikovsky, however, having received the "folk songs for him to arrange," wrote appreciatively of Tolstoy and his writings but had to point out that he couldn't manage to work with those particular songs. R. F. Christian explains: "Despite a favourable first impression, Tchaikovsky was offended by Tolstoy's persistent and outspoken criticism of Beethoven and the two men never met again."†

※

The second half of Part 5 of *Anna Karenina* came out in the December 1876 issue of the *Russian Herald*, which subscribers received on December 31.

Readers had been without a new installment since April 29. They might have remembered that Levin's brother Nikolai had just died and Kitty was pregnant. They might have wondered if Kitty and Levin were back on the estate now. And of course what was going on now with Anna and Vronsky? Anna was bored in Italy and she and Vronsky had returned to Russia. Now what?

Like the arrival of a late bus, all the impatience and anxiety is forgiven when it finally rolls up to the curb.

Here we are, serial readers of *Anna Karenina*, Chapters 21–33 of Part 5. We thank (or not) the servant who brings us the mail; Stiva Oblonsky, though friendly and warm with his valet Matvei, doesn't thank him for bringing the mail to his desk. (And I'm sorry I'm imagining us as privileged idle people with servants. But if we were subscribers to the *Russian Herald* . . . we had servants.)

Where does Tolstoy reopen the story? How are we going to spend our New Year's Eve, 1876?

With Karenin.

In Part 5, Chapter 21, Tolstoy brings us back to two days after Anna and Vronsky left Russia. To Karenin's own surprise, he cannot compose himself and there is no one to

---

* Christian, *Tolstoy's Letters*, 301–302, December 19–21, 1876.

† Christian, *Tolstoy's Letters*, 301.

whom he can appeal for consolation. He feels himself a "laughing-stock." Tolstoy opens up Karenin's whole life, back to childhood, to explain to us why Karenin cannot find help from a friend or relative. He was orphaned at age ten when his mother died. Raised by a politically well-connected uncle, he and his brother went into government service. And only now, with Anna certainly gone out of his life forever, does Tolstoy tell us how and why he got married in the first place:

> While he was governor of a province, Anna's aunt, a wealthy provincial lady, had thrown him—middle-aged as he was, though young for a governor—with her niece, and had succeeded in putting him in such a position that he had either to declare himself or to leave the town. Alexey Alexandrovitch was not long in hesitation. There were at the time as many reasons for the step as against it, and there was no overbalancing consideration to outweigh his invariable rule of abstaining when in doubt. But Anna's aunt had through a common acquaintance insinuated that he had already compromised the girl, and that he was in honor bound to make her an offer. He made the offer, and concentrated on his betrothed and his wife all the feeling of which he was capable.*

How curious! He was apparently bamboozled into marrying an extraordinary twenty-year-old. Though by nature emotionally detached, Karenin threw himself into the relationship *as far as he could*. And there, in his intimacy with Anna, he found himself at home: "The attachment he felt to Anna precluded in his heart every need of intimate relations with others. And now among all his acquaintances he had not one friend." Can we feel no sympathy for him?

It's difficult to imagine reading this a hundred and forty years ago. It's difficult to imagine reading this without the knowledge that poor Anna is going to kill herself at least partly because Karenin and others will fold up all their decency into stony hearts. Can I go back a hundred and forty years? Even if I could, I know it took me many readings to become at all sympathetic to Karenin. Because the information Tolstoy provides us here is fascinating, it only makes me wish even more that Tolstoy had also written a novel of Anna and Karenin's first years together.

Finally, the first chapter of this installment clears the way for the invasion or infection of Karenin's new friend, who will represent herself as the moral standard-bearer but

---

* *Anna Karenina*, Part 5, Chapter 21, http://www.literatureproject.com/anna-karenina/anna_145.htm.

whom we see as the representative of high-society hypocrisy: "Of his women friends, foremost amongst them Countess Lidia Ivanovna, Alexey Alexandrovitch never thought. All women, simply as women, were terrible and distasteful to him."[*]

. In Chapter 22, Lidia, who is in fact "terrible and distasteful," comes as a friend to his rescue. She will not be deterred:

> [. . .] she gave Alexey Alexandrovitch moral support in the consciousness of her
> love and respect for him, and still more, as it was soothing to her to believe,
> in that she almost turned him to Christianity—that is, from an indifferent
> and apathetic believer she turned him into an ardent and steadfast adherent of
> the new interpretation of Christian doctrine, which had been gaining ground
> of late in Petersburg. It was easy for Alexey Alexandrovitch to believe in this
> teaching. Alexey Alexandrovitch, like Lidia Ivanovna indeed, and others who
> shared their views, was completely devoid of vividness of imagination, that
> spiritual faculty in virtue of which the conceptions evoked by the imagination
> become so vivid that they must needs be in harmony with other conceptions,
> and with actual fact.[†]

Two people "completely devoid of imagination" take over the education of poor Seryozha. What a comedown for the boy. Had Anna been able to see Lidia in action, she would have absconded with her son. In Chapter 23, Tolstoy reviews Lidia's short miserably unhappy marriage and explains what seems to be her hobby of high-society busybodying and her unattractive predilection of "falling in love." More than twenty years later, Chekhov would make such a predilection comic and sympathetic in "The Darling."

Tolstoy, however, makes it impossible to sympathize with Lidia.

In Chapter 24 Tolstoy shows us the gossiping at a St. Petersburg high-society party about both Karenin and Lidia and Anna and Vronsky. Lidia finds Karenin at the party to break the news to him that Anna and Vronsky are in town. Back at home in Chapter 25,

---

[*]   *Anna Karenina,* Part 5, Chapter 21, http://www.literatureproject.com/anna-karenina/anna
      _145.htm.

[†]   *Anna Karenina,* Part 5, Chapter 22, http://www.literatureproject.com/anna-karenina
      /anna_146.htm. Was Tolstoy aware that in Lidia he was describing Alexandrine Tolstaya? In
      her letters to him from the time, she did not see herself as Lidia. Sofia did not let on that she
      saw a connection, so why do I? See insert for photos of Alexandrine Tolstaya, Tolstoy's second
      cousin and confidant, http://tolstoy.ru/media/photos/?topic[]=298.

Karenin is inclined to let Anna see Seryozha; Lidia persuades him not to permit it, and she writes Anna a perfectly calculated wounding note.

Chapters 26–30 free us from the high-society snakepit and bring us to Seryozha himself in the series of chapters that brought Sofia, recopying them, and every reader thereafter to tears. We see Karenin's lack of tact with Seryozha, and how earnestly Seryozha tries to be the boy Karenin unimaginatively imagines that he should be. Seryozha is on the eve of his ninth birthday. Meanwhile, we see the awkwardness of Vronsky and Anna's life in the capital. He can make his way anywhere, but Anna is shunned by her former friends. In Chapters 29–30, despite Lidia's denial of her request to visit, Anna, bearing toys, goes to the house to see Seryozha on his birthday. There is bustle and confusion among the servants and tutors; we and the servants weep with sympathy, and Anna flees upon Karenin's appearance at Seryozha's room.

Tolstoy keeps reminding us about *understanding* a situation.

People understand or they don't; when they do they are with God. Understanding a situation is godliness.

In that silent observing way that Serozha has in the paragraph I'm about to quote, Tolstoy is showing us how *God* would see Anna's situation, how *God* would see Anna, and that she is indeed *not* guilty:

> How often afterward she thought of words she might have said. But now she did not know how to say it, and could say nothing. [This poignant moment begins with the thoughts that Anna *will* have; this is interesting because Tolstoy in narrative mode almost never gives us a glimpse of the future.] But Seryozha knew all she wanted to say to him. He understood that she was unhappy and loved him. He understood even what the nurse had whispered. He had caught the words "always at nine o'clock," and he knew that this was said of his father, and that his father and mother could not meet. That he understood, but one thing he could not understand—why there should be a look of dread and shame in her face? . . . She was not in fault, but she was afraid of him and ashamed of something. He would have liked to put a question that would have set at rest this doubt, but he did not dare; he saw that she was miserable, and he felt for her.[*]

---

[*]   *Anna Karenina*, Part 5, Chapter 30, http://www.literatureproject.com/anna-karenina /anna_154.htm.

All right, I'm pausing here, with this moment, to make my case—my case, to Tolstoy, my hero, and it's his own case: "You believe in the moral vision of children, and *here it is*. This child Seryozha, who sees with love and understanding, he is the ultimate judge of Anna, not society or 'God' or you in your other moods—true or false?"

In Chapter 31 Anna is deflated, and so are we. She can't deny to herself that she feels little for her daughter compared to what she feels for Seryozha, and she knows that she is a pariah in St. Petersburg. She tells Vronsky they need to leave. Part 5 ends with Anna peeved with Vronsky for his privilege of having his personal connections open to him. She seems to have decided to burn all bridges back to society by going, against all sensible advice, to the theater performance of a famous singer. Vronsky is angry at her for deliberating attracting the hypocritical outrage at her shamelessness in appearing there. They retreat to Vronsky's country estate.

Reading these chapters is how I hope I would have spent my New Year's Eve before entering 1877.

11

The End of Serialization:
January–May 1877

❋

. . . and all the while he was thinking of her inner life, trying to divine her feelings. And though he had judged her so severely hitherto, now by some strange chain of reasoning he was justifying her and was also sorry for her, and afraid that Vronsky did not fully understand her.

—*Anna Karenina**

There were plenty of family and friends at Yasnaya Polyana for Christmas, which in Russia then and now follows New Year's. "Never again!" may have been what Tolstoy and Sofia said to each other as they saw off the Golokhvastovs shortly after Christmas. Sofia wrote her sister on January 4, 1877: "The Golokhvastovs' presence made everyone gloomy."

To Strakhov, who had returned to Petersburg, Tolstoy wrote: "The Golokhvastov nightmare has only now begun to let up."† Tolstoy wrote his brother Sergei, who hadn't

---

*   *Anna Karenina*, Part 7, Chapter 11, http://www.literatureproject.com/anna-karenina /anna_200.htm.

†   *PSS* 62: 304, letter of January 11–12, 1877.

come for the holidays: "Though the noise—tree, dances, mummers—was a lot, it was needed for the children. The children study well, the teachers are good, except the Russian teacher, who, it seems you didn't see. He is very good but he drinks." Tolstoy himself was fine. "I'm writing my A K, and dreaming about a new one." To the pride of all of us Anthony Trollope fans, he added: "*The Prime Minister* is excellent."* Indeed, it is. In one shocking incident, the complicated, ambitious villain (a once admired acquaintance of the prime minister's wife), commits suicide by stepping in front of a speeding train.†

Though Tolstoy was in good health for the moment, he was anxious about his brother and concerned about Sofia, who was about to leave to see a doctor in St. Petersburg about her shortness of breath; her brother Stepan, who had been with them over the holidays, would travel with her there on January 14. "Every day, especially at night when I lie in bed," Tolstoy continued in his letter to Sergei, "I torment myself by thoughts about you, that I know nothing about you." But Tolstoy couldn't visit Sergei right now because of "family; the year and work (writing) prevent me. Write me, please, about yourself and yours, in detail, and I will write you right away. Sonya is so unwell. She skates and puts up the Christmas tree and sometimes is merry, but I see that her health is undergoing misery. She coughs, she complains about pain in her side, she does not sleep nights and sweats at night."‡

Writing to Alexandrine, Tolstoy anxiously explained, "My wife is going to Petersburg to see her mother, whom she hasn't seen in three years. I remain here with the kids. If it weren't for that, I would be with my wife with you. Right now, she will be alone and she will tell you everything from me and from her. One thing that she won't tell you that I would is about my growing and growing worry about her health from the time of the deaths of our last children."§

Tolstoy wrote Fet and seemed to be wanting to make connections: "I always speak about you with Strakhov because we three are related by soul."¶

---

*   *PSS* 62: 301–302, letter of January 10–11?, 1877.

†   Anyone familiar with Trollope's novels will appreciate, especially with *Anna Karenina* in mind, the novelists' similarities in presenting multiple, interwoven plots. Trollope's pen, unlike Tolstoy's, dreamed and raced its way through his forty-seven novels. There was seemingly no agonizing or hesitating. To change the metaphor, once Trollope got on the horse, he kept the pace steady, writing about 10–12 book pages a day—almost every day for more than thirty years. As distractible and fitful as Tolstoy was, Trollope was almost undistractable and ever persistent.

‡   *PSS* 62: 300.

§   *PSS* 62: 300, letter of January 10–11, 1877.

¶   *PSS* 62: 303, letter of January 10–11, 1877.

In his letter to Strakhov, Tolstoy confessed: "I still can't get into that state of happy work as I was in before them [the Golokhvastovs]. But it seems that if no one interferes, I'll finish, I hope, in one period of work to clear out space for a new work, which keeps more and more asking for it."* Finally Tolstoy mentioned to Strakhov that "in the Decem issue of the *Russian Herald* there are errors [in *Anna Karenina*], but not very big."† He didn't identify these minor errors.

Tolstoy never described himself in the moment of writing as happy, but in the Strakhov letter he recalled "that state of happy work" from just a few weeks before. Was writing so serious a business for him that it precluded happiness? Could it activate only satisfaction or disgust? A job that required physical exertion like mowing certainly gave joy to Levin and Tolstoy. They were happier probably than the peasants they accompanied in the labor, just as amateur athletes can seem to take more pleasure in their sport than professionals. Tolstoy never wrote a passage about an artist or writer taking joy in the production of a work in the way that he described Levin's ecstatic mowing. For Tolstoy, making art didn't activate a joyful physical consciousness, and, as far as he could see, it didn't for other people, either. But what about Anna's moody portrait-painter Mikhailov? Does he ever experience "that state of happy work"? Back in Part 5, on the morning of Vronsky and Anna's first visit, Mikhailov is caught up by a painting he has been struggling with:

> Never did he work with such fervor and success as when things went ill with him, and especially when he quarreled with his wife. "Oh! damn them all!" he thought as he went on working. He was making a sketch for the figure of a man in a violent rage. A sketch had been made before, but he was dissatisfied with it. "No, that one was better . . . where is it?" He went back to his wife, and scowling, and not looking at her, asked his eldest little girl, where was that piece of paper he had given them? The paper with the discarded sketch on it was found, but it was dirty, and spotted with candle-grease. Still, he took the sketch, laid it on his table, and, moving a little away, screwing up his eyes, he fell to gazing at it. All at once he smiled and gesticulated gleefully.
>
> "That's it! that's it!" he said, and, at once picking up the pencil, he began rapidly drawing. The spot of tallow had given the man a new pose.

---

* *PSS* 62: 304, letter of January 11–12, 1877. The "new work," say the Jubilee editors, was to be "a people's novel of the 18–19th centuries."

† *PSS* 62: 304.

He had sketched this new pose, when all at once he recalled the face of a shopkeeper of whom he had bought cigars, a vigorous face with a prominent chin, and he sketched this very face, this chin on to the figure of the man. He laughed aloud with delight. The figure from a lifeless imagined thing had become living, and such that it could never be changed. That figure lived, and was clearly and unmistakably defined. The sketch might be corrected in accordance with the requirements of the figure, the legs, indeed, could and must be put differently, and the position of the left hand must be quite altered; the hair too might be thrown back. But in making these corrections he was not altering the figure but simply getting rid of what concealed the figure. He was, as it were, stripping off the wrappings which hindered it from being distinctly seen. Each new feature only brought out the whole figure in all its force and vigor, as it had suddenly come to him from the spot of tallow. He was carefully finishing the figure when the cards were brought him.

"Coming, coming!"*

One hopes that Tolstoy had such moments of excited, laughter-inducing discovery. (One wonders if he also was somehow put into the perfect fervor for writing after an argument with Sofia.) If he had such moments, they must have been few and far between, because no seems to have caught him at it.

His sister-in-law Tatyana, in her pre-marriage days, had worshiped Tolstoy almost as much as Sofia had. In her memoirs she is as lively and attractive as the character Natasha Rostova that Tolstoy modeled on her. In the mid-1860s, during the writing of *War and Peace*, when Tolstoy was in Moscow getting treatment for his injured arm, Tatyana had helped him by taking dictation. She recalled:

> I see him as clearly as though he were here now—with a look of concentration on his face, supporting his injured arm with his other hand—walking back and forth, dictating to me. Ignoring me completely, he talked aloud: "No, a cliché won't do," or he simply said: "Strike that out."
>
> His tone was commanding. There was impatience in his voice, and often while dictating he would change a passage some three or four times. Sometimes he dictated quietly, smoothly, as though dictating something he had

---

* *Anna Karenina,* Part 5, Chapter 10, http://www.literatureproject.com/anna-karenina/anna_134.htm.

memorized, but that rarely happened, and then the expression on his face would become calm. At other times he would dictate in spurts, unevenly and hurriedly. [. . .]

Our dictation usually finished with these words: "I've tortured you enough. Go skating now."*

Writing, for Tolstoy, was a most serious labor.

❋

On January 16, Strakhov wrote Tolstoy from Petersburg that "Even *advanced* teachers find that the descriptions of Seryozha include important points for the theory of education and learning."† Strakhov, bless his heart, was referring to the end of Part 5, when Seryozha is on the eve of his ninth birthday (these are scenes I skipped over in the summary in the previous chapter in order to discuss them now):

> . . . when the teacher came, the lesson about the adverbs of place and time and manner of action was not ready, and the teacher was not only displeased, but hurt. This touched Seryozha.‡

Later in 1877, when Tolstoy had just finished correcting the first complete edition of *Anna Karenina*, he told a young man that he noticed "a story makes an impression only when it's impossible to sort out with whom the author sympathizes."§ But if we look at any scene that Tolstoy wrote involving teachers and students, it's always the students who have all of Tolstoy's and our sympathy. Tolstoy brings out our sympathy for Seryozha here because we see where Seryozha's sympathy is going—toward his understandably impatient teacher. Simultaneously, Tolstoy shows us Seryozha's all too familiar childhood confusion:

---

*   Kuzminskaya, *Tolstoy as I Knew Him: My Life at Home and at Yasnaya Polyana,* 289.

†   Donskov, *L. N. Tolstoy – N. N. Strakhov,* 304, January 11, 1877, http://feb-web.ru/feb/tolstoy /texts/selectpe/ts6/ts62303-.htm?cmd=2.

‡   *Anna Karenina,* Part 5, Chapter 26, http://www.literatureproject.com/anna-karenina/anna _150.htm.

§   A. D. Obolenskiy, "Dve vstrechi s L. N. Tolstym" [Две встречи с Л. Н. Толстым], originally in Tolstoy *Tolstoy. Memories of Creation and Life.* [Толстой. Памятники творчества и жизни], Moscow, 1923, 34–35, http://feb-web.ru/feb/tolstoy/critics/vs1/vs1-239-.htm.

He felt he was not to blame for not having learned the lesson; however much he tried, he was utterly unable to do that. As long as the teacher was explaining to him, he believed him and seemed to comprehend, but as soon as he was left alone, he was positively unable to recollect and to understand that the short and familiar word "suddenly" is an adverb of manner of action. Still he was sorry that he had disappointed the teacher.[*]

Tolstoy has put us so deeply and sympathetically into Seryozha's frame of mind and feelings that it was only a few years ago that I realized that while once upon a time I had been in Seryozha's situation, I was actually by profession and habit the kvetching tutor. Tolstoy has tricked us: *All* of us sympathize with Seryozha even though all of us grown-ups—Strakhov and Tolstoy included—are most of the time the brow-beating teacher. Strakhov, who pointed out this scene, had been a teacher and was still a consultant about national education issues. From these scenes about Seryozha and his teacher, Strakhov and his fellow pedagogues gained an ability to imagine students intently thinking their own thoughts:

He chose a moment when the teacher was looking in silence at the book.

"Mihail Ivanitch, when is your birthday?" he asked all, of a sudden.

"You'd much better be thinking about your work. Birthdays are of no importance to a rational being. It's a day like any other on which one has to do one's work."[†]

Not one of the millions of readers of this scene has ever sympathized with the exasperated teacher, Mikhail Ivanovich. (And yet after we teachers close the book, the next time we walk into our classrooms we reorient ourselves into Mikhail Ivanoviches!)

Tolstoy makes us identify with Seryozha's engaged attention, not with the deadened spirit of Mikhail Ivanovich, for whom it's just another moment in the frustrating life of a teacher:

Seryozha looked intently at the teacher, at his scanty beard, at his spectacles, which had slipped down below the ridge on his nose, and fell into so deep

---

[*]   *Anna Karenina*, Part 5, Chapter 26, http://www.literatureproject.com/anna-karenina/anna
      _150.htm.

[†]   Ibid.

a reverie that he heard nothing of what the teacher was explaining to him. He knew that the teacher did not think what he said; he felt it from the tone in which it was said. "But why have they all agreed to speak just in the same manner always the dreariest and most useless stuff? Why does he keep me off; why doesn't he love me?" he asked himself mournfully, and could not think of an answer. [*]

The earnest boy is alive in spirit in this moment and the teacher is not. This was as much a revelation to the fiction-writing Tolstoy as it is to us. As a father, Tolstoy could as senselessly badger his own children when teaching them math as Mikhail Ivanovich does to his charge here.

Speaking of fathers, Seryozha sits with his father for the next lesson of the morning. Karenin goes into teacher/father-mode. As soon as that happens . . .

Seryozha's eyes, that had been shining with gaiety and tenderness, grew dull and dropped before his father's gaze. This was the same long-familiar tone his father always took with him, and Seryozha had learned by now to fall in with it. His father always talked to him—so Seryozha felt—as though he were addressing some boy of his own imagination, one of those boys that exist in books, utterly unlike himself. [†]

That's on those of us who are teachers or parents—speaking to our children as though they are or should be the ones that we fantasized we deserved:

And Seryozha always tried with his father to act being the storybook boy. [‡]

Someone could argue that students *should* pretend to be those imaginary students— *because then they might learn something.* Just act the part, and you'll be the part. But even if you argue that, you can't argue with this moment in the novel. We sympathize only with Seryozha. Nobody can be on Karenin's side.

---

[*]   *Anna Karenina*, Part 5, Chapter 26, http://www.literatureproject.com/anna-karenina/anna _150.htm.

[†]   *Anna Karenina*, Part 5, Chapter 27, http://www.literatureproject.com/anna-karenina/anna _151.htm.

[‡]   Ibid.

To rebut Tolstoy with his own words: it's impossible to *not* "sort out with whom the author sympathizes."

As the scene goes on, Seryozha gets confused and Karenin becomes annoyed. Tolstoy puts us again into Seryozha's heart and head:

> The passage at which he was utterly unable to say anything, and began fidg-
> eting and cutting the table and swinging his chair, was where he had to repeat
> the patriarchs before the Flood. He did not know one of them, except Enoch,
> who had been taken up alive to heaven. Last time he had remembered their
> names, but now he had forgotten them utterly, chiefly because Enoch was the
> personage he liked best in the whole of the Old Testament, and Enoch's transla-
> tion to heaven was connected in his mind with a whole long train of thought,
> in which he became absorbed now while he gazed with fascinated eyes at his
> father's watch-chain and a half-unbuttoned button on his waistcoat.*

Even dull Karenin, if he knew what was going on in Seryozha's head, would be touched and would lay off. He loves his son; he would not torture him as he is unconsciously doing now. That "whole long train of thought" of Seryozha's is something that Tolstoy honors and reveals in almost all his characters:

> In death, of which they talked to him so often, Seryozha disbelieved entirely. He
> did not believe that those he loved could die, above all that he himself would die.†

What do we rereaders of the novel know here? That tomorrow Seryozha is going to see his mother, who he has been told is dead (by horrid Lidia Ivanovna and his father). We also know that Seryozha in a couple of years will indeed believe in death.

In Seryozha's "whole long train of thought," death "seemed completely impossible and incomprehensible to him":

> But he had been told that all men die; he had asked people, indeed, whom
> he trusted, and they too, had confirmed it; his old nurse, too, said the same,
> though reluctantly. But Enoch had not died, and so it followed that everyone

---

*   *Anna Karenina*, Part 5, Chapter 27, http://www.literatureproject.com/anna-karenina/anna
    _151.htm.

†   Ibid.

did not die. "And why cannot anyone else so serve God and be taken alive to heaven?" thought Seryozha. Bad people, that is those Seryozha did not like, they might die, but the good might all be like Enoch.*

Tolstoy shows us that in the midst of such a profound meditation as Seryozha's, dull-witted grown-ups are trying to teach *him.*

> "Well, what are the names of the patriarchs?"
>
> "Enoch, Enos—"
>
> "But you have said that already. This is bad, Seryozha, very bad. If you don't try to learn what is more necessary than anything for a Christian," said his father, getting up, "whatever can interest you? I am displeased with you, and Piotr Ignatitch" (this was the most important of his teachers) "is displeased with you. . . . I shall have to punish you."
>
> His father and his teacher were both displeased with Seryozha, and he certainly did learn his lessons very badly.†

Again, if Karenin only knew. Yet we teachers do know better and make the same mistake: We scold our students in the midst of their actual educational experience. We scold them for sliding into their own feelings and thoughts and not reciting thoughtless unfelt words back at us.

Unless we can imagine our own stirred-up Seryozhas thinking of Enoch and death and their beloved mothers, we aren't likely to hold ourselves back: we will continue to berate and distract the students for their own damned good!

So I obtrusively pin a moral on this extraordinary piece of art.

The most important thing to remember here about Seryozha is that he's *Anna's* boy. He's dreaming of seeing her on his birthday tomorrow and we know that he will. And what of those heartbreaking chapters when Anna, despite Lidia and Karenin forbidding her to do so, has come to the house to see Seryozha on his birthday?

I summarized them above, but just go read them! They're too fine for my blunt summarizing. Copying out Chapters 29 and 30 of Part 5 made Sofia cry, and even if you're an old stick like Karenin, they'll make you cry, too.

---

*   *Anna Karenina,* Part 5, Chapter 27, http://www.literatureproject.com/anna-karenina/anna _151.htm.

†   Ibid.

✳

Let's return to Sofia and her trip to Petersburg on January 14. At the train in Moscow, Sofia was introduced to Katkov, the *Russian Herald*'s editor, by her uncle Kostya, and rode with him from Moscow.[*]

It seems hard not to think of Anna riding on the train when there Sofia was, on her own with her little brother Stepan, but Katkov, almost sixty years old, the father of eleven, famous in his own right, was no lovestruck Vronsky; he was deferential and polite and looked for her in her carriage in the morning to ask how she had slept and if she needed anything.

In St. Petersburg Sofia saw Dr. Botkin, and on January 16, she wrote her husband that Botkin was "very attentive. He said that my lungs and chest are perfectly healthy, that it's all nerves. He made a prescription, diet advice, changes and so on. I asked him, 'Could it be I'm well?' 'No,' he said. 'You're not at all well,' and kept telling me to stay a week, in order to begin the treatment with him."[†]

Botkin told her she could and should have more children (her previous doctor had warned her against doing so). "Lev Nikolaevich was thrilled at this advice,"[‡] Sofia noted, as she apparently was not:

> But no matter how spoilt or celebrated I was in Petersburg, all my thoughts, interests and attachments at this time were back with my own family at Yasnaya Polyana. I kept receiving letters from Lev Nikolaevich describing all the details about himself and the family.[§]

When we read "kept receiving" we might imagine that Tolstoy wrote her at least once a day during that week. There are only three letters, however, that have survived (or even seem to have existed), but what a good first letter he wrote on January 14 or 15:

> Yesterday after you left we went skating—D'yakov and I. The children were good and jolly, except Ilyusha, whose face, it struck me from morning, was disgusting. The whole day I was in a dark mood—and unhealthy, as my thoughts about Ilyusha tormented me. I'm embarrassed to say about D'yakov,

---

[*]   Tolstaya, *My Life*, 231.

[†]   *PSS* 83: 234, footnote 4.

[‡]   Tolstaya, *My Life*, 232.

[§]   Tolstaya, *My Life*, 233.

whom I so love, that I got tired of him. No working. At night, having put the children to bed, I went to bring D'yakov to Kozlovka. I returned—played a while and depressed lay down to sleep. I slept poorly and woke early. I went around the children. They're all well and conducting themselves well. I, in order to right myself, went riding until coffee, did gymnastics and went skating with the children.

Everyone ran around merrily. The day was frosty, but the sun warms well. Yesterday I allowed them, except Seryozha, to spend an extra hour; but today, afraid of your precision, went with them home in time. Everyone did their lessons. Ilyusha with Vl[adimir] Ivanovich. This moment, after a long wavering, I decided to speak again with Ilyusha. He cried and I cried, and, God willing, ended the consequences.

I can't do anything else today and I'm going to Yasenka bringing this letter.

Please don't hurry back. If only for the need of Botkin's advice, and simply if it's pleasant to you to be with good people. It's not worth hurrying when you have gone so far away. Please don't do that, or you'll tell me: "I would've gone, seen or heard this if I had spent another day." I'm lonely without you, but there's not that misery I'm afraid of, and I feel there won't be. And the children are in such conditions as with you. Goodbye, darling. Kiss everyone you love for me.*

No 19th-century husband left at home with the children could have written a more considerate, informative letter.

He wrote again, even more feelingly, on January 16: "As you see, we continue being all right." Their daughter Tanya prefaced his letter: "We're all well, I'm beginning because I know you're worried about us." Having Tanya lead off, he could more comfortably and reassuringly tell Sofia:

Yesterday I taught Lele and Tanya, and Tanya got me so angry I yelled at her, and I feel very ashamed. I can't work. Last night the children sat with me and painted, and I played draughts with Vladimir Ivanovich, but then played the piano the whole night, until one. For a long time I couldn't sleep and woke up early. Right now I'm going to the station. The children went skating, but today there was a strong frost; at night it was 19 degrees, but in the sun it was warm.

---

*   *PSS* 83: 233–234, letter of January 14–15, 1877.

It's so boring for me, the meals with pedagogues sulking at each other. I every moment think about you and imagine what you're doing. And, it seems to me, despite being gloomy (from my stomach), all will be well.

Please don't hurry, and even though you say you won't buy anything, don't feel shy about the money, and if you decide to buy something, get the money from Lyubov Aleksandrovna [Sofia's mother] and buy, and go on a binge!— And within three days we'll return it.

Farewell, darling, I haven't yet received the letter from you. Without you *I try not to think about you. Yesterday I went over to your desk, and I jumped up and down (as though I had touched something hot) trying not to picture you in my mind's eye. The same at night—I don't look in the direction of your {bed}.* [I've italicized Cathy Porter's translation of Sofia's excerpt in *My Life*, which is more explanatory than what I had translated for myself.] If you would only be in a strong, energetic spirit in the time of your stay, then all will be well.

A bow from me to all, especially Lyubov Aleksandrovna.

Tanya added another note: "Today we skated—little, because it was freezing. Lele was such a long time getting his skates on, and when he made a circle we saw that he was crying. We asked him about what, and he said, *"I'm cold every where."* [This phrase was set down in English by Tanya.] Annie [Phillips, the English governess] right away ran home with him and rubbed his arms and legs with eau de cologne and put a coat on him. Now he's completely warmed up."[*]

Sofia quoted from only one of Tolstoy's three letters. Let's start with her excerpts to see what she wanted to emphasize:

He wrote:

"Yesterday I taught Lelja and Tanja, and Tanja got me so angry I yelled at her, and I feel very ashamed." He also wrote about playing board-games with the children and draughts with the teacher, Vladimir Ivanovich {Rozhdestvenkij}.

He was very affectionate toward me {in his letters}. For example, he wrote me:

". . . I played the piano the whole evening until one in the morning . . . I try not to think about you. Yesterday I went over to your desk, and I jumped up and

---

down (as though I had touched something hot) trying not to picture you in my mind's eye. The same at night—I don't look in the direction of your {bed}."[*]

What did Sofia expect us to think when she quoted us this last sentence? The "bed" has been inserted by the 21st-century editors of *My Life*, but Sofia had to have expected us to understand that Tolstoy was saying that he was missing her sexually. In her frankness or lack of embarrassment she was so different from her husband, who could never catch himself thinking of sex without later chastising himself. Is it overstepping to say that she was proud of his appetite for her? And wasn't it obvious anyway? So many children, and so much desire on his part for more of them.

But why was Sofia reluctant to quote the entire letter? She only mentioned her husband's shame at getting angry with Tanya; didn't his confession of the fight and Tanya's notes on the letter show that father and daughter had reconciled, that he had done his parental work with love? She withheld giving him his due credit here. As for the money, another common marital issue—what did he say? *Go ahead, honey, spend! Take your time; no need to rush back. We're okay!* She didn't include that, either.

Day three, January 17, produced a reasonably shorter note, as he didn't even know if she would get it:

> I write you, dear friend, even though this letter won't reach you if you have left as you wished. If you're staying, it will calm you. Everything is fine. The children are well and have done nothing naughty and they study well. They went out for a walk today but didn't skate—too cold. I didn't go out all day, mostly because today I feel myself better than the previous days and I worked all morning—I finished the corrections [he was doing corrections of the first half of Part 6 of the novel for the *January* issue].
>
> Farewell, darling. About the children especially, don't worry, and when we're both home, we'll be busy with each other [. . .].
>
> But now there's nothing more to do than worry about them. We haven't received letters from you.
>
> It's now Monday, 7 in the evening. Right now I'm going to Yasenka.
>
> Yesterday I played lotto with all of them.
>
> Tanya is running the house.[†]

---

[*]   Tolstaya, *My Life*, 233.

[†]   *PSS* 83: 235, letter of January 17, 1877.

Sofia could not have complained about Tolstoy's communications to her during her trip. She returned to Yasnaya Polyana on January 22.

In Sofia's "Back at Yasnaya,"* she described an incident in which Seryozha had a concussion skating on a Yasnaya Polyana pond on January 23. Having received the news, she writes: "Lev Nikolaevich and I ran down the allee {preshpekt}, holding hands."

As I've pointed out, it's not clear in *My Life* how or when Sofia worked from her diaries and letters. Was she referring to materials at her desk that she had collected and gathered? Was she infusing into her recollections a mention from a letter? (There's no surviving diary entry here.) We don't know; we know that she wrote that she remembered the two of them running down that beautiful wide path from the house while holding hands. It's a wonderful image: it collects in one picture a concerned father and mother, a loving husband and wife.

Sergei L'vovich Tolstoy remembered the accident this way:

> Tania, Ilya, and I swept several paths on the snow-covered pond and on 1/23 chased one another on skates. . . . trying to elude Tania, I butted into her and we both fell down. She was not hurt, but I struck my head so violently against the ice that I lost consciousness and began to have convulsions. I was carried home unconscious, ice-packs were applied to my head and a leech behind the ear. When I woke up after 24 hours I had completely lost my memory which, however, I recovered after a short time.[†]

Tolstoy's letter of January 24 to Dmitry D'yakov crisply narrated the previous day's incident. "You can imagine," he wrote, "that yesterday, Sunday, the children went skating, but we stayed back." I wonder what Tolstoy expected his old friend D'yakov to "imagine"; the first thing I imagine, with the kids out of the house after his wife's healthy return, and Dr. Botkin's assurance that she was fit to get pregnant again, is that they would have been cavorting in bed. Tolstoy continued: "I go to the door, I meet the puffing breathless Mademoiselle Gachet. 'Serge has fallen. He was brought to the little house.' 'Which? How?' 'I don't know anything.'[‡] I run along the Proshpekt and meet the Russian teacher. 'What? How?' 'He was brought off without sign of life,' and he continued past. Sonya

---

*   Tolstaya, *My Life*, 234.

†   Because of the concussion, perhaps the grown-up Seryozha only remembered what he had been told of the accident? Tolstoy, *Tolstoy Remembered by His Son,* 30.

‡   I have inserted the quotation marks; I presume the last sentence was the French teacher's.

caught up to me [here's where he should mention their holding hands] and we ran to the worker-hut. When we came in, he looked around but didn't remember anything. He was brought home and a doctor was sent for. He woke up, had leeches applied, and today we've calmed down. He remembers everything and has become almost completely well. Maybe you can imagine yourself our terror and how bad this was for Sonya's nerves."*

His own peace of mind restored at least, he encouraged the D'yakovs to come for a visit.

That very day he also wrote to Alexandrine, but to her he mentioned nothing of the accident. To her, he expressed his thanks for her help to Sofia, and then, unusually, discussed Alexandrine's praise of *Anna Karenina* and why her words made him squirm: "it's very pleasant what you write about the last installment of my novel. I can't say I'm unfeeling to the praise, but with reservations. The first praise, as yours was, when I myself don't yet know whether what I've written is decent or very bad, I'm very joyful by the praise and I don't reproach myself; but when I'm praised a lot I begin to be moved by myself and make myself disgusting to me. I walk in the wood alone and I praise everything as myself. I haven't yet reached this, thank God, but I could."†

This confident man didn't like the effect that admiration had on him.‡ If his head got turned, he lost his ability to commune with his beloved woods. He spent the walk thinking about himself, and he didn't like that.§

❈

When Tolstoy wrote Strakhov to thank him for his kindnesses to Sofia while she was in Petersburg, he also wanted to discuss St. Petersburg's response to the December issue:

---

*   *PSS* 62: 305, letter of January 24, 1877.

†   *PSS* 62: 306, letter of January 24, 1877.

‡   He could have recalled Pascal's "belt of nails" that he had mentioned a year before (see above, p. 246).

§   *PSS* 62: 306. A small overlap of phrasing occurs between the letter and the novel. Tolstoy opened the letter to Alexandrine: "If you have sins, dear friend Alexandrine, they are probably forgiven you for the good that you did me in the last two letters." In Chapter 18 of Part 6, that is, the very installment he was now working on, Anna says to Dolly, "'If you had any sins,' she said, 'they would all be forgiven you for your coming to see me and these words.' And Dolly saw that tears stood in her eyes. She pressed Anna's hand in silence." (Garnett translation: http://www.literatureproject.com/anna-karenina/anna_175.htm.)

[. . .] The success of the latest installment of *Anna Karenina* also, I confess, gave me pleasure. I hadn't expected it, and really I'm surprised that such an ordinary and insignificant thing should be liked, and still more than that, being convinced that such an insignificant thing is liked, I haven't started to write any old thing at random, but have been making a choice which is almost incomprehensible even to me. I say this frankly, because it's to you, and especially because, having sent off the proofs for the January issue, I have faltered over the February issue,* and am only just getting back into my stride mentally.†

Was he modestly making light ("really I'm surprised that such an ordinary and insignificant thing should be liked") or was he, from self-consciousness, ducking Strakhov's praise and reports of others' praise? *Aw, shucks!* But we couldn't have blamed Tolstoy if he had said, *You're right, Nikolai Nikolaevich,* Anna Karenina *is the most marvelous thing a writer's ever done!*

To continue with his letter to Strakhov: Tolstoy turned to the topic of his former friend, the author Ivan Turgenev. Turgenev's faults seemed to inspire Tolstoy's thoughts about how lying betrays art. Tolstoy admitted that he hadn't read Turgenev's latest novel, but he had read everything else by him and could guess:

I haven't read the Turgenev [*Virgin Soil*], but judging from all I hear, I sincerely regret that this spring of pure and excellent water has been polluted by such trash. If he had simply recalled in detail a day of his and described it, everyone would have been full of admiration.

Turgenev was so good an author that he didn't need to be clever. He didn't need to invent. He didn't need to *lie*:

---

* The February issue (Chapters 16–32 in the book edition) that he had "faltered" over contains such episodes as Dolly's summer visit to Anna at Vronsky's modern progressive estate (16–24); Anna and Vronsky's dull life on their own in the country in the fall while Vronsky continues his political activity (25); and Levin and Kitty's move to Moscow for her confinement and Levin's reluctant involvement in provincial elections, where he unexpectedly encounters Vronsky (26–30). Anna, lonely in the country, desperately writes to Vronsky to ask him to return from the elections for the sake of their little girl, who is ill, and he returns; the child is after all just fine, but the parents are on uneasy terms (31–32). Such artistic falterings have eluded writers of fiction ever since.

† Christian, *Tolstoy's Letters,* 302–303, January 25–26, 1877.

However trite it is to say so, there is only one negative quality needed for everything in life, particularly in art—not to lie.

In life, lying is nasty, but it doesn't destroy life, it smears it over with its nastiness, but the truth of life is still there underneath, because somebody is always wanting something, something is always giving pain or pleasure; but in art, lying destroys the whole chain which links phenomena, and everything crumbles to dust.

That train of Tolstoy's thought abruptly stopped there; had it occurred to him because of what he was writing in *Anna Karenina*? Wherever it had come from, he checked himself and resumed a conversational manner with Strakhov: "What are you doing, i.e., writing? Send me your *Citizen* articles. God grant you the leisure and inclination to write."

Tolstoy was in a new good mood. I imagine it was because he knew for sure, maybe for the first time, that he was going to get *Anna Karenina* across the finish line. He could encourage his friend about writing rather than rue his own efforts. He was busy with the job and, it seems, had abandoned that daunting scholarly pursuit he had been on while depressed:

I haven't for a long time been so indifferent to philosophical questions as this year, and I flatter myself with the hope that this is good for me. I very much want to finish what I'm doing quickly and begin something new.

Goodbye; my wife sends her regards.*

To be over the "philosophical questions" seems to mean that he had crawled out of the quagmire of depression described in *Confession*.

Writing fiction resisted him more than philosophy or pedagogy, because he had to create something, not just analyze it, explain it, argue it. The greatest literary artist in the world could not perfect art. He couldn't, as he did with ideas about education, sex, war, vegetarianism, farming, figure it all out, slam the door on his predecessors, and say, "I *got* it!" Fiction, as it resisted him and forced him to be creative, was indeed good for him.

❋

---

* Christian, *Tolstoy's Letters,* 302–303, June 25–26, 1877.

The January issue of the *Russian Herald* was published on February 1. The corresponding chapters in Part 6 for us book readers are 1–15. I've already laid out the briefest of summaries of the second half of Part 6 (see above, page 304), which Tolstoy was still working on, but here we'll retreat: Dolly has brought her children with her to Levin's estate for the summer. Kitty's family overwhelms Levin: "And though he liked them all, he rather regretted his own Levin world and ways, which were smothered by this influx of the 'Shtcherbatsky element,' as he called it to himself. Of his own relations there stayed with him only Sergey Ivanovitch, but he too was a man of the Koznishev and not the Levin stamp, so that the Levin spirit was utterly obliterated."* The visitors include Varenka, Kitty's saintly friend from abroad, and, because Kitty is pregnant, Kitty's mother. Chapter 2 dramatizes the jam-making dispute between Kitty's family and Levin's longtime family housekeeper, Agafya. In Chapter 3, Kitty and Levin have their own private discussion. Chapters 4–5 show us the mushroom hunt, where Sergei Koznishev resolves to propose to Varenka and then, to his and Varenka's relief, does not do so. Chapter 6 brings Stiva and his handsome, bumbling friend Veslovsky to Levin's estate. Levin is almost immediately jealous of Veslovsky, and in Chapter 7 Kitty tries to quiet Levin's jealousy. Chapters 8–13 take in Stiva, Veslovsky, and Levin's hunting trip. Veslovsky botches the hunting and spoils the pleasure for Levin until the morning, when Oblonsky and Veslovsky are sleeping off a night of carousing with the peasants. Only then do Levin and his dog Laska have time to themselves, and Levin has success shooting birds. Back home at the estate, in Chapters 14–15, Levin grows so jealous of Veslovsky that, despite knowing he is exposing his jealousy to mockery and violating good manners, he commands Veslovsky to leave.

The installment ends: *No Anna. No Vronsky. No Karenin.*

Strakhov wrote ecstatically to Tolstoy about these chapters: "This part of the novel has left me with lively pleasure, not only upon reading it, but then in those arguments and conversations that come up every day. . . . But do you know, there's not one part of *Karenina* that has had such success as this. Your worshipers not only weep and grow excited, but they can't find the words to express all the fine charm and mastery of these idyllic scenes. . . . The successes are really unbelievable, crazy."†

---

*　*Anna Karenina,* Part 6, Chapter 1, http://www.literatureproject.com/anna-karenina/anna
　　_158.htm.

†　Donskov, *L. N. Tolstoy – N. N. Strakhov,* 311–312, beginning of February 1877, http://feb-web
　　.ru/feb/tolstoy/texts/selectpe/ts6/ts62311-.htm.

Probably before he received that letter, Tolstoy wrote Strakhov on February 3 or 4 and in a teasing tone critiqued one of Strakhov's *Citizen* essays: "I see in your article a study, excerpts from that work you're writing; but for an article about spiritualism, you did what often I sin doing: from the desire to say too much you weaken what you wanted to say."*

Tolstoy, still in his new forward mode, and seeing the end of his odyssey with Anna, tried again to patch up his friendship with his conventionally religious relative Alexandrine. He had survived his depression and was more temperately addressing her about an agitating topic:

> [. . .] the problem of religion is exactly the same for me as the one facing a drowning man—the problem of what to clutch at to save himself from the imminent death which he senses with his whole being. For a couple of years now religion has seemed to offer the possibility of salvation. [. . .] the point is that as soon as I clutch at the plank I go down with it. Somehow or other *je surnage* [I float] as long as I don't seize hold of the plank. If you ask me what stops me I won't tell you, because I would be afraid to shake your faith [. . .] and so I won't tell you, but will rejoice for you and for all those who are sailing in the boat in which I am not a passenger. I have a friend, Strakhov, a learned man and one of the best people I know. We are very much alike in our religious views: we are both convinced that philosophy has nothing to offer and that it's impossible to live without religion, but we cannot believe. This summer we intend to go to the Optina Monastery. There I shall explain to the monks all the reasons why I cannot believe.†

And what of Anna's belief? How is it that Tolstoy's heroine is seemingly not at all religious? "In Variant No. 22 (Mss. No. 17) are crossed out lines [. . .]. Feeling herself powerless to help her brother in his family estrangement, she tells him: 'There is One who knows our hearts, who can help us,' and later is said, 'Oblonsky grew silent. He knew this bombastic somewhat cloying excited tone of religiousness in his sister and was never able to continue a conversation in this tone.'"‡ In that draft, Stiva knows this fakeness of hers. He can't fake it here (though he can in the real novel). In the real novel Anna is unconcernedly unreligious. (In Variant No. 23, Dolly also remarks on Anna's overdone piety.)

---

*   *PSS* 62: 309, letter of February 3–4, 1877.

†   Christian, *Tolstoy's Letters,* 303, February 5–9, 1877.

‡   *PSS* 20: 597.

It was a significant change in Tolstoy's outlook on Anna to take away her religiousness. In the final draft, she will address God only once.

✳

In *My Life* Sofia composed a chapter titled "Lev Nikolaevich's Trip to Moscow— Zakhar'in—The Ending of *Anna*":

> In February Lev Nikolaevich went to Moscow to personally proofread *Anna Karenina*. There was something he needed to correct in order to speed up the release of the February issue of *Russkij Vestnik*. Apart from that Lev Niko-laevich's health was alarming me. He began to have hot flashes in his head, and we were both afraid he might have a stroke. [In her diary, she does not mention her worry about a stroke.]
>
> It was decided he should go see Professor Zakhar'in in Moscow, who was always ready at any moment to treat Lev Nikolaevich free of charge. There in Moscow Zakhar'in applied leeches, but the trouble didn't abate; however, it gradually passed with time.*

On February 27 Tolstoy sent a telegram home at noontime to tell Sofia that he had finished the corrections on the February issue of *Anna Karenina* and he had seen Dr. Zakhar'in (who had applied the leeches to Tolstoy's spine) and that he was fine.

Sofia's diary of that same day:

> As I was reading through some of Lyovochka's old diaries today, I realized I would never be able to write those "Notes for a Biography" [. . .]. His inner life is so complicated and his diaries disturb me so much that I grow confused and cannot see things clearly. [. . .]
>
> The other day, when I asked him to tell me about something from his past, he said: "Please don't ask about these things; it disturbs me to think of my past and I'm much too old now to relive my whole life in memories."†

It seems to me Tolstoy only meant: "Please, dear, I'm *busy*."

---

*   Tolstaya, *My Life*, 234.

†   *The Diaries of Sophia Tolstoy*, 54.

On March 1, the February installment, the second half of Part 6 of *Anna Karenina*, was published (Chapters 13–29 in the *Russian Herald*; Chapters 16–32 in the book). The most important matter is that we see that Anna is beginning to lose her grip. Dolly, her biggest advocate besides Stiva, is confused and unhappy over her friend's use of contraception and her hopelessness about a contented domestic life with Vronsky. (But why hasn't Dolly ever wondered about Anna having had only one child with Karenin? Had Anna used contraception with Karenin?)

> [. . .] "Dolly."—[Anna] suddenly changed the subject—"you say I take too gloomy a view of things. You can't understand. It's too awful! I try not to take any view of it at all."[*]

Dolly encourages her to get the divorce and marry Vronsky. Anna reacts wildly:

> "[. . .] You tell me to marry Alexey, and say I don't think about it. I don't think about it!" she repeated, and a flush rose into her face. She got up, straightening her chest, and sighed heavily. With her light step she began pacing up and down the room, stopping now and then.[†]

How alarmed, with Dolly, do we feel, and how close to Anna! We even feel her characteristic "light step." But she's beyond herself, beyond her own command:

> "I don't think of it? Not a day, not an hour passes that I don't think of it, and blame myself for thinking of it . . . because thinking of that may drive me mad. Drive me mad!" she repeated. "When I think of it, I can't sleep without morphine. [. . .]"[‡]

It's understandable why Dolly is eager to go home and can now count her own blessings. Her wonderful friend is losing her mind.

Anna is frightened, because she can't seek a divorce if it means cutting herself off from Seryozha. "Don't judge me!" is the subtitle, practically, of this section and little speech:

---

[*]   *Anna Karenina*, Part 6, Chapter 24, http://www.literatureproject.com/anna-karenina/anna _181.htm.

[†]   Ibid.

[‡]   Ibid.

"It is only those two creatures that I love, and one excludes the other. I can't have them together, and that's the only thing I want. And since I can't have that, I don't care about the rest. I don't care about anything, anything. And it will end one way or another, and so I can't, I don't like to talk of it. So don't blame me, don't judge me for anything. You can't with your pure heart understand all that I'm suffering."*

She goes and sits next to Dolly, looks in her face, takes her hand and asks what she thinks.

Before Dolly replies, Anna continues:

"I'm simply unhappy. If anyone is unhappy, I am . . ."†

She turns away and cries. We, with Dolly, understand and hear and feel her unhappiness. Then she returns to her rooms, takes her morphine, and goes happily to bed with Vronsky. The next day, with Dolly about to leave:

Only Anna was sad. She knew that now, from Dolly's departure, no one again would stir up within her soul the feelings that had been roused by their conversation. It hurt her to stir up these feelings, but yet she knew that that was the best part of her soul, and that that part of her soul would quickly be smothered in the life she was leading.‡

In the installment's last chapter, we are let in further than Dolly was and are shocked to learn what Anna can barely acknowledge to herself: suicide is an ever-tempting alternative to her suffering:

And so, just as before, only by occupation in the day, by morphine at night, could she stifle the fearful thought of what would be if he ceased to love her.§

---

* *Anna Karenina*, Part 6, Chapter 24, http://www.literatureproject.com/anna-karenina/anna _181.htm.

† Ibid.

‡ Ibid.

§ *Anna Karenina*, Part 6, Chapter 32, http://www.literatureproject.com/anna-karenina /anna_189.htm.

But books, my dear readers, will save us all, won't they?

Unfortunately, no: I realize that sometimes reading is just a mindless compulsion: a way to pass the time and *not* think; nobody in this book reads the way I'm reading *Anna Karenina*:

> Walks, conversation with Princess Varvara, visits to the hospital, and, most of all, reading—reading of one book after another—filled up her time. [*]

The scholar Eikhenbaum writes: "Obolensky recalls Tolstoi's words in 1877: 'The very best books are English; when I bring English books home with me I always find new and fresh content in them.' In spite of his secluded life at Yasnaya Polyana, Tolstoi used to receive the latest foreign works very quickly. S. Urusov was amazed: 'I do not understand; who is your bookseller from whom you receive everything both better and quicker than we do from ours?'" [†] The answer: Gautier. The Jubilee editors explain in a footnote that "Vladimir Ivanovich Gautier (1813–1887) was the owner of an old bookstore and library, established in 1799 by his father Ivan Ivanovich Gautier-Duffas, [. . .] on Kuznetsky Most. Tolstoy ordered foreign books and periodicals through him" [‡]; and so does Anna Karenina: "I got a box of books yesterday from Gautier's. No, I shan't be dull." [§]

Anna is also living under the dread of Vronsky's disapproving look. She remembers the one that he had upon leaving for the political meetings; she expects it now that he's about to arrive, and then, late in the chapter, she sees it again. She's not imagining it, but she's looking for it. It's really there.

Anna does frustrate Vronsky. He does everything right, everything honorable. He tells her:

> "Don't you know that I can't live without you?" [¶]

---

*   *Anna Karenina*, Part 6, Chapter 32, http://www.literatureproject.com/anna-karenina/anna _189.htm.

†   Eikhenbaum, *Tolstoi in the Seventies*, 153.

‡   *PSS* 62: 315, footnote 4.

§   *Anna Karenina*, Part 6, Chapter 25, http://www.literatureproject.com/anna- karenina/anna _182.htm.

¶   *Anna Karenina*, Part 6, Chapter 32, http://www.literatureproject.com/anna-karenina/anna _189.htm.

He says just what a romantic hero would say. Anna on the other hand has become so difficult that she can't stop herself from saying and doing things that she immediately knows she shouldn't have.

She is, for example, upset being left alone while Vronsky has things to do in the world:

> "If you go to Moscow, I will go, too. I will not stay here. Either we must separate or else live together."
>
> "Why, you know, that's my one desire. But for that . . ."
>
> "We must get a divorce. I will write to him. I see I cannot go on like this. . . . But I will come with you to Moscow."
>
> "You talk as if you were threatening me. [She is! I don't blame Vronsky, but he shouldn't have said anything. He should have just nodded.] But I desire nothing so much as never to be parted from you," said Vronsky, smiling. [What should he have said? He said the right words, but we know that he would at this moment rather be anywhere in the world. Should we lie directly against our very strong feelings? The other person is being completely unreasonable. To make the situation stop, should we lie? I don't blame Vronsky (I keep saying), but he should've said nothing. Because he does speak he cannot help but show his feelings to Anna—who reads him as if she were Tolstoy reading him. Even in a panic of jealousy and despair, she reads Vronsky accurately.]
>
> But as he said these words there gleamed in his eyes not merely a cold look, but the vindictive look of a man persecuted and made cruel.
>
> She saw the look and correctly divined its meaning.
>
> "If so, it's a calamity!" that glance told her. It was a moment's impression, but she never forgot it.*

She understands what Vronsky means better than he does. And Tolstoy provides here again another glimpse into the future—"*she never forgot it.*" The idea of Vronsky being fed up with her is what she's going to carry with her to the suicide.

❀

---

* *Anna Karenina*, Part 6, Chapter 32, http://www.literatureproject.com/anna-karenina/anna_189.htm.

That first day of March, Strakhov wrote offering the very help that Tolstoy was going to want with proofreading and revising the novel: "I offer you again my services, if they're convenient and needed. With great joy I'll do for you anything; I count myself your debtor."*

Tolstoy was so occupied writing and revising the "Epilogue" (which was rechristened upon publication as Part 8) and doing the corrections for the March issue, as well as dealing with a medical problem, that he hadn't had for a while one of his typical days of sending out a bushel of letters. In early March, however, he wrote Strakhov and Fet. He apologized to Strakhov for not having written or answered: "I was and am very busy, but worst of all that from the New Year (while on skis having an injury to the head from a tree by the walkway), I began having surges to the head, confusing my working. But I really want to write and as much strength as there is, I do write."†

If only Tolstoy had continued writing little autobiographical *Azbuka* stories for children, he could have composed "The Count and the Tree"! Had he been distracted? Slippery ice? He never saw the tree? Under my management of Yasnaya Polyana, that tree—or one of its descendants—would have a plaque installed below it: "Hereabouts Lev Nikolaevich Tolstoy clonked his head while skiing in 1877. *Thank God it did not kill him!*" (Strakhov *immediately* replied that he was worried about Tolstoy's head. Strakhov also observed that *Anna Karenina* was greater than any novel by Dickens or Balzac.‡)

Tolstoy's letter to Fet remarked on the long time since he had heard from him; he asked Fet to write: "Botkin has calmed me concerning my wife; the children are healthy. Only I am ill with surges to the head, but now it's better. It was burdensome enough that it hindered working."§ (There was no allusion to buying or selling horses in this note to Fet or in the next one.) His conversational fluidity resumed in the next week's letter to Fet:

> I'm dictating this letter to Seryozha because I have a headache. [. . .]
>
> I didn't receive your long letter, and you wouldn't believe how upset I am at the thought that it has gone astray. I started to write via Seryozha more as a joke. The children came in after lessons and I made Tanya take down a letter

---

* Donskov, *L. N. Tolstoy – N. N. Strakhov*, 316, March 1, 1877.

† *PSS* 62: 312, letter of March 5–6, 1877.

‡ Donskov, *L. N. Tolstoy – N. N. Strakhov*, 319, March 10, 1877.

§ *PSS* 62: 313, letter of March 5–6, 1877.

in French to Gautier, and Seryozha turned up and I began dictating to him. It's true that I have a headache and it stops me working, which is particularly annoying, because the work is not just coming, but has come to the end. There's only the epilogue left. And that is occupying me very much.*

Let's notice again what a modern father Tolstoy was. He taught Tanya by dictating in French and he included the boy in the dictation game (like an afterthought, the way Stiva includes Grisha) and, after Seryozha's exit, Tolstoy resumed the letter himself:

> I read through the first part of *Virgin Soil* and skimmed through the second. I was too bored to finish it. Eventually he [i.e., Turgenev] makes Paklin say that it's Russia's misfortune in particular that all the people who are well are bad, and the good people are unwell. That is my own, and his own, opinion of the novel. The author is unwell, and his sympathies are with people who are unwell, and he doesn't sympathize with those who are well, and so he calls what he is himself and therefore what he likes, good, and says: "What a misfortune that all the people who are well are bad, and the good people are unwell."
>
> The one thing at which he is such a master that your hand shrinks from touching the subject after him is nature. Two or three strokes and you smell it. There are 1½ pages of such descriptions all told, and nothing else. The descriptions of people are only descriptions of descriptions. [. . .]†

Tolstoy was emphasizing here a characteristic we almost always see in his fiction: a description has to be as if seen and felt by a character. Tolstoy saw no use for fine writing that was divorced from immediate individual conscious perception.

Now that he was finishing *Anna Karenina*, now that he was apparently finished with the philosophical readings that occupied him in the dark times described in *Confession*, his usual literary observations were popping up more frequently.

He wrote Fet once more in March: "You write that in the *Russ Herald* they published [Alexei] Tolstoy, but your 'Temptation' lies there. There are no other such stupid and dead editors. [. . .] My head is better now and as much as it's better that much more I work. March, the beginning of April, are my best work months, and I continue to be in

---

*　Christian, *Tolstoy's Letters*, 304, March 11–12, 1877.

†　Ibid.

excitement that what I'm writing is very important, even though I know that in a month I will be embarrassed to remember this."* He encouraged Fet and his wife to visit.

He wrote Strakhov to not be mad that he hadn't written: "Now I can say that I'm finished and hope in April to publish the last part, and I very much await and ask for your judgment."† Tolstoy meant that he wanted Strakhov's opinion of Part 7, not of the Epilogue, which he was writing and was not actually "finished" with.‡

※

On March 28, the first half of Part 7 (Chapters 1–16 in the book edition) was published.

In summary, Levin is out of sorts in Moscow at Kitty's parents' house, where everyone awaits the birth of his and Kitty's baby. Levin goes out on the town with Stiva. At a club, Stiva not only reconciles Levin to Vronsky and Vronsky to Levin, but convinces Levin to accompany him on a visit to Anna, who is lonely and unhappy because of her social isolation.

The scene where Levin meets Anna has become for me one of the most important in the novel, because it dramatizes Tolstoy's revelations about his own creation. Oddly, it's not a scene that everyone remembers. When I remind fellow readers about it, it doesn't always ring a bell, even though it's the first and only time that the two protagonists of the novel meet. It's curious that they've never met before and it's not important to the plot that they meet, and nothing changes for either of them because of the meeting. But Tolstoy, with the novel's end in sight, seemed to want to see what would happen when his protagonists came face to face. It was not part of his earlier draft plans, and we'll find that after this meeting Levin almost completely disappears from Anna's consciousness—and she from his.

Levin encountering Anna spans three chapters, starting with the end of Chapter 9, when Stiva and Levin arrive at Anna's apartment. On the other side of the dining room, in a half-dark study, there are two lamps, one of which shines on Mikhailov's "full-length" portrait of Anna.

Until I started writing this section, I hadn't even imagined Anna in the painting at full-length. Not necessarily life-size, but head to toe. What kind of shoes is she wearing?

---

*   *PSS* 62: 315–316, letter of March 22–23?, 1877.

†   *PSS* 62: 316, letter of March 23–24, 1877.

‡   On May 18, 1877, Strakhov mentioned in a letter to Tolstoy that he had not seen the Epilogue. See Donskov, *L. N. Tolstoy – N. N. Strakhov*, 335.

We only know that the dress that she is wearing is *not* the blue dress she is wearing when Levin meets her. Do we imagine a Joshua Reynolds–like gigantic portrait? No. By our knowledge of Mikhailov, from our familiarity with the Russian paintings Tolstoy admired, we can guess that the painting is not double-sized or playful or imaginative; it's serious, as serious as Tolstoy, and as penetrating as Tolstoy's portrayal of her. It catches her beauty, which is the easier part; everyone has seen that. Most importantly, it catches, for lack of a better word, her essence. She never comments on the portrait herself, but there it is, on the wall, a preview of her, an insight to her, for any of her occasional visitors:

> Another lamp with a reflector was hanging on the wall, lighting up a big full-length portrait of a woman, which Levin could not help looking at. [. . .] Levin gazed at the portrait, which stood out from the frame in the brilliant light thrown on it, and he could not tear himself away from it. He positively forgot where he was, and not even hearing what was said, he could not take his eyes off the marvelous portrait. It was not a picture, but a living, charming woman, with black curling hair, with bare arms and shoulders, with a pensive smile on the lips, covered with soft down; triumphantly and softly she looked at him with eyes that baffled him. She was not living only because she was more beautiful than a living woman can be. *

Levin is transfixed. He has still not met her, but he is taken by the artistic presentation of her. It's Tolstoy, however, not Levin, who seems to declare of the woman in the portrait that "She was not living only because she was more beautiful than a living woman can be." Tolstoy is speaking as an artist on art. Art can make beauty absolute. But then Tolstoy lets his fictional self, Levin, have an experience that he, the author, can't have, an encounter with the "living woman":

> "I am delighted!" He heard suddenly near him a voice, unmistakably addressing him, the voice of the very woman he had been admiring in the portrait. Anna had come from behind the treillage to meet him, and Levin saw in the dim light of the study the very woman of the portrait, in a dark

---

* *Anna Karenina,* Part 7, Chapter 9, http://www.literatureproject.com/anna-karenina/anna _198.htm.

blue shot gown, not in the same position nor with the same expression, but with the same perfection of beauty which the artist had caught in the portrait. She was less dazzling in reality, but, on the other hand, there was something fresh and seductive in the living woman which was not in the portrait.

Is this Levin's perception, though? Is he thinking about the artist who "caught" her beauty? Unlikely. There's something the painter Mikhailov caught (and that Tolstoy himself had caught) and then something beyond it, "something fresh and seductive" (or, as Rosamund Bartlett translates it, "new and alluring").

Chapter 9 ends with Chapter 10 completely continuously following. We're back to Levin's dazzled perceptions. Tolstoy separates himself from Levin here to show Levin's bewitchment:

> She had risen to meet him, not concealing her pleasure at seeing him; and in the quiet ease with which she held out her little vigorous hand, introduced him to Vorkuev and indicated a red-haired, pretty little girl who was sitting at work, calling her her pupil, Levin recognized and liked the manners of a woman of the great world, always self-possessed and natural.
>
> "I am delighted, delighted," she repeated, and on her lips these simple words took for Levin's ears a special significance. "I have known you and liked you for a long while, both from your friendship with Stiva and for your wife's sake. . . . I knew her for a very short time, but she left on me the impression of an exquisite flower, simply a flower. And to think she will soon be a mother!"
>
> She spoke easily and without haste, looking now and then from Levin to her brother, and Levin felt that the impression he was making was good, and he felt immediately at home, simple and happy with her, as though he had known her from childhood. [. . .]*

Reflecting on childhood is where Levin's imagination seems to go further than Tolstoy's. We understand Levin's bewitchment better, more clearly, than Vronsky's. Tolstoy

---

* *Anna Karenina*, Part 7, Chapter 10, http://www.literatureproject.com/anna-karenina/anna
_199.htm.

never gives us confidence that Vronsky knows her. Karenin, despite all his limitations as a man and husband, does actually know her; Levin instantly thinks he knows her; Mikhailov, the artist, catches her. We don't even see Vronsky's *ambition* to know her. He just cockily takes for granted that he knows her.

We're all in with Levin, who, when Stiva reenters the scene, is caught re-looking at the portrait. Levin, Stiva, and Vorkuev (a publisher) agree that the portrait's great!

Anna and Levin reengage in conversation. They talk about art—French art. But it's nothing of importance, of resonance. It's the pleasure of social conversation. When Anna turns to Stiva to ask about Vronsky, Levin observes her. He can't hear her, but he watches her animated features:

> "Yes, yes, this is a woman!" Levin thought, forgetting himself and staring persistently at her lovely, mobile face, which at that moment was all at once completely transformed. Levin did not hear what she was talking of as she leaned over to her brother, but he was struck by the change of her expression. Her face—so handsome a moment before in its repose— suddenly wore a look of strange curiosity, anger, and pride. But this lasted only an instant. She dropped her eyelids, as though recollecting something.

What does she recollect? Is it an image or a feeling? The memory of despair? The fate from which she is trying to distract herself?

Here we readers are way ahead of Levin; he doesn't suspect her terrors, as we do.

Because of the presence of her ward, the English jockey's daughter, the topic of education comes up and Anna engages Levin with her eyes to ask him for understanding:

> And she glanced again at Levin. And her smile and her glance—all told him that it was to him only she was addressing her words, valuing his good opinion, and at the same time sure beforehand that they understood each other.

He does understand, but he's not seeing deeply into her because he's dazzled. Except for a moment, she's not so intent on Levin that she can't get distracted herself, but he's so intent on her that he never looks away:

> "[. . .] And now more than ever," she said with a mournful, confiding expression, ostensibly addressing her brother, but unmistakably intending her words only for Levin, "now when I have such need of some occupation, I cannot."

And suddenly frowning (Levin saw that she was frowning at herself for talking about herself) she changed the subject.

She needs something; her attempt to educate girls didn't take—she never turns to religion or philosophy as her creator had. But writing? She has written a children's novel. But that isn't enough, either.

He sees another new expression on her face:

> [. . .] she sighed, and her face suddenly taking a hard expression, looked as if it were turned to stone. With that expression on her face she was more beautiful than ever; but the expression was new; it was utterly unlike that expression, radiant with happiness and creating happiness, which had been caught by the painter in her portrait.

He compares her again to the portrait:

> Levin looked more than once at the portrait and at her figure, as taking her brother's arm she walked with him to the high doors and he felt for her a tenderness and pity at which he wondered himself.

We also have that very same "tenderness and pity" for her, but we don't wonder at ourselves for it. Levin and Tolstoy may get over their enchantment, but most of us readers never do.

After Levin and Anna's greatly pleasurable conversation resumes, Tolstoy shows his hand, lays bare the allegory of the artist and his subject:

> While he followed this interesting conversation, Levin was all the time admiring her—her beauty, her intelligence, her culture, and at the same time her directness and genuine depth of feeling. He listened and talked, and all the while he was thinking of her inner life, trying to divine her feelings. And though he had judged her so severely hitherto, now by some strange chain of reasoning he was justifying her and was also sorry for her, and afraid that Vronsky did not fully understand her. *

---

* *Anna Karenina,* Part 7, Chapter 11, http://www.literatureproject.com/anna-karenina/anna _200.htm.

Tolstoy has brought himself from condemnatory judgment to love and admiration and curiosity. Anna Karenina is that beautiful tragic woman whose feelings we are all "trying to divine." This seems to be Tolstoy's account of how he, the novelist, was won over by his fully imagined heroine.

The evening ends; Anna sends her greetings to Kitty, and in Chapter 11, on the late night ride with Stiva back to his in-laws' house, Levin is "Still thinking of Anna, of everything, even the simplest phrase in their conversation with her, and recalling the minutest changes in her expression, entering more and more into her position, and feeling sympathy for her."[*]

Within moments of her husband's arrival, however, Kitty, having interrogated him about his night out, reads his feelings:

> "You're in love with that hateful woman; she has bewitched you!"

Vronsky found Anna more fascinating than Kitty and now Levin has too! A wife's persecution of her husband for his tender feelings for another woman is not the road to truth any more than torture is. Tolstoy has shown us what understanding feels like; Seryozha and Levin understood Anna and rightly sympathized with and adored her; but now Levin, as a dutiful husband and expectant father, has to show repentance. Levin renounces Anna to his jealous wife and never thinks of Anna again. It's fair to note, tit for tat, that Anna "liked him indeed extremely, and, in spite of the striking difference, from the masculine point of view, between Vronsky and Levin, as a woman she saw something they had in common, which had made Kitty able to love both. Yet as soon as he was out of the room, she ceased to think of him."[†]

Speaking of sympathy and understanding, in Chapter 12 we see that Vronsky is as good and sympathetic here as it is in his power to be. He tries to stop a fight with Anna:

> "Anna, what is it for, why will you?" he said after a moment's silence, bending over toward her, and he opened his hand, hoping she would lay hers in it.

---

[*]   *Anna Karenina,* Part 7, Chapter 11, http://www.literatureproject.com/anna-karenina/anna
    _200.htm.

[†]   *Anna Karenina,* Part 7, Chapter 12, http://www.literatureproject.com/anna-karenina/anna
    _201.htm.

> She was glad of this appeal for tenderness. But some strange force of evil would not let her give herself up to her feelings, as though the rules of warfare would not permit her to surrender.*

"Some strange force of evil" is not Tolstoy being clever, evasive, or deliberately vague. He didn't know what it was either, but he had experienced that perverse force himself. She confesses her real despair and fear: "If you knew how I feel on the brink of calamity at this instant, how afraid I am of myself!"

Vronsky says the right things again, but he really has no idea:

> "Come, tell me what I ought to do to give you peace of mind? I am ready to do anything to make you happy," he said, touched by her expression of despair; "what wouldn't I do to save you from distress of any sort, as now, Anna!" he said.

This is why it's not fair to feel disappointed in Vronsky: we should instead be disappointed that Tolstoy didn't make him a better man. He's a good man, in his way. He is never deliberately cruel. But he's just no match for her. He couldn't and can't imagine her "distress." I don't blame him, but Levin would have understood her. Her brother understands her and so does her son.

In the final four chapters of this installment, Levin is occupied by Kitty's pregnancy. That very next morning after Kitty's snit-fit, she wakes Levin to tell him that the birth is going to happen soon. Levin gets into a tizzy familiar to involved fathers everywhere and goes for the doctor (the women need Levin out of the way and occupied). After many hours, Kitty has the baby; she's happy and Levin is glad that she's alive and yet he remains in confusion about his feeling of estrangement from this new creature, his baby.

✳

By the time the March installment had come out on March 28, Tolstoy seems to have finished the rest of Part 7 and even nearly the Epilogue, with the aftermath of Anna's suicide. The next installment of the novel, the April issue, with the second half of Part 7, would come out in May.

---

*   *Anna Karenina,* Part 7, Chapter 12, http://www.literatureproject.com/anna-karenina/anna _201.htm.

In good spirits, Tolstoy wrote to Strakhov on April 5 about the Epilogue: "I'm completely, completely finished, I only need to correct it."*

Strakhov on about the same date wrote Tolstoy: "You and your novels—for already a long time are the best parts of my life."† How many of us have since felt this and also would have declared it to him if we could have?

Tolstoy was feeling unbound. The next week he opened a new topic with Fet . . . God:

> You won't believe how joyful it made me what you wrote in the one before last, of as you say "the existence of God." I completely agree and very much want to talk, but in a letter it's impossible and there's no time. You for the first time speak to me about a deity—God. I for a long time already haven't stopped thinking about this major problem. Don't say it's impossible to think about. Not only can one but one must. In all the centuries, the best, that is the real people, thought about it. And if we cannot do so, as they, thinking about it, we are obliged to find how. Have you read Pascal's *Pensées*?, that is, recently, with an open mind. When, God willing, you come here, we'll talk about a lot of things and I'll give you this book. [. . .]
>
> If I were free of my novel, whose end is already drafted, and I were making the corrections, I would come to you now on receiving your letter. [. . .]
>
> I'm hoping to celebrate my freedom and the end of my work around April 28.‡

This is the only instance in the course of *Anna Karenina* that Tolstoy beat an estimated time of completion. He would finish April 22.

In the meanwhile, he wrote Alexandrine:

> I'm terribly busy and I'm using my first free (and not free) day to write you a few words. I'm afraid to write about what I wanted to, because it would lure me away. I wanted to write you, objecting to the observations you made in passing on my writing. They offended me and I wanted to prove that I was completely right in what I wrote. But it's good that I then didn't answer you.

---

*   *PSS* 62: 318, letter of April 5, 1877.

†   Donskov, *L. N. Tolstoy – N. N. Strakhov,* 324, April 4–5, 1877.

‡   *PSS* 62: 320, letter of April 13–14, 1877.

I mainly would have started to prove it. At this moment, as we write, we are very persnickety. Now I'm no longer writing. Everything is sent off and it's only left to correct. On the contrary, please make observations to me, as many and as severe as possible. I'm praised too much or I don't hear how I'm scolded. But your remarks I value. You say, "Veslovsky doesn't need to be sent off." But if an impoverished Englishman in a hat came to you in the evening and was going to look at the icons, you would find it very correct that the attendants would lead him out.*

Alexandrine was confident enough and stupid enough to critique *Anna Karenina* to her friend and relative, its author. And so Tolstoy had to refight Levin's battle in Part 6, Chapter 15, and throw Veslovsky out again.

On April 21 or 22, Tolstoy finished *Anna Karenina*. But . . .

Before we celebrate that date, it hadn't all been published and he hadn't proofread it yet. It hadn't been collected into its book-format. He hadn't heard from Katkov that the *Russian Herald* wouldn't publish the Epilogue unless Tolstoy excised his criticism of the Serbian war mania.

But he had finished writing it.

Was there a letdown? Was there relief?

Tolstoy wrote Strakhov:

For the first time, today, after many days, I'm left without work: one set of corrections has been sent off, another not yet sent off, and I have no more manuscript, and I'm sad and lonely but free, and so I use the time to write you, dear Nikolay Nikolaevich.

As least as far as the letters reveal, he was in the sweetest mood he had been in since he began the novel. Whatever conclusions we can make about his depressions, his religious stirrings, his relations with Sofia, he was a Samson and he even today continues to burst all the bands we try to tie him with. While Delilah eventually wheedles the secret out of long-haired Samson, we still don't know the secret of Tolstoy's artistic power.

He had done his job; it seemed there was only the tidying up to do. He was calm, at peace. He continued to Strakhov:

I still have in my heart your last letter with the approval of the last part of Karenina. I'm afraid I don't love critiques and, even less, praises, except yours. They bring me to excitement and firm up my strength for work. I cannot help thinking, however, that you say to me more than you say to yourself, knowing how this pleases me. Summer is approaching and my hope is to see you. When is your vacation? How much of it are you sharing with us?[*]

I'm a crab for critiquing Professor Christian's edition and translation of the letters, but what was going through his mind when he left out the first twelve lines (the two quoted paragraphs above) and begins only with "Please let's go as soon as possible to the Optina Monastery"?

My point? Tolstoy had just finished *Anna Karenina*.

On the list of individual human artistic achievements, this ranks as . . . let's see, let me do the math . . . I've got it: *Number 1*. But from the way Professor Christian has clipped the letter you wouldn't know that Tolstoy had done anything that week. It sounds as if Tolstoy just wanted to get away!

To resume: Christian's excerpt continues:

You say in your last letter that you are cooling off toward your work. I refuse to believe it. You wouldn't believe how necessary your ideas are to me. I wait for them like facts and figures which are necessary to confirm beyond doubt the conclusion I've already formed. [. . . I'm cutting Tolstoy's criticism of Turgenev's translation of Flaubert and Tolstoy's praise and misquotation of Hugo.]

I'm hurrying off to Tula for Seryozha's exam.[†]

What's most important from R. F. Christian's translation's clip of the letter is Tolstoy's parting line. He may well have finished *Anna Karenina*, but he had parental responsibilities to attend to.

Sofia, in "Serezha's Examination and the Children," narrates:

That spring Lev Nikolaevich did a lot of hunting for woodcock, along with one of our guests, a German who had once taught my boys—Fedor Fedorovich.

---

[*] *PSS* 62: 323–324, letter of April 21–22, 1877.

[†] Christian, *Tolstoy's Letters*, 304–305, April 21–22, 1877.

The woodcock hunt was a favourite outing, for all of us. But that spring I wasn't up to accompanying Lev Nikolaevich. Pregnant again, I worked unceasingly—teaching the children, transcribing for Lev Nikolaevich and sewing.

I wrote my sister that I felt I had a yoke around my head and that my back was constantly aching. Besides having a lot of work to do, I was so accustomed to taking advantage of every moment of my life—for example reading an English novel while I breastfed a baby. Since I breastfed ten children, I managed to get through a lot of novels—especially English ones, so as to better study the language. There would always be some sort of book lying beside my low chair in the children's room.

[. . .]

I think {Serezha's success} was largely due to the fact that his father spent a great deal of time working with him personally and making him realize the necessity of getting into university. Lev Nikolaevich was quite strict with Serezha, sometimes even too strict.*

Sofia didn't explain what she meant about that over-strictness. We know from the Tolstoy children's memoirs that as a teacher Tolstoy could be impatient; that January, we remember, Tolstoy confessed to Sofia his shame about getting angry while teaching Tanya. (Seryozha's exams started on May 3 and, Sofia proudly recalled, he passed them all.)†

❋

In the Jubilee Edition the undated April letters to Katkov at the *Russian Herald* are bunched together but were probably written both before and certainly after the April 21–22 letter to Strakhov.

While offering apologies to Katkov for being late with his corrections, Tolstoy betrayed little anxiety about not being forgiven again for his tardiness: "With great regrets I only now can send you five chapters, which tormented me. They ought to be printed between what I sent at the beginning and what I sent after; but if it's too late, there's nothing to do and they can be placed in afterward. I'm hoping you'll be so good as to send me what

---

*   Tolstaya, *My Life*, 236.

†   Ibid.

I sent earlier in corrections. Finally, feeling guilty for the delay of the book, I don't dare ask to have it sent to me, but all the same I can hope for you and your corrections."*

The second letter enclosed more manuscript and promised two more chapters "the day after tomorrow"; he apologized for the many scrawled corrections on the manuscript.

He was not trying to offend Katkov, but he also didn't worry about offending him. He believed Katkov would accept what he had done, late or not.

But he was wrong; there are no surviving explanatory letters from Katkov; all we find is Tolstoy's shock, recounted in Tolstoy's letters to others, about Katkov's refusal to publish the Epilogue.

What was the imperious Katkov thinking as he read the passages that offended him? Did he immediately recognize that he wasn't going to publish them? Was he wracking his brain how he was going to tell his equally imperious author that he wanted to delete passages? Was he trying to think up arguments to bring Tolstoy around to a sympathetic view of the war? Did he consult friends to ask how to do this? If he had really known Tolstoy, he would have guessed that Tolstoy would not compromise. Perhaps he, like editors everywhere, would feel annoyed at being expected to grant ever more additional favors to an ever-tardy writer.

Tolstoy's third April letter to Katkov: "Despite all efforts, I couldn't finish the corrections of these 3 chapters that need to be between what I sent earlier and what was sent after, and so I'm afraid to hold you back and decided on the following: be so kind, much esteemed M.N., and send the laid out sheets as they are. If God gives me on these days 3 hours of light, I will correct them and send them, and if it's fine with you, order to assemble and print them to the end. Their transposition will not interfere with the course of the novel."†

This seems to be the last actual surviving business letter between Katkov and Tolstoy.

Katkov deserves no sympathy. The nationalistic trumped-up war that he had helped to instigate was plainly wrong; he had the world's greatest author concluding the world's greatest novel; he should have published anything Tolstoy wanted, no matter how controversial, no matter how annoyingly late.

And yet, the scholar Susanne Fusso cautions us (me, that is), "As far as we know, Katkov allowed all of Tolstoy's attacks on his favored projects to pass without objection or amendment. Just as he gave Tolstoy special treatment in financial matters, during most

---

*   *PSS* 62: 324.

†   *PSS* 62: 325.

of the publication of *Anna Karenina* he refrained from the intrusive editorial practices that had plagued Tur, Turgenev, and Dostoevsky."[*]

Tolstoy's aggravation about Katkov's surprising refusal to publish the Epilogue would not come until the third week of May.

Tolstoy's correspondence this spring was the lightest it had been over any of his *Anna Karenina* springtimes. He was busy. He was nearing completion. He was neither down in the dumps nor struggling to right himself to write. He was free from wheeling and dealing about the business of publishing other projects. He was not particularly restless.

❋

The April issue of the *Russian Herald,* the last serialized appearance of *Anna Karenina,* was published May 2.

How long would it have taken a hungry reader to read the second half of Part 7, those last devastating fifteen (in the book, divided into sixteen) chapters?

I imagine I would have sat home reading them and then taken a long tearful walk through the muddy countryside or along the Moscow River. Persuaded by my own feelings, I imagine every single one of the estimated five thousand subscribers of the *Russian Herald* (and the subscribers' novel-reading friends and families) weeping.[†] I sympathize with every stricken reader's response as they follow Anna to her last moment of consciousness. We only have the reactions of one of those *Russian Herald* subscribers, a bureaucrat named Prince Vladimir Mikhailovich Golitsyn, who responded unpretentiously and mostly uninterestingly in his diary to several of the installments.[‡]

But because Tolstoy has been showing us how we actually live and think and act, I also manage to imagine an outlier beyond Prince Golitsyn: Akaky Bobovich Durakiy. He's a middle-aged man with a graying beard who comes home after a night out. May 2 has reached midnight and turned into May 3; he picks up the copy of the *Russian Herald* from the desk in his study and takes it to his bedroom and starts to read and as he gets

---

[*]   Susanne Fusso, *Editing Turgenev, Dostoevsky, and Tolstoy: Mikhail Katkov and the Great Russian Novel* (Dekalb: Northern Illinois University Press, 2017), 193.

[†]   Mills Todd III, "V. N. Golitsyn Reads *Anna Karenina*: How One of Karenin's Colleagues Responded to the Novel," 189–200. (Note 6: ". . . while a 'thick journal' such as the *Russian Herald* might have a subscription list of only 5000 [. . .] it would be read by many more than this [. . .]. Still, even allowing for ten readers a copy, it is hard to dispute Dostoevsky's estimate that only one Russian in five hundred could read this level of literature.")

[‡]   Ibid.

to the most intense momentum of Anna's crazed determination . . . the page seems to swirl, his head becomes a sack of flour, his neck tilts forward, and he falls asleep. The agitation he feels in his sleep is not because he dreams of Anna's unhappiness but because in the dream he thinks he remembers an appointment, but he doesn't know what it's for. He arrives at a governmental building that resembles his childhood home in Kursk. A rooster is walking down the corridor from the entry-hall, and he follows it. He wakes up smacking his lips, mouths the word "Poulet!" and while he notices the bent copy of the *Russian Herald* in his bed it doesn't make him reflect for a second. At the office that day or the next, someone mentions Anna's suicide and he nods knowingly, mutters, "Terrible! So sad!" and thinks: "I should read that myself," but never does.

I can or should imagine as well Tolstoy's friends' and loved ones' reactions: they are proud that they know this man who wrote this! No matter how well they knew him, however, their relationship with him didn't overwhelm the experience they went through reading about Anna's suicide. Even so, there was something about Tolstoy that they could never have known better or more deeply than through these chapters. This was as deep as Tolstoy ever went into his own terrors.

Only Sofia could have stood off from it. Only Sofia already knew this Tolstoy. She didn't know the novel only as the gift of art. She knew it in all its painful creation; she knew it the way the characters in the novel know Anna: personally, complicatedly. It had to be more than a literary experience for her. Her artistic responses were naturally enough mixed up with her personal responses and knowledge of her husband. No one else would ever read *Anna Karenina* as she did at this time. All of us can read it more or less as Strakhov did: with amazement and awe and shock.

12

Suicidal Tendencies

✳

Not only is suicide a sin, it is the sin. It is the ultimate and absolute evil, the refusal to take an interest in existence; the refusal to take the oath of loyalty to life. The man who kills a man, kills a man. The man who kills himself, kills all men; as far as he is concerned he wipes out the world.

—G. K. Chesterton*

Tolstoy didn't see suicide as a sin. He would remark to a friend: "I can't understand why people look upon suicide as a crime. It seems to me to be a man's right. It gives a man the chance of dying when he no longer wishes to live. The Stoics thought like that."† In *The Kingdom of God Is Within You*, completed sixteen years after *Anna Karenina*, Tolstoy would write: "People are astonished that sixty thousand suicides are committed in Europe every year, reckoning only the recognized and recorded cases and excluding Russia and Turkey; but they ought rather to be surprised that there are so few. Every man of our time, if we go deep enough into the contradiction between his conscience and his life, is in a most terrible condition."‡ Anna does

---

* G. K. Chesterton, "The Flag of the World," *Orthodoxy* (London: John Lane Co., 1908).

† Goldenweizer, *Talks with Tolstoy*, 92.

‡ Leo Tolstoy, *The Kingdom of God and Peace Essays*, trans. Aylmer Maude (Oxford, UK: Oxford University Press, 1937), 157.

not survive that "most terrible condition," but Levin does and Tolstoy did. How? Why? What was the difference?

※

The final installment of *Anna Karenina* in the *Russian Herald* begins by bringing us back to Stiva's money problems. Stiva needs Karenin's help to get a better-paying position. Tolstoy doesn't want us to feel amused or charmed by Anna's brother anymore. Karenin exposes Stiva's base motivations for the position: not for service or his particular fitness but simply for the money. Stiva also needs to convince Karenin to grant Anna a divorce now; Karenin consents to consider it. Having promised Karenin he wouldn't speak to Seryozha about Anna, Stiva does, and Seryozha breaks into ashamed tears. Then, thrown off from his usual poise, Stiva finds himself too far into a game of flirtation with Betsy. Finally, at a séance hosted by Lidia, to which Stiva feels obliged to attend to get on his brother-in-law's good side, Stiva is denounced by the French spiritualist Landau, whose advice and whims Lidia and Karenin cater to. Stiva flees, unsuccessful for the first time in the novel: no help from Karenin for a position for him, no divorce for Anna.

The remaining nine chapters dramatize in unsettling hyper-focus Anna's last two days.

In Chapter 24, Vronsky tells Anna, in a newsy way, trying to keep her from getting mad, about a dinner party he has returned from and how a swimming instructor who was there demonstrated her new method of swimming. Vronsky insists that the instructor was "old and hideous"; he wants to drop the topic, but jealous Anna asks: "[. . .] did she swim in some special way, then?"[*] (Anna will compare herself, as she is about to jump under the train, to a swimmer: "A feeling such as she had known when about to take the first plunge in bathing came upon her, and she crossed herself.")

Vronsky wants to get them away from this subject:

> "There was absolutely nothing in it. That's just what I say, it was awfully stupid. Well, then, when do you think of going?"
>
> Anna shook her head as though trying to drive away some unpleasant idea.[†]

---

[*]   *Anna Karenina*, Part 7, Chapter 24, http://www.literatureproject.com/anna-karenina/anna_213.htm.

[†]   Ibid.

There is no other "unpleasant idea" for her than the one goading her toward suicide. (We might recall now Tolstoy's terrifying description in *Confession* of his impulse toward death being stronger than the usual one toward life.)*

Anna knows that she has been impossible with Vronsky, and she decides "it must be ended."

"But how?" she asked herself, and she sat down in a low chair before the looking glass.

"*How?*" We know how. We don't want her to figure it out, but we know. This is not something we want anybody to figure out. Don't give her any hints! But the answer is in her head, and Tolstoy is sweeping us readers along into her feeling of hollowness:

> [. . .] At the bottom of her heart was some obscure idea that alone interested her, but she could not get clear sight of it.

And this is where almost anybody, except the suicidal, would divert themselves from further clarifying. Anna, however, is "interested" and goes on:

> Thinking once more of Alexey Alexandrovitch, she recalled the time of her illness after her confinement, and the feeling which never left her at that time. "Why didn't I die?" and the words and the feeling of that time came back to her. And all at once she knew what was in her soul. Yes, it was that idea which alone solved all. "Yes, to die! [. . .]"

Her reason cannot bring her to the feeling of wanting to live. Even though we rereaders know what happens, most of us hope that *this time* she'll turn back from the train. As I've shown, to my own unhappiness, from her first appearance in the novel, *her fate is sealed*. A train station is where she's going to die. But Tolstoy somehow also makes us feel as if she could, after all, turn away. I don't think that's just my sentimentality. It's certainly what people in families that suffer a suicide feel. It may have seemed inevitable, but until the last moment, she could have stepped away.

In Chapter 25, Anna decides that she wants to leave Moscow. She's in a "good" mood that is teetering; the slightest vibration tips her. She cannot control or assert any balance except by sticking hard to a position.

Vronsky reacts to Stiva's letter's news of the unlikely prospects for the divorce—but Anna asserts that it doesn't matter. The person who's always flying off the handle

---

* See above, pages 201–202.

is set off by people thinking she could fly off the handle. Vronsky tries to bring up something else:

> "No," she said, irritated by his so obviously showing by this change of subject that he was irritated, "why did you suppose that this news would affect me so, that you must even try to hide it? I said I don't want to consider it, and I should have liked you to care as little about it as I do."*

She gets madder because of his tone, not his words. She has no margin for forgiveness, for patience. She is torturing him. She ignores what he says; she has lost distance from her mood; her mind and mood are too coordinated.

He, trying so hard, is bewildered and doesn't know which way to move:

> "Oh, I said: for your sake. Above all for your sake," he repeated, frowning as though in pain, "because I am certain that the greater part of your irritability comes from the indefiniteness of the position."

Vronsky is doing as well and as much as any spouse or lover could here—and it's not enough:

> "Yes, now he has laid aside all pretense, and all his cold hatred for me is apparent," she thought, not hearing his words, but watching with terror the cold, cruel judge who looked mocking her out of his eyes.

And then she goes after his mother: the worst arguing strategy in the history of domestic relationships:

> "You don't love your mother. That's all talk, and talk, and talk!" she said, looking at him with hatred in her eyes.

It's unbearable.

Vronsky's friend Yashvin drops in, and Tolstoy makes us wonder what does it mean about us human beings that in the middle of a personal catastrophe, we can flip a switch and appear as our social selves?

---

* *Anna Karenina*, Part 7, Chapter 25, http://www.literatureproject.com/anna-karenina/anna _214.htm.

Why, when there was a tempest in her soul, and she felt she was standing at a turning point in her life, which might have fearful consequences—why, at that minute, she had to keep up appearances before an outsider, who sooner or later must know it all—she did not know. But at once quelling the storm within her, she sat down and began talking to their guest.

Why, indeed! Is it shame before others? Is it our socializing reflex?

Another visitor comes by to buy a horse, and Anna exits the room. Before Vronsky leaves with his guests, he goes to her.

All her continual attacks on Vronsky are part of her suicide. Each act of her own cruelty is killing her, taking her steps closer to the abyss.

Though Vronsky is fed up, he is still responsive to her:

> "I'm not to blame in any way," he thought. "If she will punish herself, *tant pis pour elle* [too bad for her]." But as he was going he fancied that she said something, and his heart suddenly ached with pity for her.
>
> "Eh, Anna?" he queried.
>
> "I said nothing," she answered just as coldly and calmly.
>
> "Oh, nothing, *tant pis* then," he thought, feeling cold again, and he turned and went out. As he was going out he caught a glimpse in the looking glass of her face, white, with quivering lips. He even wanted to stop and to say some comforting word to her, but his legs carried him out of the room before he could think what to say.

Again with the mirror—which, unlike her face, does not lie.

When he returns that night she has her maid tell him she has a headache and doesn't wish to be disturbed.

In Chapter 26, her hopelessness sweeps her away and takes her beyond where anybody should be. Tolstoy shows us the sharpest, most painful division between a couple. One cannot see or know the obvious suffering that the other is experiencing:

> Was it possible to glance at her as he had glanced when he came into the room for the guarantee?—to look at her, see her heart was breaking with despair, and go out without a word with that face of callous composure?[*]

But wait, Anna: Was it possible to look at *Vronsky* and not see *his* suffering?

---

[*]   *Anna Karenina*, Part 7, Chapter 26, http://www.literatureproject.com/anna-karenina/anna _215.htm.

She is in a panic and sliding deeper into her depression. Again, depression is where one's mood . . . no, I don't know what it is, but Anna is sliding and can't stop herself:

> All the most cruel words that a brutal man could say, he said to her in her imagination, and she could not forgive him for them, as though he had actually said them.
>
> "But didn't he only yesterday swear he loved me, he, a truthful and sincere man? Haven't I despaired for nothing many times already?" she said to herself afterward.

Then, instead of reflecting, she comes up with a test of proof of whether he still loves her or not: sending him a note to say she has a headache:

> "If he comes in spite of what the maid says, it means that he loves me still.
> If not, it means that all is over, and then I will decide what I'm to do! . . . "

Can we knock thoughts out of somebody's head? Isn't that what I, her loving reader, want to do here? Knock that alluring suicidal thought out of her head?

She becomes possessed by the spirit of righteous indignation—it's not quite revenge because she hasn't got anything on Vronsky that he's actually done. Her need to "punish" him is a kind of self-obliteration: murder and suicide. If she's going down, he's going down. How can we sympathize with her? I don't know how or why, but I do.

This next passage is terrible:

> And death rose clearly and vividly before her mind as the sole means of bringing back love for her in his heart, of punishing him and of gaining the victory in that strife which the evil spirit in possession of her heart was waging with him.
> [. . .] The one thing that mattered was punishing him.

She imagines dying and his reaction. She lies down after an opium dose and looks around her room . . .

> . . . while she vividly pictured to herself how he would feel when she would be no more, when she would be only a memory to him.

CREATING ANNA KARENINA ※ 335

She cannot be "just a memory"! Whatever it is she "vividly pictured to herself," I'll bet it isn't the bitter grief that Vronsky will actually suffer. She probably doesn't imagine his anger and resentment and the poisoning of his memories of her. No, she imagines her own feelings of satisfied vengeance.

The only vengeance in a novel preceded by the most famous of all literary epigraphs ("Vengeance is Mine, and I will repay") is enacted by Anna.

She has a nightmarish vision as the candle goes out; then she revives and decides what everyone else knows already: she loves him, he loves her. They can go on. Is her suicide inevitable, just because Tolstoy has decided it is, that he conceived the story so?

No matter how many times I read it, I never remember this dreamy scene of her going to Vronsky's room and shining her candle on him. She decides against waking him up, lest he look at her coldly and she accuses him of something. So she goes back to her room and takes more opium and has an agitated sleep. She has the terrible recurring dream of the peasant.

Every time Anna tries to right herself, the smallest details throw her off—e.g., seeing Vronsky accept a letter from a young woman that his mother has sent over. Anna goes in to Vronsky to tell him that she's not leaving with him and he decides to disregard this nonsense, the only tactic of response that he hasn't tried before. She watches him leave. Even if he had returned to her within moments and apologized (insincerely, for nothing), she would have cracked again sooner or later. He is not to blame. Whatever Vronsky is in his own limited self, he is not to blame.

The next day, Chapter 27, Anna knows she has lost her wits. While she's beyond me and my own experiences, she's not beyond Tolstoy. Tolstoy knows and Dostoevsky knows and Chekhov knows these madnesses and they have all written about them. I only think I know because I have read those fellows.

She asks a servant where Vronsky has gone; she writes a note to send to him:

"I was wrong. Come back home; I must explain. For God's sake come! I'm afraid."*

And in a nightmare that's real, she rushes to the children's room and is disappointed and surprised to see her daughter, not Seryozha.

Anna continues to see everything, to register, like Tolstoy, all the details with startling clarity. It's then what she does with those perceptions that shows us her derangement. She sees her daughter:

---

* *Anna Karenina,* Part 7, Chapter 27, http://www.literatureproject.com/anna-karenina/anna
  _216.htm.

The little girl sitting at the table was obstinately and violently battering on it with a cork, and staring aimlessly at her mother with her pitch-black eyes.

Then, seeing Vronsky in her daughter's expression, she panics and leaves, thinking:

"Can it be all over? [. . .]"

And then, so weirdly and in a way that brought tears to her eyes, she can't remember, now anticipating Vronsky's return, whether she brushed her hair yet or not:

She felt her head with her hand. "Yes, my hair has been done, but when I did it I can't in the least remember." She could not believe the evidence of her hand, and went up to the pier glass to see whether she really had done her hair.

This—this having to confirm with her eyes what her hand knows—brought tears to *my* eyes:

She certainly had, but she could not think when she had done it. "Who's that?" she thought, looking in the looking glass at the swollen face with strangely glittering eyes, that looked in a scared way at her. "Why, it's I!" she suddenly understood, and looking round, she seemed all at once to feel his kisses on her, and twitched her shoulders, shuddering. Then she lifted her hand to her lips and kissed it.

At first, I misread the end of that in Russian; as I recopied it I was as surprised as *she*—she raises her own hand to her lips and kisses it! (I had thought she was imagining Vronsky raising it and kissing it.)

With so much of *Anna Karenina*, I think biographically of Tolstoy—but not here. Why? How does Tolstoy know this? Why don't we reject this moment as fantasy? What does it take to drive a person of supreme consciousness—Tolstoy and Anna for example—to suicide? This, apparently. It's not Vronsky's limitations or the loss of Seryozha or her ostracism from society, or even the opium: it's madness. Twice in this chapter she realizes that she's going "out of her mind" ("Why, I'm going out of my mind!"; "I shall go out of my mind").

She is in a continual panic:

"Yes, I mustn't think, I must do something, drive somewhere, and most of all, get out of this house" [. . .]

She leaves in the coach with the driver.

In Chapter 28, Anna rides through Moscow observing the street signs. It could be an aimless unimportant wandering observation. We know it's not, but it's just like one as she notices the seemingly random signs—one of which, or in combination with something, gives her a memory that we never had access to (unlike in the movies, where the stirred memory almost always comes from the events already pictured in the movie):

> And she remembered how, long, long ago, when she was a girl of seventeen, she had gone with her aunt to Troitsa.[*]

Were we thinking of Anna at seventeen? No. But she could and did. And we realize that there's all that full life she has had that we know nothing about—except this, that at seventeen she went to Troitsa with her aunt:

> "Was that really me, with red hands?"

Perfectly neutral—observed, remembered, but not judged.
But then she reflects and it gets really bad:

> "How much that seemed to me then splendid and out of reach has become worthless, while what I had then has gone out of my reach forever! Could I ever have believed then that I could come to such humiliation? [. . .]"

She resumes observing—then when Vronsky comes to mind she muses on something even more terrible:

> "What's so awful is that one can't tear up the past by its roots. One can't tear it out, but one can hide one's memory of it. And I'll hide it." And then she thought of her past with Alexey Alexandrovitch [Karenin], of how she had blotted the memory of it out of her life.

---

[*] *Anna Karenina*, Part 7, Chapter 28, http://www.literatureproject.com/anna-karenina/anna _217.htm.

And she now turns the neutral observations into cynical readings of the people she sees. She sees boys playing and remembers Seryozha and then pushes her son out of her thoughts, replaced by Vronsky.

It seems amazing that when she arrives at Dolly's house Kitty is there. This coincidence sends her thoughts back through the novel (not her *life* but the novel) and seems less believable than her thoughts that brought her back to age seventeen.

When she leaves, after some awkward moments with Dolly and Kitty, Kitty is almost infatuated again but Dolly sees something ominous:

> "She's just the same and just as charming! She's very lovely!" said Kitty, when she was alone with her sister. "But there's something piteous about her. Awfully piteous!"
>
> "Yes, there's something unusual about her today," said Dolly. "When I went with her into the hall, I fancied she was almost crying."

Our desperate friends whom we can't help! Our desperate selves, whom our friends can't help!

In Chapter 29, Anna, back in the carriage, resumes watching people, but all her thoughts become infected with despair. Seeing two men talking . . .

> "What can he be telling the other with such warmth?" she thought, staring at two men who walked by. "Can one ever tell anyone what one is feeling? I meant to tell Dolly, and it's a good thing I didn't tell her. [. . .]"*

She decides—comes to believe what we all believe when we're depressed—that no one understands anyone else. Had Tolstoy felt *this*?

A man tips his hat to Anna, then realizes she is not after all an acquaintance:

> "He thought he knew me. Well, he knows me as well as anyone in the world knows me. I don't know myself. I know my appetites, as the French say. [. . .]"

Then, because there are no innocent pleasures left, she is cynical about boys wanting ice cream. She's able to twist even that thought into a swipe at Kitty and into a proverb on perpetual hatred:

---

*   *Anna Karenina*, Part 7, Chapter 29, http://www.literatureproject.com/anna-karenina/anna _218.htm.

"If not sweetmeats, then a dirty ice. And Kitty's the same—if not Vronsky, then Levin. And she envies me, and hates me. And we all hate each other. I Kitty, Kitty me. Yes, that's the truth. [. . .]"

It's almost unbearable to watch her, feel her, in this state of mind as she goes through her house:

> She longed to get away as quickly as possible from the feelings she had gone through in that awful house. The servants, the walls, the things in that house—all aroused repulsion and hatred in her and lay like a weight upon her.

She packs for the train:

> She knew she would never come back here again.

And then there's her food aversion. What does it mean about our state of being when we lose a most fundamental appetite?[*]

> Dinner was on the table; she went up, but the smell of the bread and cheese was enough to make her feel that all food was disgusting. She ordered the carriage and went out.

She goes to the train station. From here on (maybe from even further back), all her thoughts, except until the last couple of moments, are suicidal.

In Chapter 30, we see another sign of suicidal depression: complete self-confidence:

> "[. . .] Again I understand it all!"[†]

Beware of revelations!

---

[*] Sofia wrote and told Tolstoy a dozen years later, when *he* had gone off meat: "How stupid vegetarianism is. . . . Kill life in yourself, kill all impulses of the flesh, all its needs—why not kill yourself altogether? After all you are committing yourself to *slow* death, what's the difference?"; Tolstoy, *Tolstoy: A Life of My Father*, 301–302.

[†] *Anna Karenina*, Part 7, Chapter 30, http://www.literatureproject.com/anna-karenina/anna _219.htm.

And now for the first time Anna turned that glaring light in which she was seeing everything on to her relations with him, which she had hitherto avoided thinking about.

As she is thinking of Vronsky, up pops in her consciousness the English phrase "The zest is gone." All her persecuted and persecuting nonsense is "true." Beware all infuriated insight:

This was not mere supposition, she saw it distinctly in the piercing light, which revealed to her now the meaning of life and human relations.

More build-up of nonsense:

[. . .] she opened her lips, and shifted her place in the carriage in the excite-ment, aroused by the thought that suddenly struck her. "[. . .] And where love ends, hate begins."

She mocks—or does Tolstoy mock her?—her old aspirations to happiness:

"[. . .] Come, let me try and think what I want, to make me happy. Well? Suppose I am divorced, and Alexey Alexandrovitch lets me have Seryozha, and I marry Vronsky."

Then back to her inspired clarity—she enjoys it! Yes, isn't that part of the delirium of cynicism and spite? We *enjoy* it:

And the clarity with which she saw now her and all people's lives pleased her.

In this flight of feelings and thoughts, she is conscious and clear, possessing Tol-stoy's artistic penetration; Levin is only a reflection of Tolstoy, but Anna embodies Tolstoy's consciousness.

Her second-to-last chapter ends thusly:

Then she thought that life might still be happy, and how miserably she loved and hated him, and how fearfully her heart was beating.

In Chapter 31, Anna, seated on the train at the station, in a fury of attention, notices:

A second bell sounded, and was followed by moving of luggage, noise, shouting and laughter. It was so clear to Anna that there was nothing for anyone to be glad of, that this laughter irritated her agonizingly, and she would have liked to stop up her ears not to hear it.*

These same feelings almost drove Tolstoy himself to suicide a couple of years before.

"Yes, what did I stop at? That I couldn't conceive a position in which life would not be a misery, that we are all created to be miserable, and that we all know it, and all invent means of deceiving each other. And when one sees the truth, what is one to do?"

God sees the truth, Tolstoy sees the truth, Anna sees the truth. Beware of seeing the truth. If you find it, how to escape it?

Tolstoy never ever condemns Anna for killing herself. Anna will have her moment, her last moments of existence, of regret, and will realize that she doesn't after all want to die, but Tolstoy does not condemn her.

Anna overhears a woman saying, "Why are people given reason but to save themselves?" And that clicks for her. She looks with hatred at this couple and has a Tolstoyan disgust at having Tolstoy's creative imagination—*reflexively imagining others' lives*:

Anna seemed to see all their history and all the crannies of their souls, as it were turning a light upon them. But there was nothing interesting in them, and she pursued her thought.

Tolstoy will himself react upon his own fiction this way. He became ashamed of imagining the lives of fictitious characters. What's the use of seeing the souls of other people? Her thoughts, anyway, are clear with *truth*. And they get her meditating:

"Yes, I'm very much worried, and that's what reason was given me for, to escape; so then one must escape: why not put out the light when there's nothing more to look at, when it's sickening to look at it all? But how? Why did the conductor run along the footboard, why are they shrieking, those young men

---

* *Anna Karenina,* Part 7, Chapter 31, http://www.literatureproject.com/anna-karenina/anna _220.htm.

in that train? why are they talking, why are they laughing? It's all falsehood, all lying, all humbug, all cruelty! . . ."

The truth that things are bad and that this truth is conclusive brings us to the very edge of the world, at which point we are rescued by luck or life-overflowing or . . . we "escape" and kill ourselves.

As Tolstoy wrote in *Confession*:

> The third escape is that of strength and energy. It consists in destroying life, when one has understood that it is an evil and an absurdity. A few exceptionally strong and consistent people act so. Having understood the stupidity of the joke that has been played on them, and having understood that it is better to be dead than to be alive, and that it is best of all not to exist, they act accordingly and promptly end this stupid joke, since there are means: a rope round one's neck, water, a knife to stick into one's heart, or the trains on the railways [. . .]*

This is Anna's last day, her last hour!

Tolstoy and Levin tried to find salvation in religion. Anna doesn't; for her, there is no generous, mollifying spirit:

> "No, I won't let you make me miserable," she thought menacingly, addressing not him, not herself, but the power that made her suffer, and she walked along the platform.

Now I don't know what to say:

> A feeling such as she had known when about to take the first plunge in bathing came upon her, and she crossed herself.

Wait! That physical reflex of crossing herself awakens something:

> That familiar gesture brought back into her soul a whole series of girlish and childish memories, and suddenly the darkness that had covered everything

---

* *Confession*, 41.

for her was torn apart, and life rose up before her for an instant with all its bright past joys.

Why is it too late? Why does she have to complete her "escape"?:

> But she did not take her eyes from the wheels of the second carriage. And exactly at the moment when the space between the wheels came opposite her, she dropped the red bag, and drawing her head back into her shoulders, fell on her hands under the carriage, and lightly, as though she would rise again at once, dropped on to her knees. And at the same instant she was terror-stricken at what she was doing. "Where am I? What am I doing? What for?" she tried to get up, to drop backwards; but something huge and merciless struck her on the head and rolled her on her back. "Lord, forgive me all!" she said, feeling it impossible to struggle. A peasant muttering something was working at the iron above her. And the light by which she had read the book filled with troubles, falsehoods, sorrow, and evil, flared up more brightly than ever before, lighted up for her all that had been in darkness, flickered, began to grow dim, and was quenched forever.

I had forgotten that she does after all ask God for forgiveness. Was *that* just another reflex? Doesn't Tolstoy show us that our reflexes matter?

Tolstoy resisted killing himself, but Anna did not. He had been terrified. He thought he could have done it, but he didn't.

Why not? Maybe because Anna did it for him.

13

Finishing Off:
May 7, 1877–January 1878

❋

Strakhov, Tolstoy's most important reader, wrote him on May 7:

> [. . .] I read through Anna Karenina just three days ago. The Petersburg half
> was news to me—and very impressive. How laughable and how terrible!
> Oblonsky, the representative of rationalism and Karenin and Lidia Ivanovna
> of mysticism! This is amazing and seizes the heart; such a mass of lies, such
> shallowness of mind and heart. [. . .]
>
> The second half of the story—Moscow—felt confusing to me. You have
> developed with unbelievable simplicity and clarity—the relations between
> Anna and Vronsky. Of such further realism than Flaubert (I reread him a
> bit), Zola and such ones. For example, the sticking-out little finger*, exciting
> hatred in Vronsky, and Anna understood his feelings.
>
> But you have taken from me that tenderness I experienced three years ago
> in your room and which I expected now. You're pitiless; you don't forgive Anna
> even at the moment of her death; her bitterness and rage grew up until the

---

* Andrew Donskov (*L. N. Tolstoy – N. N. Strakhov*) points us to the "little finger" in Part 7,
   Chapter 25. Garnett translates it this way: "She lifted her cup, with her little finger held apart
   [отставленный мизинец], and put it to her lips. After drinking a few sips she glanced at
   him, and by his expression, she saw clearly that he was repelled by her hand, and her gesture,
   and the sound made by her lips."

last moment, and you have deleted, as it seems to me, some places expressing
the softening of her soul and pity for herself. In such form, I didn't weep but
became very gloomily thoughtful. Yes, this is truer than what I imagined. It
is very true and more terrible.

Her reasoning and impressions were so simple and so striking! Who is right?
one asks oneself. She, seeing the final thoughts of her life, or this merchant
crossing himself and this young rascal glancing at her beneath her hat? But in
her soul it is so terrible, such a hell, that she exits it, as if this coarse, stupid,
frivolous life is the truth, more truthful than her despair.

In the newspapers the appearance of each part of Karenina comes out just
as immediately and is construed just as earnestly as about a new battle or a
new speech of Bismarck. And just as suddenly. So just yesterday I read that
Karenina decided on suicide being convinced that Vronsky loved another. You
see that otherwise they probably cannot understand by tradition, by French
novels, and not by the feeling of one's own heart.[*]

Strakhov then refuted Tolstoy's pooh-poohing of his earlier admiring criticism:

But as for my praises, I think that they make you happy only because they
are true; I don't write what I don't think. I try very hard for this; you praise
me that you give such value to my words, but I know that this applies only to
the truth. You note that I write the truth but not the whole truth. To that I
say this. I write you what is most clear in my soul. [. . .]

I know one thing: a great work in Russian literature has happened, a new
great production [. . .][†]

Tolstoy, reading that, should have nodded and admitted, *"It's true."* If his head was
turned by this praise, he didn't say so.

When Tolstoy wrote Fet in early May, he expressed all his usual pleasure about Fet's
impending visit: "Let me know exactly when you're coming and I'll send a cart to the station or even meet you a few stations up the line and ride in with you." Tolstoy explained:
"I'm completely taken up with my work or I would come to you."[‡] That is, he was working

---

[*]   Donskov, *L. N. Tolstoy – N. N. Strakhov*, 332–333, May 7, 1877.

[†]   Ibid.

[‡]   *PSS* 62: 325, letter of May 8–9, 1877.

on corrections for the May issue of *Anna Karenina*, corrections of the Epilogue that he didn't yet know would never be published by Katkov's *Russian Herald*.

On May 18, Strakhov, not having heard back from his friend, wrote again:

> The last part of Anna Karenina [Part 7, he means] has produced an especially strong impression, a veritable explosion. Dostoevsky waves his arms and calls you the God of Art. This amazes and overjoys me—he so determinedly opposed you. Stasov wrote in a pseudonymous article in New Times in which he pronounced you a great writer, equal with Gogol and Shakespeare, and ordered your everlasting fame. [. . .]
>
> It turns out that the others praise you no less than I do. With the greatest impatience I await the last part, which I still absolutely don't know, even in draft. I'm convinced that you have risen to your full height, so high that it torments me with curiosity.[*]

By May 21 or 22, Tolstoy had learned of Katkov's objections to the Epilogue and he wrote Strakhov:

> I just received your second unanswered letter and I'm ashamed.—I was prevented from writing you because I was very busy with writing and mainly because I didn't want to say anything to you until you had read through the last part. It was typeset long ago and twice already corrected by me and in a few days they're sending it to me again for a final look. But I'm afraid that all the same it's not going to come out soon. And so I want to consult with you about this and ask for your help.
>
> It seems to me that Katkov doesn't share my views and that it can't be otherwise as I blame namely such people as he; mumbling politely, he asks me to soften what's coming out; it terribly sickens me, and I've already explained to them that if they don't publish it in the way I want I absolutely won't publish it with them, and so that's what I'm doing; but despite the inconvenience of everything being published in a booklet and selling it separately, the inconvenience is the necessity of getting it past the censor. What do you advise—separately with the censor or some uncensored journal—the *Herald of Europe*, *Cornfield*, the *Wanderer*, it's all the same to

---

[*]   Donskov, *L. N. Tolstoy – N. N. Strakhov*, 335.

me—only that I want it published as soon as possible and no conversing over softenings or deletions. Please advise and help. Maybe I'll still arrange things with Katkov, but I would very much want to know what to do in the event of a disagreement.[*]

Tolstoy was in Moscow on or around May 28–29 and wrote Strakhov from there:

[. . .] I'm very grateful for your advice and offered help. I'm taking the advice and am rescuing the writing and giving it to Ris[†] to publish in Moscow. He promises that in a week it will be ready. I terribly want your help, but I don't know how it will be. Ris is coming to me right now bringing the original, and I'll ask him if he can send you the corrections. Moreover, this depends on when you're leaving Petersburg and coming to us. Of your visit I only repeat with words, thought, and heart: the sooner the better. [. . .] The proof of the sincerity of what I'm saying is that I would desire you to finish the work.—I'm finishing in two, three days; so tell me to send it after you to Tula or Kozlovka on the 3rd of June. That is, in truth, I want you to read the corrections of the epilogue without me and throw out and correct everything that you find necessary and come to us as soon as possible.

I didn't sleep at night and I'm angry and my head is weary and so this letter is confused, but I hope you understand me and forgive me.[‡]

Tolstoy wrote Sofia from Moscow: "I was completely angry and poured it out to Lyubimov [Katkov's editor in chief at the *Russian Herald*], who I met in the carriage coming to Moscow. But I didn't get too angry. I remembered: 'The spirit of patience and love.' [. . .] If I was angry, now it's gone."[§]

He said that on the advice of Strakhov's May 26 letter he would publish Part 8 separately, "without censors." It did after all go to a censor because it didn't reach 160 pages,

---

[*]   *PSS* 62: 326, letter of May 21–22, 1877.

[†]   Fedor Fedorovich Ris was the printer who had published *War and Peace* and Tolstoy's children's stories.

[‡]   *PSS* 62: 328, letter of May 28–29, 1877.

[§]   *PSS* 83: 237, letter of May 28–29, 1877.

the minimum for a book to get around a publishing law.* In the separate edition of Part 8 of *Anna Karenina* there are 127 pages.†

Tolstoy, back home, wrote Strakhov to tell him never mind about getting the corrections in Petersburg, to just come to Yasnaya Polyana as soon as possible, which Strakhov did, on June 10.‡ On that same date, Tolstoy published his angry letter, "To the Editor of *New Times*," about Katkov's rejection of Part 8 of *Anna Karenina*:

> Dear Sir,
>
> In the May issue of the *Russian Herald*, on page 472, there is a notice in the form of a completely inconspicuous footnote about the non-appearance in that issue of the last chapters of the novel *Anna Karenina*. This notice is so striking in its dutiful attitude toward the subscribers of the *Russian Herald*, its consideration toward the author of the novel and its masterly exposition, that I consider it would not be out of place to draw the attention of the public to it.
>
> "In the previous issue, the words 'to be concluded' were inserted at the foot of the novel *Anna Karenina*. But with the death of the heroine the novel proper finished. According to the author's plan a short epilogue of a couple of printer's sheets were to follow, from which the readers would learn that Vronsky, in grief and bewilderment after Anna's death, left for Serbia as a volunteer, and that all the others were alive and well, but that Levin remained in the country and was angry with the Slavonic committees and volunteers. The author will perhaps develop these chapters for a special edition of his novel."
>
> The dutiful attitude towards subscribers was expressed by the fact that, having refused to publish the ending of the novel, the editor, in his concern to satisfy the curiosity of his readers, told them the content of the unpublished part, and tried to assure them that the novel proper was finished and that there was nothing important to follow.
>
> The consideration towards the author was expressed by the fact that the editor not only did not allow the author to express harmful ideas, but indicated where his novel ought to end, and, without publishing the ending he wrote, artificially extracted and revealed to him and others the essence of that ending.

---

* See *PSS* 62: 328, footnote 2.

† *PSS* 83: 238, footnote 4.

‡ *PSS* 62: 329, letter of June 2, 1877.

The masterly exposition of the last, unpublished part of *Anna Karenina* makes one regret the fact that for three years the editor of the *Russian Herald* gave up so much space in his journal to this novel. With the same gracefulness and laconicism he could have recounted the whole novel in no more than ten lines.

But there is an error in this notice. It omits the fact that the last part of the novel was already set up and ready for printing in the May issue, but was not printed only because the author did not agree to cut out certain passages from it as the editor insisted, while the editor for his part did not agree to print it without their omission, although the author suggested that the editor might make any reservations he found necessary.

These last chapters of *Anna Karenina* are now being published separately.

I have the honour to be your obedient servant.

Count Lev Tolstoy*

What I didn't appreciate until I typed up his letter is that Tolstoy suggested that Katkov simply publish his disagreement with Tolstoy's Epilogue. That would have been the perfect compromise: point (the Epilogue), counterpoint (Katkov's nationalistic nonsense).

Sofia, however, would contend that "while Katkov did have the right not to publish in his magazine a work that he did not agree with, he did *not* have the right, after reading it, to steal the author's composition and present his own version to the magazine's subscribers. The ending of *Anna Karenina* had to be published and sold as a separate booklet. But Lev Nikolaevich's views did not ring true with every man. The public had a strong consensus as to the Serbo-Turkish war and the Russian volunteers' {participation in it}, and Lev Nikolaevich's denial of the whole scenario irritated the general public."†

At first I thought Sofia's was a fair representation of the dispute, but I was wrong. She seems to have been wanting to lay her husband out for criticism from two angles: one, he had been exposing his usual overconfidence in his own opinion; and two, as he had a blockbuster novel going, why alienate half the audience by criticizing the war?

But back to June 10 and Strakhov's arrival.

We can wish that Strakhov had kept a record of the conversations that he and his friend had over the next month. But Strakhov, as much as he loved and revered Tolstoy, was a discreet man and did not write about personal matters or his and Tolstoy's private conversations. He was more like Levin's half-brother Sergei in his dispassionate professional

---

*   Christian, *Tolstoy's Letters*, 305–306.

†   Tolstaya, *My Life*, 235.

attitude. He repeatedly proved a devoted friend, and though he appreciated as well as anyone ever has the novel that he helped not only encourage but to bring into the world, he didn't like attracting attention to himself. Chekhov later worried that the world was going to miss out on Tolstoy's everyday characteristics and conversations because he and his fellow Russians were too lazy or thoughtless to do what the English did concerning their great men, but by the late 1890s the Tolstoy house would be awash with quoters and noters. *

Fortunately for the sake of the literary record, in an 1880 "memo," Strakhov went as far as briefly describing his and Tolstoy's work at this time on the complete *Anna Karenina* manuscript:

> This volume is the copy of *Anna Karenina* from which the separate edition of 1878 was printed. It consists of sheets torn from *Russkij vestnik* [the *Russian Herald*] and includes corrections and changes in the author's own hand. But since my own hand is discernible in this too, I feel obliged to explain.
>
> In the summer of 1877 (June and July) I was visiting Lev Nikolaevich Tolstoy at Yasnaya Polyana, and suggested a review of *Anna Karenina*, with a view to preparing it for a separate edition. I set about a preliminary reading to correct punctuation and obvious errors, and to point out to Lev Nikolaevich places which for one reason or another seemed to be in need of improvement, mainly—almost exclusively, in fact—involving lack of clarity and incorrect use of language. Thus it came about that I did my reading and corrections first, and then Lev Nikolaevich did the same. It went on this way until halfway through the novel, but then Lev Nikolaevich got more and more involved in the work, overtook me, and I ended up doing my corrections after his. I would always take a look at his corrections first to make sure I had understood and interpreted [the text] in the right way, since afterward I would have to do the proofreading.
>
> Each morning, after a full discussion over coffee (which was served at noon on the terrace), we would part and sit down to work on the tasks at hand. I would work in the study, downstairs. It was agreed that an hour or a half-hour before dinner (5:00 o'clock) we should set out for a walk to refresh ourselves and work up an appetite. As pleasant as the work was for me, I, with my customary accuracy, rarely missed the appointed time and, after getting ready myself for the outing, I would go to summon Lev Nikolaevich. He almost always took

---

* Chekhov: "Goethe's words were all recorded, but Tolstoy's thoughts are being lost in the air. That, my dear fellow, is intolerably Russian. After his death they will all bestir themselves, will begin to write reminiscences, and will lie." Maxim Gorky, *Reminiscences of Leo Nikolaevich Tolstoy*, 47.

his time and sometimes it was difficult to tear him away from his work. In such cases signs of stress were all too evident. I would notice a rush of blood to the head, Lev Nikolaevich would be distracted and eat very little for dinner.

That was our daily routine for more than a month. The toilsome work bore its fruit. As much as I loved the novel in its original form, I was fairly quickly persuaded that Lev Nikolaevich's corrections were always done with amazing mastery, that they illuminated and deepened characteristics which had seemed clear enough before, and invariably blended in with the tone and spirit of the whole work. In respect to my corrections, almost all concerning language, I noticed another peculiarity which, while it did not surprise me, was quite conspicuous. Lev Nikolaevich was firm in his insistence on even his least significant turn of expression and would not agree to even the most innocent changes. From his explanations I was persuaded that he had a particular fondness for his language and that in spite of any apparent brusqueness or unevenness of flow, he carefully considered each of his words, each turn of phrase, in the same way as the most sensitive poet.

Indeed, I always marvelled at how much he thought, how much his mind worked, it struck me as something new each time we met, and it is only by such an amplitude of soul and mind that the power of his works can be explained.

St. Petersburg, April 18, 1880[*]

I'm inclined to take Strakhov's word for Tolstoy's "amazing mastery" in revising. When I review the list of revisions made by restoration editors of the Jubilee Edition, who decided that they should delete any inserted words made by Strakhov's pencil or Sofia's pen, I'm in an area where my Russian isn't good enough to judge the superiority of the corrections and clarifications in grammar and phrasing. In *A Karenina Companion*, the most significant stylistic changes that Professor C.J.G. Turner could find result only in moments of slightly higher definition or slightly different focus. For example, in Part 6, Chapter 32, the version Strakhov and Tolstoy completed reads:

"... that unavoidable business could crop up. Now, for instance, I shall have to go to Moscow about the house. ... Oh, Anna, why are you so irritable?"[†]

---

[*]   Donsko, *L. N. Tolstoy – N. N. Strakhov,* xxvii, http://feb-web.ru/feb/tolstoy/texts/selectpe /ts6/ts61013-.htm; Strakhov's second note concerned the typeset but redacted first draft of 64 pages in 1874 that features the *pre*-Anna Anna.

[†]   These are Turner's translations. (C.J.G. Turner, *A Tolstoy Companion,* 90.)

The restoration editors, V. A. Zhdanov and E. E. Zaidenshnur, replaced Strakhov's editings and, despite the likelihood that Strakhov was following Tolstoy's directions and despite that Tolstoy approved of the change, preserved this instead:

> ". . . that things could crop up, something unavoidable. Now, for instance, I shall have to go to Moscow about the house. . . . Oh, Anna, why do you get so irritated?"

One more example—and I remind myself that these two are about the biggest Turner could find:

> but there was no culprit. She suffered,

Restored:

> but there was no culprit. Even if there were no culprit, was it not possible simply to help her, to rescue her, but this too was not possible, was not necessary. She suffered,*

That "restored" version is not *better*, is it?

All the same, in the little refinements, it can be a pleasure to see Tolstoy's care and fussing. And it's useful for us to know that the language that he left us is exactly the language that he wanted. Professor Turner's point is that Tolstoy reviewed and accepted the tiny revisions and alterations made by Strakhov and Sofia *only* when they conformed to his own language, so efforts by the Soviet editors to purge the novel of Strakhov's and Sofia's emendations seem to have been mistaken. As Strakhov explained: "Lev Nikolaevich was firm in his insistence on even his least significant turn of expression and would not agree to even the most innocent changes."† And while Strakhov was impressed by the changes Tolstoy made from the *Russian Herald* serialized edition into

---

* These are Turner's translations. (C.J.G. Turner, *A Tolstoy Companion*, 91.)

† In this he was like his peasant-student Fedka: "Thus, for example, he would not allow words to be transposed; if he once said, 'I have sores on my feet,' he would not permit me to say, 'On my feet I have sores.' His soul, now softened and irritated by the sentiment of pity, that is, of love, clothed every image in an artistic form, and denied everything that did not correspond to the idea of eternal beauty and harmony." *Tolstoy on Education,* 196.

the "final form," they seem to me only a last scrubbing before presentation, except possibly in his intensifying of the final moments of Anna's life.[*]

✳

The publication of Part 8 as a booklet was dated Moscow, June 25, 1877. On page 3 was the following plainspoken note: "The last part of *Anna Karenina* comes out in a separate edition and not in the *Russian Herald* because the editors of that journal did not want to publish this part without deletions to which the author did not agree."[†]

Ever since May 2, 1877, when excited readers read the end of Part 7, there had been the question: What could possibly follow Anna's death?

If it's 1877, we would have to buy this continuation of the novel from our bookseller. It's a little longer than the journal installments, but we are not going anywhere until we finish it.

As we begin Chapter 1, Tolstoy places us in the consciousness of . . . *Sergei Ivanovich?* Readers, no matter how attentive, have to pause and remind themselves who "Sergei Ivanovich" is (no mention even of Sergei's last name to give us a clue). That's how third-string Levin's half-brother is. *His* drama? The most important thing that has happened to him recently is the loud silence that greeted his scholarly book that took him six years to write. This never happened to Tolstoy. When he wrote, readers were sensibly excited to see what he had come up with. *Anna Karenina* had cost him four years, but by the time Tolstoy wrote about Sergei's disappointment, he knew that his novel was, and would be for some time, a sensation. Poor Sergei! His book vanishes as soon as it appears. Just as it usually happens for the rest of us.

What was Tolstoy thinking in starting the last part of his famous novel with a peripheral character who is known mostly for his intellectual and emotional conventionality and coolness? Or perhaps that summation explains it?

Unlike Trollope, who is famous for addressing us, his readers, on among other topics the process of writing the very novel that he knows we are holding in our hands, Tolstoy

---

[*]   I had become convinced that Tolstoy never read the novel after it was printed as a book; then I stumbled back across a quotation of a reminiscence by L. E. Obolenskii in Turner's book: "'Willy nilly I have just been reading the proofs of my *Anna Karenina* and all the time I was thinking: what a bad man (Tolstoy used a much stronger expression) it was to write such filth. . . . Well, wasn't I right when I said that this novel was written by a very bad man?'" (See C.J.G. Turner. *A Tolstoy Companion*, 51.) This proofreading was for an 1886 edition of his *Works*. Sofia soon relied on herself and Strakhov and others to do the proofreading.

[†]   *PSS* 62: 328.

never explains why he chooses to describe one scene or character at any given moment over another.

Almost everybody (due only partly to Katkov's dismissive summary in the journal) *did* think that Anna's death was the end of the novel. Tolstoy restarting it with Levin's half-brother gives us the feeling that it could have restarted with anybody; everybody's life has gone on, even as Anna's has been extinguished. As Sergei advocates for Russian military involvement in Serbia, we return to her story, as if by accident.

In Chapter 2, Sergei and an unnamed princess are talking at a Moscow train station when Stiva comes along. Stiva is his usual social self—but we know, that is, remember, that though he is caught up in the public enthusiasm for the war, he is still conscious of his dear sister. He is distracted:

> But the fact that Sergey Ivanovitch and the princess seemed anxious to get rid of him did not in the least disconcert Stepan Arkadyevitch. Smiling, he stared at the feather in the princess's hat, and then about him as though he were going to pick something up.*†

The princess mentions to Stiva that Vronsky is leaving on this train. Now watch this: he is affected for a moment but then forgets his suffering over Anna. I do not and never did—I think—believe it:

> For an instant Stepan Arkadyevitch's face looked sad, but a minute later, when, stroking his mustaches and swinging as he walked, he went into the hall where Vronsky was, he had completely forgotten his own despairing sobs over his sister's corpse, and he saw in Vronsky only a hero and an old friend.‡

If I had been in Strakhov's shoes, I would have squawked: *No! That's not true, my most esteemed Lev Nikolaevich! Stiva has* not *forgotten! You know that Anna Pirogova's mangled*

---

* Garnett's translation "as though he were going to pick something up" puzzled me. The Maudes (and almost everyone else) translate this phrase [как будто припоминая что-то] as "as if trying to remember something." I like, in any case, that Garnett reminds us that remembering is an attempt to put our finger on something.

† *Anna Karenina*, Part 8, Chapter 2, http://www.literatureproject.com/anna-karenina/anna_222.htm.

‡ Ibid.

body that you saw in the local station has been haunting you ever since January 1872! Stiva could not have forgotten his dear sister's fate.

Anna's autopsy is sharply recalled in Stiva's imagination, but then—by Tolstoy's pen—immediately purged. I refuse to believe it, but Stiva, the golden boy of the first half of the novel, our always favorite company, is so out of favor with his creator by now that Tolstoy won't even allow him a normal bout of grief. Good grief!

In Chapter 3 Tolstoy exposes the thoughtlessness and hypocrisy of Sergei's and his friend Katavasov's support for the war (again, there's no doubt where Tolstoy's sympathies lie), and then in Chapter 4, still at the station, Sergei goes and talks to Vronsky's mother. Tolstoy has pulled us a couple of degrees of separation away from Anna . . . to talk about her.

This was not just an artistic decision; I think Tolstoy needed to pull away, to get away from the middle of the rushing stream and find eddies. Sergei and Madame Vronsky are eddies. Madame Vronsky lets her resentment out, which is understandable, if you like, in that she's a horribly mean old woman:

> "[. . .] You know, of course, that he had shot himself once already on her account," she said, and the old lady's eyelashes twitched at the recollection. "Yes, hers was the fitting end for such a woman. Even the death she chose was low and vulgar."[*]

Any reader who condemns Anna's morality should have to explain why Tolstoy puts that argument into the mouth of the novel's vilest woman. Nevertheless, Madame Vronsky's recounting of getting the news is chilling and sets me atremble:

> "[. . .] my Mary told me a lady had thrown herself under the train. Something seemed to strike me at once. I knew it was she. [. . .]"[†]

And Madame Vronsky goes on! How *damaged* Vronsky was! She is understandable in her hatred if she would just focus on her son, but her contempt of Anna reminds us again that Madame V is a nasty piece of work:

---

[*]   *Anna Karenina,* Part 8, Chapter 4, http://www.literatureproject.com/anna-karenina/anna _224.htm.

[†]   Ibid.

"Oh, why talk of it!" said the countess with a wave of her hand. "It was an awful time! No, say what you will, she was a bad woman. Why, what is the meaning of such desperate passions? It was all to show herself something out of the way. Well, and that she did do. She brought herself to ruin and two good men—her husband and my unhappy son."[*]

On and on. She rues her destroyed son by condemning Anna:

"[. . .] No, say what you will, her very death was the death of a vile woman, of no religious feeling. God forgive me, but I can't help hating the memory of her, when I look at my son's misery!"[†]

That religious woman then thanks God for having sent them the Serbian war to rouse her son a little.

She has also mentioned in her conversation with Levin's half-brother that "Karenin came to the funeral. But we tried to prevent his meeting Alexey." Hearing of such a scene secondhand, I realize that Trollope, Dickens, Dostoevsky, and Hugo would have given us the funeral: we would have seen Karenin and Vronsky over her coffin. I think of what Trollope did for Glencora Palliser, who, we discover when we open *The Duke's Children*, the sixth and final novel in the Palliser series, has died! All through that novel, she scarcely leaves her husband's or children's memories—or Trollope's. We continuously recall her follies, her wit, her personality. But Tolstoy doesn't roll that way.

He has us revisit the memory of Anna, but only several weeks after her death, and it's grim, grim, grim.

In Chapter 5, Tolstoy makes the usual genius stroke that no one else in the world ever would have thought of: Vronsky, grieving, organizing troops to go to Serbia with him, has a terrible toothache. At a moment when the tormented Vronsky is grateful for Sergei's cheerful encouragement, he perceives beside him, along the rails, a big wheel of a train rolling in:

And all at once a different pain, not an ache, but an inner trouble, that set his whole being in anguish, made him for an instant forget his toothache. As he glanced at the tender and the rails, under the influence of the conversation

---

[*]   *Anna Karenina*, Part 8, Chapter 4, http://www.literatureproject.com/anna-karenina/anna_224.htm.

[†]   Ibid.

with a friend he had not met since his misfortune, he suddenly recalled *her*—that is, what was left of her when he had run like one distraught into the cloak room of the railway station—on the table shamelessly sprawling out among strangers, the bloodstained body so lately full of life; the head unhurt dropping back with its weight of hair, and the curling tresses about the temples, and the exquisite face, with red, half-opened mouth, the strange, fixed expression, piteous on the lips and awful in the still open eyes, that seemed to utter that fearful phrase—that he would be sorry for it—that she had said when they were quarreling.*

It goes on—Vronsky tries to remember Anna as she was at the *beginning*, but he instead remembers *everything* and sobs. Poor man![†] He didn't know her as much as we seemed to, but he is now in his suffering beyond us. We can have tears in our eyes, but we don't have his suffering. As wrecked as we know we would be in real life, we are only reading a novel and can return to her again and again in all her vividness; we can remember her as she was in the beginning, as she *is* in her vitality up to her very death.

Vronsky's breakdown is for me another end of the novel.

But where is Levin? In Chapter 6, Sergei and Katavasov travel to Levin's estate. Levin's suicidal-thoughts drama creates no tension.

All that spring he was not himself, and went through fearful moments of horror.

"Without knowing what I am and why I am here, life's impossible; and that I can't know, and so I can't live," Levin said to himself.

"In infinite time, in infinite matter, in infinite space, is formed a bubble-organism, and that bubble lasts a while and bursts, and that bubble is Me."

It was an agonizing terror, but it was the sole logical result of ages of human thought in that direction.

This was the ultimate belief on which all the systems elaborated by human thought in almost all their ramifications rested. It was the prevalent conviction,

---

* *Anna Karenina*, Part 8, Chapter 5, http://www.literatureproject.com/anna-karenina/anna_225.htm.

† And what of Tolstoy's acquaintance, the landowner Bibikov and *his* Anna? Bibikov must have seen the same crushed body that Tolstoy saw, but *he* was not deflected from marrying the lover who had supplanted desperate Anna Pirogova. Vronsky certainly is a more romantic hero than the real-life Bibikov.

and of all other explanations Levin had unconsciously, not knowing when or how, chosen it, as anyway the clearest, and made it his own.

But it was not merely a falsehood, it was the cruel jeer of some wicked power, some evil, hateful power, to whom one could not submit.

He must escape from this power. And the means of escape every man had in his own hands. He had but to cut short this dependence on evil. And there was one means—death.

And Levin, a happy father and husband, in perfect health, was several times so near suicide that he hid the cord that he might not be tempted to hang himself, and was afraid to go out with his gun for fear of shooting himself.

But Levin did not shoot himself, and did not hang himself; he went on living.[*]

There is on the other hand tension in Tolstoy's description in *Confession* of his own very similar situation:

> It was indeed terrible. And to rid myself of the terror I wished to kill myself. I experienced terror at what awaited me—knew that that terror was even worse than the position I was in, but still I could not patiently await the end. However convincing the argument might be that in any case some vessel in my heart would give way, or something would burst and all would be over, I could not patiently await that end. The horror of darkness was too great, and I wished to free myself from it as quickly as possible by noose or bullet. That was the feeling which drew me most strongly toward suicide.[†]

Anna has the same conviction, logic, and terror as Tolstoy described there. But when this same exact string of events happens to *Levin*, it doesn't touch me and it sure doesn't touch Tolstoy; it's as if he's reviewing last year's bad storm. When Tolstoy is talking about his terrors in *Confession*, the effect is the same as when he presents them as Anna's.

So why is Levin able to go on living when Anna couldn't?

---

[*] *Anna Karenina*, Part 8, Chapter 9, http://www.literatureproject.com/anna-karenina/anna_229.htm.

[†] *Confession*, 22–23.

In Chapter 12: "Levin strode along the highroad, absorbed not so much in his thoughts (he could not yet disentangle them) as in his spiritual condition, unlike anything he had experienced before."*

I remember being completely caught up in Levin's joyful clear understanding—and I used to feel his joy as he triumphs over the cunning cheat called Reason:

> [. . .] he briefly went through, mentally, the whole course of his ideas during the last two years, the beginning of which was the clear confronting of death at the sight of his dear brother hopelessly ill.
>
> Then, for the first time, grasping that for every man, and himself too, there was nothing in store but suffering, death, and forgetfulness, he had made up his mind that life was impossible like that, and that he must either interpret life so that it would not present itself to him as the evil jest of some devil, or shoot himself.†

My comment at the moment of rereading this was "Does this have *anything* to do with Anna?" It is a comment rather than a question, because I'm suggesting that Tolstoy doesn't have Anna on his mind anymore, either. Even though readers are still thinking about her, to Levin, *she is out of sight, out of mind.* Levin does not think of her in connection to himself and suicide, and Tolstoy does not think of Levin's suicidal thoughts in connection to Anna.

Why not? Why wouldn't the smitten Levin remember suicidal Anna when he himself—so soon after—became suicidal?

Nikolai Gudziy, in his account of the drafts of the novel, points out that in Variant 198, Levin went to see Anna's dead body.‡

In her study of the editor Katkov's influence on the history of great Russian novels, Susanne Fusso points out that despite Katkov's many faults, particularly concerning this novel and its epilogue, "He makes the keen-eyed observation that [. . .] the characters seem strangely unaffected by her terrible death. [In his *Russian Herald* article "What Happened after the Death of Anna Karenina"] Katkov inserts his journal into the fictional world of the characters: 'Quite a few people have gathered at the family home of the Liovins [In

---

* *Anna Karenina*, Part 8, Chapter 12, http://www.literatureproject.com/anna-karenina/anna _232.htm.

† Ibid.

‡ *PSS* 20: 639.

Slavic studies, *Liovin* has become the new English rendering of *Levin*], Sergei Ivanovich is there, and Katavasov, and the old prince, and Dolly with her children, they talk about a lot of things, but for this whole company it is as if the terrible episode which so struck even readers who knew Anna only from stories, and not from personal acquaintance like these people, had not happened. As if the fourth issue of the *Russian Herald* had not yet reached Liovin's estate.'"*

Tolstoy had had Anna on his mind the entire time that he was going through his suicidal period. So *Anna* saved Tolstoy. Who or what saved Levin?

Why is Levin, a person who has everything going for him, having to hide a gun from himself?

[. . .] it was clear to him that he could only live by virtue of the beliefs in which he had been brought up.

"What should I have been, and how should I have spent my life, if I had not had these beliefs, if I had not known that I must live for God and not for my own desires? I should have robbed and lied and killed. Nothing of what makes the chief happiness of my life would have existed for me." And with the utmost stretch of imagination he could not conceive the brutal creature he would have been himself, if he had not known what he was living for.

"I looked for an answer to my question. And thought could not give an answer to my question—it is incommensurable with my question. The answer has been given me by life itself, in my knowledge of what is right and what is wrong. And that knowledge I did not arrive at in any way, it was given to me as to all men, *given*, because I could not have gotten it from anywhere.

"Where could I have gotten it? By reason could I have arrived at knowing that I must love my neighbor and not oppress him? I was told that in my childhood, and I believed it gladly, for they told me what was already in my soul. But who discovered it? Not reason. Reason discovered the struggle for existence, and the law that requires us to oppress all who hinder the satisfaction of our desires. That is the deduction of reason. But loving one's neighbor reason could never discover, because it's irrational."†

---

* She spells Levin *Liovin*, which may have been how Tolstoy pronounced Levin. Susanne Fusso, *Editing Turgenev*, 201.

† *Anna Karenina*, Part 8, Chapter 12, http://www.literatureproject.com/anna-karenina/anna_232.htm.

If that's not a good philosophy, it's at least a good dramatization of how we satisfy ourselves with homespun philosophizing.

> "This new feeling has not changed me, has not made me happy and enlightened all of a sudden, as I had dreamed, just like the feeling for my child. There was no surprise in this, either. Faith—or not faith—I don't know what it is—but this feeling has come just as imperceptibly through suffering, and has taken firm root in my soul.
>
> "I shall go on in the same way, losing my temper with Ivan the coachman, falling into angry discussions, expressing my opinions tactlessly; there will be still the same wall between the holy of holies of my soul and other people, even my wife; I shall still go on scolding her for my own terror, and being remorseful for it; I shall still be as unable to understand with my reason why I pray, and I shall still go on praying; but my life now, my whole life apart from anything that can happen to me, every minute of it is no more meaningless, as it was before, but it has the positive meaning of goodness, which I have the power to put into it."*

Levin's happy and inspiring resolution is satisfying and gives us hope.

Tolstoy followed Anna, on the other hand, to the ultimate end. He imagined suicide as far as the imagination can go. Doing so, he pulled himself up just short of the abyss.

✳

In the beginning of July Tolstoy wrote a gossipy letter to Fet about his old friend D'yakov's wedding: "I went off to my sister at Kresta and there found out striking news—D'yakov was marrying Sofesh, his former governess. My wife writes me that she's going to the wedding and calls me. I went to Nikol'ski and from there to D'yakov's, where I was present at an unpleasant to me wedding of a fifty-five-year-old old fellow to a thirty-two-year-old young woman and at his caresses and such in front of his married daughter. It's impossible to judge; but to me it was oppressive and awkward."† (At the moment, Tolstoy was a forty-eight-year-old old fellow; Sofia, a thirty-two-year-old young woman.)

---

*   *Anna Karenina*, Part 8, Chapter 19, http://www.literatureproject.com/anna-karenina/anna_239.htm.

†   *PSS* 62: 332, letter of July 4–5, 1877.

He wrote Strakhov: "My adventures without you are the following: I went to an unpleasant for me wedding, then, having returned, found guests, went hunting, and *played croquet* [my italics] and received guests, and despite all this succeeded in rereading and redoing Karenina—so that in three days I hope to finish. Yesterday Ris was here, he brought the last part. There are mistakes, but the edition is good."*

It's important for me to remember, and which I do wish Tolstoy would have specifically mentioned in *Confession*: In the midst of his searching for the meaning of life in the 1870s, he was also taking trips, attending weddings, hunting, writing the greatest novel in history, *and using a mallet to hit little round wooden balls through tiny gates.* Chekhov might describe in stories such details as that, but not Tolstoy.

In Tolstoy's letters from the end of June and here, on July 11–12, he had moved on from buying horses from Fet to buying dogs from him. He asked Fet to send along to him "that dog."

In late July, Tolstoy and Strakhov set off for the Optina Monastery, where they had wanted to visit the previous summer. Tolstoy wrote Sofia a note from there about his plans and return. Strakhov and Tolstoy were at Fet's on July 29–30.† Did Strakhov feel as if he was one of the boys, or an extra?

Tolstoy wrote Sofia a note from Tula in the beginning of August mentioning Katkov's response to his letter to *New Times*, "but," he declared, "I won't be further annoyed."‡

Tolstoy was back home by August 10–11, intending to take up again a novel about the Decembrists. He seems never to have written a creative word in July or August, so his impressive excuse to Strakhov for *not* starting, which came in the midst of his indulgence in his passionate pastime ("I've been hunting, and also to my brother's, and tomorrow I'm going hunting again a long way off for wolves"), should be taken with a pood of salt: "There's now only the family here—just Styopa—and I would like to begin work but I can't because of the war. Whether I'm in a good or bad frame of mind, the thought of the war overclouds everything for me. Not the war itself, but the problem of our insolvency which must be resolved at once. [. . .]"§

Sofia sympathized with his writer's block. She recalled him explaining to her at the time of this Turkish war: "I can't do any work. I can't write while the war is on. Just as

---

*   *PSS* 62: 333, letter of July 10, 1877.

†   *PSS* 62: 332, footnote 1.

‡   *PSS* 83: 240.

§   Christian, *Tolstoy's Letters*, 306, August 10–11, 1877.

when a fire is raging somewhere, there's nothing that can be accomplished."* Nothing except visiting a monastery and hanging out with friends and hunting wolves.

In mid-August, Tolstoy wrote and thanked Strakhov again:[†] "How grateful I am to you for your work on Anna Karenina.—I read through [Katkov's] *Russian Herald* article and was very annoyed at this confident impudence [. . .] but now I've calmed down."[‡]

About *Anna Karenina* being blamed for a perceived increase of suicide, Strakhov wrote Tolstoy: "In the *Voice*, from August 14, a columnist writes: 'but suicide doesn't stop and even more often ones are throwing themselves on the rails, like Anna Karenina; isn't this the influence of this novel?'—this is strange! I would think that at the time of war there wouldn't be suicides."[§]

Not only that, but could anyone be persuaded to commit suicide by *Anna Karenina*? How many suicides besides Tolstoy's own did it *prevent*?

Strakhov, still devotedly on the job, wrote Tolstoy: "If it would at all alleviate you that you don't read the corrections of *Anna Karenina*, I'd be very glad to, because, really, that work is especially pleasant to me. I very much love that finally it will be published spaciously and clearly so that it will be doubly easy for the reader; I attribute a lot to my punctuation—and I imagine with how much delight the readers will be who are reading it for the first time."[¶] Tolstoy of course accepted his pal's offer.

In a September letter, in the midst of proofreading the novel, Strakhov summarized for Tolstoy the reviews of Part 8, and had a suggestion:

> Of the reproaches that they have made, only one has sense. Everyone noticed that you don't want to dwell on Karenina's death. And you told me that you were against heightening that pity which was excited there. I ever since have not understood that feeling that has guided you. Maybe I can guess, but help me. The latest version of that death-scene is so dry that it's frightening. I, however, think that it's scarcely comfortable to offer readers a new edition when all the details of that ending have already been etched into their memories. I am sending you both editions—copied out, and I'm ashamed to trouble you,

---

*   Tolstaya, *My Life*, 237.

†   Donskov, *L. N. Tolstoy – N. N. Strakhov*, 353.

‡   *PSS* 62: 337, letter of August 15–16, 1877.

§   Donskov, *L. N. Tolstoy – N. N. Strakhov*, 356, August 16–17, 1877.

¶   Donskov, *L. N. Tolstoy – N. N. Strakhov*, 359, August 25, 1877.

tearing you away from your new work [*ha!*]—I ask you to look again whether you want to leave the second?

The printing is going along all right, though the typography does not do what it could. I, however, am corresponding with Ris.*

Strakhov's assessment of Anna's death as "dry" is one that has puzzled me. Tolstoy drives with Anna down to Hell. Tolstoy's revisions for the book edition only heightened the intensity, and this upset Strakhov.

Here is Anna's suicide in the *Russian Herald*:

> The first wagon came, the second only began to come up. Taking off from her arm the red little bag, she went even closer and bent under the wagon. And feeling that she was completing something important, more important than anything that she had done in her life, she as by habit raised her hand, crossed herself and leaning with her hands on her shoulders on the crossties, went down on her knees and bent her head. The customary gesture of crossing herself called up in her soul a whole series of memories of the important moments of her life, particularly as a girl and child. She felt that she loved life in a way she had never loved it before. "Where am I? What am I doing? Why?" She wanted to get up, but something gigantic, relentlessly merciless, gripped her, pushed and dragged her by the back. "Lord, forgive me all!" she said. *The dirty sand and coal came nearer to her sight. She fell face first onto them.* A peasant saying something worked on the iron. And the candle by which she was reading the book filled with anxiety, misery, insults and evil, flickered, flared, reddened, and completely extinguished.†

Those two sentences I italicized did not get into the novel. They provide a hard detail. It's a true detail, but Tolstoy didn't after all want it. It would dirty Anna, if only superficially.

If the magazine scene was not as intense as in the final version, it was because in Tolstoy's head her suicide was not over. There was more he had to see and imagine, and Strakhov was shocked—because the final version is even more devastating. There's no gainsaying Strakhov's argument that Anna's death wouldn't have etched itself into the memories of the readers, but its intensification or heightening (increased "dryness"?) would

---

* Donskov, *L. N. Tolstoy – N. N. Strakhov*, 364, September 8, 1877.

† Gusev, *Materials*, 320–321.

be felt rather than compared to the original. Her death is so overwhelmingly, terrifyingly *experiential*. There's nothing comparable to it in the arts except perhaps Don Giovanni's being dragged into Hell near the end of Mozart's opera.

Tolstoy replied:

> I didn't answer your last two letters, dear Nikolay Nikolaevich. You think up excuses to apologize to me, and I in the whole letter don't know how to begin thanking you, and I'm not thanking you because otherwise the whole letter would be filled with only thanks: and you're bored probably for all your work on this edition, and for the unusual attention that you give to it, and for the summations of the journals about Karenina, which I wouldn't want to read but know that I'm very pleased. [. . .] As to your proposal to add the words to the corrections, I'm grateful, but if possible have them send them to me and I'll look. [. . .] You understood from my letter that I was at work. No. I hunt and I assemble, but I can't sit at my desk other than to write letters. [. . .]
>
> I feel myself today in bad spirits and I'm writing poorly and, I'm afraid, coldly, but I always want to express how much I feel for you—always with a carefully respectful tenderness.[*]

The Jubilee editors write that Strakhov's proposal was to restore Anna's confused exclamations: "Where am I? What am I doing? What for?" in the last paragraph of Part 7. Tolstoy had cut them from the book edition but he relented to Strakhov's request and restored them.[†] I could do without them.

✳

Sofia wrote to her sister on September 28 about Tolstoy's mood: "Levochka is somewhat gloomy. He either spends whole days hunting or he sits in the room silently reading; if he argues or speaks he's gloomy and unhappy. The war very much disturbs him and so he can't write."[‡] That same day, from where he was attending to regional election business, he sent Sofia a telegram to say that he would be home the next day.[§] Occasionlly we can

---

[*]   *PSS* 62: 343, letter of September 22–23, 1877.

[†]   *PSS* 62: 344, footnote 4.

[‡]   *PSS* 62: 344, footnote 5.

[§]   *PSS* 83: 241, letter of September 28, 1877.

see for a fleeting moment Tolstoy as Vronsky and Sofia as forlorn Anna. But unimaginative Vronsky, even though he once shot himself, never got depressed, or even gloomy, or sat at a desk *not* composing a novel. And Sofia, though she would try several times over the next four decades to kill herself, never committed suicide.

In mid-October Tolstoy corresponded with Strakhov about the *Anna Karenina* corrections for the complete book, which would be called "the second edition," as opposed to the "first edition," which was the magazine serialization. "I'm ashamed to look at the last page of *Anna Karenina* which you copied out," Tolstoy told Strakhov. "Of course I agree with you and with the insertion. [. . .] I'm still doing nothing except hunting and shooting hares, and feel ill physically and morally. I'm depressed. But still I often think about you, as always, and love you."*

Strakhov was working away at the corrections and Tolstoy was again in the dumps. He was free of what he thought of as the disgusting novel, which he had been blaming for his depression and sense of purposelessness—but he was now free of it and doing what he did in other fall-times: hunting! doing business! feeling low! He hadn't decided to give up fiction, but the grand "people's novel" was not coming to him and neither would the novel of the Decembrists.

So was *Anna Karenina* really a distraction?

No.

He wrote out his own suicide in it and thereby prevented it from really happening. To disentangle his depression, the supreme literary artist needed the challenge of composing the novel; art forced him to reach his cleverest, deepest, best self. He complained about the novel being an obstacle, but it was exactly what he needed. Its flower was Anna.

Depressed, he wrote again to Strakhov, who was grieving over the death of a friend:

> I only wanted to write you, dear Nikolay Nikolaevich, namely in order to ask you what you're doing with yourself, whether or not you are in woe, if you really couldn't be attracted to work, when I received your letter.
>
> I'm very sorry for you; by the tone in which you spoke about the deceased, I feel that he was very close to you and dear.—It seems to me that from what I know about him from you that I clearly understand his character, and he is very sweet to me. The more I feel for you the less I'm able to cheer you up, and I very lately was in the same depression, sadness, beaten state of soul. Really, I don't know where it came from; if I knew, I would fight it. But the two main

---

* Christian, *Tolstoy's Letters*, 307, October 19, 1877.

pretexts of my sadness are my idleness and complete shame, and the situation of my wife, sick and pregnant, in preparation of a December birth. A much less important reason: this tormenting war.[*]

I know that it's wrong of me to complain, but I do so in my own heart, and to no one but you. It's agonising and humiliating to live in complete idleness and it's repulsive to console myself by saying that I'm sparing myself and waiting for inspiration. It's all petty and worthless. If I were alone I wouldn't be a monk, I would be a yurodivy [a holy fool], i.e., I wouldn't value anything in life and wouldn't do anybody any harm.

Please don't try to console me, especially by saying that I'm a writer. I've been consoling myself like this for too long already, and better than you can, but it has no effect; just listen to my complaints and that will console me. [. . .][†]

They were *both* in low spirits.

Tolstoy resorted to his usual remedies: first, the complete indulgence of his passion for hunting. Sofia remembered: "Lev Nikolaevich was alarmed by my situation [her pregnancy; she couldn't walk "without assistance"]. He often said there was an emptiness in his head and he couldn't work. So all during October he would go on daily hunts either with the borzois or with the hounds. Every feast-day and every Sunday he would take with him his elder sons, Serezha and Ilya. Neither the weather or any sort of fatigue would stop Lev Nikolaevich—except for guests, but sometimes not even then."[‡]

But the weather did finally interfere with his outdoor recreation, she recalled: "When hunting got uncomfortable, in November Lev Nikolaevich began taking up music once again, and would play for up to several hours at a time. Sometimes we would play four-handed pieces. I was not a skillful player to begin with, and my large tummy kept making this activity more and more impossible. My situation kept causing more and more embarrassment and alarm for Lev Nikolaevich."[§]

Can we imagine Tolstoy embarrassed and alarmed by her pregnancy? Was he always like this? Sofia had been pregnant at least nine times. Does she mean that he worried she would bump the unborn baby's head as she leaned into the keyboard? Where does the *embarrassment* come into it? Were they playing for company and was her pregnancy

---

[*]   *PSS* 62: 347, letter of November 6, 1877.

[†]   Christian, *Tolstoy's Letters,* 308, November 6, 1877.

[‡]   Tolstaya, *My Life,* 241.

[§]   Ibid.

especially conspicuous at the piano? Did she simply mean us to understand that he was fussy and annoying when she was pregnant, a "situation" that he had put her in?

On November 11, Strakhov wrote to complain about the slowness of the printing of *Anna Karenina* by Ris. It was only half-done and Ris wasn't answering Strakhov's letters.* Tolstoy replied to Strakhov to say that for his part he was just sitting around, feeling disgusted by the war and playing the piano.

We learn from his letter to his brother from the second half of November that Sofia was due December 2, "carries very heavily," and "is quite unwell."† Tolstoy communicated much the same about Sofia's health to Fet.‡

Her health was plenty to worry about, but we seem to be in a different atmosphere. The *creating* of *Anna Karenina* has gone clear out of his head.

And what does that mean?

It means that when Tolstoy-the-artist's work was done he was no longer in that spirit. It's not exactly the shoemaker's reaction to having made another pair of shoes; it's more like an architect's having completed a project and now that it's done, he doesn't have much to do with when or how the tenants move in.

But his mood continued to be gloomy. So Tolstoy bought more horses. In late November he wrote Fet again, asking him to send him the stallion "about which we spoke" and wondering if Fet would sell the gray mares. He added: "I recognize that I've fallen out of spirits and I'm not even fighting it. I wait."§

Sofia gave birth to their son Andrey at three in the morning on December 6.

Tolstoy wrote to D'yakov and to his sister on the birth date to give them the news. It was, he told Maria, "easier than we expected."¶ Sofia, however, remembered it differently: "The labor was difficult and dragged on for an extended period of time. The baby's head was exceptionally large, and it took me a fairly long time to recover after the birth."**

✳

---

*   Donskov, *L. N. Tolstoy – N. N. Strakhov*, 376.

†   *PSS* 62: 350.

‡   On November 16, 1877.

§   *PSS* 62: 351–352, letter of November 23–24, 1877.

¶   *PSS* 62: 354.

**   Tolstaya, *My Life*, 242.

I confess that even after I had been working for years on this book I became so accustomed to the renunciating Tolstoy that I kept ignoring all the evidence that he was an active businessperson. We are used to believing in Tolstoy's dramatic breaks from his past because he himself made such a big deal of them. But Tolstoy, like all the rest of us, never stopped being himself. There was business to be taken care of, and sometime in the week after his son Andrey's birth, he wrote a good business note to Nikolay Nagornov. (It was also about family business, as Tolstoy told his niece's husband that baby Andrey hadn't even been named yet.) He insisted to Nagornov that he wouldn't pay a bookseller of *Anna Karenina* 35% but only the agreed-upon 30%.

He was not on a religious crusade or a guilt trip. He was wheeling and dealing again, but his interest in business feels surprising, similar to finding out that one's priest or rabbi or imam is good at poker. But why am I surprised when for forty years I have been reading how Levin, Tolstoy's conventional alter-ego, alertly does business?

Is it that *Anna Karenina* is for me a holy book, a work of art, and so how could its creator think of money?

No.

Reading of *Trollope*'s life, I always admire his publishing negotiations; I root for him to get the largest sums for his novels, and so I do here, for Tolstoy.

Tolstoy wrote V. A. Islavin about buying land for him. He also mentioned that Sofia had just had a baby: "And though for me it's an old thing, it always excites and touches and makes me feel joyful."*

On the same day as his letter to Islavin, he wrote Strakhov. He mentioned his wife's childbirth and that he had started writing. The Jubilee editors say that he was working not only on the Decembrists novel but on an unfinished religious-philosophical work, by which I believe they mean *Confession*.

The third letter of the day, the longest and most personal, was to B. N. Chicherin, an old acquaintance who had sent him a book. It's on these days of multiple letters that we can see the evidence of Tolstoy's mood and audience. We can't really see that in the novel. We can't point at a sentence or paragraph or chapter and say: *Tolstoy was in a bad mood, a feisty mood, a cheerful mood.* We can make those assessments with the letters. Tolstoy would soon develop an unpleasant attitude about child-death (they're better off!), but here he was speaking as one with experience of suffering. The Chicherins had lost their infant children a few years before:

---

*   *PSS* 62: 356, letter of December 10, 1877.

I heard about your woe, and both my wife and I sympathize. I'm glad that you now have hope and a goal in life, but my judgment argues with yours. I don't agree that for the health and safety of the baby it's more convenient to live in Moscow. In the village the doctor is far but God is much closer than in the city. At least it always seems so to me. Especially in the Samara region, where we were living with a baby at the breast 130 versts from town. And this baby died within a month after we returned—in the hands of a doctor.

I'm writing you from the birth room of my wife, who 5 days ago gave birth to a little one, the 9th baby in all, of whom 6 are living and the oldest boy already speaks with a bass and translates Cicero.[*]

He was in an energetic mood as he encouraged the Chicherins not to give up on having children nor to worry too much about *where* to have the children.

He wrote his brother to invite him to Andrey's christening.[†]

In late December, Strakhov wrote Tolstoy about the final corrections of the novel:

Maybe you're finding *Karenina* a strange juxtaposition to your new baby. But for me it is so. Three days ago I sent off the last sheet of corrections—and ever since then I'm still full up with Karenina; toward the end of the reading of corrections, the excited delight continued (for me) and I was nearly in tears. I fell terribly in love with your novel. When I hear judgments of it, which continue (in *The Voice* three articles by Martov I still haven't read), everything comes to my thought from the old princess about Levin: "He's so light-minded!" That's absolutely the way all the judges understand your novel—judging your light-mindedness by their own.

I say only the seriousness of your tone is simply frightening. There has never been such a serious novel in the world.

In reward I ask you—have them send me two copies of the novel—one for me, the other to give to *reading*.[‡]

---

[*]   *PSS* 62: 358, letter of December 10, 1877.

[†]   *PSS* 62: 362, letter of December 20–23, 1877.

[‡]   Donskov, *L. N. Tolstoy – N. N. Strakhov*, 387–388, December 24–27, 1877.

Strakhov is reminding us that amid its everlasting attractions, *Anna Karenina* is most terribly serious and that despite his own recent wholly absorbed work on it, he knows that he will want to read it again. There is no literary experience like it.

✳

As 1877 came to a close, *Anna Karenina* remained seemingly completely out of Tolstoy's head and heart. Whatever labor he had put into it, whatever feeling he had poured into it, it was past. The novel came to represent a kind of life and type of fiction that he could not approve of; it was full of his life during an unhappy and difficult time. It evoked *shame*. In 1881, he wrote V. V. Stasov: "Concerning *Karenina*, I assure you that for me that abomination does not exist, and it is only annoying to me that there are people to whom it is of any value."*

The Jubilee editors tell us that in the *Moscow News* of December 25, 1877, an advertisement appeared: "In the bookstore of Ivan Grigor'evich Solov'ev, on Strastniy Boulevard, in the house of Alekseev, is the just published and put out for sale book Anna Karenina. Novel. (In 8 parts, 3 volumes.) By Count L'ev Nik. Tolstoy. Cost 6 rubles, by post 7 rubles. At the same time for sale: The Works of Count Tolstoy, 11 volumes, in which are placed Childhood, Boyhood, Youth, stories, War stories, War and Peace and the novel Anna Karenina. Price 16 rubles, 50 kop., by post 18 rubles."†

But is it possible that Solov'ev had *advance* copies on December 25? Or was he just tantalizing the appetites of his customers for the mid-January publication? According to Strakhov, after all, the last corrections had only just been made.

On December 29, Tolstoy was in Moscow "to look for a new teacher,"‡ recalled Sofia, after they had fired the drunk tutor Jules Rey, who, Tolstoy wrote Strakhov, "had become intolerable because of his rudeness and bad character."§

Poor Rey never wrote his own account of living with the Tolstoys and neither did their other employees, except one German governess. Why didn't they? By the 1890s, they would have understood that Lev Tolstoy was world famous. The Tolstoys' tutors and governesses were discreet in ways that many visitors, relatives, friends, and future biographers would not be.

✳

---

*   Eikhenbaum, *Tolstoi in the Seventies*, 142.

†   *PSS* 62: 355.

‡   Tolstaya, *My Life*, 243.

§   Christian, *Tolstoy's Letters*, 310, January 3, 1878.

Cover of the first book edition of *Anna Karenina*.[*]

The appearance of *Anna Karenina* in book form did not shake the world and inspire Russian-language learning. But it should have. In my own time-traveling fantasies, I like to think that I would have been the first in line at Solov'ev's shop the morning it went on sale and that I would have celebrated by reading it right away, cover to cover.

In 1878 there were no publication parties or bookstore signings. Sofia, however, recalled how she came by her "Anna Karenina ring":

> When the novel *Anna Karenina* was completely finished and published, I asked Lev Nikolaevich for a small gift in return for all my zealous transcribing. And when he went to Moscow [she does not indicate the date], he bought me a very fine ring, with a ruby in the centre and two diamonds—one on either side. I always liked any kind of jewelry, finery and sparkling stones, and I am wearing this ring right now on my finger.[†]

Sofia's "Anna Karenina" ring.[‡]

---

[*]   *Anna Karenina* book cover, 1878, Wikipedia, https://en.wikipedia.org/wiki/Anna_Karenina #/media/File:AnnaKareninaTitle.jpg; accessed July 27, 2017.

[†]   Tolstaya, *My Life*, 235.

[‡]   "History of the Tolstoy Family." Google Arts & Culture, accessed July 27, 2017, https://www .google.com/culturalinstitute/beta/exhibit/7QJSm-9ITJOWKA.

I can imagine Tolstoy at a bookstore or toy store, but how about at a jewelry store? Was he a tough customer, or did clever salespeople (sales*men*, I suspect) rub their hands in happy anticipation?

✳

Tolstoy's comments on the novel would be few and far between, but a couple of weeks after publication of the complete edition, he was provoked into a famous statement by a teacher, S. A. Rachinsky. Tolstoy wrote:

> Your opinion about *Anna Karenina* seems to me wrong. [Christian's note: "Rachinsky had complained of a fundamental weakness in the construction of *Anna Karenina*. 'There is no architecture in it. Two themes are developed side by side, and developed magnificently, which are in no way connected with each other.'"] On the contrary, I'm proud of the architecture—the arches have been constructed in such a way that it is impossible to see where the keystone is. And that is what I was striving for most of all. The structural link is not the plot or the relationships (friendships) between the characters, but an inner link. Believe me, this is not unwillingness to accept criticism—especially from you whose opinion is always too indulgent; but I'm afraid that in skimming through the novel you didn't notice its inner content. I wouldn't quarrel with the man who said "que me veut cette sonate" ["what does this sonata want me to do"], but if you wish to speak about the lack of a link, then I can't help saying—you are probably looking for it in the wrong place, or we understand the word "link" differently; but what I understand by link—the very thing that made the work important for me—this link is there—look for it and you will find it. Please don't think that I'm touchy—really, I'm not writing because of that, but because when I got your letter I began to think about all this and wanted to tell you. And the first impulse est le bon [is the good one].*

Having considered all of Tolstoy's numerous restarts and revisions of the novel (not to mention his misgivings and expressions of disgust), this post-game claim of his about its architectural "keystone" and the all-important "link" is puzzling. Did we miss something? Tolstoy never let on what link or keystone it was that he meant.

---

* Christian, *Tolstoy's Letters*, 311, January 27, 1878.

To guess what he meant, I have to retreat to what has kept the novel as powerful and significant as it is: simply his discovery of Anna and the ensuing creation of her. The novel's other characters spring to life because she is the sun and they are the planets revolving around her. Despite her being so alive, or frighteningly because she is so alive and conscious, she descends into suicidal thoughts that she cannot escape. Fortunately, because of his realization of her tragedy, Tolstoy after all survived his own descent into depression. The keystone, then, is the Anna Karenina that Tolstoy discovered and created.

Works Cited

✳

Bartlett, Rosamund. *Tolstoy: A Russian Life*. London: Profile Books, 2010.

Behrs, C. A. [Stepan Bers]. *Recollections of Count Leo Tolstoy*. Translated by Charles Edward Turner. London: William Heinemann, 1896.

Biryukoff, Paul [Pavel Ivanovich Biriukov]. *Leo Tolstoy, His Life and Work: Autobiographical Memoirs, Letters and Biographical Material*. New York: Charles Scribner's Sons, 1911.

Chekhov, Anton. *Anton Chekhov's Life and Thought: Selected Letters and Commentary*. Selected by Simon Karlinsky. Translated by Michael Henry Heim and Simon Karlinsky. Berkeley: University of California Press, 1973.

Chesterton, G. K. *Orthodoxy*. London: John Lane Co., 1908.

Chesterton, G. K. *What's Wrong with the World*. New York: Dodd, Mead and Co., 1910.

Christian, R. F., ed. and trans. *Tolstoy's Diaries. Vol. 1: 1847–1894*. New York: Charles Scribner's Sons, 1985.

Christian, R. F., ed. and trans. *Tolstoy's Letters*. New York: Charles Scribner's Sons, 1978.

Donskov, Andrew. Л. Н. Толстой—Н. Н. Страхов. Полное собрание переписки [L. N. Tolstoy – N. N. Strakhov. Complete Correspondence]. Vol. 1. Ottawa: University of Ottawa, 2003.

Donskov, Andrew. *Tolstoy and Tolstaya: A Portrait of a Life in Letters*. Ottawa: University of Ottawa, 2017.

Dostoievsky, F. M. [sic]. *The Diary of a Writer*. Translated by Boris Brasol. New York: George Braziller, 1954.

Eikhenbaum, Boris. *Tolstoi in the Seventies*. Translated by Albert Kaspin. Ann Arbor: Ardis, 1982.

Fusso, Susanne. *Editing Turgenev, Dostoevsky, and Tolstoy: Mikhail Katkov and the Great Russian Novel*. Dekalb: Northern Illinois University Press, 2017.

Goldenweizer, A. B. *Talks with Tolstoy*. Translated by S. S. Koteliansky and Virginia Woolf. New York: Horizon Press, 1969.

Gorky, Maxim. *Reminiscences of Leo Nikolaevich Tolstoy*. Translation by S. S. Koteliansky and Leonard Woolf. New York: B. W. Huebsch, 1920.

Gusev, N. N. *Letopis' zhizni i tvorchestva L'va Nikolaevicha Tolstogo, 1828–1890*. Moscow: Gosudarstvennoe Izdatel'stvo Khudozhestvennoi Literatury, 1958.

Gusev, N. N. *Lev Nikolaevich Tolstoi: Materialy k Biografii s 1870 po 1881 god*. Moscow: Izdatel'stvo Akademii Nauk SSSR, 1963.

Harper, Samuel Northrup. *Russian Reader*. 6th ed. Chicago: University of Chicago Press, 1932.

Holmes, Richard. "A Quest for the Real Coleridge." *New York Review of Books*. December 18, 2014.

Kuzminskaya, Tatyana A. *Tolstoy as I Knew Him: My Life at Home and at Yasnaya Polyana*. New York: Macmillan, 1948.

Maude, Aylmer. *The Life of Tolstoy: First Fifty Years*. London: Archibald Constable and Co., 1908.

McLean, Hugh. *Nikolai Leskov: The Man and His Art*. Cambridge, MA: Harvard University Press, 1977.

Morrison, Simon. *Bolshoi Confidential: Secrets of the Russian Ballet from the Rule of the Tsars to Today*. New York: Liveright, 2016.

Mudrick, Marvin. *Books Are Not Life But Then What Is?* New York: Oxford University Press, 1979.

Obolenskiy, A. D. "Dve vstrechi s L. N. Tolstym." Originally in Толстой. Памятники творчества и жизни [Tolstoy. Memories of Creation and Life]. Moscow, 1923. http://feb-web.ru/feb/tolstoy/critics/vs1/vs1-239-.htm.

Orwin, Donna Tussing. *Simply Tolstoy*. New York: Simply Charly, 2017.

Polner, Tikhon. *Tolstoy and His Wife*. Translated by Nicholas Wreden. New York: W.W. Norton and Co., 1945.

Popoff, Alexandra. *Sophia Tolstoy: A Biography*. New York: Free Press, 2010.

Roser, Max. Our World in Data. "Literacy rates around the world from the 15th century to present." https://ourworldindata.org/literacy/. Accessed 8 July 2016.

Schuyler, Eugene. "On the Steppe." *Hours at Home: A Popular Monthly of Instruction and Recreation*. Vol. 9. New York: Charles Scribner and Co., 1869.

Simmons, Ernest. *Leo Tolstoy*. Vol. 1. New York: Vintage, 1960.

Todd III, William Mills. "V. N. Golitsyn Reads *Anna Karenina*: How One of Karenin's Colleagues Responded to the Novel." In *Reading in Russia*. Edited by Damiano Rebecchini and Raffaella Vassena. Milan: Ledizioni, 2014.

Tolstoy, Alexandra. *Tolstoy: A Life of My Father*. Translated by Elizabeth Reynolds Hapgood. New York: Harper and Brothers, 1953.

Tolstoy, Leo. *Anna Karenin*. Translated by Constance Garnett. New York: McClure, Phillips and Co., 1901. http://www.literatureproject.com/anna-karenina/anna_1.htm.

Tolstoy, Leo. *Anna Karenina*. Translated by Rosamund Bartlett. Oxford: Oxford University Press, 2014.

Tolstoy, Leo. *Anna Karenina*. Translated by Louise and Aylmer Maude. London: Oxford University Press, 1918.

Tolstoy, Leo. *Anna Karenina*. Translated by Richard Pevear and Larissa Volokhonsky. New York: Penguin Books, 2000.

Tolstoy, Leo. *Anna Karenina*. Translated by Miriam Schwartz. New Haven, CT: Yale University Press, 2014.

Tolstoy, Leo. *Anna Karenina*. Edited by V. A. Zhdanov and E. E. Zaidenshnur. Moscow: Nauka, 1970.

Tolstoy, Leo. *The Complete Works of Count Tolstoy*. Translated by Leo Wiener. London: J. M. Dent, 1905.

Tolstoy, Leo. *Confession*. Translated by Aylmer Maude. London: Oxford University Press, 1971.

Tolstoy, Leo. "Master and Man." Translated by Aylmer and Louise Maude. http://www.gutenberg.org/files/986/986-h/986-h.htm.

Tolstoy, Leo. *Tolstoy on Education*. Translated by Leo Wiener. Chicago: University of Chicago Press, 1972.

Tolstoy, Leo. *What Is Art?* (1898) In *What Is Art and Essays on Art*. The World's Classics edition. Translated by Aylmer Maude. London: Oxford University Press, 1950.

Tolstoy, Lev. *Polnoe sobranie sochinenii* [abbreviated as *PSS*]. Edited by V. G. Chertkov. 90 volumes. Moscow, 1928–1958.

Tolstoy, L. N., and sister and brothers. *Perepiski Russkikh Pisateley: Perepiska L. N. Tolstogo s sestroy i brat'yami*. Moscow: Khudozhestvennaya Literatura, 1990.

Tolstoy, Sergei. *Tolstoy Remembered by His Son Sergei Tolstoy*. Translated by Moura Budberg. New York: Atheneum, 1962.

Tolstaya, Sofia Andreevna. *My Life*. Translated by John Woodsworth and Arkadi Klioutchanski. Edited by Andrew Donskov. Ottawa: University of Ottawa Press, 2010.

Tolstoy, Sophia. *The Diaries of Sophia Tolstoy*. Translated by Cathy Porter. New York: Random House, 1985.

Tolstoy, Tatyana. *Tolstoy Remembered*. Translated from the French by Derek Coltman. McGraw-Hill: New York, 1977.

Trollope, Anthony. *An Autobiography*. New York: Dodd, Mead and Company, 1916.

Turner, C.J.G. *The Tolstoy Companion*. Waterloo, Ontario: Wilfrid Laurier University Press, 1993.

Wettlin, Margaret. *Reminscences of Lev Tolstoi by His Contemporaries*. Translated by Margaret Wettlin. Moscow: Foreign Languages Publishing House. [No date, but this edition was published after 1960.]

Acknowledgments

✳

I wouldn't have written this book if not for the translators whose work allowed me to read my book of books in English more than forty years ago. I read *Anna Karenina* in at least a half-dozen different translations before deciding I had better try to do the heavy lifting myself and, at the age of forty-five, learn Russian. I was inspired at that time by a friend who had taken up Russian in his forties. If he could do it, I could do it. Well, if I had been as smart as he and known the difficulty and time it would take, I would not have started. Along the way I was encouraged and guided by tutors in St. Petersburg and at Yasnaya Polyana, among them Albina Kuznetsova and Svetlana Voloshchikova, but especially and most regularly over the last fifteen years in New York City by Dina Kupchanka. *Bolshoe spasibo!*

I eventually had to have enough Russian to be able to read not only Анна Каренина but the hundreds of letters by Tolstoy in these years that were not translated by R. F. Christian, whose 1978 two-volume collection of letters by Tolstoy remains the only large sampling in English of Tolstoy's letters to various correspondents. I beg his forgiveness for occasionally carping at his selections or the incompleteness of his excerpts. I am an amateur in Russian in all senses of the word (the first being "lover"), and the errors in my translations are, I hope, only in rough sense and not in spirit. For almost two decades Michael A. Denner has encouraged me in my efforts to understand and appreciate Tolstoy, not only through his gift of letting me review books for *Tolstoy Studies Journal*, my favorite periodical in the world, but through guidance to the fundamental Russian texts that would give me the most abundant details about Tolstoy's life and writings.

I never met the late Hugh McLean of the University of California, Berkeley, but his writings on Tolstoy, collected in *In Quest of Tolstoy*, continually reminded me that the primary and best form of criticism is to be as straightforward and as engaged as one can be as a reader. Literary theories be damned!

The biographers of Tolstoy I have most learned from and leaned upon include Rosamund Bartlett, who was kind enough to engage in email correspondence about the great man, and Tikhon Polner, whose *Tolstoy and His Wife* was probably the first biography of a literary figure I ever read. I was probably twenty-one, by which age I had already read *Anna Karenina* a half-dozen times. Polner whetted my curiosity to keep learning about the author of the most vital book of my life. Ernest Simmons's two-volume biography, as well as Aylmer Maude's, gave me the happy illusion of completeness, but as Tolstoy says, there can't be a complete biography of anybody. In Russian, I owe the backbone of this biographical study to Nikolai Gusev, whose *Materials* and *Chronicle* of Tolstoy's life describe his day-to-day interactions and movements, and never neglects Tolstoy's wife Sofia Tolstaya's input, as so many other sources have. For the translations of her *My Life* and *Diaries* and the married couple's selected correspondence, I have to thank John Woodsworth, Arkardi Klioutchanski, Cathy Porter, and Liudmila Gladkova. For her appreciative recent *Sophia Tolstoy: A Biography*, scholars and readers should thank Alexandra Popoff.

As a reviewer, I have had several editors who were kind enough to indulge me and assign me books about and by Tolstoy, thus contributing to my knowledge and appreciation of my hero: at the *San Francisco Chronicle*, Oscar Villalon and then John McMurtrie; at the *Christian Science Monitor*, the late and generous Marjorie Kehe; and most wonderfully, Boris Dralyuk at the *Los Angeles Review of Books*. Christopher Edgar at Teachers & Writers Collaborative oversaw our edition of *Tolstoy as Teacher: Leo Tolstoy's Writings on Education* and Stephen Mitchell at Prometheus brought my edition of Tolstoy's children's stories to light. At Dover Publications, John Grafton and Susan Rattiner allowed me to include important essays by Tolstoy in various anthologies.

Readers of various drafts of this biography include Ian Frazier, Ross Robins, and John Wilson, whose comments and suggestions greatly sharpened a more discursive and less-focused work. Kia Penso and Max Schott, to whom I dedicate this book, each patiently and painstakingly read and critiqued a couple of versions, each time helping to encourage me while steering me back on track and into greater clarity. Jessica Case, deputy publisher of Pegasus, seemed to understand better than I what I was hoping to show of Tolstoy's achievement and suggested important improvements, including the title. I have very much appreciated Mary Hern for her editing and for her astute queries and apt suggestions; the remaining errors or awkwardnesses are all mine. Maria Fernandez has expertly designed the pages, for which I am grateful.

Sections or early versions of parts of this book have appeared in *Russian Life*, *Changing English: Studies in Culture and Education*, the *Tolstoy Commons*, New York University's Jordan Center's *All the Russias' Blog*, and *Former People*. Thank you to, among others, Paul E. Richardson, Susan Alice Fischer and Jane Miller, Ani Kokobobo, and Maya Vinokour.

To work on language and biographical projects at Tolstoy's estate at Yasnaya Polyana and home in Moscow, I thank the reviewers of my fellowship leave and the granters of three PSC-CUNY research awards. Galina Vasil'evna Alekseeva, the director of Yasnaya Polyana's academic research, shared her expert opinions and information about Tolstoy's relationships to American and British authors. My attendance at the City University of New York's Biography Clinic at the Leon Levy Center for Biography in 2015 was useful. My chair at Kingsborough Community College (CUNY), Dr. Eileen Ferretti, was generous in her support for my sabbatical project to begin writing this biography. My colleague Dr. Lea Fridman ever kindly encouraged me throughout every stage. My friend Caroline Allen of the Literature faculty at the College of Creative Studies at the University of California, Santa Barbara, invited me to speak to her class about Tolstoy and the novel as did my sister Carol Blaisdell's reading group in Silver Spring, Maryland, where I learned why *Anna Karenina* indeed still matters. My dear friend the author Jervey Tervalon invited me to speak at LitFest Pasadena in May 2020 so that I could discuss with the novelist Janet Fitch and Professor Vadim Shneyder of UCLA the meaningfulness of Tolstoy's relationship to his heroine. (Maybe next year!)

Finally, I thank Suzanne Carbotte for her emotional support and patience throughout my studies and travels. As happy as Lev and Sofia Tolstoy were in the first ten years of their marriage, I have been as happy in the almost three decades of ours.

Bob Blaisdell
New York City
March 1, 2020

Index

✳